Memoirs
of an
imaginary
friend

Memoirs of an imaginary friend

MATTHEW GREEN

sphere

SPHERE

First published in Great Britain in 2012 by Sphere
Reprinted 2012 (twice)

Copyright © Matthew Dicks 2012

The moral right of the author has been asserted.

A CIP catalogue record for this book
is available from the British Library.

ISBN 978-0-7515-4787-0

Printed and bound in Great Britain by
Clays Ltd, St Ives plc

Papers used by Sphere are from well-managed forests
and other responsible sources.

MIX
Paper from
responsible sources
FSC® C104740
www.fsc.org

Sphere
An imprint of
Little, Brown Book Group
100 Victoria Embankment
London EC4Y 0DY

An Hachette UK Company
www.hachette.co.uk

www.littlebrown.co.uk

For Clara

CHAPTER 1

Here is what I know:

My name is Budo.

I have been alive for five years.

Five years is a very long time for someone like me to be alive.

Max gave me my name.

Max is the only human person who can see me.

Max's parents call me an imaginary friend.

I love Max's teacher, Mrs Gosk.

I do not like Max's other teacher, Mrs Patterson.

I am not imaginary.

CHAPTER 2

I am lucky as imaginary friends go. I have been alive for a lot longer than most. I once knew an imaginary friend named Philippe. He was the imaginary friend of one of Max's classmates in preschool. He lasted less than a week. One day he popped into the world, looking pretty human except for his lack of ears (lots of imaginary friends lack ears), and then a few days later, he was gone.

I'm also lucky that Max has a great imagination. I once knew an imaginary friend named Chomp who was just a spot on the wall. Just a fuzzy, black blob without any real shape at all. Chomp could talk and sort of slide up and down the wall, but he was two-dimensional like a piece of paper, so he could never pry himself off. He didn't have arms and legs like me. He didn't even have a face.

Imaginary friends get their appearance from their human friend's imagination. Max is a very creative boy, and so I have two arms, two legs, and a face. I'm not missing a single body part and that makes me a rarity in the world of imaginary friends. Most imaginary friends are missing something or other and some don't even look human at all. Like Chomp.

Too much imagination can be bad, though. I once met an imaginary friend named Pterodactyl whose eyes were stuck on the ends of these two gangly, green antennas. His human friend probably thought they looked cool, but poor Pterodactyl couldn't focus on anything to save his life. He told me that he constantly felt sick to his stomach and was always tripping over his own feet, which were just fuzzy shadows attached to his legs. His human friend was so obsessed with Pterodactyl's head and those eyes that he had never bothered to think about anything below Pterodactyl's waist.

This is not unusual.

I'm also lucky because I'm mobile. Lots of imaginary friends are stuck to their human friends. Some have leashes around their necks. Some are three inches tall and get stuffed into coat pockets. And some are nothing more than a spot on the wall, like Chomp. But thanks to Max, I can get around on my own. I can even leave Max behind if I want.

But doing so too often might be hazardous to my health.

As long as Max believes in me, I exist. People like Max's mother and my friend, Graham, say that this is what makes

3

me imaginary. But it's not true. I might need Max's imagination to exist, but I have my own thoughts, my own ideas and my own life outside of him. I am tied to Max the same way that an astronaut is tied to his spaceship by hoses and wires. If the spaceship blows up and the astronaut dies, that doesn't mean that the astronaut was imaginary. It just means that his life support was cut off.

Same for me and Max.

I need Max in order to survive, but I'm still my own person. I can say and do as I please. Sometimes me and Max even get into arguments, but nothing ever serious. Just stuff about which TV show to watch or which game to play. But it *behooves* me (that's a word that Mrs Gosk taught the class last week) to stick around Max whenever possible, because I need Max to keep thinking about me. Keep believing in me. I don't want to end up *out of sight, out of mind*, which is something Max's mom sometimes says when Max's dad forgets to call home when he is going to be late. If I am gone too long, Max might stop believing in me, and if that happens, then poof.

CHAPTER 3

Max's first-grade teacher once said that houseflies live for about three days. I wonder what the lifespan of an imaginary friend is? Probably not much longer. I guess that makes me practically ancient in the imaginary friend world.

Max imagined me when he was four years old and, just like that, I popped into existence. When I was born, I knew only what Max knew. I knew my colors and some of my numbers and the names for lots of things like tables and microwave ovens and aircraft carriers. My head was filled with the things that a four-year-old boy would know. But Max also imagined me much older than him. Probably a teenager. Maybe even a little older. Or maybe I was just a boy with a grown-up's brain. It's hard to tell. I'm not much taller than Max, but I'm definitely different. I was more together than Max when I was born. I could make sense of things that still confused him. I could see the answers to problems that Max could not. Maybe this is how all imaginary friends are born. I don't know.

Max doesn't remember the day that I was born, so he can't remember what he was thinking at the time. But since he imagined me as older and more together, I have been able to learn much faster than Max. I was able to concentrate and focus better on the day I was born than Max is able to even today. On that first day I remember Max's mother was trying to teach him to count by even numbers, and he just couldn't get it. But I learned it right away. It made sense to me because my brain was ready to learn even numbers. Max's brain wasn't.

At least, that's what I think.

Also, I don't sleep, because Max didn't imagine that I needed sleep. So I have more time to learn. And I don't spend all my time with Max, so I've learned lots of things that Max has never seen or heard before. After he goes to bed, I sit in the living room or the kitchen with Max's parents. We watch television or I just listen to them talk. Sometimes I go places. I go to the gas station that never closes, because my favorite people in the world, except for Max and his parents and Mrs Gosk, are there. Or I go to Doogies hot-dog restaurant a little ways down the road or to the police station or to the hospital (except I don't go to the hospital anymore because Oswald is there and he scares me). And when we are in school, I sometimes go to the teachers' lounge or another classroom, and sometimes I even go to the principal's office, just to listen to what's going on. I am not smarter than Max, but I know a lot more than him just because I am awake more and go places that Max can't. This is good. Sometimes I can help Max when he doesn't understand something so well.

Like last week Max couldn't open a jar of jelly to make a peanut butter and jelly sandwich. 'Budo!' he said. 'I can't open it.'

'Sure you can,' I said. 'Turn it the other way. Lefty loosy. Righty tighty.'

That is something I hear Max's mom say to herself sometimes before she opens a jar. It worked. Max opened the jar. But he was so excited that he dropped it on the tile floor, smashing it into a million pieces.

The world can be so complicated for Max. Even when he gets something right, it can still go wrong.

I live in a strange place in the world. I live in the space in between people. I spend most of my time in the kid world with Max, but I also spend a lot of time with adults like Max's parents and teachers and my friends at the gas station, except they can't see me. Max's mom would call this *straddling the fence*. She says this to Max when he can't make up his mind about something, which happens a lot.

'Do you want the blue popsicle or the yellow popsicle?'

she asks, and Max just freezes. Freezes like a popsicle. There are just too many things for Max to think about when choosing.

Is red better than yellow?

Is green better than blue?

Which one is colder?

Which one will melt fastest?

What does green taste like?

What does red taste like?

Do different colors taste different?

I wish that Max's mom would just make the choice for Max. She knows how hard it is for him. But when she makes him choose and he can't, I sometimes choose for him. I whisper, 'Pick blue,' and then he says, 'I'll take blue.' Then it's done. No more straddling the fence.

That's kind of how I live. I straddle the fence. I live in the yellow world and in the blue world. I live with kids and I live with adults. I'm not exactly a kid, but I'm not exactly an adult either.

I'm yellow *and* blue.

I'm green.

I know my color combinations, too.

CHAPTER 4

Max's teacher is Mrs Gosk. I like Mrs Gosk a lot. Mrs Gosk walks around with a meter stick that she calls her meter-beater and threatens students in a fake British accent, but the kids know she's just trying to make them laugh. Mrs Gosk is very strict and insists that her students work hard, but she would never hit a student. Still, she is a tough lady. She makes them sit up straight and work on their assignments in silence, and when a child misbehaves, she says, 'Shame! Shame! Let all the boys and girls know your name!' and 'You will get away with that nonsense when pigs fly, young man!' The other teachers say Mrs Gosk is old-fashioned, but the kids know that she is tough because she loves them.

Max doesn't like many people, but he likes Mrs Gosk.

Last year Max's teacher was Mrs Silbor. She was strict, too. She made the kids work hard like Mrs Gosk does. But you could tell that she didn't love the kids like Mrs Gosk, so no one in the class worked as hard as they do this year. It's strange how teachers can go off to college for all those years to learn to become teachers, but some of them never learn the easy stuff. Like making kids laugh. And making sure they know that you love them.

I do not like Mrs Patterson. She's not a real teacher. She's a paraprofessional. This is someone who helps Mrs Gosk take care of Max. Max is different than other kids so he doesn't spend the whole day with Mrs Gosk. Sometimes he works with Mrs McGinn in the Learning Center with other kids who need extra help, and sometimes he works on his speech with Mrs Riner, and sometimes he plays games with other kids in Mrs Hume's office. And sometimes he reads and does homework with Mrs Patterson.

As far as I can tell, no one knows why Max is different from the rest of the kids. Max's father says that Max is just a late bloomer, but when he says that, Max's mom gets so angry that she stops talking to him for at least a day.

I don't know why everyone thinks Max is so complicated. Max just doesn't like people in the same way other kids do. He likes people, but it's a different kind of liking. He likes people from far away. The farther you stay away from Max, the more he will like you.

And Max doesn't like to be touched. When someone touches Max, the whole world gets bright and shivery. That's how he described it to me once.

I can't touch Max, and Max can't touch me. Maybe that's why we get along so well.

Also, Max doesn't understand when people say one thing but mean another. Like last week Max was reading a book at recess and a fourth grader came over and said, 'Look at the little genius.'

Max didn't say anything to the boy, because he knew if he said something, the fourth grader would stay there longer and keep bothering him. But I know that Max was confused, because it sounded like the boy was saying that Max was smart even though the boy was actually being mean. He was being sarcastic, but Max doesn't understand sarcasm. Max knew the boy was being mean, but only because that boy is always mean to Max. But he couldn't understand why the boy would call him a genius, since being called a genius is usually a good thing.

People are confusing to Max, so it's hard for him to be around them. That's why Max has to play games in Mrs Hume's office with kids from the other classes. He thinks it's a big waste of time. He hates having to sit on the floor around the Monopoly board, because sitting on the floor is not as comfortable as sitting in a chair. But Mrs Hume is trying to teach Max to play with other kids, to understand what they mean when they sarcasm or joke around. Max just doesn't understand. When Max's mom and dad are fighting, Max's mom says that his dad can't see the forest for the trees. That's like Max except with the whole world. He can't see the big things because of all the little things that get in his way.

Today Mrs Patterson is absent. When a teacher is absent, it usually means that the teacher is sick or her child is sick or someone in her family has died. Mrs Patterson had someone in her family die once. I know this because sometimes the other teachers will say nice things to her like, 'How are you holding up, dear?' and sometimes they whisper to each other after she has left the room. But that was a long time ago. When Mrs Patterson is absent, it usually means that it is Friday.

There's no substitute for Mrs Patterson today so Max and I get to stay with Mrs Gosk all day, which makes me happy. I don't like Mrs Patterson. Max doesn't like her either, but he doesn't like her in the same way he doesn't like most of his teachers. He doesn't see what I see because he's too busy looking at the trees. But Mrs Patterson is different than Mrs Gosk and Mrs Riner and Mrs McGinn. She never smiles for real. She's always thinking something different in her head than what is on her face. I don't think she likes Max, but she pretends that she does, which is even scarier than just not liking him.

'Hello, Max, my boy!' Mrs Gosk says as we walk into the classroom.

Max doesn't like when Mrs Gosk calls him *my boy*

because he is not *her boy*. He has a mother already. But he won't ask Mrs Gosk to stop calling him *my boy* because asking her to stop would be harder than listening to Mrs Gosk say *my boy* every day.

Max would rather say nothing to everyone than something to one person.

But even though Max doesn't understand why Mrs Gosk calls him *my boy*, he knows that she loves him. He knows that Mrs Gosk is not being mean. Just confusing.

I wish I could tell Mrs Gosk not to call Max *my boy*, but Mrs Gosk can't see or hear me and there's nothing I can do to make her see or hear me. Imaginary friends can't touch or move things in the human world. So I can't open a jelly jar or pick up a pencil or type on a keyboard. Otherwise I would write a note asking Mrs Gosk not to call Max *my boy*.

I can bump up against the real world, but I can't actually touch it.

Even so, I am lucky because when Max first imagined me, he imagined that I could pass through things like doors and windows even when they are closed. I think it's because he was afraid that if his parents closed his bedroom door at night, I might get stuck outside the room, and Max doesn't like to fall asleep unless I'm sitting in the chair next to his bed. This means that I can go anywhere by walking through the doors and windows, but never through walls or floors. I can't pass through walls and floors because Max didn't imagine me that way. That would've been too strange for even Max to think about.

There are imaginary friends who can walk through doors and windows like me, and some who can even walk through walls, but most can't walk through anything and get stuck in places for a long time. That's what happened to Puppy, a talking dog who got stuck in the janitor's closet overnight a couple of weeks ago. It was a scary night for his human friend, a kindergartener named Piper, because she had no idea where Puppy was.

But it was even scarier for Puppy, because getting locked in a closet is how imaginary friends sometimes disappear for ever. A boy or girl accidentally (or sometimes *accidentally on purpose*) locks an imaginary friend in a closet or a cabinet or basement and then *Poof!* Out of sight, out of mind. The end of the imaginary friend.

Being able to pass through doors can be a life-saver.

Today I want to stay put in the classroom because Mrs Gosk is reading *Charlie and the Chocolate Factory* aloud to the class, and I love it when Mrs Gosk reads. She has a whispery, thin voice, so all the kids must lean in and be absolutely silent in order to hear, which is great for Max. Noises distract him. If Joey Miller is banging his pencil on his desk or Danielle Ganner is tapping her feet on the floor like she does all the time, then Max can't hear anything but the pencil or the feet. He can't ignore sounds like the other kids can, but when Mrs Gosk reads, everyone must be perfectly quiet.

Mrs Gosk always chooses the best books and tells the best stories from her own life that somehow relate to the book. Charlie Bucket does something crazy and then Mrs Gosk tells us about a time when her son, Michael, did something crazy, and we all laugh our heads off. Even Max sometimes.

Max doesn't like to laugh. Some people think it's because he doesn't think things are funny, but that is not true. Max doesn't understand all funny things. Puns and knock-knock jokes make no sense to him, because they say one thing but mean another. When a word can mean a bunch of different things, he has a hard time understanding which meaning to choose. He doesn't even understand why words have to mean different things depending on when you use them, and I don't blame him. I don't like it much, either.

But Max finds other things hilarious. Like when Mrs Gosk told us how Michael once sent twenty cheese pizzas and the bill to a schoolyard bully as a joke. When the police officer came to their house to scare Michael, Mrs Gosk told the police officer to 'Take him away' to teach her son a lesson. Everyone laughed at that story. Even Max. Because it made sense. It had a beginning, a middle, and an end.

Mrs Gosk is also teaching us about World War II today, which Mrs Gosk says is not in the curriculum but should be. The kids love it, and Max especially loves it because he thinks about wars and battles and tanks and airplanes all the time. Sometimes it is the only thing that he thinks about for days. If school was only about war and battles and not math and writing, then Max would be the best student in the whole wide world.

Today Mrs Gosk is teaching us about Pearl Harbor. The Japanese bombed Pearl Harbor on 7 December 1941. Mrs Gosk said that the Americans were not ready for the sneak attack because they couldn't imagine the Japanese attacking us from so far away.

'America lacked imagination,' she said.

If Max had been alive in 1941 things might have been different because he has an excellent imagination. I bet that Max would have imagined Admiral Yamamoto's plan perfectly, with the midget submarines and the torpedoes with the wooden rudders and everything else. He could have warned the American soldiers about the plan because that is what Max is good at. Imagining things. He has a lot going on inside of him all the time so he doesn't worry so much about what is going on outside him. That's what people don't understand.

That's why it's good for me to stick around Max whenever I can. Sometimes he doesn't pay enough attention to the things around him. Last week he was about to get on the bus when a big gust of wind blew his report card right out of his hands and between bus 8 and bus 53. He ran out of line to get it, but he didn't look both ways when he did, so I yelled, 'Max Delaney! Stop!'

I use Max's last name when I want to get his attention. I learned that from Mrs Gosk. It worked. Max stopped, which was good, because a car was passing by the school buses at that moment, which is illegal.

Graham said that I saved Max's life. Graham is the third imaginary friend at the school right now, as far as I know, and she saw the whole thing. Graham is a girl but she has a boy's name. She looks almost as human as I do, except her hair stands up like someone on the moon is pulling on each individual strand. It doesn't move. It's as solid as a rock. Graham heard me yell at Max and tell him to stop, and then after Max was back in line, she walked over to me and said, 'Budo! You just saved Max's life! He would've been squished by that car!'

But I told Graham that I saved my own life, because if Max ever died, I think I would die, too.

Right?

I think so. I've never known an imaginary friend whose human friend died before he disappeared. So I'm not sure.

But I think I would. Die, I mean. If Max died.

CHAPTER 5

'Do you think I'm real?' I ask.

'Yes,' Max says. 'Hand me that blue two-pronger.'

A two-pronger is a kind of Lego. Max has names for all the Lego pieces.

'I can't,' I say.

Max looks at me. 'Oh, yeah. I forgot.'

'If I'm real, then why are you the only one who can see me?'

'I don't know,' Max says, sounding irritated. 'I think you're real. Why do you keep asking me?'

It's true. I ask him a lot. I do it on purpose, too. I'm not going to live for ever. I know that. But I'm going to live as long as Max believes in me. So if I force Max to keep insisting that I'm real, I think he will believe in me longer.

Of course, I know that by constantly asking him if I'm real, I might be putting in his head the idea that I am imaginary. It's a risk. But so far, so good.

Mrs Hume once told Max's mom that it's 'not uncommon for kids like Max to have imaginary friends, and they tend to persist longer than most imaginary friends'.

Persist. I like that word.

I persist.

Max's parents are fighting again. Max can't hear because he is playing video games in the basement and his parents are screaming at each other in whispers. They sound like people who have been yelling for so long that they have lost their voices, which is actually half true.

'I don't care what the fucking therapist thinks,' Max's dad says, his cheeks turning red as he whisper-yells. 'He's a normal kid ... he's just a late bloomer. He plays with toys. He plays sports. He has friends.'

Max's dad is not correct. Max doesn't have any friends other than me. The kids at school either like Max or hate Max or ignore Max, but none of them are his friend, and I don't think he wants any of them to be his friend. Max is happiest when he is left alone. Even I bother him sometimes.

Even the kids at school who like Max treat him differently. Like Ella Barbara. She loves Max, but she loves him in the same way a kid loves a doll or a teddy bear. She calls him 'my little Max' and tries to carry his lunchbox to the cafeteria and zip up his coat before recess, even though she knows that Max can do those things for himself. Max hates Ella. He cringes every time she tries to help him or even touch him, but he can't tell her to stop because it's easier for Max to cringe and suffer than speak up. Mrs Silbor kept Ella and Max together when she sent them on to third grade because she thought that they were good for each other. That's what she told Max's mom at the parent–teacher conference. Max might be good for Ella, because she gets to play with him like he's a doll, but Ella is most definitely not good for Max.

'He is not a late bloomer and I wish you'd stop saying that,' Max's mom says in the tone she uses when she's trying to stay calm but is having a hard time doing so. 'I know it kills you to admit it, John, but that's just the way it is. How could every expert we meet be wrong?'

'That's the problem,' Max's dad says, his forehead turning red and blotchy. 'Not every expert agrees and you know it!' When he speaks, it's like he's firing his words from a gun. 'No one knows what is going on with Max. So how is my guess any worse than the opinions of a bunch of experts who can't agree on a thing?'

'The label isn't important,' Max's mom says. 'It doesn't matter what is wrong with him. He needs help.'

'I just don't get it,' Max's dad says. 'I played catch with him in the backyard last night. I've taken him camping. His grades are good. He doesn't get in trouble at school. Why are we trying to fix the poor kid when there's nothing wrong with him?'

Max's mom starts to cry. She blinks and her eyes fill with tears. I hate when she cries, and so does Max's dad. I have never cried before, but it looks awful.

'John, he doesn't like to hug us. He can't make eye contact with people. He flips out if I change the sheets on his bed or switch brands of toothpaste. He talks to himself constantly. These are not normal kid behaviors. I'm not saying he needs medication. I'm not saying that he won't grow up and be normal. He just needs a professional who can help him deal with some of his issues. And I want to do it before I get pregnant again. While we can focus on just him.'

Max's dad turns and leaves. He slams the screen door behind him on the way out. It goes whack-whack-whack before it stops moving. I used to think that when Max's dad walked away from an argument, it meant that Max's mom had won. I thought his dad was retreating like Max's toy soldiers retreat. I thought he was surrendering. But even though he is the one who retreats, it doesn't always mean that he has surrendered. He has retreated lots of times before, slamming that door and making it go whack-whack-whack, but then nothing changes. It's like Max's dad has pressed the pause button on the remote control. The argument is paused. But it is not over.

Max, by the way, is the only boy I have ever seen who makes toy soldiers retreat or surrender.

Every other boy makes them die instead.

I'm not sure if Max should see a therapist and, to be honest, I'm not exactly sure what a therapist does. I know some things that they do, but not everything, and it's the everything that makes me nervous. Max's mom and dad are probably going to fight about this again and again, and even though neither one will ever say, 'Okay, I give up!' or 'You win!' or 'You're right,' Max will eventually go to the therapist because, in the end, Max's mom almost always wins.

I think Max's dad is wrong about Max being a late bloomer. I spend most of the day with Max and I see how he is different from the other kids in his class. Max lives on the inside and the other kids live on the outside. That's what makes him so different. Max doesn't have an outside. Max is all inside.

I don't want Max to see a therapist. Therapists are people who trick you into telling the truth. They can see inside your head and know exactly what you are thinking, and if Max is thinking about me when he's talking to the therapist, the therapist will trick Max into talking about me. Then maybe he'll convince Max to stop believing in me.

But I still feel bad for Max's dad, even if Max's mom is the one who's crying now. Sometimes I wish I could tell Max's mom to be nicer to Max's dad. She is the boss of the house, but she's also the boss of Max's dad, and I don't think it's good for him. It makes him feel small and silly. Like when he wants to play poker with friends on a Wednesday night but he can't just tell his friends that he will play. He has to ask Max's mom if it's okay for him to play, and he has to ask at the right time, when she is in a good mood, or he might not be able to play.

She might say, 'I could really use you at home that night,' or 'Didn't you play last week?' Or, worse, she might just say, 'Fine,' which really means, 'It is not fine and you know it and if you go, I am going to be mad at you for at least three days!'

It reminds me of how Max would have to ask permission to visit a friend, if Max ever wanted to play with anyone but me, which he doesn't.

I don't understand why he has to ask permission, but I really don't understand why Max's mom would want to make him ask permission. Wouldn't it be better if Max's dad just got to choose what he did?

It's doubly worse because Max's dad is a manager at Burger King. Max thinks that this is one of the best jobs in the world, and if I ate bacon double cheeseburgers and small fries, then I'd probably feel the same way. But in the adult world, a Burger King manager is not a good job at all, and Max's dad knows it. You can tell by the way he doesn't like to tell people about his job. He never asks people what their job is, and that's the most popular adult question ever asked in the history of the world. When he has to tell someone what his job is, he looks at his feet and says, 'I manage restaurants.' Getting him to say the words *Burger King* is like trying to get Max to choose between chicken noodle and vegetable beef soup. He tries everything he can not to say those two words.

Max's mom is a manager, too. She manages people at a place called Aetna, but I can't figure out what they make at her job. Definitely not bacon double cheeseburgers. I went to her job once, to try to figure out what she did all day, but everyone just sits in front of computers in these tiny boxes without lids. Or they sit around tables in stuffy rooms and tap their feet and look at the clock while some old man or woman talks about stuff that nobody cares about.

But even though it's boring and they don't make bacon double cheeseburgers, you can tell that Max's mom has a better job because the people in her building wear shirts and dresses and ties, and not uniforms. She never complains about people stealing or not showing up to work like Max's dad does. And sometimes Max's dad works at five in the morning, and sometimes he works all night long and comes home at five in the morning. It's weird because even though Max's dad's job seems a lot harder, Max's mom makes more money and adults think she has a much better job. She never looks at her feet when she tells people what she does.

I'm glad that Max didn't hear them arguing this time. Sometimes he does. Sometimes they forget to whisper-shout and sometimes they fight in the car, where it doesn't matter if you whisper-shout. When they fight, it makes Max feel sad.

'They fight because of me,' he said to me once. He was playing with Lego, which is when Max likes to talk about serious things the most. He doesn't look at me. He just builds airplanes and forts and battleships and spaceships while he talks.

'No they don't,' I said. 'They fight because they're grown-ups. Grown-ups like to argue.'

'No. They only argue about me.'

'No,' I said. 'Last night they argued about what show to watch on the television.'

I had been hoping that Max's dad would win so we could watch the crime show, but he lost and we had to watch some stupid singing show.

'That was not an argument,' Max said. 'That was a disagreement. There's a difference.'

These were Mrs Gosk's words. Mrs Gosk says that it's okay to disagree but that doesn't mean you are allowed to argue. 'I can stomach a disagreement,' she likes to say to the class. 'But I can't stand to listen to an argument in my presence.'

'They only argue because they don't know what's best for you,' I said. 'They're trying to figure out what is right.'

Max looked at me for a minute. He looked mad for a second, and then his face changed. It got softer and he looked sad. 'When other people try to make me feel better by twisting words, it only makes me feel worse. When you do it, it makes me feel worst of all.'

'Sorry,' I said.

'It's okay.'

'No,' I said. 'I'm not sorry for what I said, because it's true. Your parents really are trying to figure out what is right. I meant that I'm sorry that your parents argue about you, even if it's only because they love you.'

'Oh,' Max said and he smiled. It wasn't an actual smile, because Max never really smiles. But his eyes opened a little wider and he tilted his head a tiny bit to the right. That's Max's version of a smile. 'Thanks,' he said, and I knew that it was a real thanks.

CHAPTER 6

Max is in the bathroom stall. He is making a poop, which Max does not like to do outside the home. He almost never makes a poop in a public restroom. But it's 1.15 and there are still two hours of school left and he couldn't hold it anymore. He always tries to poop before going to bed every night, and if he can't, he tries again in the morning before he leaves for school. He actually pooped this morning right after breakfast, so this is a bonus poop.

Max hates bonus poops. Max hates all surprises.

Whenever he poops at school, Max tries to use the handicapped bathroom near the nurse's office so he can be alone, but today the janitor was cleaning puke off the floor because when a kid says that he's going to be sick, the nurse always sends him to that bathroom.

When Max has to use the regular bathroom, I stand outside the door and warn him if someone is coming. He doesn't like to have anyone in the bathroom when he is pooping, including me. But he doesn't like even more to be surprised, so I am allowed to come in, but only if it's an emergency.

An emergency means that someone is coming to use the bathroom.

When I tell him that someone is coming, Max lifts his feet up off the floor so no one can see him and waits until the bathroom is empty again before he finishes pooping. If he is lucky, the person never even knows that Max is on the toilet, unless the person has to poop, too, and knocks on the door to the stall. Then Max puts his feet back on the floor and waits until the person leaves.

One of Max's problems with pooping is that it takes him a long time, even when he is sitting on his own toilet at home. He has been in the bathroom for ten minutes already and he is probably not close to being finished. It's possible that he hasn't even started. He could still be carefully arranging his pants on top of his sneakers so they don't touch the floor.

That's when I see trouble come walking down the hall-way. Tommy Swinden has just left his classroom at the far end of the hall and is heading in my direction. As he walks, he swipes the maps of the thirteen colonies off the bulletin board outside Mrs Vera's class. He laughs and kicks the papers across the floor. Tommy Swinden is in fifth grade and he does not like Max.

He has never liked Max.

But now he doesn't like Max even more. Three months ago, Tommy Swinden took his Swiss Army knife to school to show it off to his friends. Tommy was standing at the edge of the woods, whittling a stick to show the other boys how sharp his knife was, and Max saw the knife and told the teacher. But Max doesn't know how to be quiet about these kinds of things. He ran up to Mrs Davis and shouted, 'Tommy Swinden has a knife! A knife!' A whole bunch of kids heard Max, and a few of the little kids screamed and ran in the direction of Tommy, which scared them even more. Tommy Swinden got in a lot of trouble. He was kicked out of school for a week, kicked off the bus for the rest of the school year, and had to go to these after-school classes to learn about being a good person.

That's a lot of trouble for a fifth grader.

Even though Mrs Davis and Mrs Gosk and the rest of the teachers all told Max that he did the right thing by reporting the knife (because weapons are not allowed at school and this is a very serious rule), none of them bothered to teach Max about how to tell on a kid without letting everyone on the playground know that you did. I don't get it. Mrs Hume spends all this time teaching Max how to take turns and ask for help but no one takes the time to teach Max something so important. Don't the teachers know that

Tommy Swinden is going to kill Max for getting him in so much trouble?

Maybe they don't because most of the teachers in Max's school are girls, and maybe they never got into any trouble when they were in school. Maybe none of them ever brought a knife to the playground or had trouble pooping in the bathroom. Maybe they don't know what it is like to be a kid in a lot of trouble, and that's probably why they spend their lunch hours saying things like, 'I don't know what that Tommy Swinden was thinking when he brought that knife to school.'

I know what he was thinking. He was thinking that his friends might stop calling him Tommy the 'Tard for not being able to read if he could show them that he knew how to whittle a stick with his Swiss Army knife. That's the kind of thing kids do. They try to cover up their problems with things like Swiss Army knives.

But I don't think the teachers understand this, which is probably why no one taught Max how to tell a teacher that a fifth grader has a knife without telling the entire world at the same time. So now Tommy Swinden, the fifth-grade boy who can't read and owns a knife and is twice as big as Max, is heading for the bathroom while Max is inside, trying to poop.

'Max!' I say as I pass through the restroom door. 'Tommy Swinden is coming!'

Max lets out a groan as his sneakers disappear from the crack between the stall and the floor. I want to pass through the stall door and stand alongside him, so he isn't all alone, but I know I can't. He wouldn't want me to see him on the toilet, and he knows that I can be more helpful outside the stall, where I can see what he can't.

Tommy Swinden, who is as tall as the art teacher and almost as wide as the gym teacher, comes into the bathroom and walks over to one of the toilets on the wall. He takes a quick peek under the stalls, sees no feet, and probably thinks he's alone. Then he looks back at the door to the bathroom, looks right through me, and reaches back, pulling his underwear from the crack in his butt. I see people do this all the time, because I spend a lot of time with people who think they are alone. When your underwear is stuck in the crack of your butt, it's called a wedgie and it can't be too comfortable. I've never had a wedgie because Max didn't imagine me with a wedgie. Thank goodness.

Tommy Swinden turns back to the toilet on the wall and pees. When he's done, he shakes his thing a little before buttoning and zipping his jeans. Not the way I once saw a kid shaking his thing in the handicapped bathroom near the nurse's office when Max asked me to check and see if anyone was in there. I have no idea what that boy was doing, but it was more than just a shake. I don't like to peek in on people using the bathroom, especially when they are tugging on their thing, but Max hates to knock on the bathroom door because he never knows what to say when someone knocks on the door when he's in there. He used to say, 'Max is pooping!' but then he got in trouble when a kid told the teacher what he said.

The teacher told Max that it's not appropriate to say that you're pooping. 'Just say *I'm in here* the next time someone knocks,' she told Max.

'But that sounds silly,' he said. 'The person won't know who *I* am. I can't just say *I'm* in here.'

'Fine,' the teacher said in a way that teachers tell kids to do ridiculous things when they're frustrated and don't want to talk anymore. 'Tell them who you are, then.'

So now when someone knocks on the bathroom door, Max says, 'Occupied by Max Delaney!' It makes people either laugh or stare at the door with a funny expression.

I don't blame them.

Tommy Swinden is finished at the toilet and is now standing at the sink, reaching for the faucet, just about to turn the knob and fill the bathroom with the sound of running water, when he hears a *plop!* from the stall where Max is hiding.

'Huh?' he says, bending down again to see if there are any feet in the stall. He doesn't see any, so he walks over to the first stall and bangs on the door real hard. Hard enough to make the whole stall shake. 'I know you're in there!' he says. 'I can see you through the cracks!'

I don't think Tommy knows that it's Max behind the door, because the cracks between the door and the wall are too small to see his whole face. But that's what is good about being one of the biggest kids in school. You can bang on a stall door and not worry about who is behind it, because you can beat up just about every kid at school.

Imagine what that must feel like.

Max doesn't answer, so Tommy bangs again. 'Who's in there? I want to know!'

'Don't say anything, Max!' I say from my spot by the door. 'He can't get in there. He'll have to leave eventually!'

But I'm wrong, because when Max doesn't answer the second time, Tommy gets down on his hands and knees and peeks his head under the door.

'Max the Moron,' he says, and I can hear the smile on his face. Not a nice smile. A rotten one. 'I can't believe it's you. It's my lucky day. What's the matter? Couldn't hold that last one in?'

'No,' Max shouts, and I can already hear the panic in his voice. 'It was already halfway out!'

Everything about this situation is bad.

Max is trapped inside a public bathroom, a place that already frightens him. His pants are wrapped around his ankles and he probably hasn't finished pooping. Tommy

Swinden is on the other side of the stall door, and Tommy definitely wants to hurt Max. They are alone. Except for me, of course, but they might as well be alone for all the help that I can be.

It's the way Max answered Tommy that scares me the most. There was more than panic in his voice. There was fear. Like when people in the movies see the ghost or the monster for the first time. Max just saw a monster peek underneath the stall door and he is frightened. He might already be close to getting stuck, and that is never good.

'Open this door, dickhead,' Tommy says, pulling his head back and standing up. 'Make this easy on me and all I'll do is bowl you.'

I don't know what *bowl* means, but I have visions of Tommy Swinden rolling Max's head across the bathroom like a bowling ball.

'Occupied by Max Delaney!' Max shouts, his voice screeching like a little girl. 'Occupied by Max Delaney!'

'Last chance, moron. Open it up or I'm coming in!'

'Occupied by Max Delaney!' Max screams again. 'Occupied by Max Delaney!'

Tommy Swinden gets back down on his hands and knees, ready to crawl under the door, and I don't know what to do.

Max needs more help than most kids in his class, and I am always there for him, ready to lend a hand. Even on the day that he tattled on Tommy Swinden, I was there, telling him to whisper, begging him to 'Slow down! Don't rush! Stop yelling!' Max wouldn't listen to me that day because there was a knife at school and that was such an important rule to break that he could not control himself. It was like the whole world was broken and he needed to find a teacher to fix it. I didn't stop him that day, but I tried.

At least I knew what to do.

But I don't know what to do now. Tommy Swinden is about to crawl under the door and enter a tiny bathroom stall where Max is trapped, probably perched on top of the toilet, knees in his chest, pants around his ankles, frozen in place. If he's not crying yet, he soon will be, and by the time Tommy has made it all the way under the door, Max will probably be screaming, a high-pitched, breathless scream that paints his face red and fills his eyes with tears. He will ball his hands into fists and bury his face behind his forearms, closing his eyes, and screaming the wispy, almost silent screams that make me think of a dog whistle. Full of air but almost no sound at all.

Before any teacher gets here, Tommy Swinden will bowl Max, whatever that means. Even though I'm sure that being bowled would be bad for any kid, it's going to be a lot worse for Max, because that is how Max is. Things stay with Max for ever. He never forgets. And even the tiniest, littlest things can permanently change him. Whatever *bowling* is, it's going to change Max for ever and ever. I know it and I don't know what to do.

'Help!' I want to scream. 'Someone help my friend!'

But only Max would hear.

Tommy's head disappears under the stall and I shout, 'Fight, Max! Fight! Don't let him in there!'

I don't know what makes me say it. I'm surprised by the words as they come out of my mouth. It's not a great idea. It's not smart or even original. It's just the only thing left to do. Max must fight or he will be bowled.

Tommy's head and shoulders are now under the stall and I can see that he is about to pull his hips and legs under in one quick movement, and then he will be inside the stall with Max, standing over his small, shaking body, ready to hurt him. Ready to bowl him.

I stand like a dummy outside the stall. Part of me wants to go in, to stand by my friend, but Max does not like it when people see him naked or pooping. I am as stuck as Max has ever been.

Then there is another scream, and this time it's not Max. This time it is Tommy who screams. It's not Max's terrified, locked-up scream. It's a different kind of scream. A more knowing scream. Not panicked or frightened, really, but the scream of someone who can't believe what has just happened. As he screams, Tommy starts to say something and he tries to stand up, forgetting the door above him, and he slams his back into the bottom of the door, causing him to scream again, this time in pain. Then the door flies open and Max is standing there, pants nearly pulled up but not buttoned or zipped, his legs straddling Tommy's head.

'Run!' I shout and he does, stepping on Tommy's hand, causing Tommy to scream again. Max runs past me, yanking his pants up the rest of the way, and then he is out the door. I follow. Instead of turning left toward his classroom, he turns right, buttoning and zipping his pants without stopping.

'Where are you going?'

'I still need a bathroom,' he says. 'Maybe the nurse's bathroom is clean now.'

'What happened to Tommy?' I ask. 'What did you do?'

'I pooped on his head,' Max says.

'You pooped with someone else in the bathroom?' I ask.

I can't believe it. The fact that he pooped on Tommy Swinden's head is unbelievable, but the fact that he managed a poop in the presence of another human person is even more amazing.

'Just a little one,' Max says. 'I was almost finished when he came in.' He takes a few more steps down the hall before adding, 'I pooped this morning, so this was a lot less poop this time. Remember? It was a bonus poop.'

CHAPTER 7

Max is worried that Tommy will tell on him the same way that he told on Tommy about the Swiss Army knife. But I know that he won't. No kid wants his friends or even his teachers to know that he was pooped on. Tommy will want to kill Max now. Actually kill him. Make his heart stop beating and whatever else it takes to kill a human person.

But we'll worry about that day when it comes.

Max can live with the fear of death just as long as he doesn't get in trouble for pooping on Tommy Swinden's head. Kids are afraid of dying all the time, so for Max, being afraid that Tommy Swinden might choke him to death or punch him in the nose is normal. But kids don't get suspended from school for pooping on the head of a fifth grader. That would happen only in a broken world.

I tell Max not to worry about getting in trouble. He only half believes me, but that's enough for him to stay unstuck.

Besides, Max pooped on Tommy Swinden three days ago

and we haven't seen Tommy since. At first I thought he was absent from school, so I went to Mrs Parenti's classroom to see if he was there, and he was. Sitting in the first row, closest to the teacher, probably so she can keep an eye on him.

I'm not sure what Tommy is thinking. Maybe he is so embarrassed about having poop on his head that he has decided to forget about the whole thing. Or maybe he's so angry that he is planning to torture Max before he kills him. Like the kids who burn ants with magnifying glasses at recess instead of just stepping on them and smearing them on the bottom of their sneakers.

That's what Max thinks, and even though I tell him that he's wrong, I know he is probably right.

You can't poop on the head of a kid like Tommy Swinden and expect to get away with it.

CHAPTER 8

I saw Graham today. I passed her on the way to the cafeteria. She waved to me.

She's starting to fade away.

I can't believe it.

I could see her spiky hair and toothy grin through her hand as she waved it back and forth in front of her face.

Imaginary friends can take a long time to disappear or a short time to disappear, but I don't think Graham has much time left.

Her human friend is a girl named Meghan, and she is six years old. Graham has been alive for only two years, but she is my oldest imaginary friend and I don't want her to go. She is the only real friend I have except for Max.

I am afraid for her.

I am afraid for me, too.

Someday I will raise my hand in front of my face and see Max's face on the other side of it, and then I'll know that I am fading away, too. Someday I am going to die, if that's what happens to imaginary friends.

It must be. Right?

I want to talk to Graham, but I don't know what to say. I wonder if she knows that she is disappearing.

If she doesn't know, should I tell her?

There are lots of imaginary friends in the world who I never get to meet because they do not leave their houses. Most imaginary friends aren't lucky enough to be able to go to school or walk around on their own like me and Graham. Max's mom brought us to one of her friends' houses once and I met three imaginary friends. They were all sitting in tiny chairs in front of a chalkboard. Their arms were crossed and they were frozen like statues while this little girl named Jessica recited the alphabet to them and asked them to answer math problems. But the imaginary friends couldn't walk or talk. When I walked into the playroom, they just blinked at me from their chairs. That was it.

Just blinked.

Those kinds of imaginary friends never last long. I once saw an imaginary friend pop up in Max's kindergarten classroom for fifteen minutes and then just disappear. It was like someone inflated her in the middle of the room. She got bigger and bigger and bigger like one of those people-shaped balloons they sell at parades until she was almost as big as me. A big, pink girl with pigtails in her hair and yellow flowers for feet. But when story time was done, it was like someone popped her with a pin. She shrank and shrank until I couldn't see her anymore.

I was scared watching that pink girl disappear. Fifteen minutes is nothing.

She never even heard the whole story.

But Graham has been around for so long. She has been my friend for two years. I can't believe that she is dying.

I want to be mad at her human friend, Meghan, because it is Meghan's fault that Graham is dying. She doesn't believe in Graham anymore.

When Graham dies, Meghan's mother will ask Meghan where her friend has gone, and Meghan will say something like, 'Graham doesn't live here anymore,' or 'I don't know where Graham is,' or 'Graham went on vacation.' And her mother will turn and smile, thinking her little girl is growing up.

But no. That is not what's going to happen. Graham is not going on any vacation. Graham is not moving to another city or country.

Graham is going to die.

You stopped believing, little girl, and now my friend is going to die. Just because you are the only human person who can see and hear Graham doesn't mean that she is not real. I can see and hear Graham, too. She is my friend.

Sometimes when you and Max are in class, we meet at the swing set to talk.

We used to play tag when you and Max had recess together.

Graham called me a hero once when I stopped Max from running out in front of a moving car, and even though I don't think I was a hero, it still felt good.

And now she is going to die because you don't believe in her anymore.

We are sitting in the cafeteria. Max is in music class and Meghan is eating lunch. I can tell by the way that Meghan is talking to the other girls at her lunch table that she doesn't need Graham like she used to. She is smiling. She is laughing. She is following the conversation with her eyes. She is even talking every now and then. She is part of a group now.

She's a whole new Meghan.

'How are you feeling today?' I ask, hoping this might get Graham to mention the disappearing first.

She does.

'I know what's happening if that's what you mean,' she says. She sounds so sad, but it also sounds like she has given up, too. Like she has already surrendered.

'Oh,' I say, and then I don't know what to say for a moment. I stare at her, and then I pretend to look around, over my shoulder and to my left, acting as if a sound in the corner of the cafeteria has caught my attention. I can't look at her because it means I'm looking through her. Finally, I turn back to her. I force myself to look. 'What does it feel like?'

'It doesn't feel like anything.'

She holds up her hands to show me, and I can see her face, no smile this time, on the other side of her hands. It is as if her hands were made of wax paper.

'I don't get it,' I say. 'What happened? When you talk to Meghan, can she still hear you?'

'Oh yeah. And she can still see me, too. We just spent the first ten minutes of recess playing hopscotch together.'

'Then why doesn't she believe in you anymore?'

Graham sighs. Then she sighs again.

'It's not that she doesn't believe in me. She doesn't *need* me anymore. She used to be afraid to talk to kids. When she was little, she had a stutter. It's gone now, but when she stuttered, she missed out on a lot of time talking with kids and making friends. But she's catching up now. A couple weeks ago she had a play date with Annie. It was her first play date ever. Now she and Annie are talking all the time. They even got in trouble in class yesterday for talking when they were supposed to be reading. And when the girls saw us playing hopscotch today, they came over and played, too.'

'What's a stutter?' I ask. I wonder if Max has a stutter, too.

'It's when words don't come out right. Meghan used to get stuck on words. She knew what the word was but couldn't make her mouth say it. A lot of times I would say the word really slowly for her, and then she could say it. But now she only stutters when she's afraid or nervous or surprised.'

'She was cured?'

'Sort of,' Graham says. 'She worked with Mrs Riner during the week and with Mr Davidoff after school. It took a long time but now she can talk just fine, so she's making friends.'

Max works with Mrs Riner, too. I wonder if he can be cured. I wonder if Mr Davidoff is the therapist who Max's mom wants him to see.

'So what are you going to do?' I ask. 'I don't want you to disappear. How can you stop it?'

I'm worried about Graham, but I feel like I need to ask these questions for me, too, in case she disappears right in front of me. I need to ask them while I still can.

Graham opens her mouth to talk and then she stops. She closes her eyes. She shakes her head and rubs her hands over her eyes. I wonder if she is stuttering now. But then she starts to cry. I try to remember if I have ever seen an imaginary friend cry.

I don't think so.

I watch as she dips her chin into her chest and sobs. Tears

stream down her cheeks, and when one finally drips off her chin, I watch as it falls, splashes on the table and then vanishes completely.

Like Graham will do before long.

I feel like I'm back in the boys' bathroom. Tommy Swinden is crawling under the stall. Max is standing on top of the toilet, his pants around his legs. And I am standing in the corner, not knowing what to say or what to do.

I wait until Graham's sobs turn to sniffles. I wait until the tears stop running. I wait until she can open her eyes again.

Then I speak. 'I have an idea.' I wait for Graham to say something.

She only sniffles.

'I have a plan,' I say again. 'A plan to save you.'

'Yeah?' Graham says, but I can tell that she doesn't believe me.

'Yes,' I say. 'All you need to do is be Meghan's friend.'

But that's not right and I know it as soon as I say it.

'No, wait,' I say. 'That's not right.'

I pause. The idea is there. I just have to find a way to say it right.

Say it without stuttering, I think.

Then I know.

'I have a plan,' I say again. 'We need to make sure that Meghan still needs you. We have to find a way to make it impossible for Meghan to live without you.'

46

CHAPTER 9

I can't believe we didn't think of this sooner. Meghan's teacher, Mrs Pandolfe, gives her class a spelling test every Friday, and Meghan does not do well on these tests.

I don't think that Max has ever spelled a word wrong, but Graham says that Meghan spells about six words wrong each week, which is about half of the words on her test, even though Graham didn't know that half of twelve is six. I thought it was kind of weird that she didn't know this, because it seems so obvious. I mean, if six plus six equals twelve, how could you not know that half of twelve is six?

Then again, I probably didn't know what half of twelve was when Max and me were in first grade together.

But I think I did.

Graham and I spent Meghan's lunch period making a list of all of Meghan's problems. I told Graham that we needed to find a problem that she could fix, and then, after she fixed it, Meghan would see how much she still needed Graham.

Graham thought it was a great idea. 'That might work,' she said, her eyes wide and bright for the first time since she started disappearing. 'That's a great idea. It might really work.'

But I think that Graham would think that any idea is a great idea, because she is fading away more and more by the minute.

I tried to make her laugh by telling her that her ears had already disappeared, since she never had any to begin with, but she didn't even smile at my joke. She's scared. She says she feels less real today, like she's going to fall into the sky and just float away. I started to tell her about satellites in space and how their orbits can decay and they can float away, too, to see if that is how she feels, but then I stopped.

I don't think she wants to talk about it.

Max taught me about decaying orbits last year. He read about it in a book. I am lucky because Max is smart and reads a lot, so I get to learn a lot, too. That's why I know that half of twelve is six and that satellites can fall out of orbit and float away for ever.

I am so glad that Max is my friend and not Meghan. Meghan can't even spell the word *boat*.

So we made a list of Meghan's problems. Of course, we

couldn't write the list down on paper, since neither one of us can pick up a pencil, but it was short enough that we were able to memorize it.

Stutters when she's upset.

Afraid of the dark.

Bad speller.

Can't tie her shoelaces.

Throws a temper tantrum every night before bed.

Can't zip up her coat.

Can't kick a ball past the pitcher.

It is not a good list, because Graham can't help her with a lot of these problems. If Graham could tie shoelaces or zip a zipper, she might be able to tie Meghan's sneakers or zip her coat, but she can't. I know only one imaginary friend who could touch and move things in the human world, and he wouldn't help us even if I begged him.

And I'm too afraid of him to go see him, anyway.

I didn't know what a temper tantrum was, so Graham had to explain it to me. It sounds a lot like when Max gets stuck. Meghan doesn't like to go to bed, so when her mom says that it's time to brush her teeth, she starts screaming and stamping her feet, and sometimes her daddy has to pick her up and carry her into the bathroom.

'This happens every night?' I ask Graham.

'Yeah. She turns red and gets all sweaty and eventually she starts crying. She cries herself to sleep a lot of nights. I feel so bad for her. Nothing that her parents or I say can make it any better.'

'Wow,' I say, because I can't imagine how annoying it must be to listen to someone have a temper tantrum every night.

Max doesn't get stuck too often, but when he does, it's like he is throwing a temper tantrum on the inside. He gets quiet and his hands make fists and he shakes a little, but he doesn't turn red or sweat or scream. I think he is doing all of those things on the inside, but on the outside he just gets stuck. And sometimes it takes a long time before he gets unstuck.

But at least it's not loud or annoying when it happens. And it never happens just because it's time to go to bed. Max likes to go to bed as long as it's the right time.

Eight-thirty.

If it's too early or too late, he gets upset.

I couldn't think of a way that Graham could help Meghan with her temper tantrums, so that didn't leave much else on the list. And that's what brought us back to the spelling tests.

'How can I help her with spelling?' Graham asked.

'I'll show you.'

Mrs Pandolfe keeps the weekly spelling words hanging on chart paper in front of the room, just like Mrs Gosk does in her classroom. She takes the list down on Thursday afternoon, so Graham and I spend the last hour of the day standing in front of the chart paper, memorizing each word. I've never paid a lot of attention to Max's spelling tests, and I don't really listen to Mrs Gosk's spelling lessons, so it was harder than I thought it would be. A lot harder.

But after an hour, Graham knew how to spell the words perfectly.

Tomorrow she'll stand next to Meghan as she takes the test, and when Meghan spells a word wrong, Graham will tell her how to spell it right. It's an especially good plan because Meghan has to take a spelling test every week, so this won't just be a one-time thing. She can help Meghan every week. Maybe she can even start helping Meghan on other tests, too.

I think this might really work, if Graham doesn't disappear tonight. An imaginary friend named Mr Finger once told me that most imaginary friends disappear when their human friends are asleep, but I think he was probably making that up to impress me. How could anyone know that? I almost told Graham to try to keep Meghan awake tonight, just in case Mr Finger was telling the truth, but Meghan is only six years old, and little kids like that can't stay up all night. She would eventually fall asleep no matter what Graham did.

So I'm just hoping that Graham makes it through the night.

CHAPTER 10

Max is mad at me because I have been spending so much time with Graham. He doesn't actually know that I've been with Graham. He just knows that I have been someplace else, and he is mad. I think this is good. I always get a little nervous when I don't see Max for a while, but if he's mad at me for not being around enough, that means he's been thinking about me and misses me.

'I had to go pee and you weren't there to check the bathroom,' Max says. 'I had to knock on the door.'

We are riding on the bus now, going home, and Max is hunkered down in his seat, whispering to me so the other kids don't hear us talking. Except they do. They always do. Max can't see what the other kids can see, but I can. I can see the forest for the trees.

'I had to go pee and you weren't there to check the bathroom,' Max says again.

Max repeats himself if you don't answer his questions,

because he needs an answer before he can say the next thing. Except that Max doesn't always ask his questions like questions. Lots of times he just says something and expects you to know it's a question. If he has to repeat himself three or four times, which he never has to do for me but sometimes has to do for his teachers and his dad, he gets really upset. Sometimes this makes him get stuck.

'I was in Tommy's classroom,' I say. 'I was trying to figure out what he plans on doing next. I wanted to make sure that he wasn't going to get his revenge this week.'

'You were spying,' Max says, and I know that this is a question, too, even if he doesn't say it like a question.

'Yes,' I say. 'I was spying.'

'Okay,' Max says, but I can tell that he's still a little mad.

I can't tell Max that I was with Graham because I don't want Max to know that other imaginary friends exist. If he thinks that I'm the only imaginary friend in the whole wide world, then he'll think I'm special. He'll think that I'm unique. That is good, I think.

It helps me persist.

But if Max knew that there were other imaginary friends, and he was mad at me, like he is now, then maybe he would just forget about me and imagine a new imaginary friend. And then I would disappear like Graham is disappearing right now.

It's been hard, because I want to tell Max about Graham.

At first I wanted to tell him because I thought he could help. I thought that maybe Max could give me a good idea to help Graham because Max is so smart. Or maybe he could help us solve one of Meghan's problems, like teaching her to tie her own shoes, and then he could tell Meghan that it was Graham's idea, so Graham would get all of the credit.

But now I want to tell Max about Graham because I'm scared. I'm afraid that I might lose my friend and I don't have anyone to talk to about it. I guess I could talk to Puppy, but I don't know Puppy very well, and definitely not as well as I know Max or Graham. And even if Puppy can talk, talking to a dog is weird. Max is my friend, and he should be the one I talk to when I'm sad or afraid, but I can't.

I just hope that Graham comes to school tomorrow and we aren't too late.

Max's father likes to tell people that he and Max play catch every night in the backyard, like they are doing tonight. He tells everyone he can, sometimes more than once, but he usually waits until Max's mom isn't around before he says it. Sometimes he says it just after she leaves the room if he knows that she's coming right back.

But he and Max don't really play catch. Max's dad throws the ball to Max, and Max lets it hit the ground and roll, and when it stops moving, he picks it up and tries to throw it back. Except Max's dad never stands close enough for Max to reach him, even though he tells Max to 'Step into it!' and 'Throw with your body!' and 'Give it your all, son!'

Whenever they play catch, Max's dad calls Max *son* instead of Max.

But even if Max *steps into it* or *gives it his all* (I don't know what either of those things mean, and I don't think Max does either), the ball never reaches his dad.

If Max's dad wants the ball to reach him, why doesn't he just stand closer?

Max is in bed now. He is sleeping. No temper tantrum, of course. He brushed his teeth, put on his Thursday-night pajamas, read one chapter in his book, and laid his head down on the pillow at exactly eight-thirty. Max's mom is at a meeting tonight so Max's dad gave Max a kiss on the forehead and said good night. Then he turned out the light in Max's room and switched on the nightlights.

There are three.

I sit in the dark beside Max's bed, thinking about Graham. Wondering if there is anything left to think about. Wondering if there is anything else I can do.

Max's mom comes home a little later. She sneaks into the room, tiptoes over to Max's bed, and kisses him on the forehead. Max allows his mom and dad to kiss him, but it has to be quick and always on the cheek or forehead, and Max always cringes whenever they do it. But when Max is asleep like this, his mom can give him a longer kiss, usually on the forehead but sometimes on the cheek, too. Sometimes she goes to his room to kiss him two or three times a night before she goes to bed, even if she was the one who put him to bed and kissed him already.

One morning at breakfast, Max's mom told Max that she had given him a kiss good night after he was asleep. She said, 'You looked like such an angel last night when I went to kiss you good night.'

'Dad put me to bed,' Max said. 'Not you.'

This was one of Max's questions-that's-not-a-question, and I knew it. So did Max's mom. She always knows. She knows even better than me.

'Yes,' she said. 'I was visiting Grandpa at the hospital, but when I came home, I tiptoed into your bedroom and gave you a kiss good night.'

'You gave me a kiss good night,' Max said.

'Yes,' his mom said.

Later on, while we were riding the bus to school, Max hunkered down and said, 'Did Mom kiss me on the lips?'

'No,' I said. 'On the forehead.'

Max touched his forehead, rubbed it with his fingers and then looked at his fingers. 'Was it a long kiss?' he asked.

'No,' I said. 'It was super-short.'

But that wasn't the truth. I don't lie to Max very often, but I lied that time because I thought it would be better for Max and better for his mother if I did.

Max still asks me if his mom gives him a long kiss on the nights when she is not home to put him to bed. I always say, 'Nope. Super-short.'

And I've never told Max about all the extra kisses his mom gives him before she goes to bed.

But that's not a lie, because Max has never asked me if she gives him extra kisses.

Max's mom is eating dinner. She heated the plate of food that Max's dad made for her from the leftovers. Max's dad is sitting at the table across from her, reading a magazine. I am not a very good reader but I know this magazine is called *Sports Illustrated* because Max's dad gets it from the envelope and magazine delivery man every week.

I'm annoyed because it doesn't look like Max's mom and dad are going to watch television soon, and I want to watch television. I like to sit on the couch next to Max's mom and watch the television show and listen to them talk about the show during the commercials.

Commercials are tiny little shows in between the big show, but most of them are stupid and boring, so no one really watches them. People use the commercials to talk or go to the bathroom or fill their glass with more soda.

Max's dad likes to complain about the television shows. He thinks that they are never good enough. He says the stories are *ridiculous* and that there were too many *missed opportunities*. I'm not really sure what this means, but I think it means that the television shows would be better if he was allowed to tell the people on the show what to do.

Max's mom sometimes gets annoyed at the complaining because she just likes to watch the shows and not look for the *missed opportunities*.

'I just want to take a break from the day,' she says, and I agree. I don't watch the shows to find a way to make them better. I just like the stories. But most of the time Max's mom and dad just laugh at the shows that are funny and bite their nails when the shows are scary or suspenseful. I don't think Max's mom and dad know that they both bite their nails at the exact same time when they watch television.

They also love to predict what will happen on the next show. I'm not sure, but I think that Max's mom and dad must have had Mrs Gosk as a third-grade teacher, because she is always asking her students to make a prediction about the book that she is reading, and it seems like making predictions is what Max's mom and dad like to do the best. I like to make predictions, too, because then I can wait and see if I'm right. Max's mom likes to predict that good things are going to happen even when everything looks bad. I usually predict the worst possible ending, and sometimes I'm right, especially when we watch movies.

That's why I'm so nervous tonight about Graham. I can't stop thinking about the worst.

Some nights I have to sit in the cozy chair because Max's dad sits next to Max's mom and puts his arm around her, and she squeezes in real close and they smile. I like those nights because I know they are happy, but I feel a little left out at the same time. Like I don't belong. Sometimes on those nights I just leave, especially if they are watching a show without a story, like the one where people decide who sings the best and the winner gets a prize.

Actually, I think it's more fun to figure out who is singing the worst.

Max's mom and dad are quiet for a long time. She is eating and he is reading. The only sounds are the tinkles of the fork and knife on the plate. Max's mom is never this quiet unless she wants Max's dad to talk first. Usually she has lots and lots to say, but sometimes, when they are fighting, she likes to wait and see if Max's dad will talk first. She's never told me this, but I've watched them for so long that I just know.

I don't know what they are fighting about tonight, so it's almost like watching a television show. I know they are going to argue soon, but I don't know what it will be about. It's a mystery. I predict that it will have something to do with Max, because that's what they argue about the most.

When she is finished with her dinner, Max's mom finally speaks. 'Have you thought about seeing a doctor?'

Max's dad sighs. 'You really think we need to?' He doesn't look up from his magazine, which is a bad sign.

'It's been ten months.'

'I know, but ten months isn't a long time. It's not like we had any trouble in the past.' Now he is looking at Max's mom.

'I know,' she says. 'But how long should we wait, then? I don't want to wait a year or two before we talk to some-one and then find out that there's a problem. I'd rather know now, so we can do something about it.'

Max's dad rolls his eyes. 'I just don't think ten months is that long to wait. It took Scott and Melanie almost two years. Remember?'

Max's mom sighs. I can't tell if she is sad or frustrated or something else.

'I know,' she says. 'But it wouldn't hurt to just speak to someone. Right?'

'Yeah,' Max's dad says, and now he sounds angry. 'That'd be fine if speaking to someone was all we had to do. But talking to a doctor isn't going to help if we have a problem. They're going to want to do tests. It's only been ten months.'

'But don't you want to know?'

Max's dad doesn't answer. If Max's mom was Max, she would repeat the question, but sometimes adults answer questions by not answering them at all. I think that this is what Max's dad is doing.

When he finally speaks, he answers Max's mom's first question instead of her last. 'Okay, we can go see a doctor. Will you make the appointment?'

Max's mom nods. I thought she would be happy that Max's dad agreed to go to the doctor, but she still looks sad. Max's dad looks sad, too, but neither one of them looks at the other. Not once. It is like there are a hundred dining room tables between them instead of just one.

I feel sad for them, too.

If they had just watched television, this would never have happened.

CHAPTER 11

I tell Max that I'm going to check on Tommy Swinden again. He doesn't mind because he made a poop this morning, so he won't need me to check the bathroom until lunch. And Mrs Gosk has started the day by reading aloud to the class. Max loves it when Mrs Gosk reads aloud. He becomes so focused on her voice that he forgets everything else, so he probably won't even know I'm gone.

I don't go to Tommy Swinden's class. I go to Mrs Pandolfe's classroom. I almost don't want to go, because I'm afraid of what I will find. Or what I won't find.

I step into her classroom, which is much neater and more organized than Mrs Gosk's classroom. All the desks are in perfectly straight rows and there are no sliding mountains of papers on Mrs Pandolfe's desk. It's almost too clean.

I look from one side of the room to the other and then back again. Graham is not here. I look in the corner behind the bookshelf and in the coatroom. She is not there.

The children are sitting in their rows, staring at Mrs Pandolfe, who is standing at the front of the classroom. She is pointing at a calendar and talking about the date and the weather. The chart paper with the list of this week's spelling words is gone.

I see Meghan. She sits near the back of the classroom. Her hand is raised. She wants to answer Mrs Pandolfe's question about the number of days in October.

It's thirty-one. I know that answer.

I don't see Graham.

I want to walk over to Meghan and ask her if she stopped believing in her imaginary friend last night.

'Did you stop believing in the pointy-haired girl who kept you company when you didn't know how to talk and everyone made fun of you?'

'Did you forget about your friend when you forgot how to stutter?'

'Did you even notice that she was fading away?'

'Did you kill my friend?'

Meghan can't hear me. I'm not her imaginary friend. Graham is.

Graham was.

Then I see her. She's standing just a few steps away from Meghan, near the back of the class, but I can barely see her. I was looking right through her, straight through to the windows, and I didn't even know it. It's like someone painted her picture on the window a long time ago and now it's all faded and worn. I don't think I would have even noticed her, had she not blinked. It was the movement that I saw first. Not her.

'I didn't think you'd see me,' Graham says.

I don't know what to say.

'It's all right,' Graham says. 'I know how hard it is to see me. When I opened my eyes this morning, I couldn't see my own hands at first. I thought I had disappeared.'

'I didn't know you sleep,' I said.

'Yeah. Of course I do. You don't?'

'No,' I say.

'Then what do you do when Max is asleep?'

'I hang out with his parents until they go to sleep,' I say. 'Then I go for walks.'

I don't tell her about my visits to the gas station on the corner and Doogies and the hospital and the police station. I have never told any imaginary friends about my visits. I feel like they are mine. My own special thing.

'Wow,' Graham says, and I notice for the first time that her voice is starting to fade, too. It sounds wispy and thin, like she's talking through a door. 'I never knew that you didn't need to sleep. I feel bad for you.'

'Why?' I ask. 'What good is sleep?'

'When you sleep, you dream.'

'*You* dream?' I ask.

'Of course,' Graham says. 'Last night I dreamed that Meghan and I were twin sisters. We were playing in the sandbox together, and my fingers could touch the sand. I could hold it in my hands and let it run though my fingers, just like Meghan does.'

'I can't believe you dream,' I say.

'I can't believe you can't.'

Neither one of us says anything for a minute.

There is a boy at the front of the classroom named Norman, and he is talking about his visit to a place called Old Newgate Prison. I know what a prison is, so I know that Norman is lying about his trip. Kids aren't allowed to visit prisons. But I can't figure out why Mrs Pandolfe isn't making Norman tell the truth. If Mrs Gosk heard Norman telling this story, she would say, 'Shame! Shame! Let all the boys and girls know your name!' Then Norman would have to tell the truth.

Norman has a rock in his hand, and he says it came from the prison. He says it came from *a mine*. That doesn't make any sense, either. A mine is a bomb that soldiers bury in the ground so that when other soldiers pass by, they will step on it and blow up. Max pretends to dig minefields for his toy soldiers, so that's how I know. So how could Norman get a rock from a mine?

But Norman has everyone fooled, because all the kids in the class want to touch the rock now, even though it's just rock that he probably found on the playground this morning. Even if he really did find the rock on a mine, it's still just a rock. Why is everyone so excited? Mrs Pandolfe has to tell the class to 'sit back and relax'. When Mrs Gosk wants her kids to relax, she says, 'Don't get your knickers in a bunch.' I don't know what this means, but it sounds funny.

Mrs Pandolfe tells all the kids to sit down again. She promises that everyone will get a chance to hold the rock if they are just patient.

It's just a stupid rock, I want to yell.

All this nonsense going on while my friend is dying.

'When is the spelling test?' I finally ask.

'Next, I think,' Graham says, and her voice is even wispier than before. It sounds as if she's standing behind three doors now. 'She usually gives the test right after show and tell.'

Graham is right. After Norman is done lying about his fake trip to the prison and everyone has had a chance to touch his stupid rock, Mrs Pandolfe finally passes out the white-lined paper for the spelling test.

I stand at the back of the room during the test while Graham stands beside Meghan. I can barely see her anymore. When she stands still, she almost disappears completely.

I'm standing in the back, hoping that Meghan makes at

least one mistake. Even though Meghan is a rotten speller, Graham said that she's also spelled all the words on some tests correctly. If she spells them all correctly today, we won't have time to make a new plan.

I feel like Graham could disappear at any second.

Then it happens. Mrs Pandolfe says *giant* and Meghan writes the word on her paper. A second later, Graham leans over, points to it, and says something. Meghan has spelled the word wrong, probably with a *j* instead of a *g*, and I feel giddy as I watch her erase the word and rewrite it.

Three words later, the same thing happens again, this time on the word *surprise*. By the time the test is finished, Graham has helped Meghan spell five words correctly and I am just waiting for the fading to reverse. In minutes, I expect that I will no longer lose sight of her unless she is moving. Any second now, my friend will appear whole again. She will be safe once more.

I wait.

Graham waits.

The test is over. We sit at a small table at the back of the room. We stare at each other. I wait for the moment when I can jump up and shout, 'It's happening! You're coming back!'

Mrs Pandolfe has moved onto math and we still wait.

But it's not happening. In fact, I think she's fading away

even more. Graham is sitting three feet in front of me and I can barely see her.

I want to doubt my eyes. They must be playing tricks on me. But then I know it's true. Graham is still fading away. She's becoming more and more transparent by the second.

I can't tell her. I don't want to tell her that the plan didn't work, because it should have worked. It had to work.

But it didn't. Graham is disappearing. She is almost gone.

'It didn't work,' she finally says, breaking the silence. 'I can tell. It's okay.'

'It had to work,' I say. 'She spelled all those words right because of you. She needs you. She knows that now. It had to work.'

'It didn't,' Graham says. 'I can tell. I can feel it.'

'Does it hurt?'

As soon as I say it, I wish I hadn't asked it. I feel bad asking it, because I'm asking it for me. Not for my friend.

'No,' Graham says. 'Not at all.' Even though it's hard to see her, I think she is smiling. 'It feels like I'm floating away. Like I'm free.'

'There must be something else we can do,' I say.

I sound frantic. I can't help it. I feel like I am on a ship sinking into the ocean and there are no little boats to save me.

I think that Graham is shaking her head, but I can't tell. It's so hard to see her now.

'There has to be something that we can do,' I say again. 'Wait. You said that Meghan is afraid of the dark. Go tell her that a monster lives under her bed, and it only comes out at night, and that you're the reason she hasn't been eaten yet. Tell her that every night you protect her from the monster, and that if you die she will be eaten.'

'Budo, I can't.'

'It's a rotten thing to do, I know, but you're going to die if you don't. You have to try.'

'It's okay,' Graham says. 'I'm ready to go.'

'What does that mean you're ready to go? Go where? You know what happens when you disappear?'

'No, but it's okay,' she says again. 'Whatever happens, I'll be fine and Meghan will be fine.'

I can barely hear her now.

'You have to try, Graham. Go over there and tell her that she needs you. Tell her about the monster under the bed!'

'That's not it, Budo. It doesn't have to do with Meghan needing me. We were wrong. Meghan's just growing up. First it's me, and then it'll be the tooth fairy, and next year it will be Santa Claus. She's a big girl now.'

'But the tooth fairy isn't real and you are! Fight, Graham. Fight! Please! Don't leave me!'

'You've been a good friend to me, Budo, but I have to go now. I'm going to go sit next to Meghan now. I want to spend my last few minutes with her. Sitting next to my friend. It's the only thing I'm really sad about.'

'What?'

'That I won't be able to look at her anymore. See her grow up. I'm going to miss Meghan so much.' She is quiet for a moment and then she adds, 'I love her so much.'

I start crying. I don't know it at first, because I have never cried before. My nose is suddenly clogged with boogers and my eyes feel wet. I feel warm and sad. So very sad. I feel like a hose with a kink in it, just waiting to let go and spray water everywhere. I feel like I am going to burst open with tears. But I'm glad that I'm crying, because I don't have the words to say goodbye to Graham, and I know that I must. Graham will be gone very soon and I am going to lose my friend. I want to say goodbye and tell her how much I love her, too, but I don't know how. I hope that my tears say it for me.

Graham stands up and smiles at me. She nods her head. Then she walks over to Meghan. She sits behind her and speaks in her ear. I don't think Meghan can hear her anymore. Meghan is listening to Mrs Pandolfe and smiling.

I stand up. I go to the door. I want to leave. I don't want to be here when Graham disappears. I look back one more time. Meghan has her hand raised again, ready to answer another question. Answer without stuttering. Graham is still sitting behind her, perched in a tiny first-grade chair. I can barely see her now. If Mrs Pandolfe opened the window and let a breeze in, I think that it might be enough to blow the last little bit of Graham away for ever.

I look one more time before I leave. Graham is still smiling. She's staring at Meghan, craning her neck to see the little girl's face, and she's smiling.

I turn. I leave my friend behind.

CHAPTER 12

Mrs Gosk is teaching math. The kids are spread out around the room, rolling dice and calculating with their fingers. It takes me a minute to check all the corners of the room, but Max is not here. This is good. Max hates these games. He hates to roll dice and listen to kids scream when they roll two sixes. He just wants to solve his math problems and be left alone.

I'm not sure where Max is supposed to be right now. He could be in the Learning Center with Mrs McGinn and Mrs Patterson, or he could be in Mrs Hume's office. It's hard to keep track of Max because he sees so many teachers during the day. I'm also not very good at telling the time when a clock has hands on it, and that's the only kind of clock that Mrs Gosk has in her classroom.

I check in Mrs Hume's office first because it is the closest to Mrs Gosk's room but Max is not there. Mrs Hume is talking to the principal about a boy who sounds a lot like

Tommy Swinden except his name is Danny and he is in second grade. The principal sounds worried. She uses the word *situation* three times when talking about Danny. When adults use *situation* a lot, it means that things are serious.

The principal's name is Mrs Palmer. She's an older lady who doesn't like to punish kids or give out consequences, so she talks to Mrs Hume a lot about *alternative ways* to make the students behave. She thinks that if she makes a kid like Tommy volunteer in a kindergarten classroom, he will learn to behave.

I think that just gives Tommy Swinden a chance to be mean to even smaller kids.

Mrs Hume thinks that Mrs Palmer is crazy, but she doesn't tell Mrs Palmer. But I've heard her say it more than once to other teachers. Mrs Hume thinks that if Mrs Palmer would just give a kid like Tommy Swinden detention more often, he might not try to bowl kids like Max in the bathroom.

I think Mrs Hume is right.

Max's mom says that the right thing is usually the hardest thing. I don't think Mrs Palmer has learned that lesson yet.

I walk down the hallway and check the Learning Center, but Max isn't there either. Mrs McGinn is working with a boy named Gregory. Gregory is a first grader who has a disease called seizures. He has to wear a helmet all the time just in case he falls on his head when he's having a seizure. A seizure is a like a combination of a temper tantrum and getting stuck.

Maybe if I had figured out a way for Graham to help Meghan with her temper tantrums, Graham would still be here. Maybe Meghan didn't care about spelling. Maybe we needed to fix something even bigger than a spelling test.

Max is probably in the bathroom near the nurse's office. He probably had a bonus poop after all. If that's what happened, Max is going to be mad. That's two days in a row that he had to knock on the door.

But Max isn't in the bathroom either. It's empty.

Now I'm worried.

The only other place where Max could be is in Mrs Riner's office, but Max works with his speech teacher only on Tuesdays and Thursdays. Maybe he's working with her today for some special reason. Maybe Mrs Riner has to go to a wedding next Tuesday and won't be able to see Max. It's the only place he could be. But Mrs Riner's room is on the other side of the school, and I'll have to walk by Mrs Pandolfe's classroom to get there.

I hadn't thought about Graham for three whole minutes and I was starting to feel better. Now I'm wondering if Graham has completely disappeared. If I walk by the classroom, I wonder if I will look inside and see her still sitting behind Meghan. Maybe I will see just a few wisps left of my friend.

I want to wait until Max gets back to Mrs Gosk's classroom, but I know I should meet him in Mrs Riner's classroom. It would make him happy to see me, and, to be honest, I want to see Max, too. Watching Graham disappear makes me want to see Max more than ever, even if it means walking by Mrs Pandolfe's classroom.

But I never get there.

Just as I'm passing the gym, which separates the little kids' side of the school from the big kids' side of the school, I see Max. He is walking into the school, passing through a set of double doors that lead to the outside. It doesn't make sense. It's not recess time, and those aren't even doors that lead to the playground. They face the parking lot and the street. I have never seen a kid go through those doors.

Mrs Patterson walks in behind him. She stops as she enters the building and looks left and right, like she was expecting to see someone waiting by the doors.

'Max!' I say, and he turns and sees me.

He doesn't say anything, because he knows if he does, Mrs Patterson will start asking questions. Some adults talk to Max like he's a baby when they ask him questions about me. They say, 'Is Budo with us right now?' and 'Does Budo have anything he wants to say to me?'

'Yes,' I always tell Max. 'Tell them that I wish I could punch them in the nose.'

But he never does.

Then there are other adults that look at Max like he's sick when he tells them about me. Like there's something wrong with him. Sometimes they even look a little frightened of him. So we almost never talk in front of people, and when someone sees Max talking to me from a distance, on the playground or on the bus or in the bathroom, he just says that he was talking to himself.

'Where were you?' I ask, even though I know that Max won't answer.

He looks back outside toward the parking lot. His eyes widen to tell me that, wherever he was, it was good.

We walk in the direction of Mrs Gosk's classroom, Mrs Patterson leading the way. Just before we reach the classroom door, Mrs Patterson stops. She turns around and looks at Max. Then she leans down so that she and Max are eye to eye.

'Remember what I said, Max. I want only what's best for you. Sometimes I think I'm the only one who knows what's best for you.'

I'm not sure, but I think Mrs Patterson said that last part more to herself than to Max.

She's about to say something else when Max interrupts. 'When you tell me the same thing over and over again, it bothers me. It makes me think that you don't think I'm smart.'

'I'm sorry,' Mrs Patterson says. 'I didn't mean that. You're the smartest boy I know. I won't say it again.'

She pauses for a second, and I can tell that she's waiting for Max to say something. This happens a lot. Max doesn't notice the pauses. Someone will be speaking to him, and when the person stops, expecting Max to say something, he just waits. If there is no question to answer and nothing that he wants to say, then he just waits. The silence does not make him squirm like it makes other people squirm.

Mrs Patterson finally speaks again. 'Thank you, Max. You really are a smart and a sweet young man.'

Even though I think that Mrs Patterson is telling the truth, that she really believes that Max is smart and sweet, she is using that same baby talk that some people use to speak to Max about me. She sounds fake because she sounds like she is trying to be real instead of just being real.

I do not like Mrs Patterson one bit.

'Where did you go with Mrs Patterson today?' I ask.

'I can't tell you. I promised I would keep it a secret.'

'But you've never kept a secret from me.'

Max grins. It's not exactly a smile, but it is as close as Max gets to smiling. 'No one has ever asked me to keep a secret before. This is my first.'

'Is it a bad secret?' I ask.

'What do you mean?'

'Did you do something bad? Or did Mrs Patterson do something bad?'

'No.'

I think for a moment. 'Were you helping someone?'

'Kind of, but it's a secret,' Max says, and he grins again. His eyes get wide. 'I can't tell you anything else.'

'You're really not going to tell me?' I ask.

'No. It's a secret. It's my first secret.'

CHAPTER 13

Max did not go to school today. It is Halloween, and Max does not go to school on Halloween. The masks that the kids wear during their Halloween parties scare him. In kindergarten Max got stuck after seeing a boy named JP walk out of the bathroom wearing a Spiderman mask. It was the first time he got stuck at school and the teacher didn't know what to do. I don't think I've ever seen a teacher so scared.

Max's mom and dad sent him to school on Halloween in first grade, hoping that he had grown out of it. *Grown out of it* means that his parents couldn't figure out what to do, so they didn't do anything except hope that things had changed because Max was taller and wearing bigger sneakers.

But as soon as the first kid put on a mask, Max got stuck again.

Last year he stayed home from school on Halloween, and he is doing the same today. Max's dad took the day off, too, so they could spend the day together. He called his boss and said that he was sick. An adult doesn't have to be sick to say that he is sick, but if a kid wants to stay home from school, he has to be sick.

Or afraid of Halloween masks.

We're going to the pancake house on the Berlin Turnpike. Max likes the pancake house. It's one of his four favorite restaurants. Max will eat at only four restaurants.

A List of Max's Four Favorite Restaurants

1. International House of Pancakes.
2. Wendy's (Max can't eat at Burger King anymore because his father once told him a story about a customer eating a fish sandwich with a bone in it and now Max is worried that everything at his father's Burger King will have a bone in it).
3. Max Burger (there are actually a bunch of Max restaurants, with names like Max Fish and Max Downtown, and Max thinks it's great that they share his name. But Max's parents brought him to Max Burger first, and now it's the only one where he will eat).
4. The Corner Pug.

If Max goes to a new restaurant, he cannot eat. Sometimes he even gets stuck. It's hard to explain why. To Max, the pancakes at the pancake house on the Berlin Turnpike are pancakes, but the pancakes at the diner across the street aren't really pancakes. Even though they look the same and probably taste the same, they are a completely different food for Max. He would tell you that the pancakes across the street at the diner are pancakes, but not his pancakes.

Like I said, it's hard to explain.

'Do you want to try blueberries in your pancakes today?' Max's father asks.

'No,' Max says.

'Okay,' Max's dad says. 'Maybe next time.'

'No.'

We sit quietly for a while, waiting for the food to come. Max's dad flips through the menu even though he has already ordered his food. The waitress stuck the menus behind the syrup when Max and his dad were done ordering, but Max's dad took one back out as soon as she left. I think he likes to have something to look at when he doesn't know what to say.

Max has a staring contest with me. We do this a lot.

He wins the first game. I get distracted when a waitress drops a glass of orange juice on the floor.

'Are you happy to have the day off from school?' Max's father asks just as we are beginning another staring contest. His father's voice startles me and I blink.

Max wins again.

'Yes,' Max says.

'Do you want to try trick-or-treating tonight?'

'No.'

'You wouldn't have to wear a mask,' Max's dad says. 'No costume at all if you don't want.'

'No.'

I think that Max's dad sometimes gets sad talking to Max. I can see it in his eyes and hear it in his voice. The more they talk, the worse it gets. His shoulders slump. He sighs a lot. His chin sinks into his chest. I think that he thinks that Max's one-word answers are all his fault. Like he is to blame for Max not wanting to talk. But Max doesn't talk unless he has something to say, no matter who you are, so if you ask him only yes or no questions, you're going to get only yes or no answers.

Max doesn't know how to chat.

Actually, Max doesn't want to know how to chat.

We sit in silence again. Max's dad is looking at the menu.

An imaginary friend enters the restaurant. He's walking behind a set of parents and a little girl with red hair and freckles. The imaginary friend actually looks a lot like me. He looks almost like a human person, except his skin is yellow. Not a little yellow. Yellow like someone painted him with the yellowiest yellow they could find. He's also missing eyebrows, which is pretty common for imaginary friends. But otherwise he could pass for a human person, if anyone except for the little redhead and I could see him.

'I'm going to check out the kitchen,' I say to Max. 'Make sure it's clean.'

I do this a lot when I want to explore. Max likes it when I make sure places are clean.

Max nods. He's drumming his fingers on the table in patterns.

I walk over to the yellow boy, who has taken a seat beside the girl. They are on the other side of the restaurant, and Max can't see me from here.

'Hello,' I say. 'I'm Budo. Would you like to talk?'

The yellow boy is so startled that he almost falls off the bench. I get this a lot.

'You can see me?' the yellow boy says.

He has a little girl's voice, which is also common with imaginary friends. Kids never seem to imagine their imaginary friends with deep voices. I guess it's just easier to imagine a voice like your own.

'Yes,' I say. 'I can see you. I'm like you.'

'Really?'

'Yes.'

I don't use the words *imaginary friend* because not every imaginary friend knows this name, and it scares some of them when they hear it for the first time.

'Who are you talking to?'

This is the little girl. Maybe three or four years old. She has heard the yellow boy's half of the conversation.

I see the panic in the yellow boy's eyes. He doesn't know what to say.

'Tell her that you were talking to yourself,' I say.

'Sorry, Alexis. I was talking to myself.'

'Can you get up and walk away?' I ask. 'Is that something you can do?'

'I have to go to the bathroom,' the yellow boy says to Alexis.

'Okay,' Alexis says.

'Okay what?' asks the woman sitting across from Alexis. Alexis's mom, no doubt. The two look so much alike. Red hair and freckles times two.

'Okay that Jo-Jo can go to the potty,' Alexis says.

'Oh,' Alexis's dad says. 'Jo-Jo's going to the potty. Huh?'

Jo-Jo's dad is using the baby talk. I don't like him already.

'Follow me,' I say, and I lead Jo-Jo through the kitchen, down a set of stairs, and into the basement.

I've explored this place before. With only four restaurants, and three that we go inside, it isn't hard to cover them all. There is a walk-in freezer to my right and a stockroom to my left, though it's not really a room. It's just a space surrounded by a chain-link fence. The fence starts at the floor and goes to the ceiling. I pass through the door, which is also made from chain-link fence, and sit on one of the boxes on the other side.

'Whoa!' Jo-Jo says. 'How did you do that?'

'Can't you pass through doors?'

'I don't know.'

'If you could, you would know,' I say. 'It's okay.'

I pass back through the door and take a seat on a plastic pail in the corner by the stairs. Jo-Jo stands by the wire fence for a moment longer, staring at it. He reaches out to touch it, moving his hand slowly as if he's afraid to be electrocuted. His hand stops at the chain-link. He doesn't touch the fence. He doesn't move the wire with his hand. His hand just stops. It's not the fence that blocks him from entering. It's the idea of the fence.

I've seen this before, too. It's the same reason I don't fall through the floor. When I walk, I don't leave footprints because I'm not actually touching the ground. I'm touching the idea of the ground.

Some ideas, like floors, are too strong for imaginary friends to pass through. No one imagines an imaginary friend who slides through the floor and disappears. The idea of the floor is too strong in a little kid's mind. It's too permanent. Like walls.

Lucky for us.

'Sit,' I say, motioning to a barrel.

Jo-Jo does.

'I'm Budo. Sorry to scare you.'

'It's okay. You just look so real.'

'I know,' I say.

I have frightened lots of imaginary friends when they realize that I am talking to them because I look so real. You can usually tell that someone is an imaginary friend by their yellow skin or missing eyebrows.

Most of the time, they don't look a human person at all.

But I do. That's why I can be a little scary. I look real.

'Can you tell me what's happening?' Jo-Jo says.

'What do you already know?' I ask. 'Let's start with that, and then I'll fill in the missing pieces that I know.' This is the best way to talk to an imaginary friend for the first time.

'Okay,' Jo-Jo says. 'But what should I tell?'

'How long have you been alive?' I ask.

'I don't know. A little while.'

'More than a few days?' I ask.

'Oh, yes.'

'More than a few weeks?'

Jo-Jo thinks for a moment. 'I don't know.'

'Okay,' I say. 'Probably a few weeks then. Has anyone told you what you are?'

'Mom says that I'm Alexis's imaginary friend. She doesn't say that to Alexis, but I heard her say it to Dad.'

I smile. Lots of imaginary friends think of their human's parents as their parents, too.

'Okay,' I say. 'So you know, then. You're an imaginary friend. The only people who can see you are Alexis and other imaginary friends.'

'Is that what you are, too?'

'Yes.'

Jo-Jo leans closer to me. 'Does that mean we aren't real?'

'No,' I say. 'It just means that we are a different kind of real. It's a kind of real that adults don't understand, so they just assume that we're imaginary.'

'How come you can walk through fences and I can't?'

'We can do what our human friends imagined us to do. My friend imagined that I look like this and can walk though doors. Alexis imagined that your skin is yellow and you cannot walk through doors.'

'Oh.'

It's the kind of *Oh* that says, 'You just explained a gigantic thing to me.'

'Do you really use the bathroom?' I ask.

'No. I just tell Alexis that if I want to look around a little.'

'I wish I had thought of that.'

'Do any imaginary friends use the bathroom?' he asks.

I laugh. 'None that I've ever met.'

'Oh.'

'You should probably get back to Alexis, now,' I say, thinking that Max is probably wondering where I am as well.

'Oh. Okay. Will I see you again?'

'Probably not. Where do you live?'

'I don't know,' he says. 'In the green house.'

'You should try to find out your address, in case you ever get lost. Especially because you can't pass through doors.'

'What do you mean?' he asks. He looks worried. He should be.

'You have to be careful that you don't get left behind. Make sure that you climb into the car as soon as the door is opened. Otherwise they could drive away without you.'

'But Alexis wouldn't do that.'

'Alexis is a little kid,' I say. 'She's not the boss. Her parents are the bosses, and they don't think that you are real. So you have to take care of yourself. Okay?'

'Okay,' he says, but he sounds so small when he speaks. 'I wish I could see you again.'

'Max and I come here a lot. Maybe I'll see you here again. Okay?'

'Okay.' It sounds almost like a wish.

I stand. I'm ready to get back to Max. But Jo-Jo is still sitting on the pail.

'Budo,' he asks. 'Where are my parents?'

'Huh?'

'My parents,' he says. 'Alexis has parents but I don't.

Alexis says they're my parents, too, but they can't see me or hear me. Where are my parents? The ones who can see me?'

'We don't have parents,' I tell him. I want to say something better, but there is nothing better. He looks sad when I say this, and I understand, because it makes me sad, too. 'That's why you have to take care of yourself,' I say.

'Okay,' he says, but he still doesn't stand. He sits on the pail, staring at his feet.

'We have to go now. Okay?'

'Okay.' Finally he stands. 'I'll miss you, Budo.'

'Me too.'

Max begins screaming at exactly 9.28 p.m. I know this because I am watching the clock, waiting for 9.30 when Max's mom and dad will change the channel to my favorite show of the week.

I don't know why he is screaming, but I know that it is not normal. He hasn't woken up from a nightmare or seen a spider. This is not a normal scream. I know that he's probably going to get stuck no matter how fast his parents run up the stairs.

Then I hear it.

Three bangs coming from the front of the house. Hitting the house. There might have been a bang right before Max started screaming, too. The television was on a commercial, and commercials are loud.

Then I hear two more bangs. Then the sound of glass breaking. A window, I think. A window is broken. Max's bedroom window is broken. I don't know how I know it, but I do. Max's mom and dad are already on the second floor. I can hear them running down the hall toward Max's room.

I'm still sitting in the cushy chair. I'm stuck for a second, too. Not like Max, but the screams and the bangs and the breaking of glass have me stuck in place. I don't know what to do.

Max says that a good soldier is *good under pressure*. I am not good under pressure. I am bad under pressure. I don't know what to do.

Then I do.

I get up and go to the front door. I pass through the door and step out onto the front porch. I catch a glimpse of a boy just as he disappears behind the house across the street. It's the Tylers' house. Mr and Mrs Tyler are old people. They don't have little boys, so I know this boy is just using their backyard to escape. I think about chasing him for a second, but I don't need to.

I know who it is.

Even if I caught up to him, there is nothing that I could do.

I turn and look at the house. I expect to see holes in the house. Maybe sparks and fire. But it's just eggs. Eggshells and yolk are running down the frame around Max's bedroom window. And his window is broken. The glass on part of the window is gone.

I don't hear Max screaming anymore.

He's stuck.

There is no screaming when he is stuck.

When Max gets stuck, there's nothing anyone can do for him. His mom will rub his arm or stroke the hair on his head, but I think that this only helps his mom feel better. I don't think Max even notices. Max eventually gets unstuck on his own. And even though Max's mom is worried that this will be *the worst episode that Max has ever had*, Max never gets more stuck or less stuck. He just gets stuck. The only thing that changes is how long he gets stuck. Since Max has never had his bedroom window break and glass land on his bed while he was sleeping, I think he's going to be stuck for a while this time.

When Max gets stuck, he sits with his knees pulled really tight into his chest and he rocks back and forth and makes a whining sound. His eyes are open, but it's like they can't see anything. He really can't hear anything either. Max once told me that when he's stuck, he can hear the people around him, but it sounds like they are coming from a television in the neighbors' house – fake and far away.

Kind of like how Graham sounded before she disappeared.

So there's nothing I can say or do to help.

That's why I'm going to the gas station. I'm not being mean. I'm just not needed here.

I waited for the police to show up and ask Max's mom and dad a bunch of questions. The police officer, who was much shorter and skinnier than the police officers on television, took some pictures of the house and the window and Max's room, and wrote everything down in a little notepad. He asked Max's parents if they knew why someone might egg our house and they said no.

'It's Halloween,' Max's dad said. 'Don't lots of people get egged?'

'They don't have their windows broken with rocks,' the little police officer said. 'And it looks as if the person throwing the eggs was aiming specifically at your son's window.'

'How would they know it was Max's window?' his mom asked.

'You told me that the window was full of *Star Wars* decals,' the little police officer said. 'Right?'

'Oh. Yes.'

Even I knew the answer to that one.

'Is Max having trouble with anyone at school?' the police officer asked.

'No,' Max's dad said, talking so fast that Max's mom didn't have a chance to speak. Like he was afraid to give her a chance to speak. 'Max does well in school. No problems at all.'

Unless you count pooping on a bully's head.

CHAPTER 14

The gas station is at the end of the street and six blocks over. It's open all the time. It never closes like the grocery store and the other gas station down the street, and that's why I like it so much. I can go out in the middle of the night and still find people who are awake. If I made a list of my favorite places in the whole wide world, I think Mrs Gosk's classroom would win, but I think the gas station would be second.

When I walk through the door tonight, Sally and Dee are on duty. Sally is usually a girl's name, but this Sally is a boy.

For a second, I think of Graham, my girl friend with a boy's name.

I once asked Max if Budo is usually a boy's name and he said yes, but he crinkled his eyebrows when he said it, so I don't think that he was sure.

Sally is even skinnier and even shorter than the police

officer who visited the house tonight. He is practically tiny. I don't think that his real name is Sally. I think that people call him Sally because he's smaller than most girls.

Dee is standing in the candy bar and Twinkie aisle, putting more candy bars and Twinkies out for people to buy. Twinkies are little yellow cakes that everyone makes fun of but everyone eats, so Dee is always filling up the Twinkie shelf. Her hair is always wrapped up in tight curls and she is chewing gum. She is always chewing gum. She chews gum like she is chewing with her whole body. Everything moves when she chews. Dee is always happy and angry at the same time. She gets mad at lots of little things but always smiles while she is yelling about them. She loves to yell and to complain, but I think the yelling and complaining make her happy.

I just think that she is funny. I love her. If I made a list of all the human persons except for Max who I would like to talk to, I think Mrs Gosk would win, but I think Dee would win, too.

Sally is behind the counter, holding a clipboard and pretending to count the boxes of cigarettes that hang in a plastic case over his head. He is actually watching the small television on the back counter. He does this all the time. I don't recognize the show, but it has police officers in it, like most of the shows on television.

There's one customer in the store. An older man who is

94

wandering in the back of the store near the coolers, peeking through the glass for the right bottle of juice or soda. He is not a regular. A regular is someone who comes to the gas station all the time.

Every day for some of them.

Dee and Sally don't mind the regulars, but Dorothy, who sometimes works overnights, too, hates the regulars. She says, 'Of all the places these deadbeats can be spending their time, why would they want to hang out in a godforsaken gas station?'

I guess I'm a regular here, too. Out of all the places that I could spend my time, I come here, too.

I don't care what Dorothy thinks. I love this place. This was the first place where I felt safe when I started leaving Max at night.

It was Dee who made me feel safe.

I'm standing over by Dee when she notices that Sally isn't working. 'Hey, Sally! You gonna stop playing with yourself and finish inventory?'

Sally holds his hand up and points at Dee with his middle finger. He does this a lot. I used to think that he was raising his hand to ask a question, like Max does when he wants to ask Mrs Gosk a question or like Meghan was doing when I saw Graham for the last time. But I think it means more than that because Sally never seems to have a question to ask. Sometimes Dee points her middle finger back at him, and when she does it, she sometimes adds the phrase *Fuck you*, which I know is inappropriate because Cissy Lamont once got caught saying it to Jane Feber in the cafeteria and got in a lot of trouble for it. It's almost like Sally and Dee are high-fiving each other without touching. But I think it's supposed to be a way of acting rude, like sticking your tongue out at a person when you don't like them, because Sally does this only when Dee is being mean to him. But Sally never does it when a customer is being mean and I've seen customers be ten times meaner than Dee. So I'm still not sure.

I can't ask Max, because he doesn't know that I come here.

Actually, Sally and Dee like each other a lot. But whenever a customer is inside the store, they pretend to fight. Nothing too bad. Max's mom would call it bickering, which means fighting without the danger of hating each other at the end of the fight. That's what Sally and Dee do. They bicker. But as soon as the customer leaves, they go back to being nice to each other. When someone is watching, I think they like to put on a show.

Max would never understand this. He has a hard time understanding that you have to act differently in different situations.

Last year Joey came over to the house for a play date and Max's mom said, 'Do you boys want to play with Max's video games?'

'I can't play video games until after dinner,' Max said.

'Oh no. It's okay, Max. Joey is here. You can play.'

'I'm not allowed to play video games until after dinner, and for only thirty minutes.'

'It's okay, Max,' his mom said. 'You have a friend over. It's different today.'

'I can't play video games before dinner.'

Max and his mom went back and forth until Joey finally said, 'It's okay. Let's go play catch outside.'

That was Max's last play date.

The customer leaves and Sally and Dee switch back to nice.

'How's your ma?' Sally asks. He's back to counting cigarettes, but probably because there's a commercial on the television.

'She's okay,' Dee says. 'But my uncle had his foot amputated when he had diabetes, and I'm worried that they might have to do that to my mom, too.'

'Why would they do that?' Sally asks. His eyes are wide.

'Bad circulation. She's already got it a little bit. The foot sort of dies, and they've got to chop it off.'

'Damn,' Sally says in that way that means he's still thinking about what Dee just said and still can't believe it.

I can't believe it, either.

This is why I love hanging out at the gas station. Before I came into the store, I didn't know that a foot could die and get chopped off. I thought if one part of a human person dies, everything dies.

I'll have to ask Max what bad circulation means, and I have to make sure he doesn't catch it. And I want to know who *they* are.

The foot-chopping people.

As they talk more about Dee's mom, Pauley walks in the door. Pauley is a man who works at Walmart and likes to buy scratch tickets. I love scratch tickets, and I love when Pauley comes in to buy them, because he always scratches them right here on the counter, and if he wins, he hands the money right back to Dee or Sally or Dorothy for more scratch tickets.

Scratch tickets are like tiny television shows, even shorter than commercials but a whole lot better. Every scratch ticket is like a story. Pay one dollar and try to win a million dollars, which is a lot of money. Pauley's whole life could change with just one scratch. In one second he could become rich, which would mean he wouldn't have to work at Walmart anymore and could spend more time here. And when I'm here, I get to watch him scratch. I stand right over his shoulder and watch those little shavings get pushed off the card by his lucky quarter.

Pauley has never won more than five hundred dollars, but even that made him very happy. He tried to pretend like nothing big happened, but his cheeks turned bright red and he could barely stand still. He shuffled his feet and rubbed his hands, like a kindergartener who has to pee real bad.

Someday I think Pauley is going to win *the big prize*. He buys so many scratch tickets that he has to win eventually.

I worry that he's going to win when I'm not here, and I'll only hear about it later from Dee or Sally.

Pauley says that when he hits it big, we won't ever see him again, but I don't believe him. I don't think Pauley has a better place to be than the gas station. Why else would he come every night, buy scratch tickets and a coffee and stay for an hour? I think Sally and Dee and even Dorothy are Pauley's friends, even if Sally and Dee and Dorothy don't know it.

But I think Dee knows it. I can just tell by the way she talks to Pauley. I don't think she wants to be Pauley's friend, but she needs to be Pauley's friend. For Pauley.

That's why Dee is my favorite person in the world except for Max and his mom and his dad. And maybe Mrs Gosk.

I watch Pauley scratch ten tickets. He doesn't win anything and now he has no more money.

'Tomorrow is payday,' he says. 'I'm a little low on funds.'

This is how Pauley asks for free coffee. Dee tells him to take a cup. Pauley drinks his coffee slowly, standing near the counter and watching the television with Sally, who isn't even pretending to count cigarettes anymore. It's 10.51, which means that the show must be near the end, and that's the worst time to miss something on a TV show. You can skip the first ten minutes if you want, but you can't miss the last ten minutes, because that's where all the good stuff happens.

'I swear that if you don't turn off that goddam TV, I'm going to tell Bill to throw it away,' Dee says.

'Five minutes!' Sally says, not taking his eyes off the screen. 'Then I'll turn it off. I promise.'

'Have a heart,' Pauley says.

When the show ends (a smart policeman catches a thinks-he's-so-smart bad guy), Sally goes back to counting, Pauley finishes his coffee, waits for two more customers to leave, and then says goodbye. He gives a big wave, stands at the door for a moment as if he doesn't want to leave (and I don't think he ever does), and then tells us that he'll be back tomorrow.

Someday I should follow Pauley. See where he lives.

It's still Halloween, and even though it's late and most kids are in their beds, I'm not surprised when the man walks in wearing the mask. It's a devil mask. Red with two plastic horns on top. Dee is stocking the shelf on the far side of the store with Band-Aids and aspirin and tiny tubes of toothpaste. She is down on one knee, so she doesn't see the man in the devil mask come in. Sally is counting scratch tickets

---

100

now. The man in the devil mask comes in the door closest to Sally and walks up to the counter.

'Sorry, no masks allowed in the store. It's a—'

It sounds like Sally wants to say something else but he stops. Something is wrong.

'I will blow your fucking head off unless you open your register and give me the money now.'

This is the voice of the devil man. He is holding a gun. It's black and silver and looks heavy. He is pointing it at Sally's face. I know that the bullet can't hurt me, but I duck anyway. I'm afraid. The devil man's voice sounds so loud even though it is not.

As I duck, Dee rises up next to me, tubes of toothpaste in her hand. We pass each other at the halfway point, and as our faces flash by one another, I suddenly want to tell her to stop. To duck.

'What's going on?' she asks, her head rising above the shelves.

Then I hear a crash. A bang that is so loud that it would hurt my ears if they could hurt. It makes me scream. Not a long scream but a quick scream. A surprised scream. Even before I finish my scream, Dee falls. It's like she is pushed backwards, and she falls into a shelf of potato chips. She falls backwards and turns at the same time, and I see the blood on her shirt as she turns. This is not like television. The blood is on her shirt but tiny drops are on her face and arms, too. Red is everywhere. And Dee doesn't say anything. She just falls into the potato chips, face first, little tubes of toothpaste landing around her.

'Fuck!'

This is the man. The devil man. Not Sally. It's not an angry *fuck*. It is a scared *fuck*.

'Fuck! Fuck!'

He screams these last two *fucks*. He's still afraid, but he also sounds like he can't believe what he is seeing. Like he was suddenly popped into a television show as the bad guy without anyone telling him that this would happen.

'Get up!'

He shouts these words, too. He is back to angry now. I think he's talking to me, so I do. I stand up. But he's not talking to me. Then I think he's talking to Dee, who has slid off the potato chip shelf and onto the floor. But he's not talking to Dee, either. He is shouting at the counter, trying to peek over it, but the counter is tall. It is on a stage, and there are three stairs that you have to climb to get behind the counter. Sally is on the other side of the counter, I think. On the floor. But the devil man can't see him from where he's standing.

'Fuck!'

He shouts again and makes a growling sound, and then he turns and runs. He opens the door that he walked through a minute ago before Dee was bleeding and he runs into the dark.

I stand for a minute, watching him run away. Then I hear Dee. She's on the floor next to my feet, wheezing, like Corey Topper when he's having an asthma attack. Her eyes are open. It looks like she is looking straight into my eyes, but she can't see my eyes. But part of me swears that she can. I think she is looking right at me. She looks so afraid. This is not like television. There is so much blood.

'Dee has been shot,' I say, and somehow this makes me feel a tiny bit better, because being shot is a lot better than being dead. 'Sally!' I yell.

But Sally can't hear me.

I run over to the counter, climb the three steps, and look behind the counter. Sally is lying on the floor. He is shaking. Shaking even more than Max shakes when Max is stuck. At first I think Sally has been shot, too, but then I remember that I heard only one bang.

Sally is not shot. Sally is stuck. He needs to call the hospital or Dee will die. But Sally is stuck.

'Get up!' I shout to Sally. 'Hurry! Get up!'

Sally is stuck. He is as stuck as Max has ever been. He's curled up into a ball and he is shaking. Dee is going to die because Sally won't move and I can only watch. One of my most favorite people in the whole wide world is bleeding and I can't do a thing.

The door closest to me opens. The devil man is back. I look, expecting to see his gun and his pointy horns, but it is not the devil man. It's Dan. Big Dan. Another regular. Not as nice as Pauley but more normal. Not so sad. Dan walks in and, for a moment, I think he is looking at me, because he is. He's looking straight through me, and he looks confused because he sees no one.

'Dan!' I shout. 'Dee's shot!'

'Hello?' Big Dan looks around. 'Guys?'

Dee makes a sound. Dan can't see her, because she is on the floor behind the shelves, and for a second I don't think Dan has heard her. Then he looks in her direction and says, 'Hello?'

Dee makes another sound, and suddenly I am happy. So happy. Dee is still alive. I shouted that Dee has been shot because it was better than saying that Dee is dead, and now I know that she is not dead. She is making a wheezing sound, and, even better, she's trying to answer Big Dan. That means she is awake.

Dan walks over to the aisle where Dee has fallen. When he sees Dee on the floor, he says, 'Oh my God! Dee!'

Big Dan moves fast. He opens his cellphone and presses numbers as he moves into the aisle and kneels down beside Dee. He acts like Big Dan, a guy who stops at the gas station every night for a Doctor Pepper to keep him awake on his ride home to a place called New Haven. Big Dan, who doesn't linger in the gas station a moment longer than necessary, but who is friendly just the same.

I love Pauley and his scratch tickets and the way he tries to drink his coffee as slowly as possible, but, in an emergency I love Big Dan.

CHAPTER 15

The ambulance people took Dee and Sally away in two separate vans. Dee was taken first, but Sally left right after her, even though he wasn't hurt at all. I tried to tell the ambulance people that Sally was just stuck, and no one needs to ride in the ambulance van just because they are stuck, but they couldn't hear me, of course.

An ambulance man with bushy hair used an old-fashioned cellphone with a big antenna to tell someone at the hospital that Dee is in a critical condition. This means that Dee might die, especially if she got a good look at the devil man who shot her. It seems like the more you know about the person who shot you, the more likely you are to die.

The police closed the gas station even though it's never supposed to close, so after Dee and Sally were taken away, I went home.

Max is still stuck. His dad has to work at five tomorrow morning so he went to bed. Max's mom is still awake, sitting in a chair next to Max's bed.

My chair.

But I don't mind. I want to sit with Max's mom, too. I want her to stay in Max's room all night. I just saw my friend get shot with a real gun and a real bullet and I can't stop thinking about it.

I wish that Max's mom would stroke my hair back and kiss me on the forehead, too.

Max wakes up on Saturday morning. He is unstuck.

'Why are you sitting there?'

I think he's talking to me. I'm sitting on the end of his bed. I've been sitting here all night, thinking about Dee and Sally and the devil man, and staring at Max's mom, because it makes me feel better.

But Max isn't talking to me. He's talking to his mother. She fell asleep in my chair, and his voice wakes her. She jumps up like someone pinched her.

'What?' she says, looking around like she doesn't know where she is.

'Why are you sitting there?' Max asks again.

'Max, you're awake.'

And then the eggs and the rocks and the broken window and Max getting stuck seem to fall out of the sky and fill her up like air in a balloon. She pops up out of the chair, all inflated and awake, and she quickly answers Max.

'I'm sitting here because you were upset last night, and I didn't want you to be alone.'

Max looks at the window beside his bed. It's covered with clear plastic. Max's dad tacked it up last night.

'I was stuck?' he asks.

'Yes,' his mother says. 'For a little while.'

Max knows that he was stuck, but he always asks if he was stuck anyway. I don't know why. It's not like he has amnesia, which is a disease that turns a person's brain off so it can't record what the person sees or does. It happens a lot on television, and I think it's real, even though I've never met anyone with amnesia before. It's like Max is double-checking, to make sure everything is okay. Max is a big fan of double-checking.

'Who broke my window?' he asks, still looking at the plastic.

'We don't know,' his mom says. 'We think it was an accident.'

'How could someone break my window by accident?'

'Kids do crazy things on Halloween,' his mom says. 'They threw eggs at our house last night. And rocks, too.'

'Why?'

From the tone of his voice, I can tell that Max is upset about this. I'm sure that his mom can tell, too.

'It's called a prank,' she says. 'Some kids think that it's okay to pull pranks on Halloween.'

'Pull?'

'Make pranks. Do pranks,' she says. 'People use the expression *pull pranks* sometimes.'

'Oh.'

'Do you want breakfast?' his mom asks. Max's mom is always worried about Max eating enough, even though he eats plenty of food.

'What time is it?' Max asks.

Max's mom looks at her watch. It's the kind with hands on it, so I can't read it well.

'It's eight-thirty,' she says, looking relieved.

Max can eat breakfast only before nine. After nine, he must wait until twelve to eat lunch.

This is Max's rule. Not his mom's.

'Okay,' Max says. 'I'll eat.'

His mom leaves to make the pancakes and let Max get dressed. He does not eat breakfast in pajamas. This is also Max's rule.

'Did Mom kiss me last night?' Max asks.

'Yes,' I say. 'But only on the forehead.'

I want to tell Max that the devil man shot my friend last night, but I can't. I don't want Max to know that I go to the gas station and the diner and the police station and the hospital. I don't think he would like it if he knew I went to those places. He likes to think that I am sitting beside him all night or at least somewhere in the house in case he needs me. I think it would make him mad to know that I have other friends in the world.

'Was it a long kiss?' Max asks.

For the first time ever, this question makes me mad. I know how important it is for Max to know that his mom's kiss was not too long, but the length of a mom's kiss is not that important. It's a tiny thing compared to guns and blood and friends in ambulance vans, and he shouldn't have to ask me every day. Doesn't he know that a mom's long kiss is not a bad thing?

'Nope,' I say, like I always do. 'It was super-short.'

But when I say it this time, I do not smile. I frown. I say it through clenched teeth.

Max doesn't notice. He never notices these things. He's still looking at the plastic that is covering the window.

'Do you know who broke my window?' Max asks.

I do, but I don't know if I should tell Max. I don't know if this is like his mom's long kisses and I should lie. I'm still mad at him for worrying about the long kisses, so even though I want to do the right thing for him, I don't want to do the right thing, too. I don't want to hurt Max, but I'm not in the helping mood either.

I take too long to answer.

'Do you know who broke my window?' Max asks again.

He hates it when he has to ask me questions twice, so now he is angry, too.

I decide to answer honestly, not because I think it's the best thing for Max to hear, but because I am mad and don't want to think about what is right.

'It was Tommy Swinden,' I say. 'I ran outside after I heard your window break and I saw him running away.'

'It was Tommy Swinden,' Max says.

'Yes,' I say. 'It was Tommy Swinden.'

'Tommy Swinden broke my window and threw eggs at our house.'

Max says this to his mother while he is eating his pancakes. I can't believe that he told her. I didn't expect him to say it. How is he going to explain it? Suddenly I'm not angry at Max anymore. I'm worried. Worried about what he will say. Now I'm angry at myself for being so stupid.

'Who is Tommy Swinden?' Max's mom asks.

'He's a boy who is mean to me at school. He wants to kill me.'

'How do you know that?' His mom doesn't sound like she believes him.

'He told me.'

'What did he say exactly?' She's still washing the frying pan, so I know that she still does not believe him.

'He said he was going to bowl me,' Max says.

'What does that mean?'

'I don't know, but it's bad.' Max is staring at his pancakes because when Max eats, he stares at his food.

'How do you know it's bad?' his mom asks.

'Because everything Tommy Swinden says to me is bad.'

His mom doesn't say anything for a minute, and I think she is going to forget the whole thing. Then she speaks again.

'How do you know that Tommy threw the eggs and the rocks?'

'Budo saw him.'

'Budo saw him.'

This time it is Max's mom who is saying something that didn't sound like a question but was still a question.

'Yes,' Max says. 'Budo saw him.'

'Okay.'

I feel like the elephant in the room. This is an expression that means there is something two people know that is as big as an elephant but no one wants to talk about it. Max's mom uses this expression a lot when she is talking to Max's dad about Max and his *diagnosis*.

It took me for ever to figure out what the elephant in the room thing meant.

Max and his mom eat for a little while, and then his mom asks, 'Is Tommy Swinden in your class?'

'No, he's in Mrs Parenti's class.'

'Third grade?'

'No,' Max says. He sounds annoyed. He thinks that his mom should know that Mrs Parenti doesn't teach third grade, because in Max's world, knowing who teaches what grade is a big deal. 'Mrs Parenti is a fifth-grade teacher.'

'Oh.'

Max's mom doesn't say anything else about Tommy Swinden or the eggs or the rocks or getting bowled or me, which is bad. It means she is planning on doing something.

I can feel it.

CHAPTER 16

Dee and Sally are not back on Saturday or Sunday night. A man who Dorothy calls Mr Eisner is working instead. I've never seen Mr Eisner before but Dorothy seems nervous around him. They barely speak to each other.

Mr Eisner reminds me of Max's principal. Mrs Palmer is in charge of the school and dresses in fancier clothing than most of the teachers, but I don't think that she could actually teach kids if she had to take over a classroom.

Mr Eisner is the same. He wears a tie, and he takes the money from the customers and fills the Twinkie shelf like Dee, but you can tell that he has to think too much about what he is doing instead of just doing it.

Dee is not dead. I know this because the regulars like Pauley and Big Dan came in on Saturday night to ask about Dee. Actually, they would have come in anyway, since they are regulars, but even Big Dan hung around for a little while longer than normal, asking questions about Dee. Mr

Eisner didn't talk to them very much, so it was hard for them to hang around. Everything felt different. Not right.

Dee is in a place called I See You. I think it's a place where they watch you carefully to make sure that you don't die. Dorothy says it is not certain that Dee is going to *make it*, which I think means that she could die.

I wonder if she will come back to the gas station and if I will ever see her again.

I hope so. I feel like everyone is disappearing.

CHAPTER 17

I'm worried about Max. It's Monday and we are back at school.

I think that Max's mom has something planned for today. She is worried about Tommy Swinden, and I am afraid that she might make things worse. I'm hoping that Tommy Swinden got his revenge on Friday night and now Max is safe again. Max got Tommy in a lot of trouble with the knife even before he pooped on him, so maybe Tommy thinks that Max deserves more revenge. He probably does, but it will just be worse if Max's mom gets involved.

Parents are like Max. They don't know how to do things quietly.

Mrs Gosk is funny today. She wrote a story about what it's like to be a Thanksgiving turkey and she is reading it to the class. She is walking around the room, making turkey sounds while she reads, and even Max is grinning. Not smiling, but almost. Mrs Gosk is scratching the ground with her foot and flapping her arms like wings. No one can take their eyes off of her.

Mrs Patterson arrives at the classroom door and motions to Max to join her. It takes her a moment to get Max's attention because Mrs Gosk is so funny. I'm expecting to see Max frown, because Mrs Gosk is not finished with her story yet, but Max's eyes get wide when he sees Mrs Patterson. He looks excited. I don't understand.

I want to stay with Mrs Gosk and see what she will do next. Instead, I follow Max and Mrs Patterson down the hall in the direction of the Learning Center. Except when we get to the spot where we should turn left, Max and Mrs Patterson go straight on, and Max does not say a thing. This is even more surprising than Max wanting to leave Mrs Gosk because Max does not like change, and this is a definite change in the way that we go to the Learning Center. It's a silly change, too, because it means we have to walk around the auditorium and by the gym, which makes the walk twice as long.

But then we stop at the same doors that I saw Max and Mrs Patterson enter through last week. We're behind the auditorium now, in a hallway that doesn't have classrooms or offices, but Mrs Patterson still looks left and right before she opens the door. Then she places her hand on Max's back to nudge him outside. Max is walking out the door on his own, but Mrs Patterson wants Max to move faster, and this makes me nervous. It's like she needed him to pass through the doors quickly before someone saw him.

Something is not right.

I try to follow. But as Max walks down the cement path toward the parking lot, he turns and looks at me. I'm standing outside now, too. He looks at me and shakes his head back and forth. I know what this means. It means *No way, José.*

He doesn't want me to follow him. Then he waves me back with his hand.

He wants me to go back inside the school.

I almost always do what Max asks me to do, because that is sort of my job. He needs my help, and so I give it to him. There have been other times when he has asked to be alone, like when he's reading a book or making a poop. Lots of times, in fact. But this time is different. I know it. Max is not supposed to be outside the school, and he is most definitely not supposed to be going out these side doors toward the parking lot.

Something is not right.

I go back inside like Max has told me to, but I stand against the wall beside the doors, so I can peek out. Max and Mrs Patterson are walking in the parking lot now, in the aisle between the parked cars. I think these are the teachers' cars, since the kids can't drive. They must be. Then I see Max and Mrs Patterson stop next to a small, blue car. Mrs Patterson looks around again. It's the kind of look-ing around that someone does when they want to make sure no one is watching. Then she opens up the back door of the car and Max climbs in. Mrs Patterson looks around again before getting into the front seat. The side with the steering wheel. The side where the person who is driving sits.

She is driving away with Max.

Except she's not. The car isn't moving. They are sitting in the car. Max is in the back seat. Mrs Patterson is in the front. Mrs Patterson is talking, I think, and Max keeps ducking his head down. Not to hide, but to look at some-thing on the seat, I think. He looks busy. He is doing something.

A moment later Mrs Patterson steps out of the car and looks around again. She is making sure that no one is watching. I know it. I have been around too many people who do not know that I'm watching them to know when someone is being sneaky, and Mrs Patterson is being sneaky. Then she opens the door for Max and he steps out, too. Together, they walk back to the doors. Mrs Patterson uses a key to unlock the doors and they come back in again. I take a few steps down the hall, away from the doors, and I sit with my back against the wall so that Max will think that I have been here the whole time. Not watching.

I want him to think that I don't know where he and Mrs Patterson went, and, more important, I want him to think I don't care. I do not want him to suspect that I am worried, because the next time Mrs Patterson takes Max out to her car, I am going, too.

If Mrs Patterson takes him out to her car again (and I think she will), it won't be the same as this time. I don't know what it will be, but it will be more. It will be worse. I know it. Mrs Patterson wouldn't break the rules for five minutes in her car with Max. Something else is going to happen.

I can't explain it, but I'm more worried about Mrs Patterson than I am about Tommy Swinden now.

A lot more worried.

CHAPTER 18

We are sitting inside Dr Hogan's office. Dr Hogan is smart. Max has been here for a long time and Dr Hogan has not tried to make him talk once. She has been sitting here, watching him play with these plastic and metal pieces that she called *newfangled thinker toys*. I could tell by the way she said it that *newfangled* isn't really part of their name, but I don't understand what it means.

I know what *new* means, but what's a *fangled*?

Max loves these toys. Max's mom would say that Max is *engaged*, which means that he has stopped paying attention to everything around him. Max gets engaged a lot, which is good because it means that he is happy, but it also means that he forgets everything else. When Max is engaged, it is like only one thing exists. Ever since he sat down on the carpet in front of the coffee table and started playing with these toys, I don't think he's looked up once.

Dr Hogan is smart enough to let Max play. Every now

and then she asks a question, and so far all of her questions have only needed yes-or-no and one-word answers, so Max has been answering most of them.

That's smart, too. If Dr Hogan had tried to get Max to just talk, without the thinker toys and the quiet time, he would have probably *clammed up*, which is what Mrs Hume says about Max when he won't talk to her. But Max is slowly getting used to Dr Hogan and eventually he might be able to talk to her if she waits long enough. Especially if she doesn't make him feel like she's staring at him and recording everything that he says. Most of the time adults start out slow with Max but eventually they lose their patience and mess things up.

Dr Hogan is pretty. She's younger than Max's mom, I think, and she isn't dressed too fancy. She is wearing a skirt and a T-shirt and sneakers, like she's going for a walk in the park. This is smart, too, because she looks like just another girl. Not a real doctor.

Max is afraid of doctors.

Best of all, she hasn't asked one single question about me. Not one. I was worried that she would be asking Max about me for the whole time, but instead, it seems like she's more interested in Max's favorite food (macaroni) and his favorite flavor of ice cream (vanilla) than his imaginary friend.

'Do you like school?' Dr Hogan asks.

Dr Hogan told Max that he could call her Ellen, but that

is too weird for me. Max hasn't had to say her name yet, so I don't know what he has decided to do, but I bet he will call her Dr Hogan, too. If he can remember her name. If he was listening when she told him.

'Kind of,' Max says.

His tongue is sticking out of the corner of his mouth and he is squinting, staring at two pieces of thinker toys, trying to figure out how they go together.

'What's your favorite part of school?'

Max doesn't say anything for ten seconds, and then he says, 'Lunch.'

'Oh,' Dr Hogan says. 'Do you know why lunch is your favorite part of school?'

See how smart she is? She doesn't ask Max why lunch is his favorite until she knows that he knows. If Max can't explain why lunch is his favorite part of school, then he can just say no, and he doesn't have to feel dumb for not knowing the answer. If Dr Hogan asks a question that makes Max feel dumb, she might never get him to talk.

'No,' Max says, and Dr Hogan doesn't seem surprised one bit.

I'm not surprised either. But I think I know why Max likes lunch best. I think it is because it's the part of the school day when he is left alone. No one bothers him, and no one tells him what to do. He sits at the end of the lunch table, all alone, reading his book and eating the same thing every day: a peanut butter and jelly sandwich, a granola bar, and an apple juice. The rest of the school day is unpredictable. You never know what might happen. Things are always changing, and teachers and kids are always surprising Max. But lunch is always the same.

This is only a guess. I don't know why Max likes lunch the best, because I don't think Max knows. Sometimes you can feel something but not know why you feel that way. Like the way I feel about Mrs Patterson. I knew I did not like her as soon as I met her, but I can't explain why. I just knew. And now that she and Max have a secret, I like her even less.

'Who is your best friend, Max?' Dr Hogan asks.

Max says 'Timothy' because that is what Max always says when someone asks him who his best friend is, even though I know that I am his real best friend. But Max knows that if he says my name, people will ask him questions and tell him that I don't exist. Timothy is a boy who spends time in the Learning Center when Max is there, and sometimes Timothy and Max work together. Max says that Timothy is his best friend because they don't fight. Neither one likes working with other kids, so when their teachers make them work together, they try to find a way to work alone together.

Mrs Hume once told Max's mom that it is sad that Max's best friends are the kids who leave him alone, but Mrs

Hume doesn't understand that Max is happy when he is alone. Just because Mrs Hume and Max's mom and most people are happiest when they are with their friends doesn't mean that Max needs friends to be happy. Max doesn't like other people, so he is happiest when people just leave him alone.

It's like me with food. I don't eat. I've never met an imaginary friend who eats. I was visiting the hospital one night, because the hospital never closes, and I was spending time with Susan, a lady who does not eat food with her mouth anymore. She has a straw that goes straight into her belly, and the nurses feed her pudding through the straw. Susan's sisters were visiting, and when they were in the hallway outside Susan's room, her fat sister said it was sad that Susan could not eat anymore because there is so much joy in food.

'No there's not!' I said, but no one heard me.

But it's true. I'm glad that I don't eat, no matter what Susan's fat sister says. Eating seems like a pain in the butt to me. Even if the food tastes good, you have to worry about having enough money to buy the food and cooking the food and not burning the food and eating the right amount without getting fat like Susan's sister. Plus all the time it takes to cook the food and clean the dishes and cut the mango and peel the potatoes and ask the waiter for milk instead of cream. The dangers of choking on food or being allergic to certain foods. It all seems so complicated. I don't care how good the food might taste. It wouldn't be worth all the trouble. Maybe Susan feels this way, too, now that she eats with a belly straw, which seems a lot easier than cooking dinner every night. But even if she doesn't feel this way, I still feel this way. If I was given a chance to eat food right now, I'd say no, because I wouldn't want to get in the habit of eating food and starting all of that rigmarole, which is one of Mrs Gosk's favorite words.

Even though I don't eat, I'm still happy, even if there is so much joy in food. Because there is joy in not worrying about food, too. More joy, I think.

For Max, there's joy in being alone. He's not lonely. He just doesn't like people very much. But he is happy.

'What is your least favorite food?' Dr Hogan asks.

Max stops for a moment, his hands sort of frozen in midair, and then he says, 'Peas.'

I would have guessed zucchini. I bet he forgot about zucchini.

'What's your least favorite part of school?' Dr Hogan asks.

'Gym,' Max says, quickly this time. 'And art. And recess. It's a tie.'

'Who is your least favorite person at school?'

Max looks up for the first time. His face is pinched.

'Is there anyone at school who you don't like?' Dr Hogan asks.

'Yes,' Max says, and then his eyes go back to the thinker toys.

'Who do you not like the most?'

Now I understand what Dr Hogan is doing. She's trying to talk to Max about Tommy Swinden, and Max is about to open the door and let her inside. It's bad enough that Max's mom knows about Tommy Swinden. This could make things even worse.

'Ella Wu!' I say, hoping that Max will repeat what I say.

'Tommy Swinden,' Max says instead, not looking up as he says it.

'Do you know why you don't like Tommy Swinden?'

'Yes,' Max says.

'Why don't you like Tommy Swinden?' Dr Hogan asks, and I can see that she is leaning forward ever so slightly. This is the answer she has been waiting for.

'Because he wants to kill me,' Max says, still not bothering to look up.

'Oh no,' Dr Hogan says, and it sounds like she really means it, like she's really surprised, even though I think that she knew about Tommy Swinden all along. She probably heard all about him from Max's mom.

This appointment was one giant trap, and Max just fell in.

Dr Hogan doesn't say anything for a little bit, and then she asks, 'Do you know why Tommy Swinden wants to kill you, Max?'

Adults always stick Max's name at the end of their questions when they think their questions are important.

'Maybe,' Max says.

'Why do you maybe think that Tommy Swinden wants to kill you, Max?'

Max stops moving again. He has a chunk of newfangled thinker toy in his hand and he just stares at it. I know the look on his face. It is the look that says he's going to lie. Max is not a good liar, and it always takes him a long time to think of a lie.

'He doesn't like boys named Max,' Max says.

But he says it too fast, and his voice sounds different, so I'm sure that Dr Hogan knows it is a lie. Max probably got this idea from a fifth grader who once told Max that he has a stupid name. Even though there was a real kid who didn't like his name, I do not think this is a good lie. No one wants to kill someone because of their name.

'Is there anything else?' Dr Hogan asks.

'What?' Max says.

'Is there any other reason why you maybe think this boy wants to kill you?'

Oh,' Max says, and then he pauses again. 'No.'

Dr Hogan doesn't believe him. I want Dr Hogan to

believe him, but she does not. I can tell. Max's mom has talked to her. I know it. I wonder when Max's mom and dad decided to send Max here. I wonder when Max's dad lost this fight.

Maybe when I was at the gas station last night.

But even if Max's mom didn't talk to her, Dr Hogan would still know that Max is lying. He is the worst liar on the planet.

And Dr Hogan is really smart. That scares me even more.

I wonder what she plans on doing next.

I wonder if I can find a way to get her to talk to Max about Mrs Patterson.

CHAPTER 19

I'm following Max. He told me to wait by the doors again, but this time I am going to sneak up to Mrs Patterson's car and see what's going on inside. I don't care what he says. Something is not right.

Max and Mrs Patterson are halfway to the parking lot when I pass through the glass doors and leave the school. There is a tree to the right of the walkway, and I go there first and hide behind it. I don't usually have to hide like this. I can't remember ever hiding from Max, and no one else can see me, so in a way I am always hiding from everyone except Max.

This is the first time I am hiding from everyone.

There's another tree down the walkway a bit, this one on the left side and a little farther off the path, so I run there next. If I actually touched the ground when I ran, I would be walking instead, tiptoeing so that Max would not hear me. But when I move, I am silent, even to Max, so running is a better idea, because it means I will stay unhidden for less time.

I peek around the tree. Max and Mrs Patterson have almost reached the car. Mrs Patterson is moving fast, much faster than adults who don't ask kids to keep secrets and bring them out to their cars in the middle of the school day. From the tree, I am going to have to crawl over to the parking lot. There is a row of cars in front of me, about thirty steps away. If I crawl, I can stay hidden behind the row of cars, especially since Max is so short and cannot see over the tall cars. It's funny, because as I crawl, every little kid in the two classrooms behind me should be able to see me, crawling through the grass in front of the school. It feels strange, hiding in front of so many faces.

I hear a car door open. Max and Mrs Patterson have reached the car.

I have an idea. I'm crouched behind a little red car, the first one in the row, and I'm peeking through the windows, trying to see if Max is inside Mrs Patterson's car yet. I can't quite see Mrs Patterson's car, which is farther down and in the opposite row of cars across the aisle. But I can pass through the cars in front of me, because they all have doors. This is my idea. Instead of walking down the aisle, I will crawl through the cars.

I climb into the red car and crawl over the seats. This is

a messy car. The front seat is piled with books and papers and there are empty soda cans and paper bags on the floor. This is probably Mrs Gosk's car. It reminds me of her classroom. It is full and messy. I like it. I sometimes think that neat and organized people spend too much time planning and not enough time doing. I don't trust neat and organized people.

I bet that Mrs Patterson is a neat and organized person.

I pass through the door on the opposite side of the red car and then pass through five more cars until I am crouched over inside a big car with four doors plus a door in the back. I can see Mrs Patterson's car through the back window. Mrs Patterson pulled her car in face first, not like crazy Mrs Griswold who spends five minutes every morning backing into a spot while all the kids laugh at her. This is good because it means that she and Max are looking away from me, which is perfect for me to sneak up on them. I pass through the back door of the big car and run over to Mrs Patterson's car, crossing the pavement between the two rows of cars. I keep my head low in case Max turns around.

Mrs Patterson's window is open. It is warm and her car is not running, so she probably opened the window for fresh air. I want to look in the back seat and see what Max is doing, but I can hear Mrs Patterson's voice from where I am standing. She is talking on her phone. I get down on my hands and knees and crawl over to the side of the car with Mrs Patterson's door, so I can hear better. I am crouched alongside the car, in between the front and back doors.

'Yes, Mom,' I hear Mrs Patterson say.

Then there is a pause.

'Yes, Mom,' she says again. 'I love you so much.'

Another pause.

'No, Mom, I won't get into any trouble. You're my mom, and I should be able to talk to you during the day. Especially since you are so sick.'

Another pause.

'I know, Mom. You're right. You're always right.'

Mrs Patterson laughs a little, and then she says, 'I am so lucky to have this young man helping me.' Then she laughs again. Neither laugh sounds real. 'His name is Max,' she says. 'He is the kindest, smartest boy I know.'

She pauses for a second or two and then says, 'Yes, Mom, I will be sure to tell Max how grateful you are about his help. I love you so much, Mom. And I hope you feel better real soon. Bye bye.'

Nothing about the conversation sounds right. I have heard Max's mom and dad talk on the telephone many times, and it never sounded like this. Everything about it was wrong. Her laugh wasn't real. The amount of time that she was listening and not speaking was too short. She said

133

the word *Mom* too many times. Everything she said came out perfect.

No ums. No stutters.

It sounded like a first-grade teacher reading a book to her class. It sounded like everything she said was for Max and not for her mom.

I start to move, crawling backwards, trying to get to the back of the car again, when Max's door opens. I'm on my hands and knees right in front of his door, and the bottom part of the door passes right through me as it opens because it is a door.

As he gets out, Max sees me. His smile turns to a frown. His eyes first widen and then shrink to slits, little wrinkles popping up between them. He is mad. But he says nothing, because Mrs Patterson's door opens a second later and she steps out of the car. I feel foolish, crouched on my hands and knees between them, but I'm too embarrassed and ashamed to stand up. I just stay there as Mrs Patterson closes her door and reaches for Max's hand. He takes one more look at me, and then he takes her hand. I have never seen Mrs Patterson hold Max's hand before and it looks odd. Max hates to hold hands. Max does not look back. I stand up and watch him enter the school. He disappears down the hallway. He never looks back.

I look inside Mrs Patterson's car. There is a blue

backpack on the back seat where Max had been sitting. It is closed, so there's no way for me to see inside. There is nothing else in the car except the backpack. The car is clean and empty.

I was right. Mrs Patterson is neat and organized.

She cannot be trusted.

CHAPTER 20

Max won't talk to me. He didn't even look at me for the rest of the school day, and when I try to sit with him on the bus ride home, he shakes his head and gives me his *No way, José* look. We have never sat apart on the bus before. I take a seat in front of Max, right behind the bus driver. I want to turn around and look at Max, smile at him and try to get him to smile at me, but I can't bring myself to do it. Because I know he won't smile back.

I have to talk to Max about Mrs Patterson when he's not mad at me anymore. I still don't understand what is happening, but I know that it is not good. I am even more convinced of it now. The more I think about Max sitting in that car with that blue backpack in the middle of the school day, and that phone call from Mrs Patterson that didn't sound like a phone call, and especially the way that she and Max were *holding hands*, the more afraid I become.

For a while, I thought I might be overreacting. I thought

that maybe this was like one of those television shows where all the clues point to one killer but then it turns out to be another person. A surprise killer. Maybe Mrs Patterson is a sweet lady and there is a perfectly good reason why she and Max sit in that car. But now I know that I am right. I am not overreacting. I can't explain how I know, but I know. This is probably how those characters on television feel, too. The ones who think it's one killer when it is really another. Except this is real life. There are no television makers sprinkling lots of fake clues for me. This is real life, and real life can't have this many fake clues all in a row.

The only good news is that tomorrow is Friday, and Mrs Patterson almost never comes in on Friday. It makes the principal, Mrs Palmer, crazy. I once heard her talking about Mrs Patterson to a lady who nodded and hummed and said that Mrs Patterson has a right to use her sick days if she is sick, and that was the end of the conversation. I don't know why Mrs Palmer didn't tell the suit lady that no one gets sick once a week on the same day, but she didn't. After the suit lady left, Mrs Palmer blamed it on the *damunion*. I still can't figure out what the *damunion* is, and when I asked Max, he didn't know either.

So Mrs Patterson will probably be sick tomorrow, or pretending to be sick, and I'll have the weekend to get Max to forgive me so we can talk.

I was scared for a little while, wondering if Max might stop believing in me since he is so mad and refuses to talk to me. But then I realized that Max couldn't be mad at someone who didn't exist, so I actually think that this is a good sign. He must really, really believe in me to be this mad.

Maybe I should have found a way to make Meghan mad at Graham. Maybe that would have saved Graham's life.

I've been thinking about Graham a lot, lately. I think about how she doesn't exist anymore, and how everything that she ever said or did doesn't mean anything to Meghan anymore. Even if Graham still means something to me and Meghan, and maybe even Puppy, none of that matters because she doesn't exist anymore.

That's the only important fact of Graham's nonexistence.

When Max's grandmother died, Max's dad said that Grandma would live on in Max's heart, and as long as they remembered Grandma, she would remain alive in their memories. That is fine for Max, and maybe it made him feel a little better, but it didn't help Max's grandmother at all. She is gone, and even if Max is keeping her alive in his heart, she doesn't exist anymore. She doesn't care what's going on in Max's heart, because she can't care about anything anymore. Everyone gets so worried about the people who are still living when the people who are really hurting are the dead ones. People like Grandma and Graham.

They don't exist anymore.

There is nothing worse than that.

Max hasn't talked to me all night long. He worked on his homework, played his video game for thirty minutes, read about a world war from a book as big as his head and then went to sleep without saying a word. I am sitting in the chair beside his bed, waiting for him to fall asleep, hoping to hear his small voice say, 'Budo, it's okay.' But he never speaks. Eventually his breathing gets steady and he is asleep.

I hear the door open. Max's mom is home. She had a doctor's appointment so she didn't put Max to bed. She comes into the room and kisses Max, pulls the covers up to his neck and kisses him three more times.

She leaves.

I follow.

Max's dad is watching a baseball game. He presses the mute button on the remote control when Max's mom enters the living room, but he doesn't take his eyes off the screen.

'So? What did she say?' Max's dad asks. He sounds annoyed.

'She said that it went well. They talked a little, and Max answered some questions. She thinks she can eventually get him to trust her and open up, but it's going to take a while.'

'You don't think Max trusts us?'

'C'mon, John,' Max's mom says. 'Of course he trusts us. But that doesn't mean he tells us everything.'

'What kid tells his parents everything?'

'This is different,' Max's mom says. 'And I'm sorry if you can't see it.'

Except she doesn't sound like she's sorry at all.

'Explain to me how it's different,' Max's dad says.

'I don't feel like I know my own son. He's not like other kids. He doesn't come home telling us stories from school. He doesn't play with other kids. He thinks that someone in his school wants to kill him. He still talks to his imaginary friend. For God's sake, he barely lets me touch him. I have to kiss him after he's asleep. Why can't you see him for who he is?'

Her voice gets louder as she talks, and I think that she is going to either cry or scream or both. I think she is probably already crying on the inside but holding it back so she can keep on fighting with Max's dad on the outside.

Max's dad says nothing. It's that silence that adults use to say stuff they don't want to say.

When Max's mom talks again, her voice is soft and calm. 'She thinks he's very smart. Smarter than he is able to show us. And she thinks that there is real progress to be made.'

'She could tell all that after forty-five minutes?'

'She sees kids like Max all the time. She's not saying

anything absolutely yet. She was just guessing. Based upon what she's seen and heard so far.'

'How long will insurance cover it?' Max's dad asks.

I'm not sure what this means, but I can tell by his voice that he is not asking to be helpful.

'Ten sessions to start, and then it depends on what she finds.'

'What's the co-pay?' Max's dad asks.

'Really? We're getting our son some help and you're worried about how much they'll charge?'

'I was just wondering,' Max's dad says, and I can tell that he feels bad for asking.

'Fine,' Max's mom says. 'It's twenty bucks. Okay?'

'I was just wondering,' he says. 'That's all.' He pauses a minute, and then he smiles and adds, 'But if Max is seeing her for only forty-five minutes and the co-pay is twenty bucks, you have to wonder how much she's actually getting paid an hour. Right?'

'She's not working at a liquor store,' Max's mom says. 'She's a doctor, for Christ's sake.'

'I was just joking,' Max's dad says and laughs.

This time I believe him. And I think that Max's mom does, too. She smiles, and then after a second she sits down beside Max's dad.

'What else did she say?' Max's dad asks.

'Nothing, really. Max answered almost all her questions,

which she said was good. And he didn't seem nervous being in the office by himself, which she said was unusual. But he still thinks that someone at school is going to kill him. Tommy Swinden. Do you know the name?'

'No.'

'Max said Tommy doesn't like his name and that's why he wants to kill him, but Dr Hogan doesn't believe him.'

'She doesn't believe that Tommy Swinden wants to kill him, or she doesn't believe that he doesn't like Max's name?'

'She's not sure,' Max's mom says. 'But she didn't think that Max was telling the whole truth about Tommy, and it was the only time she got the sense that Max wasn't being honest.'

'What should we do?' Max's dad asks.

'I'm going to call the school tomorrow. Max is probably misinterpreting something, but I want to be safe.'

'Helicopter Mom to the rescue?'

Max's dad has called Max's mom a helicopter mom before, but I don't get it. I know what a helicopter is, but I've never seen Max's mom drive one or even play with any of Max's toy helicopters, and he has a lot of them.

Max's mom smiles, and this makes me even more confused. When Max's dad tells Max's mom that she is a helicopter mom, it usually makes her angry, but sometimes she thinks it's funny, and I can't figure out why.

'If Tommy Swinden has threatened my son,' Max's mom says, 'I'll bring the whole goddam air force down on his ass if necessary. Helicopter Mom and all.'

'You're a little crazy sometimes,' Max's dad says. 'Possibly a little neurotic. And you're capable of overreacting from time to time. But Max is very lucky to have you.'

Max's mom reaches over and takes Max's dad's hand and squeezes it. For a moment, I think they're going to kiss, which always makes me feel a little weird, but instead Max's mom speaks.

'Dr Hogan wants to meet with me again after two more sessions. Do you want to come to the next one?'

'Will that cost us another co-pay?'

This time they do kiss, so I look away. I wish I knew what a co-pay was. The first time Max's dad mentioned it, Max's mom got angry. But now it made her want to kiss him.

This is why I understand Max so well. I am sometimes as confused as he is.

CHAPTER 21

Mrs Patterson is not in school today. Mrs Palmer might be mad about it, but I am relieved. Max is still not talking to me, but at least I have the weekend to convince him to forgive me.

It has been a strange day. Max won't even look at me. We started off in Mrs Gosk's room, working on multiplication tables (which Max memorized two years ago), and then we went to art class, where Ms Knight showed Max how to weave different colored pieces of paper into a pattern. Max didn't seem to like it very much, because he barely paid attention to Ms Knight's instructions, and Max usually loves things involving patterns.

He has just finished his snack in Mrs Gosk's classroom and is now walking to the Learning Center. Even though I'm walking right beside him, he won't even look in my direction. I'm actually feeling a little angry now. He is over-reacting, I think.

Like Max's mom sometimes.

All I did was follow him to Mrs Patterson's car.

'Max, do you want to play army after school?' I ask. 'It's Friday, we could set up a huge battle and play all day tomorrow.'

Max does not answer.

'This is ridiculous,' I say. 'You can't be mean to me for ever. I just wanted to know what you were doing.'

Max walks faster.

We're taking the long way to the Learning Center again, the way that Mrs Patterson took him the other day. I guess this is the new way, even though it takes longer. Maybe Max thinks it is a better way because it means he has to spend less time in the Learning Center.

When we reach the glass doors that lead to the parking lot, Max stops and looks outside. His face is so close to the glass that the window fogs up from his breath. He's not just looking. He's looking for something. He's searching for something. I look, too, to see what he sees, and then he sees it.

I don't.

I don't know what he sees, but he sees something, because he stands up straighter and pushes his nose right up against the glass. And there's no fog on the glass now. He's holding his breath. He sees something, and he is holding his breath. I look again. I don't see anything. Just two rows of cars and the street beyond.

'Stay here,' Max says. It's been so long since he has spoken to me that I jump a little.

'Where are you going?' I ask.

'Stay here,' he says again. 'I'll be right back. I promise if you stay here and wait here for me, I'll be right back.'

Max is lying. I know he is lying just like Dr Hogan knew that Max was lying in her office the other day. But Max is talking to me again. He's talking to me and he doesn't sound angry, so I am feeling happy again. I want to believe him, because if I do everything will be all right again. Max won't be mad at me, and even though I don't have Graham or Dee or Sally or a mom or a dad, I will have Max back, and that's good enough.

'Okay,' I say. 'I'll wait here. I'm sorry I didn't listen to you last time.'

'Okay,' Max says.

Then he looks left and right, checking the hallway to see if anyone is coming. He reminds me of Mrs Patterson, and I suddenly feel worried. Afraid.

Max is lying and something is wrong.

No one is coming, so Max opens the doors and leaves the school. He walks down the cement path toward the parking lot, walking fast but not running.

I look again. What does he see? I look in the direction that he is headed and I don't see anything. Just cars and the street. A few trees with yellow and red leaves. Grass.

Nothing.

Then I see it.

Mrs Patterson's car. I see it now. It's pulling out of a spot behind a silver truck. It was invisible behind that big truck. And she is pulling out face first. Mrs Patterson backed her car into the parking spot next to the silver truck so she could pull out face first, and that's when I know that something is really wrong, because only Mrs Griswold is silly enough to back into a parking spot. But Mrs Patterson did today, and it feels wrong and sneaky and planned. And somehow I know that Max knew all about it.

The car pulls in front of Max, and Max opens the back door and climbs in. Max is inside Mrs Patterson's car.

I pass through the glass doors and run down the cement path. I yell Max's name. I yell for him to stop. I wish I could tell him that he is being tricked and I know it way down deep inside. I can't explain how I know it but I do and he can't see it because he is Max and Max can't see the forest for the trees but there is no word that says all this so I just yell, 'Max!'

The car is moving now, down the row of cars to the street, and I can't catch up. It is definitely Mrs Patterson because I saw her before the car turned down the aisle. She is speeding up, as if she can see me coming in her rear-view mirror, and I can't catch the car in time. The car reaches the end of the row and turns left onto the street and drives away. I keep running until I reach the street. I turn down the sidewalk and run until I can't see the car anymore. I want to keep running because I don't know what else to do, but finally I stop.

Max is gone.

CHAPTER 22

I sit on the curb and wait. I don't care if Max knows that I tried to follow him. I am going to wait until he gets back, and then I am going to tell him that he should never get in Mrs Patterson's car again. I am not a teacher, but even I know that teachers are not supposed to drive kids around in their cars in the middle of the school day.

If I knew that Max would be back soon, I would not be so worried. But I am worried. There is so much to make me feel worried.

Mrs Patterson was absent from school today.

She drove to school just to pick up Max.

She backed her car into the parking spot so that she could drive away quickly.

She parked behind the big truck so no one inside the school would see her car.

She and Max made a plan to meet.

Max knew she was coming.

She was waiting for him.

He held his breath when he saw her.

No one saw them leave.

I keep hoping that I am just overreacting like a character on television, the kind that accuses his friend of a terrible crime and then realizes that he was wrong. I must be overreacting, because Max is with a teacher, and even if she is breaking the rules, she is still a teacher.

But she was absent today and came to pick up Max anyway. I can't stop thinking about that. It's the worst part, I think.

I hear a bell ring. It's the first recess bell. I have been sitting on the curb for more than an hour. Max's class is walking down the hallway to the cafeteria right now. I wonder if Mrs Gosk knows that Max is missing. Even though she is a good teacher, the best teacher, Max has so many teachers that maybe Mrs Gosk thinks that Max is with Mrs Riner or Mrs Hume or Mrs McGinn, and maybe Mrs Hume and Mrs Riner think that Max is with Mrs Gosk.

Maybe Mrs Patterson knew that Max's teachers would think like this, and that's why she chose today to pick him up.

This makes me worry even more.

It's hard to not worry, because trying not to worry reminds me that I should be worried. And when you're sitting on a curb, waiting for your friend to come back, it is hard to forget why you are sitting on the curb in the first place.

Every time a car drives by, every time a bird chirps, every time a recess bell rings, I get more worried. Each car, each chirp, and each bell is one more in between the last time I saw Max and now. Each one makes it feel more like for ever.

Four bells have rung since Max left, which means that Max has been gone for two hours. I'm wondering if there is a back entrance to the school that no one ever told me about. Maybe there is a road through the back woods that ends in the parking lot, and maybe Mrs Patterson brought Max back on this road, since no one would see them together way back there. I'm wondering if I should get up and go look for a back entrance, or maybe go inside and see if Max has come back, when I hear Max's name called on the intercom. The intercom plays inside the school and outside on the playground, which is on the other side of the building, but I can still hear Max's name being called. It's the principal. Mrs Palmer.

'Max Delaney, please report to your classroom immediately.'

Max is not back. Or maybe he is back and is walking to Mrs Gosk's room right now. I think about staying on the curb, waiting like I swore I would, but now that Mrs

Palmer knows that Max is missing, maybe it would be better if I go inside and wait.

I want to find out what is going on, too.

Mrs Gosk, Mrs Riner, and Mrs Hume are standing in Mrs Gosk's classroom. There are no kids in the classroom. They are in music class, I think. They have music on Friday afternoons. All three teachers look worried. They are staring at the classroom door, and when I walk in I think they are looking right at me. For a second, I think they can see me.

I enter the classroom. If I could look in a mirror, if I had a reflection, I think I would have the same worried face as the teachers.

Mrs Palmer walks in a second later. 'He hasn't shown up?' she asks. She looks worried, too.

'No,' Mrs Gosk says.

I have never heard Mrs Gosk sound so serious, and she only said one word. She said, 'No,' and I could tell that she is the worriedest she has ever been.

'Where could he be?' Mrs Hume asks. She is worried, too.

Good, I think. They should all be worried.

'Okay, stay here,' Mrs Palmer says and she leaves the room.

'What if he's run away?' Mrs Hume asks.

'Max isn't a runner,' Mrs Gosk says.

'I honestly don't think he's in the building, Donna,' Mrs Hume says.

Donna is Mrs Gosk's first name. Kids can never use a teacher's first name but teachers can use it whenever they want.

'He wouldn't just leave the building,' Mrs Gosk says, and she is kind of right. Max would never leave the building unless a teacher tricked him into leaving, which is exactly what happened.

I am the only one who knows what happened, and I can't tell anyone. Max is the only human person who I could tell, but Max isn't here, because Max is the one who disappeared.

Mrs Palmer's voice comes on the intercom again.

'Staff members, please take a moment and look around you and the area that you are in. Max Delaney from Mrs Gosk's classroom has lost his way somewhere in the building and we want to be sure that he finds his way back to his classroom. If you see Max, please call the office immediately. And Max, if you can hear me, please go to your classroom. If you're stuck somewhere, please call out and we'll find you. No need to worry, boys and girls. It's a big school and kids can sometimes get a little lost.'

Yeah, right, I think.

'I don't think he's in the building. I think we need to call the police,' Mrs Hume says. 'He doesn't live too far away. Maybe he walked home.'

'That's true,' Mrs Riner says. 'We should call his parents. He could be on his way home.'

'Max would not leave the building,' Mrs Gosk says.

Mrs Palmer returns. I can't believe how calm she looks.

'I have Eddie and Chris checking the basement and opening all the closets. The cafeteria staff are searching the kitchen. Wendy and Sharon are doing a sweep of the outside.'

'He's gone,' Mrs Hume says. 'I don't know how or why, but he's not here. It's been too long. This is Max we're talking about.'

'We don't know that,' Mrs Palmer says.

'She's right,' Mrs Gosk says. Her voice is softer. She doesn't sound as certain as she did a second ago. She sounds absolutely terrified. 'I can't believe that Max would ignore all those announcements.'

'You think he left the building?' Mrs Palmer asks.

'Yes. I don't know how he disappeared, but I think he's gone.'

I told you Mrs Gosk was smart.

CHAPTER 23

The whole school is in something called *lockdown*. This means that no one is allowed to leave the school until the police officers let them leave. Even teachers. Even Mrs Palmer. It's weird because I am the only one who knows that Mrs Patterson took Max, but I'm also the only one who can leave the school. I feel like I should be the one who is locked down, but I am the only one who is not.

Even though I know what happened to Max, I still don't know where Mrs Patterson took him, and even if I did, I still wouldn't know what to do. There is nothing I can do. So I'm just as stuck as all the people who don't know anything.

Except I'm probably the most worried. Everyone is worried. Mrs Gosk is worried, and so are Mrs Hume and Mrs Palmer. But I think I am more worried than all of them, because I know what happened to Max.

Even the policemen are worried. They look at each other

with squinty eyes and talk in whisper voices so the teachers and Mrs Palmer can't hear. But I can hear. I can stand right next to them and listen to every word they say, but I can't get any of them to listen to a single word I say. I am the only one who could help Max, but nobody can hear me.

When I was born, I tried to get other people like Max's mom and dad to listen to me, because I didn't know that they couldn't hear me. I thought they were ignoring me.

I remember one night when Max and his mom went out and I stayed home with Max's dad. I was afraid to go with Max because I had never left the house before, so Max's dad and I sat on the couch together for the whole night. I screamed and yelled at him for the whole time. I thought that if I shouted long enough, he would at least look at me and tell me to be quiet. I begged him to listen to me and talk to me, but he just kept staring at the baseball game like I wasn't even there. Then, as I was screaming, he laughed. I thought for a second that he was laughing at me, but he must have been laughing at something the man on the television had said, because the other man on the television was laughing now, too. And then I realized that it would be impossible for Max's dad to hear the man on the television because I was screaming so loud and right into his ear. That was when I understood that no one could hear me except Max.

Later on I met other imaginary friends and eventually

figured out that they could hear me. The imaginary friends who could hear, at least. Not all can.

I once met an imaginary friend that was just a hair bow with two eyes. I didn't even know that she was an imaginary friend until she started blinking her eyes at me, like she was trying to send me a signal. She just looked like a little bow in a little girl's hair. A pink bow. That's how I knew she was a girl. But she couldn't hear anything I said because the little girl never imagined her that way. Even when kids forget the ears on imaginary friends, most of them still imagine that their imaginary friends can hear, so they can. But not this little bow. She just blinked at me and I blinked back. She was afraid, too. I could tell by the look in her eyes and the way that she blinked, and even though I tried, I couldn't tell her that everything would be okay. All I could do was blink. But even those back-and-forth blinks seemed to make her a little less afraid. A little less alone.

But only a little.

I'd be afraid too if I was a little deaf hair bow stuck on a kindergartener's head.

Little pink hair bow girl disappeared the next day, and even though I think that not existing is the worst thing that could ever happen to someone, I think that little pink hair bow girl was probably happier after she disappeared. At least she wasn't so afraid anymore.

*

The police think that Max ran away from school. That's what they say when they stand in a circle and whisper. They don't think that Mrs Gosk is telling the truth. They think that Max probably left her classroom earlier in the morning than Mrs Gosk says he did, and that is why they haven't found Max yet.

'She just lost track of the kid,' one of the policemen said, and everyone in the circle nodded their heads.

'If that's the case, there's no telling how far he could've walked,' another policeman said, and everyone nodded again.

Policemen are not like kids. They always seem to agree with each other.

The police chief said that he has officers and community volunteers (which is just a fancy word for people) looking in the forest behind the school and walking the neighborhood streets searching for Max. They are knocking on the doors of all the houses to see if anyone has seen Max. I thought about going outside to search, too, but I am going to stay inside the school for now. Even though I am not locked down, I am staying locked down. I am waiting for Max to come back. Mrs Patterson can't keep him for ever.

I just wish the police would figure out that Mrs Patterson took Max. I keep thinking that the police on television would have already figured it out.

I have seen a lot of police officers over the last few days. First there was the policeman who came to the house after Tommy Swinden broke Max's window, and then there were the policemen and one policewoman who came to the gas station when Dee got shot and Sally got stuck. And now there are policemen and police-women all over the school. Bunches of them. But none of them look like the police officers on television, so I'm worried that none of them are as smart. The real-world policemen are all a little shorter, a little fatter and a little hairier than the ones on TV. One even has hair in his ears. Not the girl policeman, though. One of the boy policemen. I have never seen such normal-looking police officers on TV. Who do the television-maker people think they're fooling?

Who do they think they're fooling? That's a Mrs Gosk question. She asks it a lot. Mostly to the bad boys when they try to tell her that they forgot their homework on the kitchen table. She says, 'Who do you think you're fooling, Ethan Woods? I wasn't born yesterday.'

I would like to ask Mrs Patterson who she thinks she is fooling, but it looks like she is fooling everyone.

Mrs Palmer is annoyed that the school is locked down. I heard her say it to Mrs Simpson after the police finished searching the school. Mrs Palmer thinks that Max ran away, so she doesn't understand why the whole school has to be locked down for all this time. The police already searched every room and every closet and even the basement, so they know that Max is not here. I think they are just being careful. The police chief said that if one child can disappear from a school, others could, too.

'Maybe someone took the boy,' he said to Mrs Palmer when she tried to complain. 'If that's the case, someone in the school might know something about it.'

I don't think he really believes that someone took Max. He is just being careful. He is playing just-in-case. That's why Mrs Palmer is mad. She doesn't think there is a just-in-case. She thinks that Max went for a walk and didn't come back. That's what the police chief thinks, too.

I keep thinking that every minute the police search the basement and the forest and knock on doors is another minute that I lose Max for ever.

I don't think Max is dead. I don't even know why that idea keeps popping in my head, because I don't believe it. I think Max is alive and just fine. He's probably sitting in the back seat of Mrs Patterson's car with that blue backpack. I think he is fine, but I also keep thinking that he is not dead. I wish I could stop thinking about him being not dead and just think about him being alive.

But if Max was dead, would I ever know? Or would I just poof away without even knowing what happened? I keep holding my breath, waiting to poof, but if I was going to poof, I wouldn't even know it. I would just poof. One second I would exist and the next second I would not. So waiting for it to happen is silly. But I can't help it.

I keep hoping that maybe there is a reason why Mrs Patterson took Max. Maybe they went for ice cream and got lost, or maybe she is bringing Max on a field trip and forgot to tell Mrs Gosk, or maybe she took Max to meet her mother. Maybe they will pull into the driveway any second and Max will be back.

Except I don't think Mrs Patterson was talking to her mother yesterday.

I don't think Mrs Patterson even has a mother.

I wonder if Max's mom knows yet. And his dad. Probably. Maybe they are searching the forest right now.

Mrs Palmer comes into the classroom. Mrs Gosk has been reading *Charlie and the Chocolate Factory* to the kids again, which I usually love, but Max is missing the story now and he loves it when Mrs Gosk reads to the class. Plus Veruca Salt just disappeared down a garbage chute and I do not think Mrs Gosk should be reading stories about disappearing kids right now.

Mrs Gosk stops reading and looks up at Mrs Palmer.

Mrs Palmer says, 'Could I speak to the class for a moment, Mrs Gosk?'

Mrs Gosk says yes, but her eyebrows rise, which means that she is confused.

'Boys and girls, I am sure that you heard us call Max Delaney to the office a little while ago. And you know that we are in lockdown. I'm sure you have lots of questions. But there is nothing to worry about. We just need to make sure that we find Max. We think he may have wandered off or got picked up early and forgot to tell us. That's all. So I am wondering if anyone knows where Max might have gone. Did he say anything to anyone today? Anything about leaving the school early?'

Mrs Gosk already asked these questions to her kids a little while ago, when the kids saw the police cars pull up in front of the school and Mrs Palmer asked teachers to 'begin lockdown protocols until further notice'. But she lets Mrs Palmer ask anyway.

Briana raises her hand. 'Max goes to the Learning Center a lot. Maybe he got lost going there today.'

'Thank you, Briana,' Mrs Palmer says. 'Someone is checking on that right now.'

'Why are the police here?' This is Eric, and he did not raise his hand. Eric never raises his hand.

'The police are here to help us find Max,' Mrs Delaney says. 'They are good at finding lost children. I'm sure that he will turn up soon. But did he say anything to anyone today? Anything at all?'

Kids shake their heads. No one heard Max say anything because no one talks to Max.

'Okay. Thank you, boys and girls,' Mrs Palmer says. 'Mrs Gosk, could I speak to you for a moment?'

Mrs Gosk puts down the book and meets Mrs Palmer in the doorway to the classroom.

I follow.

'You're sure he didn't say anything to you?' Mrs Palmer asks.

'Nothing,' Mrs Gosk says. She sounds annoyed. I would be, too. The police chief has asked Mrs Gosk this question twice already.

'And you are sure about the time he left the classroom?'

'I'm sure,' Mrs Gosk says, even more annoyed.

'Okay. If the kids think of anything, let me know. I'm going to see about lifting the lockdown. We have a bunch of parents on the street already, waiting to pick up their kids.'

'The parents already know?' Mrs Gosk asks.

'The police have been knocking on doors for two hours, and the PTO is organizing volunteers to search the neighborhood. An Amber Alert went out. There's a news van outside already. There are bound to be more before six.'

'Oh,' Mrs Gosk says, and she sounds a lot less annoyed. She sounds like a little kid who has just been punished. Mrs Gosk never sounds like this. She sounds scared and confused, and this scares me.

Mrs Palmer turns and leaves Mrs Gosk standing in the

doorway. I follow Mrs Palmer down the hallway. I want to hear what she says to the police chief, and I do not want to hear what happens to that nasty Veruca Salt.

I don't care how rotten she is. Disappearing kids don't seem so funny anymore.

As Mrs Palmer crosses through the lobby and turns toward the office, one of the front doors to the school opens. The policeman standing beside it is holding it open.

Mrs Patterson walks in.

I stop.

I can't believe it. Mrs Patterson is walking into the school. I wait for Max to follow behind her, but the policeman closes the door.

No Max.

CHAPTER 24

'Karen, I can't believe the news,' Mrs Patterson says. 'What could have happened?'

Mrs Palmer and Mrs Patterson hug in the middle of the lobby.

Mrs Palmer is hugging Mrs Patterson and Max is not here.

I thought about running out to Mrs Patterson's car to see if Max was still in the back seat, but I decided not to. Mrs Patterson said that she couldn't believe the news about Max disappearing, and since she was the one who disappeared him, I know she is lying. Max isn't in her back seat anymore.

For a second, I thought he was dead, and my whole body filled with sadness. I thought that I might be dead for a minute, too. Then I remembered that I am still here, so Max must still be alive.

Here's the thing: if Max was dead (which he is not) and

I was still alive, that would mean that I won't disappear when Max dies or when Max stops believing in me.

I don't want Max to be dead, and I don't think he is dead (because he isn't), but if he was dead and I wasn't dead, that would mean something. It would be the saddest thing ever in the history of all things, but it would mean something, too. Something important about me. I'm not saying I want Max to be dead, because I do not and he is not. But if he ever was dead and I still existed, that would be an important thing to know.

I only keep thinking that he might be dead because I watch too much television.

Mrs Patterson and Mrs Palmer finish hugging just as the police chief comes around the corner. It was a long hug. I think they like each other now, even though they didn't like each other before Max disappeared. And I think Mrs Palmer has forgotten all about the *damunion*. They look like best friends, standing in the middle of the lobby. Sisters even.

'Ruth Patterson?' the police chief asks.

I don't know if he is really a police chief but he is in charge today and he has a big belly, so he looks like a police chief. His real name is Bob Norton, which is not a television show police officer kind of name. It doesn't make me feel good about his chances of finding Max.

Mrs Patterson turns. 'Yes, that's me.'

'Can we speak in Mrs Palmer's office?'

'Of course.'

Mrs Patterson sounds worried. The police chief probably thinks she is worried about Max, but I think she is
worried about getting caught. Maybe she is trying to make
worried-about-getting-caught sound like worried-about-
Max-disappearing.

Mrs Patterson and Mrs Palmer sit on one of the couches
together, and the police chief sits on the couch on the other
side of the coffee table. He has a pad of yellow paper on his
lap and a pen in his hand.

I sit next to the police chief. Even though he doesn't
know it, I am on his team.

'Mrs Patterson,' the police chief says. 'You are Max
Delaney's paraprofessional. Is that correct?'

'Yes. I spend a lot of time with Max. But I have other students, too.'

'You're not with him all day long?' the police chief asks.

'No. Max is a smart boy. He doesn't need assistance all
day.'

Mrs Palmer nods as Mrs Patterson is speaking. I have
never seen her be so agreeable around Mrs Patterson before.

'Can I ask why you were absent from work today?' the
police chief asks.

'I had a doctor's appointment. Two appointments,
actually.'

'Where was your appointment?'

'The first was just down the street,' Mrs Patterson says, pointing in the direction of the front of the school. 'At the walk-in clinic. They have a physical therapy center located in the building. I had physical therapy this morning for a shoulder problem. Then I had an appointment on Farmington Avenue. That's where I was when Nancy called.'

'Mrs Palmer says you miss a lot of work, especially on Fridays. Is it because of the physical therapy?'

Mrs Patterson looks at Mrs Palmer for a second, and then she turns back to the police chief and smiles.

She has stolen Max and is sitting in front of a police chief, and she is smiling.

'Yes,' she says. 'I mean, sometimes I'm ill, and sometimes I have doctor's appointments.' She pauses, takes a deep breath, and then says, 'No one knows this, but I have lupus, and it's caused me to have some health problems over the past couple years. Sometimes a five-day work week is just too much for me.'

Mrs Palmer makes a little gasping sound. 'Ruth, I had no idea.'

She reaches out and touches Mrs Patterson on the shoulder. It's the kind of touch that Max's mother would like to give to Max when he is upset, if Max would ever let her touch him like that. I can't believe that she is touching Mrs Patterson like this. Max disappears and Mrs Patterson says she has something called lupus and suddenly Mrs Palmer wants to hug her and pat her on the shoulder.

'It's okay,' Mrs Patterson says to Mrs Palmer. 'I didn't want people to worry.'

'Is there anything that you can tell us that might help us find Max?' the police chief asks. He sounds a little annoyed, and I am glad.

'I can't think of anything,' Mrs Patterson says. 'Max has never been a runner, but he's always been a curious boy, and he asks lots of questions about the forest. But I can't imagine that he would go there alone.'

'A runner?' the police chief asks.

Mrs Palmer speaks this time. 'Some of our special needs children have a propensity for running away from us. If they make it to the doors, they will sometimes run for the street. But Max isn't a runner.'

'Max has never been a runner?' the police chief asks.

'No,' Mrs Patterson says. 'Never.'

I can't believe how calm she is. Maybe lupus makes people good liars.

The police chief looks down at his yellow pad. He clears his throat. I don't know how I know, but I can tell that he is about to ask important questions now. Tougher questions.

'Max was supposed to go from Mrs Gosk's class to the Learning Center today, but he never made it there. Is this a walk he usually does by himself?'

'Sometimes,' Mrs Patterson says, but that is not true. I am always with him when he walks to the Learning Center. 'If I'm in school, I'll pick him up, but he doesn't need an escort.'

'We are trying to get Max to be more independent,' Mrs Palmer says. 'So even when Ruth is here, we will sometimes have Max travel around the building on his own.'

'But on Fridays,' Mrs Patterson says, 'I am scheduled to work with Max in the Learning Center, so I would normally escort him there because I need to be there, too.'

'Do you think it's possible that Max could have left Mrs Gosk's class early?'

'Maybe,' Mrs Patterson says. 'He can't read an analog clock. Did Donna send him on time?'

'She says she did,' the police chief says. 'I'm just wondering if she could have sent him early by mistake, or if he could've left the class without telling her or without her noticing.'

'It's possible.'

'She's lying!' I shout, only because I can't stop myself. Mrs Gosk never sends kids early. If anything, she forgets to send them at all. She gets too busy with her books and her teaching. And Max would never leave the room without permission. Never ever.

The more Mrs Patterson lies, the more frightened I become. She is so good at it.

'What about Max's parents?' the police chief asks. 'Is there anything I should know about them?'

'What do you mean?'

'How are they as parents? Do they get along? Do they get Max to school on time? Does he seem well cared for? Things like that.'

'I don't understand,' Mrs Patterson says. 'Do you think they did something to Max? I thought he was at school today.'

'He was, and it's likely he just went for a walk and he'll turn up any minute, playing on someone's backyard swing set or hiding in the forest. But if Max didn't take a walk, then someone took him, and it's almost always someone who the child knows. Most often a family member. Can you think of anyone who might want to take Max? Could his parents be involved?'

Mrs Patterson doesn't answer this question as quickly as the others, and the police chief notices. He leans forward at the same time I do. He thinks he is about to hear something important, and I do, too. But the police chief thinks that he is about to get an important fact.

I think it's going to be an important lie.

'I've always worried about Max being here at school.'

She talks like she is lifting a heavy backpack. All her words sound heavy and light at the same time.

'Max is a very sensitive boy and he doesn't have any friends. Kids pick on him from time to time. Sometimes he loses track of what he is doing and is unsafe. Runs out in front of a school bus or forgets that he's allergic to tree nuts. I don't know if I would send Max to a public school if I were his parent. I think it's too dangerous. I have a hard time thinking that good parents would send a boy like Max to school.'

Mrs Patterson pauses. She's looking at her shoes. I don't think she realizes what she has been saying, because when she looks back up, she seems surprised to be looking at the police chief.

'But I don't think they would do anything to hurt Max,' she says.

Too quickly, I think.

Mrs Patterson doesn't like Max's mom and dad. I didn't know that before, but I do now. And I don't think she wanted anyone to know it.

'But there is nothing specific about his parents that would cause you concern?' the police chief asks. 'Other than that they send Max to a public school?'

Mrs Patterson pauses, and then says, 'No.'

The police chief asks Mrs Patterson questions about the Learning Center teachers, Max's classmates, and everyone else who Max sees every day, which is not too many people. She says that she cannot imagine anyone at school taking Max.

The police chief just nods.

'I'm going to ask you to walk the path that Max usually

takes to the Learning Center with one of my officers, to see if anything jogs your memory. If it does, you'll let me know. And he's going to get some contact information from you, and ask you a few questions about anyone else who Max might come into contact with on a daily basis. Okay?'

'Okay,' Mrs Patterson says. 'Would it be all right if I go home, after I answer his questions? At least for a little while. The physical therapy and the doctor's appointment took a lot out of me, and I'd like to rest. Or maybe I could just lie down on a couch in the faculty room if you'd prefer I stay at school.'

'No, that's fine. We'll contact you if we need anything. If Max doesn't turn up by this evening, we'll probably need to talk to you again. Sometimes people don't realize what they might know that could help us.'

'I'll do whatever I can to help,' Mrs Patterson says. She starts to rise from the couch and then stops. 'You think you're going to find him. Right?'

'I hope so,' the police chief says. 'Like I said, I think he'll probably turn up within the hour, playing in someone's backyard. So yes, I think we'll find him.'

I know I will.

I'm going home with Mrs Patterson.

CHAPTER 25

Max's mom and dad are standing behind the counter in the office. I see them first because I walk out of Mrs Palmer's office first. Then Mrs Patterson sees them, but I don't think she recognizes their faces. I don't think she even knows them. She stole their son and told the police chief that they are bad parents and she doesn't even know who they are. I don't think Max's parents know who she is either. They know her name, but they have never seen her face to face until now. They have meetings with people like Mrs McGinn and Mrs Riner and Mrs Gosk.

Not Mrs Patterson. Never paraprofessionals.

Mrs Patterson doesn't stop to talk to them. She walks to the left, out the office's side door, where a policeman is waiting for her. He's an old man with a brown spot on his neck, and he doesn't look like he could stop a bad guy even if the bad guy was Mrs Patterson, which she is.

Then Mrs Palmer comes out of her office, and she sees Max's parents.

'Mr and Mrs Delaney,' she says, sounding surprised. She walks over to the counter and opens the swinging door that separates the space where regular people stand from the space where the office people stand. 'Come in. Please.'

Max's mom is usually the boss, but she does not look like the boss right now. Her hands are shaking, and her face is pale. She looks limp, a little bit like a doll. I know it sounds silly, but even her curly hair looks less curly. She doesn't look sharp like she usually does. She looks scared. Hungry, even. Hungry for news, I think.

It is Max's dad who looks like the boss now. He has his arm around Max's mom, and he is looking around the office like Mrs Gosk looks when she is taking attendance. Checking to see who is here and who is not.

They move past the counter and toward Mrs Palmer's office, but I don't think Max's mom would be moving if Max's dad was not pushing her along.

'Do you have any news?' Max's dad asks before they even make it to Mrs Palmer's office.

He sounds like the boss, too. His words are like arrows. They shoot straight at Mrs Palmer, and you can tell that they are full of extra stuff. He isn't just asking a question. He is yelling at Mrs Palmer for losing Max even though he is not yelling and all he did was ask if there was any news.

'Come into my office,' Mrs Palmer says. 'Chief Norton is waiting, and he can answer all your questions.'

'Chief Norton wasn't here when Max disappeared,' Max's dad says.

More arrows. Sharp ones.

'Please,' Mrs Palmer says. 'Step inside.'

We step into Mrs Palmer's office. This time Max's parents sit on the couch where Mrs Patterson and Mrs Palmer were sitting a couple minutes ago. I wish I could tell them that they are sitting in the same place where the person who stole Max was sitting a few minutes ago.

Mrs Palmer moves over to the couch where the police chief is still sitting. There is no room for me, so I stand beside the couch that Max's parents are sitting on. Even though there are no sides here, because there is no bad guy in the room like before, I still feel like there are sides, and something tells me that I want to be on Max's parents' side.

The police chief stands up to shake Max's parents' hands. He introduces himself and then everyone sits down except me.

'Mr and Mrs Delaney, I'm Chief Norton. I've taken charge of the search for your son. Let me tell you where we are so far.'

Max's mom nods but Max's dad doesn't. He doesn't move at all. I think he does this on purpose. If he moved, if he even nodded, then there would be no more sides in the room. Everyone would be on the same side. They would be a team.

He doesn't move an inch.

The police chief tells Max's parents about the search of the school and the people who are searching the neighborhood. He says that they are *operating under the assumption* that Max has run away and will be found soon, which sounds like he is hoping that Max has run away and will be found soon, otherwise he will not know what to do.

'Max has never run away before,' Max's dad says.

'No,' the police chief says. 'But his teachers think it's possible, and it's more likely than any other scenario.'

'Like what?' Max's dad asks.

'I'm sorry?' the police chief says.

'What other scenarios are you talking about?'

The police chief pauses for a moment. When he speaks, his words come slowly. 'Well, it's far more likely that he ran away from the school than he was abducted.'

Max's mom lets out a tiny whimper when he says *abducted*.

'I don't mean to frighten you, Mrs Delaney. Like I said, I expect my phone to ring at any moment, telling me they found Max playing in someone's backyard or lost in a patch of woods behind a neighbor's house. But if he isn't found, we will have to look into the possibility that some-one has taken him. I've already started the preliminary work in the event that this ends up being the situation. We're exploring both possibilities simultaneously, just in case.'

'Is it possible that he ran away and then got picked up by someone while he was on the street?'

Mrs Palmer asks this question, and I can tell by the look on her face and the police chief's face that they both wish she had not asked it. At least not in front of Max's parents. She looks at Max's mom, who looks like she is about to cry. 'I'm sorry,' she says. 'I don't mean to frighten you.'

'It's not likely,' the police chief says. 'It would be quite a coincidence if Max decided to run away at the same time a child abductor was driving by the school. But we're look-ing into all options, interviewing all staff members that come into contact with Max and trying to see if someone new has recently come into contact with him.'

'Why was Max alone?' Max's mom asks.

This is a good question. An arrow question that should have hit Mrs Palmer right between the eyes, but instead the question sounds like jello. There's nothing behind it. Max's mom even looks like jello. She is all wobbly and weak.

'Max's paraprofessional was out today, and Max had walked to the Learning Center many times on his own,' Mrs Palmer says. 'In fact, one of his IEP goals is to become more independent in regards to moving around the building and following a schedule, so it wasn't unusual for him to be traveling from his classroom to the Learning Center alone.'

'And that's when you think he disappeared?' Max's father asks. 'In between his classroom and the Learning Center?'

'Yes,' the police chief says, speaking quickly. I think he wants Mrs Palmer to be quiet, so he is covering up all the spaces where she could speak. 'Max was last seen in his regular classroom. He never made it to the Learning Center, but since his paraprofessional was absent today, the Learning Center teachers didn't notice that Max had never arrived, since she is the one who works with him there. And his teacher, Mrs Gosk, assumed that your son was in the Learning Center, so Max could've been gone for as long as two hours before anyone noticed.'

Max's dad runs his hands through his hair. He does this when he is stopping himself from saying something bad. He does this a lot when he argues with Max's mom. Usually right before he slams the screen door and leaves.

'We'd like to get some information from you,' the police chief says. 'Names of people who come into contact with

Max on a regular basis. Anyone new in his life. Daily routines. Any medical information we might need to know.'

'You said you thought you'd find him any minute,' Max's mom says.

'Yes, I know, and I still believe that. We have more than two hundred people searching the area right now, and the media are spreading the word for us as well.'

The police chief is about to say something else when there is a knock on the door and a policewoman pokes her head inside the office.

'Mrs Patterson is ready to go home unless you need her.'

'Nothing on the walk-through?' the police chief asks.

'No.'

'And we have her contact information?'

'Yes.'

'Fine then,' he says. 'She can go.'

'You're letting the bad guy go!' I shout, but no one hears me.

It is like when Max's dad or Sally shout at the television as they watch a detective let the bad guy go free by mistake, except on TV the bad guys usually get caught. This is the real world, and I don't think the television rules work here. Bad guys like Tommy Swinden and Mrs Patterson can win in the real world. All that Max has is me, and I am useless.

'Okay, I'll send her home,' the policewoman says.

That means it is time for me to go, too, even though a big part of me wants to stay here with Max's mom. The only way to help her is to help Max, but leaving her now seems wrong. She seems so weak. Like only half of her is here.

Still, I have to find my friend.

I pass through the office door and re-enter the main office. I do not see Mrs Patterson. The policewoman who told Chief Norton that Mrs Patterson was ready to leave is on the phone now. She is sitting at the desk where the secretary lady usually sits. I don't know where Mrs Patterson is, but I know where she parks her car, and I'm worried that she might already be walking to the parking lot so I start to run out of the office when I hear the police-woman say, 'You can tell her that she can go now. But tell her that she needs to leave her phone on in case we need her.' She says this to the person on the other end of the telephone.

Good. Mrs Patterson hasn't left yet.

Still, I want to be inside her car before she gets there, so I run.

I once knew an imaginary friend who could pop. Instead of walking to a place, he could just disappear from one place and reappear in the other place, as long as he had been to the other place before. I thought this was amazing, because it was like he stopped existing for a second and then existed again a second later. I asked him what it was like to stop existing because I wanted to know if it hurt, but he did not understand my question.

'I don't stop existing,' he said. 'I just pop from one place to the other.'

'But what does it feel like to stop existing for that second before you reappear?'

'It doesn't feel like anything,' he said. 'I just blink my eyes and I am in the new place.'

'But how does it feel when your body disappears from the place that you start?'

'It doesn't feel like anything.'

I could tell that he was getting angry so I stopped asking. I was a little jealous of him for being able to pop, except that he was only as tall as a Barbie doll and his eyes were blue. All blue. No white part at all. It was like he was looking through a pair of dark blue sunglasses, so he could barely see, especially on a cloudy day or when the teacher turned out the lights to show a movie. And he had no name, which is not uncommon in imaginary friends but still a little sad. And he is gone now. He stopped existing over Christmas vacation when Max was still in kindergarten.

I wish I could pop right now. Instead, I run through the halls, following the same path that Max and I followed earlier today when Mrs Patterson stole him. Right back to those glass doors where Max left earlier today.

Mrs Patterson's car is not in the parking lot. I run up and down the row but I can't find it. But there is only one way to the parking lot, only one hallway and one set of doors, and I know that Mrs Patterson could not have beaten me here because I ran the whole way and Mrs Patterson would not run because it would make her look suspicious.

Then I figure it out. She has two cars. She drove a different car back to the school. One without the blue backpack and all the evidence that Max was inside. Like a hair from his head or dirt from his sneakers or his fingerprints. All the stuff that the scientists can use to prove that Max was sitting in the back seat. That must be it. She drove a different car back to school just in case the police wanted to inspect her car. That would be sneaky-smart and I think Mrs Patterson is the sneakiest-smartest person I have ever met. She will be coming out those doors any second and getting into a different car. One I have never seen before. Maybe the one I am standing in front of right now.

I look around to see if I can find a new car in the parking lot. One I have never seen before. Then I see it. Not a new car that I have never seen before but Mrs Patterson's old car. The one with the blue backpack and Max's hair and Max's dirt. It is in the circle in front of the school. It is parked in the circle, right in front of the doors to the school, even though it is illegal to park in the circle when kids are in school. I know this because sometimes Mrs Palmer comes on the intercom and asks for the person who is parked in the circle to move their car *immediately*. She says *immediately* in a way to let the person who parked the car know that she is annoyed. She could just say, 'Please move your car from the circle. And whoever you are, I am annoyed that you parked there,' but instead she says *immediately*, which seems nicer and not so nice at the same time.

But it is always a parent or a substitute teacher who parks in the circle because teachers know better. Mrs Patterson knows better. So why is Mrs Patterson parked in the circle now? There are police cars in the circle, too, but police are allowed to break the rules.

Then I see that Max's parents' car is parked in the circle, too. It is parked behind Mrs Patterson's car, but then it is not parked behind Mrs Patterson's car because Mrs Patterson's car starts moving. It is driving around the back of the circle and toward the street.

I run. I run as fast as I can, which is only as fast as Max imagined that I could run, which is not that fast. I want to yell, 'Stop! Wait! You weren't supposed to park in the circle!' But she would never hear me, because her windows are up and she is so far away and I am imaginary, and only imaginary friends and my friend who she stole can hear me.

I cross the driveway without looking both ways or using the crosswalk and then I run across the front lawn to the other side of the circle, but Mrs Patterson is pulling into the street and turning right. I wish I could pop. I close my eyes and try to imagine the back seat of Mrs Patterson's car, with the blue backpack and the hair from Max's head and the dirt from his sneakers, but when I open my eyes a second later I am still running across the front lawn and Mrs Patterson's car is disappearing down a hill and around a bend.

I slow down and then I stop. I am standing in the middle of the front lawn, underneath a pair of trees. Yellow and red leaves are falling around me.

I lost Max.

Again.

CHAPTER 26

Chief Norton told Max's mom and dad that he has not given up hope on finding Max somewhere in the neighborhood, but that he is 'shifting the focus of the investigation in a different direction'.

This means he doesn't think that Max ran away anymore.

He sent Max's parents to the teacher's lounge with a policewoman to answer some more questions. Then he told the police officer with the brown spot on his neck to call Burger King and Aetna to make sure that Max's mom and dad were working when Max disappeared. He has to make sure that it wasn't Max's mom or dad who stole Max. I'm not surprised. The police always have to check out the parents first.

It seems like parents are always the bad guys on TV.

The officer comes back into the office and tells Chief Norton that Max's mom and dad were at work all day and were 'in plain sight', which means that they could not have driven to the school, stolen Max and driven back without someone noticing that they were gone.

The chief looks relieved.

I guess it is better to search for a stranger who steals little boys than to find out that a mom or dad stole their own little boy. But I also know from television that the people who hurt and steal kids are usually not strangers, which is true today, too. Mrs Patterson is not a stranger. She is just smart.

About twenty minutes before dismissal, the chief ended the lockdown and let the kids put on their coats and line up for the buses. But the lines were short today. Lots of the kids got picked up by parents who were biting their nails and twisting their wedding rings and walking faster than normal, as if the kidnapper was hiding behind the trees on the front lawn, waiting to scoop up even more kids.

I tried to talk to Puppy before he went home on the bus with Piper, but I had only a couple minutes before her bus was called.

'Mrs Patterson stole Max,' I said to him.

We were standing in Piper's classroom, watching her move the papers in her cubby to her backpack. Actually, Puppy was standing. I have to sit on the floor when I talk to Puppy, since he is a puppy.

'She stole him?' he asked.

It always looks weird when Puppy talks, because dogs are not supposed to talk, and he looks like a real dog. When he speaks, his tongue hangs out of his mouth and it makes him lisp. And he scratches himself a lot, even though as far as I know there is no such thing as imaginary fleas.

'Yes,' I said. 'Max went out to her car and then she drove away.'

'So she didn't steal him. Maybe they went for a ride.'

'Yeah, but I don't think Max knew what was going on. I think Mrs Patterson tricked him.'

'Why?' Puppy asked. 'Why would a teacher trick a little kid like that?'

This is another reason why I do not like to talk to Puppy. He doesn't understand things like I do. Piper is only in first grade, and Puppy almost never leaves her side, so he does not get to see the adult world. He doesn't go to the gas station or the hospital at night and he doesn't watch television with Piper's parents. He's too much like Piper. He hasn't learned anything like why a teacher might steal a kid.

'I don't know why Mrs Patterson would trick him,' I say, not wanting to explain bad guys to him. 'But I don't think that Mrs Patterson likes Max's parents. Maybe she thinks they are bad people.'

'Why would Max's parents be bad people? They're parents.'

See what I mean?

I wish Graham was here right now. I miss her so much. I think I'm the only who misses her. If Meghan missed her, Graham would still be here. I wonder if Meghan even remembers Graham.

No matter what happens, I don't think that anyone will remember me when I disappear. It will be like I was never here. There will be no proof that I ever existed. When Graham was disappearing, she said that the only thing that she was sad about was that she could not watch Meghan grow up. If I disappeared, I would be sad about not being able to see Max grow up, but I would also be sad about not watching me grow up.

Except you can't be sad if you disappear, because disappeared people can't feel sad.

They can only be remembered or forgotten.

I remember Graham, so it still matters that she was here. She has not been forgotten. But there is no Graham to remember me.

The police ordered Chinese food for Max's parents and Chief Norton just delivered it.

'We have some more questions, but we should be done soon. Can you hang on for another hour and then we'll send you home with a couple officers?'

'We can stay as long as you need us to,' Max's mom says.

She sounds like she wants to stay here all night. I don't blame her. As long as she does not go home, she can keep thinking that Max will be found any minute. Going home means that they know they won't find Max tonight.

Unless they go to Mrs Patterson's house, they are not going to find him.

The police officer with the brown spot on his neck leaves with Chief Norton. Chief Norton says that he wants to give Max's parents a few minutes to eat and be alone.

I do not leave. Without Max, Max's mom and dad are the only people I have.

As soon as the door closes, Max's mom starts to cry. It's not a big cry like the kindergarteners do on their first day of school. Just a little cry. Lots of sniffles and tears but that's it. Max's dad puts his arm around her. He doesn't say anything, and I don't understand why. They just sit there together. Maybe they hurt so much that the only way they can say it is to say nothing.

I hurt so much, too, but if I could I would talk.

I would tell them how stupid I feel for letting Mrs Patterson leave without me. How stupid and guilty and rotten I feel. I would tell them how worried I am that today is Friday and I won't be able to ride in Mrs Patterson's car until Monday afternoon. I would tell them how afraid I am that Mrs Patterson won't ever come back to school on Monday and I will never be able to find her or Max again.

If I could talk to Max's parents, I would tell them that Mrs Patterson tricked Max and stole him from the school and lied about it and now Max is in trouble. If I could tell them all that, then Max could be saved. If only I could touch their world and let them know.

It's why I've been thinking about Oswald, the man at the hospital. The mean imaginary friend man who I never want to see again.

Except now I might have to.

CHAPTER 27

There are two police officers at the house tonight, and they are the kind of police officers who don't sleep. I have seen this kind of police officer at the police station before. They can stay awake all night because the police station never closes.

They are sitting in the kitchen, drinking coffee and watching television. It feels weird to have two strangers in the house with us, especially with Max not here. It must be weird for Max's mom and dad, too, because they went to their bedroom early tonight instead of sitting in the living room and watching television.

Max's dad wanted to go out searching for Max, but Chief Norton told him to go home and get some sleep. 'We have patrol cars and volunteers walking the neighborhood, and we need you well rested if you're going to be any help to us tomorrow.'

'What if Max is hurt somewhere?' Max's dad asked, and

there was anger in his voice, but it was the kind of anger that someone has when they are afraid. It sounded more nervous and rushed. It was like fear dressed up in a loud voice and red cheeks. 'What if he slipped and fell and banged his head and now he's lying unconscious under a bush, out of sight of your patrol cars? Or what if he fell through an open sewer grate or even tried to climb down on his own? What if he is lying in a puddle under some street, bleeding to death right now?'

Max's mom is crying again, and it stopped Max's dad before he could say anything else about Max dying or being dead.

'Those are all things that we have considered,' Chief Norton said.

Even though Max's dad was almost yelling, Chief Norton's voice stayed quiet. He knew that Max's dad wasn't mad at him. He might have even known that Max's dad was not really angry at all but just afraid. His name might be Chief Norton, but I think he is smarter than I thought.

'We've actually checked every sewer grate within three miles of the school, and we're expanding that radius now. Yes, it's possible that Max has managed to get himself stuck in a place that is difficult for our teams to see him, but I've made sure that everyone who is searching knows this and they are leaving no stone unturned.'

Max's dad was right. Max is stuck in a place where

nobody can see him. But I don't think it matters how hard they look.

So Max's mom and dad went home, and after they showed the police officers where the coffee pot and bathroom and telephone and remote control were, they said that they were going to bed.

Max's mom and dad have not turned on the television, even though I cannot remember the last time they did not spend the evening watching TV. Max's mom took a shower and now she is sitting on the bed, brushing her hair. Max's dad is sitting on the edge of the bed, too, turning his telephone over and over in his hands.

'I just can't stop thinking about how afraid he must be,' Max's mom says. She has stopped combing her hair.

'I know,' Max's dad says. 'I keep thinking that he's stuck somewhere. Maybe he got himself trapped in the basement of an abandoned house or maybe he found a cave somewhere in the forest and he can't get out. Wherever he is, I keep thinking about how alone and how afraid he must be.'

'I keep hoping that he has Budo with him.'

I let out a little cry when I hear Max's mom say my name. I know she thinks I'm imaginary, but for that split second I almost felt like she thought I was real.

'I hadn't thought of that,' Max's dad says. 'Anything to make him feel better. Feel less scared.'

Max's mom starts to cry, and a second later Max's dad

does, too. But Max's dad cries on the inside. You can tell that he is crying, but you can also tell that he doesn't think you can tell that he's crying.

'I'm trying to think of what we did wrong,' Max's mom says, still crying. 'I keep thinking that this is somehow our fault.'

'Stop it,' Max's dad says, and I can tell that he is done crying. At least for now. 'That goddam teacher lost track of Max, and he probably took a walk and got lost. And then he got curious about something that he saw and got stuck somewhere. We have enough to worry about without blaming ourselves.'

'You don't think someone took him?'

'No,' Max's dad says. 'I can't believe that. No, they are going to find him at the bottom of a well or trapped inside the basement of some abandoned house somewhere or locked in some shed in someone's backyard. And you know Max. He's probably heard people shouting his name already but won't answer because he doesn't like to talk to people and he doesn't like to shout. He's going to be cold and wet and scared, but he is going to be fine. That's what I believe. I believe it in my heart.'

Max's dad's words sound good. They are bursting with hope and I think he really believes everything he said. I think Max's mom is starting to believe it, too. For a second, even I believe it. I want to believe it.

Max's mom and dad hug and don't let go. After a few seconds it feels weird to be sitting next to them so I leave. They will probably be asleep soon, anyway.

I do not want to go to the gas station tonight. Dee and Sally won't be there, and I can't stand to be reminded of all the people who I have lost in my life. Graham. Dee. Sally. Max. The gas station used to be one of my favorite places, but not anymore.

I can't stay here, either. Not all night. I do not feel right sitting in Max's parents' room and I do not want to sit in Max's room alone. And I can't sit in the living room or kitchen because the police officers are there and they are watching one of those shows where a man talks to a bunch of people who think he is funnier than the people watching on television do.

Plus it feels strange to have these strangers in our house.

I need to talk to someone. And there are not many places where an imaginary friend can go to talk to someone, especially at night.

But I know one place.

CHAPTER 28

The Children's Hospital is across the street from the regular hospital, but I don't go to the regular hospital anymore. Not since I met the mean man imaginary friend. Sometimes I get nervous just coming to the Children's Hospital, because it is so close to the adult hospital.

But the Children's Hospital is the best place to find imaginary friends. Even better than school. A school is full of kids, but most of them leave their imaginary friends at home, because it is hard to talk or play with an imaginary friend when teachers and other kids are around. They might bring them to school on the first day of kindergarten, but unless it is someone like Max, the kids figure out fast that talking to someone who no one else can see is not a good way to make friends. This is the time when most imaginary friends stop existing.

Kindergarten kills them.

But the Children's Hospital has always been a good place

to find other imaginary friends. I came here when Max was in first grade because Max's first-grade teacher, Mrs Kropp, told us that hospitals never close. She was teaching the class about 911, which is a number that you can press on a phone if there is an emergency.

If I could press numbers I would have pressed that number today when Mrs Patterson stole Max.

Mrs Kropp said that you can press 911 anytime, because the ambulances and hospitals are always open. So one night I decided to skip the gas station and walk to the hospital instead, which is like six gas stations away.

The kids at the Children's Hospital are always sick. Some are sick for just a day or two. They fall off their bikes and hit their heads or catch something called pneumonia, but there are also kids who have been at the hospital for a long time because they are really sick. And lots of these kids, especially the really sick ones, have imaginary friends, probably because they need them. Some of the kids are pale and skinny and have no hair, and some wake up in the middle of the night crying softly so no one will hear them and worry about them. Sick kids know that they are sick, and really sick kids know they are really sick, and all of them are scared. So lots of them need imaginary friends to keep them company when their parents go home and they are left with the beeping machines and flashing lights.

The elevator in the hospital is tricky for me, because I cannot go through the elevator doors. I can pass through glass doors and wooden doors and bedroom doors and even car doors, but I cannot pass through elevator doors. I think it is because Max is afraid of elevators and never, ever goes inside one, so he probably does not think of the elevator doors as regular doors. They are more like trapdoors to him.

But I want to go to the fourteenth floor, and it is easier for me to take the elevator. Fourteen floors is a lot of stairs. But that means I need to make sure that there is room in the elevator for me, because even though people can't see me or feel me, they can bump me and squish me into a corner if there are too many of them.

That's not quite right. I don't bump into them. I bump into the idea of them, which means that I feel them but they do not feel me. But there have been times when the elevator fills up with people and I am so squished into the corner that I start to feel how Max must feel when he is in an elevator. All tight and trapped and suffocated, even though I don't actually breathe. I look like I breathe, but all I breathe is the idea of air, which is always there.

It's very strange to be an imaginary friend. You can't be suffocated and you can't get sick and you can't fall and break your head and you can't catch pneumonia. The only thing that can kill you is a person not believing in you. That happens more than all the suffocating and bumps and pneumonia combined.

I wait for a person in a blue costume to press the button. She walked into the hospital right behind me. I have to wait for someone to use the elevator since I cannot press the button that tells the elevator that someone is waiting. And then I have to hope that the person is getting off on a floor close to mine. The woman in the blue costume presses the number eleven, which isn't bad. If no one else gets on the elevator, I will get off on the eleventh floor, too, and climb the stairs to the fourteenth floor.

No one gets on the elevator before we reach the eleventh floor, so I step off and climb the last three flights of stairs.

The fourteenth floor is shaped like a spider, with a circle in the center where all the doctors work, and four hallways stretching out from it. I walk down the hallway, toward the middle circle, past open doors on both sides of the hallway. This is another good thing about the Children's Hospital. The doctors do not close the doors to the kids' rooms all the way, so imaginary friends who cannot pass through doors don't get stuck inside overnight.

It is late so the hallway is quiet. The whole floor is quiet. Most of the rooms are dark. There are a bunch of girl doctors in the middle circle, sitting and standing behind counters, writing down numbers and words in notepads and going to rooms when buzzers buzz. They are like the police officers that never sleep. They can stay awake all night but they do not look like they want to.

At the other end of one of the spider's legs is a room with couches and cushy chairs and lots of magazines and games. This is where the sick kids have recess during the day. At night, this is where the imaginary friends who do not sleep meet.

I used to think that all imaginary friends did not sleep, but Graham said that she slept at night, so maybe there are imaginary friends sleeping with their friends tonight in their hospital rooms.

I imagine Graham sleeping in a bed next to Meghan and it makes me want to cry again.

There are three imaginary friends in the recess room tonight, which is not a lot. All three look like imaginary friends. There is a boy who looks a lot like a person except that his legs and feet are tiny and fuzzy and his head is too large for his body. He looks like one of the Red Sox bobble-head dolls that Mrs Gosk has on her desk. But he has ears and eyebrows and fingers, so this makes him look more like a person than most imaginary friends. Still, his head is so big that I wonder what he looks like when he walks.

Sitting next to the bobble-headed boy is a girl who is about as tall as a bottle of soda. She has yellow hair and no nose or neck. Her head is sitting on her body like a snow-man. She doesn't blink.

The third looks like a boy-sized spoon with two big, round eyes, a tiny mouth and stick-figure legs and arms. He is silver all over and wearing no clothes, but he doesn't need to wear clothes because, except for his arms and legs, he looks just like a spoon.

Actually, I'm not even sure if it's a he or a she. Sometimes imaginary friends are neither. I think it might just be a spoon.

As I enter, they stop talking and stare at me. But they do not look into my eyes, probably because they think I am a human person.

'Hello,' I say and the spoon gasps. The bobble-headed boy jumps and his head bobbles just like Mrs Gosk's bobble-head doll.

The little tiny girl doesn't move. She doesn't even blink.

'I thought you were real,' the spoon says. He is so surprised that it sounds like he is choking on his words. He has a boy's voice, so I think it's a he.

'Me too!' the bobble-head boy says. He sounds very excited.

'Nope. I'm like you. My name is Budo.'

'Wow. You look so real,' the spoon says. He can't stop staring.

'I am real. As real as you.'

Every time I talk to imaginary friends I have this same conversation. They are always surprised that I am not a human person and they always say how real I look. Then I have to remind them that they are real, too.

'Sure,' the spoon says. 'But you look like a real human.'

'I know,' I say.

After a moment of silence, the spoon speaks. 'I'm Spoon,' he says.

'I'm Klute,' the bobble-head boy says. 'She is Summer.'

'Hi,' the little girl says in a teeny tiny voice. All she says is 'Hi,' and I can already tell that she is sad. As sad as I have ever seen someone. Sadder than Max's dad when Max won't play catch right.

Maybe as sad as I still feel about Graham.

'Do you have someone here?' Spoon asks.

'What do you mean?'

'Do you have a human friend at the hospital?'

'Oh, no,' I say. 'I came to visit. I come here sometimes. It's a good place to find imaginary friends.'

'That's true,' Klute says, shaking his head and making it bobble around. 'Me and Eric have been here for a week and I have never seen so many imaginary friends.'

'Eric is your human friend?' I ask.

Klute bobbles a yes.

'How long have you been alive?' I ask.

'Since summer camp,' Klute says.

I count back to the beginning of summer. 'Five months?' I ask.

'I don't know. I don't count months.'

'How about you?' I ask Spoon.

'This is my three year,' Spoon says. 'Preschool, kindergarten and now first grade. That's three years. Right?'

'Yes,' I say. I'm shocked that Spoon is so old. Imaginary friends who don't look like human people don't usually last very long. 'Three years is a long time,' I say.

'I know,' Spoon says. 'I've never met anyone older.'

'I'm almost six,' I say.

'Six what?' Klute asks.

'Six years,' I say. 'Max is in third grade now. Max is my human friend.'

'Six years?' Spoon asks.

'Yes.'

No one says anything for a moment. They just stare at me.

'You left Max?' This is Summer speaking. Her voice is tiny, but it surprises me.

'What do you mean?' I ask.

'You left Max at home?'

'Actually, no. Max isn't home. He's away.'

'Oh.' Summer is silent for a moment, and then she asks, 'Why didn't you go with Max?'

'I couldn't. I don't know where he is.'

I am about to explain what happened to Max when Summer speaks again. Her voice is still tiny but somehow it is loud, too.

'I could never leave Grace,' she says.

'Grace?' I ask.

'Grace. My human friend. I could never leave her. Not even for a second.'

I open my mouth again to explain what happened to Max but Summer speaks first.

'Grace is dying.'

I look at Summer. I open my mouth to say something but nothing comes out. I do not know what to say.

'Grace is dying,' Summer says again. 'She has leukemia. That's bad. It's like the worst flu a human person could ever get. And now she is dying. The doctor man told Mommy that Grace is going to die.'

I still don't know what to say. I try to think of something to make her feel better or make me feel better, but Summer speaks again before I can.

'So don't leave Max for too long, because he might die someday, too. And you wouldn't want to miss out on playing with him when he is still alive.'

I suddenly realize that Summer's voice hasn't always been this tiny or this sad. It is tiny and sad because Grace is dying, but there was a time when Summer was smiling and happy. I can see that happy version of Summer now, like a shadow around this sad version of her.

'I mean it,' she says. 'Human friends don't live for ever. They die.'

'I know,' I say.

I don't tell her that Max dying is all I can think about.

Instead, I tell Summer and Spoon and Klute about Max. I start by describing Max. How much he loves Lego and Mrs Gosk. The way he gets stuck. His bonus poops. His parents. His fight with Tommy Swinden. Then I tell them about Mrs Patterson and what she did to him. How she tricked Max. How she tricked everyone except for me.

Except she tricked me, too, or I would be with Max right now.

I can tell by the way that they listen that Spoon understands what I say the best, but that Summer understands how I feel the best. She is scared for Max, almost as much as I am, I think. Klute listens, but he reminds me of Puppy. I don't think he understands at all. He is just trying to keep up.

'You have to find him,' Spoon says when I'm done explaining. He says it with the same voice that Max uses when he talks to his toy soldiers. He doesn't just say it. He orders it.

'I know,' I say. 'But I don't know what to do when I find him.'

'You have to help him,' Summer says. Her voice is not tiny anymore. It's still soft, but it is not tiny.

'I know,' I say again. 'But I don't know how. I can't tell the police or Max's parents where Max is.'

'I didn't say to help the police people,' Summer says. 'I said to help Max.'

'I don't understand,' I say.

'First you have to find him,' Spoon says.

I watch Klute's head bobble around as he turns from me to Summer and to Spoon and back to me.

He's barely keeping up, I think.

'You have to help him,' Summer says, and now she sounds annoyed. Angry, even. 'You have to help him get back to his mommy and daddy.'

'I know, but if I can't tell the police or his parents, it's—'

'*You* have to do it,' Summer says.

It's like she's screaming even though she is talking in her same tiny voice. It sounds the same but it isn't tiny anymore at all. It's huge. Summer seems huge. She is still the size of a soda bottle but she seems bigger now.

'Not the police,' she says. 'You. You have to save Max. Do you know how lucky you are?'

'What do you mean?' I ask.

'Grace is dying. She is going to die and I can't help her. I can sit by her and try to make her smile, but I can't save

Grace. She is going to die and be gone for ever and I can't help her. I can't save her. But you can save Max.'

'I don't know what to do,' I say.

I'm staring down at this tiny little girl with the tiny little voice but I'm the one who feels tiny now. It's as if Summer has all the answers. I am the oldest imaginary friend maybe in the world but this little girl knows everything and I do not know anything.

That's when I realize that she may know the answer to the question.

'What will happen to you when Grace dies?' I ask.

'Are you worried that Max might die?' she asks. 'That the teacher will die him?'

'Maybe,' I say. I feel bad for thinking it, but I know it's true. Not thinking about things doesn't make them not true.

'Are you worried for Max or for you?' Summer asks.

I think about lying but I can't. This tiny little girl with the tiny little voice knows everything. I know it.

'Both,' I say.

'You can't worry about yourself,' she says. 'Max might die, and you have to save him. You might save yourself by saving Max, but that's not important.'

'What will happen when Grace dies?' I ask again. 'Will you die?'

'It doesn't matter,' Summer says.

'Why?' I ask.

'Yeah. Why?' Spoon asks.

Klute bobbles in agreement. We all want to know.

Summer says nothing, so I ask again. I'm afraid to ask. I'm a little afraid of Summer now. I can't explain why, but it's true. I'm afraid of this tiny girl with this tiny voice. But still, I have to ask.

'Will you die when Grace dies?'

'I think so,' she says, looking at her tiny feet. Then she looks up at me. 'I hope so.'

We stare at each other for a long time, and finally she speaks.

'Are you going to save Max?' she asks.

I nod.

Summer smiles. It is the first time I have seen her smile. It lasts for just a second, and then it is gone.

'I'll save Max,' I say. And then, because I think it is important to say, especially to Summer, I add, 'I promise.'

Spoon nods.

Klute bobbles.

Summer smiles again.

CHAPTER 29

I ride the elevator down with a man who is pushing a machine on wheels. He stops the elevator on the fourth floor and I decide to get out. Just because the elevator was heading down doesn't mean that it won't change its mind and go back up. I have seen elevators do this before. I have seen this elevator do it before.

I step off the elevator and turn right. The stairs are around the corner. As I turn, I notice the sign on the wall. It has a list of words with little arrows pointing left and right. I am not the best reader, but I can read some of the words:

→ WAITING ROOM
→ ROOMS 401–420
← ROOMS 421–440
← RESTROOMS

And below *Restrooms*, the letters ICU with an arrow pointing right.

I see the letters as a word and say it aloud.

'Ickuh? Ick-you?'

Then I notice that all the letters are capitalized. This means that it is not a word. Each letter stands for a word. They are initials. I learned this in first grade.

I say the initials aloud. 'ICU.' I stare at the letters for a second more, and then I read them again. 'I See You.'

It takes me a second to remember where I've heard these initials before. Then I remember. Dee went to the I See You when she was shot. Except it wasn't the I See You.

It was the ICU.

Dee could be here. In this building. On this floor. To the right.

I go right.

There are doors on the left and right of the hallway. I look at the little name tags next to each one as I pass. I am looking for the letters ICU or three words that start with these letters.

I find the words at the end of the hall. There are two doors blocking the hallway. A name tag on the doors reads *Intensive Care Unit*.

ICU.

I do not know what *Intensive* means, but I bet it means a room for people who were shot by guns.

I pass through the doors. The room is big. There is a long counter in the middle of the room with three doctors sitting behind it. All ladies. The lights are on over the desk but nowhere else. The rest of the room is not dark but dim. There are lots and lots of machines in this room. They are all on wheels. They remind me of little fire trucks, sitting still and quiet but always ready to move.

Around the edges of the room are shower curtains hanging from the ceiling. They wrap halfway around the room. Some are closed. The ones that are open have empty beds behind them.

There are two closed curtains. Dee could be behind one of them.

I walk to the first curtain and try to pass through but cannot. I am stopped by the curtain, even though it doesn't move when I bump up against it.

Max doesn't think of shower curtains as doors. At least he didn't when he imagined me. Even though Max is disappeared, I feel like he is here right now, stopping me at the shower curtain. I feel like we are still together even though we are apart.

It feels like a reminder that he is still alive.

I crouch down and crawl under the space between the shower curtain and the floor. There is a girl in the bed behind the curtain, but she is not Dee. She is a little girl. She looks like she could be in Puppy's first-grade class. She is asleep. There are wires and tubes running from little machines over to her arms and under her blankets. Her head is wrapped in a white towel. Her eyes are black and blue. There is a Band-Aid on her chin and above her eyebrow.

She is alone. No mother or father sitting in the chairs next to her bed. No doctor person checking on her.

I think about Max. I wonder if he is alone tonight, too.

'When will she wake up?'

A little girl who looks almost exactly like the little girl in the bed is sitting in a chair to my right. I did not see her when I crawled under the curtain. She stands up when I look at her.

I am surprised that she did not mistake me for a human person like most imaginary friends do. Maybe she knows that I am imaginary because I crawled under the shower curtain and all the human people step through the curtain.

'I don't know when she will wake up,' I say.

'Why won't the other people talk to me?'

'Who?' I ask, looking around. For a second, I think that someone else is behind the curtain. Someone else I didn't notice.

'The other people,' she says again. 'I ask them when she will wake up but no one will talk to me.'

I understand now. 'Do you know her name?' I ask, pointing at the little girl in the bed.

'No,' the girl says.

'When did you meet her?' I ask, pointing again.

'In the car,' she says. 'After the accident. After the car hit the other car.'

'Where were you before you were in the car?' I ask.

'Nowhere,' she says. She looks confused and embarrassed. She stares at her shoes.

'When did the girl go to sleep?' I ask.

'I don't know,' she says, still looking confused. 'The people took her away. I waited by the doors and when she came back she was asleep.'

'Did you talk to her at all?' I ask.

'Yes. In the car. Mommy and Daddy wouldn't answer her, so she asked me to help. I stayed with her. I talked to her. We waited until the men with the machine got her out. It was loud and it made fire.'

'I'm glad you got out of the car,' I say.

I don't want her to be afraid, and I think my questions are making her afraid. But I still have a few more to ask.

'Have you seen Mommy and Daddy since you got out of the car?' I ask.

'No,' she says.

'What is your name?' I ask.

'I don't know,' she says, and now she sounds sad. She might cry, I think.

'Listen. You are a special friend. An imaginary friend.

That means that she is the only one who can see or hear you. She needed you in the car when she was scared so that is why you are here. But everything is going to be fine. You just need to wait until she wakes up.'

'Why can you see me?' she asks.

'Because I am like you,' I say. 'I am an imaginary friend, too.'

'Oh. Then where is your little girl?' she asks.

'My friend is a little boy. His name is Max, but I don't know where he is.'

She stares at me. She says nothing so I wait. I don't know what to say either. We just stare at one another over the beeps and hums from the machines beside the bed. The silence seems like for ever. Finally I speak.

'I lost him. But I'm looking for him.'

She keeps staring at me. This little girl has existed for only a day but I know what she is thinking.

She thinks that I am a bad friend for losing Max.

'I have to go now,' I say.

'Okay. When will she wake up?'

'Soon,' I say. 'Just wait. She will be awake soon.'

I crawl back under the shower curtain before the little girl can say anything else. There is another closed curtain a few steps away but I know that Dee is not behind it. This is the Children's Hospital. There is probably an ICU in the grown-up hospital, too, and Dee is probably there.

I wonder if Max is all alone like the little girl behind the shower curtain. She has no mommy or daddy sitting in the chairs next to her bed. Maybe they are hurt, too.

Maybe they are dead. But I do not think so because that would be too terrible a thing to think.

At least she has her imaginary friend. She may not have a name, yet, but she is waiting by the bed, so the little girl is not alone.

I keep thinking about what Max's mom said. 'I keep hoping that he has Budo with him.'

But I am not with Max.

That little girl has her brand-new imaginary friend with her tonight, but Max is alone somewhere. He is alive because I am still here and Max being dead would be too terrible a thing to think.

But he is alone.

CHAPTER 30

Max's mom will not stop crying. It is not a sad cry. It is a scared cry. It reminds me of the crying that babies do when they can't find their mothers.

Except this time a mother can't find her baby.

Max's dad holds her. He does not say anything because there is nothing to say. He is not crying but I know that he is crying inside again.

I used to think that these were the three worst things in the world:

1. Tommy Swinden
2. Bonus poops
3. Not existing

Now I think these are the three worst things in the world:

1. Waiting
2. Not knowing
3. Not existing

It is Sunday night, which means that tomorrow I can go to school and find Mrs Patterson and Max.

As long as Mrs Patterson goes back to school.

I think she will. Otherwise she would look suspicious. If Mrs Patterson was a bad guy on a television show, she would definitely go to school on Monday. She might even offer to help the police chief search for Max.

I bet she will. She is sneaky-smart.

I spent the weekend looking for Max, but now I feel like all I did was waste my time. I don't know where Mrs Patterson lives, but I couldn't just sit at home for two days doing nothing, and I couldn't spend any more time around the police officers because too many of them keep wondering aloud (but never around Max's parents) if Max is dead.

So I started searching for Max inside people's houses, hoping that one of the houses would be Mrs Patterson's house. I know that Mrs Grady and Mrs Paparazo live close enough to the school that they sometimes walk to work together, so I thought that maybe most of the teachers lived close by (even though I know Mrs Gosk lives in a faraway place on the other side of the river, which is why she is sometimes late). So I started my search with the houses closest to the school. I made circles through the neighborhood like the ripples that a stone makes when Max tosses one into the lake.

Max doesn't swim, but he loves to throw rocks into the water.

I knew it would be almost impossible for me to find Mrs Patterson's house like this, but I had to do something. But it didn't do any good. I didn't find Max or Mrs Patterson. All I found were parents who did not lose a child. Families sitting around dinner tables and raking leaves in the backyard and arguing about money and cleaning their basements and watching movies on television. All of them seemed so happy. It was like they didn't know that Mrs Patterson could just drive to school one day and steal their little boy or little girl.

Monsters are bad things, but monsters that do not walk and talk like monsters are the worst.

I thought about going back to the hospital to see Spoon and Summer again, but I am afraid that Summer will be mad because I have not found Max yet.

I don't know why I should be afraid of a little girl the size of a soda bottle, but I am. Not afraid like she will hurt me, but afraid in the same way that Max is afraid to disappoint Mrs Gosk, even though he does it all the time and doesn't even know it.

I am also afraid to find out that Summer's human friend has died and she has died, too.

Disappeared, I mean. Stopped existing.

Last night I stopped at the gas station to see if Dee was back.

She wasn't. Sally wasn't there either, but I don't think I will ever see Sally again. Getting shot might kill a person but I don't think it would stop someone from going back to work someday. But getting stuck like Sally might stop a person from ever coming back to work, even to say hello to old friends.

I don't think it will ever be the same at the gas station. There were three people working last night but I didn't know any of them. Pauley came in to buy scratch tickets, and I could tell that he feels the same way. He didn't even stay to scratch his tickets. He stood at the counter for a second, thinking about it, and then he just left with his head down.

It's not our place anymore.

But it's not a new place, either.

It's not a special place for anyone anymore. The people who work there now just work. There was a girl working last night who looked like she needed to make two or three bonus poops. Her face was all scrunched up and serious. And the other people, both old men, barely spoke to one another. And everyone works. No more goofing around. No more television behind the counter. No more talking to customers and knowing their names. No more Dee telling Sally to get back to work.

I don't know if I will ever go back to the gas station. I would like to see Dee again. Maybe in the ICU someday, if I ever find the courage to go to the adult hospital. But I don't think even Dee could make the gas station like it used to be.

I have to leave early tomorrow morning. I am worried that the bus will not stop at our bus stop, because Max will not be standing by the tree, touching it with one hand at all times so he doesn't accidentally wander into the street. That was my idea, but when he told his mother the idea so that he could wait by himself, he said that it was his idea.

I didn't care. I was his idea, so in a way my idea was his idea, too.

I could walk to the school if I had to, like I did this weekend when I was searching for Max, but I have always ridden on the bus to go to school, and I feel like it would be good luck for me to ride it tomorrow. Like I'm telling the world that I am on the bus because I know that Max will be back soon.

I have a list of things to do tomorrow. I've been thinking about them all night. Memorizing them. Sometimes I really, really wish I could hold a pencil and write things down. I have to be much more careful this time. On Friday I was not careful and Mrs Patterson drove away without me. So I have to be sure to do exactly the right thing tomorrow.

My things-to-do list is short:

1. Leave the house when Max's mom wakes up.
2. Walk to the Savoys' house and wait with them for the bus.
3. Ride the bus to school.
4. Go straight to the parking lot where Mrs Patterson parks her car.
5. Wait for Mrs Patterson.
6. When Mrs Patterson parks her car, get inside Mrs Patterson's car.
7. Don't leave the car no matter what.

I just hope that Mrs Patterson comes to school tomorrow. I tried to make a list of things to do if Mrs Patterson does not come to school but I could not think of anything to put on the list.

If she does not come back to school, I think Max will be lost for ever.

CHAPTER 31

The blue backpack is not on the back seat anymore. I am sitting in the spot where it was the last time I saw it.

Thursday. The last time I saw it was Thursday.

Four days ago. It feels like forty days ago.

Mrs Patterson pulled into the parking lot before the first bell. She parked her car in her usual spot and walked inside like it was a normal school day. A kidnapper is now walking around the halls of the school and no one knows it except for me. I keep wondering if she is planning on stealing another kid soon. Is she tricking other boys and girls like she tricked Max?

Did she want Max because he is Max or because she is collecting kids?

Both ideas scare me.

My list of things to do says to stay in the car no matter what, but the school day is long and it is still early. The first recess bell hasn't even rung yet. I don't think Mrs Patterson will leave early because that would look suspicious. And I made the list so I can change it if I want. It is not like the rules about not running in the hallways or staying silent during a fire drill or not eating peanut butter at the peanut-free table. It's my rule so I can break it if I want. So I will.

I just want to see what is going on inside the school.

I want to see Mrs Gosk.

There is a man sitting at a desk in the lobby. There has never been a desk in the lobby before, and there has never been a man sitting at a desk in the lobby before. He is not wearing a uniform but I can tell that he is a policeman. He looks serious and bored at the same time, just like those police officers who work overnight at the police station.

A lady just walked through the front doors and the police officer is waving her over to his desk. He is asking her to sign her name on a clipboard. While she is signing, he asks her to explain why she is here today.

She is carrying a tray of cupcakes.

He must not be a very good policeman. Even a kindergartener would know why this lady is here.

I walk down the hall to Mrs Gosk's classroom. She is teaching when I walk in. Just hearing her voice in the hallway makes me feel a little better.

She is standing in front of the class and talking about a boat called the *Mayflower*. She has a map rolled down in front of the chalkboard, and she is whacking it with her meter stick and asking where North America is. I know the answer to this question because Max loves maps. He loves to plan imaginary battles with imaginary armies on real maps, so I know the names of all the continents and oceans and lots of the countries.

Max's desk is empty. It is the only empty desk in the classroom. No one else is absent today. It would be better if someone else was absent today. It would make Max's desk seem less empty.

Someone should have stayed home sick.

I sit at Max's desk. The chair is pulled out enough so that I can sit without feeling squished by the idea of the desk and the idea of the chair. Mrs Gosk has stopped whacking the map. Jimmy answered the question about North America and a bunch of kids seem relieved that he knew the answer. They were afraid that Mrs Gosk would ask them where North America was, and they could tell that this is the kind of question that even a dummy should be able to answer. Now she is showing the kids a picture of the *Mayflower*, except it looks like someone has chopped the boat in half. We can see the inside of the boat. Little rooms filled with little tables and little chairs and little people.

The *Mayflower* was a big boat.

Mrs Gosk looks up from the picture to the class and says, 'Imagine that you are leaving your home for ever. Just like the Pilgrims. You're sailing to America and all you can bring is one small suitcase. What would you pack inside?'

Hands fly up. This is the kind of question that everyone can answer. No one needs Jimmy for this one. Even someone who hasn't been listening can raise their hand and answer this question without sounding like a dummy. Mrs Gosk asks these kinds of questions a lot. I think she wants all the kids to have something to talk about, and she loves to make the kids feel like they are a part of the story.

Kids start answering. Mrs Gosk laughs when Malik says, 'Lots and lots of underwear,' and Leslyan says, 'My cell-phone charger. I always forget it when we go on vacation.'

I'm surprised that Mrs Gosk is laughing. And I'm mad. Mrs Gosk is acting just like Mrs Gosk. She is not acting like the Mrs Gosk who is missing a student and who the police tried to blame two days ago. In fact, I think she is even more like Mrs Gosk than she ever was. She is like Mrs Gosk times two. She's practically bouncing around the room. It's like her shoes are on fire.

Then I understand.

Mrs Gosk is *acting* like Mrs Gosk. She is smiling and asking good questions and swinging her meter-beater around because she is not the only one who is sad or worried about Max. The kids are worried, too. A lot of them don't know Max very well and a lot of them are mean to him, some on purpose and some on accident, but they all know that Max disappeared and they must be worried and scared. Maybe even sad, too. Mrs Gosk knows this, so even though she is probably the most worried and most afraid person in the whole school, she is pretending to be Mrs Gosk times two for the kids. She is worried about Max but she is also worried about the twenty other kids in the classroom, so she is putting on a show for them. She is trying to make it the best, most normalest day that they ever had.

I love Mrs Gosk.

I might love her more than Max does.

I'm glad I came inside. Just seeing Mrs Gosk makes me feel better.

I go back to Mrs Patterson's car. I want to stop in the office and see what Mrs Palmer is doing today. I want to see if the police chief is still sitting on her couch. I want to see if Max's parents are coming to school today to answer more questions. I want to go to the faculty room and see what the teachers are saying about Max. I want to see if Mrs Hume and Mrs McGinn and Mrs Riner are as worried as I am. I want to find Mrs Patterson and see if she is acting normal today or if she is lying to kids like she lied to Max. Most of all I want to spend more time in Mrs Gosk's classroom.

But if Mrs Gosk can pretend to be herself today, I can wait inside a car until Mrs Patterson comes back.

Waiting is one of the three worst things in the world, but the waiting will be over soon.

If I just sit and wait in Mrs Patterson's car, I will find Max.

CHAPTER 32

Mrs Patterson opens the door and climbs into the driver's seat. The last bell rang about five minutes ago and there are still buses in the circle, waiting to fill up with children. But Mrs Patterson is not a teacher who is responsible for kids. She does not have to worry about how they get home or if they are getting picked up by a babysitter or an uncle or a grandmother. She doesn't even have to worry if they have friends to play with or eat enough lunch or have a warm coat for the winter.

Only teachers like Mrs Gosk can be trusted with this stuff, so teachers like Mrs Patterson can leave when the last bell rings. This must seem good to teachers like Mrs Patterson but they don't know how much the kids love Mrs Gosk.

Kids can't love you if you teach them for only an hour a week.

Or if you steal them.

Mrs Patterson starts the car and turns left out of the circle so she does not get stuck behind the buses. You are not allowed to pass a bus if it has its little stop sign switched on.

I remember the day when Max ran out between the buses and almost got hit by someone who was driving through the circle and breaking the little stop sign rule.

Graham was there that day. Graham and Max. It seems so long ago.

Mrs Patterson just drives. She does not turn on the radio. She does not make a phone call. She does not sing or hum or even talk to herself. She keeps both of her hands on the steering wheel and just drives.

I watch her. I think about climbing into the front seat next to her but I don't. I have never sat in the front seat before and I do not want to sit next to her. I want to follow her. I want her to lead me to Max so I can save him. But I do not want to sit next to her.

I was going to save Max even if I never met Summer. I love Max and I am the only one who can save him. But I still think about Summer a lot when I think about saving Max. I think about the promise that I made to her. I don't know why, but I do.

I watch for clues while Mrs Patterson drives. I wait to hear her speak. I have been alone in the car with Max's mom and dad before, and I have been alone in rooms with lots and lots of people who think they are alone, and they are usually doing something. Eventually everyone does something. They turn on the radio or hum or groan or fix their hair in the little mirror that is pasted onto the windshield or drum their fingers on the steering wheel. Sometimes they talk to themselves. They make lists or complain about someone to no one or talk to the other people who are driving in cars around them like the other people can hear them through the glass and metal.

Sometimes people are gross. They pick their noses in the car. This is gross even though the car seems like one of the best places to pick a nose, because no one is around and you can get rid of your boogers before you get home. Max's mom yells at Max for picking his nose, but Max says that some boogers won't come out with a tissue, and I think he must be right because I have seen Max's mom picking her nose, too. But never when someone else is watching.

That's what I tell Max.

'Picking your nose is like pooping,' I say to him. 'You have to do it in private.'

Max still picks his nose around people sometimes, but not as much as he used to.

Mrs Patterson does not pick her nose. She does not scratch her head. She does not even yawn or sigh or sniffle. She keeps her eyes forward and takes her hands off the steering wheel only to switch on the flashing arrow when she turns. She is serious about driving.

Serious about everything, I think. *A serious customer*, Mrs Gosk would say, and that makes me even more scared. Serious people do serious things and don't make mistakes. Mrs Gosk says that Katie Marzik is a serious customer because Katie always gets 100 percent on her spelling tests and solves all the math problems without any help. Even the ones that the rest of the class can't solve with help.

If Katie Marzik wanted to be a kidnapper when she grew up, she would be a good one.

I bet Katie Marzik will drive just like Mrs Patterson someday, with her eyes on the road and her hands on the steering wheel and her mouth closed.

If Mrs Patterson is driving to her house, and I think she is, I am worried about what she has done to Max. How did she keep him stuffed away for the whole day while she was at school?

She could have tied Max up with rope, and that would be bad. Max does not like to be held still. He will not sleep in a sleeping bag because it is too tight. It squishes him, he says. And he says that turtleneck shirts choke his neck, even though they don't but somehow do at the same time. He doesn't go into closets even if the door is wide open and never pulls blankets over his head. He wears only seven pieces of clothing at one time, not counting shoes. Never more than seven, because more than seven is too much. 'It's too much!' he yells. 'Too much! Too much!'

This means that when it is very cold outside, Max's mother can get Max to wear only underwear, pants, a shirt, a coat, two socks and a hat. Never any gloves or mittens. And even if she took away the socks or the hat and underwear, which I sometimes think she would if she could, he still would not wear the gloves or mittens because he does not like his hands all bundled up and squished inside a glove. So Max's mom sews fur linings into all of his coat pockets and Max just puts his hands in his pockets to stay warm.

If Mrs Patterson tied Max up or locked him in a closet or inside a box for the day, that would be very, very bad.

I'm mad at myself for not thinking about this before, but I am glad that I did not think about it before, too, because it would have worried me even more.

Maybe Mrs Patterson has someone helping her. Maybe Mrs Patterson is married and her husband is stealing Max, too. Maybe it was his idea. Maybe Mrs Patterson told Mr Patterson that they would be better parents for Max than Max's parents, so Mr Patterson has been pretending to be a dad by watching Max all day, which would be better than tying Max up or locking him in a cupboard, but still bad because Max does not like strangers or strange places or new foods or different bedtimes or anything that is different.

Mrs Patterson turns on her blinking arrow but there is

no street ahead to turn on to. Just houses. One of these houses must be her house. Max is inside one of these houses. I can barely sit still now. I am finally almost there.

She drives past three driveways and then finally turns right. There is a long driveway in front of us. At the top of the hill is a blue house. It is small but it looks perfect. Like a picture from a book or a magazine. There are four big trees on her front lawn but not one single leaf on the grass even though there is not one single leaf in the trees either. No leaves sticking out of the gutters or bunched around the edges of the house, either. There are two baskets of flowers sitting on the stoop by the front door. The same kind that the parents sell every year at school. Tiny yellow flowers in baskets. Maybe Mrs Patterson bought them from the parents last week when they were on sale. Every tiny flower in the baskets looks perfect. Her driveway is perfect, too. No cracks or patches at all. There is a pond behind her house. A big pond, I think. I can see little bits of it around the corners of the house.

As she drives up the hill, she picks up a remote control and presses a button. The garage door opens. She drives into the garage and turns off the car. A second later I hear the garage door rattling and humming. It is closing.

I am inside Mrs Patterson's house.

I hear Summer's voice in my head again, making me promise to save Max.

'I know,' I say.

Mrs Patterson can't hear me. Only Max can hear me, and soon he will hear me for real. He is somewhere in this house. He is close by, and I am going to find him. I can't believe I have made it this far.

Mrs Patterson opens the door and climbs out of the car.

I step out of the car.

It is time to find my friend.

'Time to save Max,' I say.

I try to sound brave but I am not.

CHAPTER 33

I do not wait for Mrs Patterson. She stops in a little room just inside the garage to take off her coat and scarf. There are hooks for hanging things and a neat row of boots and shoes along the floor and a washer machine and dryer machine but no Max, so I walk past her into a living room.

There are chairs and a couch and a fireplace and a television hanging on the wall and a little table with books and photographs in silver frames, but there is no Max.

There is a hallway and staircase to my right so I turn and climb the stairs. I climb them two at a time. I do not need to hurry now because I am finally inside Mrs Patterson's house, but I do anyway. I feel like every second counts.

There is a hallway at the top of the stairs and four doors. Three of the doors are open and one is closed.

The first door on the left is open. It is a bedroom, but it is not Mrs Patterson's bedroom. There is no stuff in it. Just a bed and a dresser and a nightstand and a mirror. Furniture but no stuff. Nothing on the dresser. Nothing on the floor. No robe or jacket hanging from the hooks on the door. Too many pillows on the bed. A mountain of pillows. It is just like the bedroom that Max's mom and dad have at the end of the upstairs hall. The guest bedroom, they call it, but Max's mom and dad have never had a guest. Probably because Max would not like a sleep-over guest. It's like a pretend bedroom. A bedroom that you only look at but never use. Like a bedroom in a museum.

There is a closet next to the bed so I check it. I pass through the door into a dark space. I can't see anything because it's so dark so I whisper. 'Max? Are you here?'

He is not. I know it before I even whisper his name.

I don't know why I whisper his name since Max is the only person who can hear me. Max's mom would say that I have watched too much television, and she is probably right.

The second door on the left is also open. It is a bathroom. This bathroom looks like a pretend room, too. A museum bathroom. There is no stuff in here, either. Nothing on the sink or floor. The towels are all hanging perfectly on the rods and the toilet seat is closed. It is a guest bathroom, I think, even though I have never heard of a guest bathroom before.

I walk down the hall to the door that is closed. If Max is upstairs, he would be in a room with a closed door, I think. I pass through the door. Max is not in the room. It is a baby's room. There is a crib and a toy box and a rocking chair and a bureau with a basket of diapers on top. There are blocks on the floor and a little blue train engine and a little plastic farm with little people and little animals.

Max would not like the little plastic farm because the people do not look real. They are little pegs with faces, and he does not like those kinds of toys. He likes realistic toys. But the little farm animals and the little people are standing outside the little plastic barn, so the baby must like it.

Then I realize it. Mrs Patterson has a baby. I can't believe it.

There is a closet in this room, too. A long closet with sliding doors, but one of the sliding doors is open. There are shelves stuffed with tiny shoes and tiny shirts and tiny pants and tiny balls of socks.

But no Max.

Mrs Patterson has a little baby. This does not seem right. Monsters are not supposed to have little babies.

I leave the baby's room and walk into the room on the

other side of the hallway. This is Mrs Patterson's bedroom. I know it right away. There is a bed and a dresser and another television hanging on the wall. The bed is made but it is not piled with pillows and there is a bottle of water and a book on the headboard. There is a little table beside the bed with a clock and a pile of magazines and a pair of glasses. There is stuff in this room. Not like the guest bedroom.

There is a bathroom attached to the bedroom and a big closet without any doors. The closet is almost as big as Max's bedroom. Lots of clothes and shoes and belts but still no Max.

I shout, 'Max! Are you here? Can you hear me?' Just in case I didn't see him.

No one answers.

I leave Mrs Patterson's bedroom. I stop in the hallway and look up to see if there is a trapdoor on the ceiling leading to an attic. Max's mom and dad have a trapdoor with stairs attached, so when you pull a cord, the trapdoor opens and the stairs unfold and you can climb up into the attic. There is no trapdoor. No attic.

I go back down the stairs.

Instead of turning back into the living room, I turn left. There is a hallway to the left that leads to the kitchen and there is another living room across the hallway. Couches and cushy chairs and little tables and lamps and another fireplace and a shelf full of books, but no Max.

I walk through the living room and turn left into a dining room. A long table with chairs. A little table with more photographs and a tray of bottles. I turn left again and walk into the kitchen. Lots of kitchen stuff but no Max.

The first floor is a living room, another living room, a dining room, and a kitchen. That is it. No Max anywhere.

No Mrs Patterson.

I walk through the house again, faster this time. I find a bathroom that I did not see the first time because the door was closed and a coat closet was by the front door.

No Max.

Then I find the door that I am looking for in the hallway to the kitchen.

The basement door.

Mrs Patterson is in the basement with Max. I know it.

I pass through the door and onto stairs. The lights in the stairway and in the room at the bottom of the stairs are turned on. The room at the bottom of the stairs is carpeted and looks like another living room. There is a big, green table in the middle of the room with no chairs around it and a little net stretched across it. It looks like a tiny tennis court. Like a tennis court for dolls. There are couches and chairs and a television down here, too, but not Max.

And no Mrs Patterson.

There is an open door on the other side of the room. I pass through it into a room that looks like a normal basement. The floor is made of stone and there are big, dirty machines in the corner. One is a furnace, which heats the house, and one is a water pipe machine, but I do not know which is which. There is a table with hammers and saws and screwdrivers hanging on the wall above it, all just as neat as Mrs Patterson's closet and lawn. The whole house is neat. The water bottle on the headboard was the only thing that looked out of place in the whole house.

That's it. There are no closets or stairs down here or anything.

No Max. And no Mrs Patterson.

I lost her again. In her own house.

I run upstairs into the kitchen and shout Max's name. I run to the garage to check if Mrs Patterson's car is still in the garage. It is. The engine is making the ticking sound that cars sometimes make after they are turned off. Her coat is still on the hook next to the washer machine.

Maybe she is outside. I am being silly because I can't lose a person inside her own house, but I still feel like I should panic. Something is wrong. I know it. Even if Mrs Patterson is outside, where is Max?

I hold my hand up in front of my face and look at it closely, checking to see if I can see through it.

It's still solid. I am not disappearing. Max must be okay.

He is somewhere and he is okay. Mrs Patterson knows where Max is so I just need to find Mrs Patterson and I will eventually find Max.

I go outside. I pass through the sliding glass doors in the dining room and step out onto a deck at the back of the house. Steps lead from the deck to a small patch of grass and down to another set of steps and the pond. It is a long, narrow pond. I can see houses on the other side of the pond, and I can see the lights from other houses to the left and right of Mrs Patterson's house through the trees. Mrs Patterson's neighbors don't live very close to Mrs Patterson, but I don't think she would ever bring Max outside.

There is a dock in the water at the bottom of the steps and a little boat floating next to it. A paddle boat. Max's mom tried to get Max to ride in one when we went to Boston last summer but he would not. He almost got stuck before his mom finally stopped asking him to give it a try. It was one of those times when I thought Max's mom might cry because all the other little boys and girls were having fun in the boats with their parents but Max would not.

Mrs Patterson is not on the deck. There is a table with an umbrella and a bunch of chairs but no Max and no Mrs Patterson.

I jump off the side of the deck and run around the house. I run and look and run until I have gone all the way around the house and am back on the deck, staring out at the pond again. The sun is low in the sky so all the shadows are long. The sunlight makes sparkles on the water.

I shout Max's name as loud as I have ever shouted anything in my life. I shout again and again and again.

The birds in trees answer my calls, but they are not answering me. Only Max can hear me, and Max is not answering.

I feel like I have lost my friend all over again.

CHAPTER 34

I go back inside the house. I must have missed a room or a closet or a cupboard. I stand in the dining room and shout Max's name again. My voice does not echo because the world cannot hear my voice. Only Max can hear my voice. But if the world could hear my voice, it would repeat it now. It would echo again and again. That is how loud I yell Max's name.

I walk through the downstairs again, slower this time, making a loop from dining room to kitchen to living room and back to dining room. I stop in the living room with the television and look at the photographs in the silver frames. There is a baby boy in all three pictures. He is crawling in one picture and standing up in another, holding onto the side of a bathtub. He is smiling in all three pictures. He has brown hair and big eyes and a chubby face.

I still can't believe that Mrs Patterson has a baby. A baby boy. I say it aloud to make it seem more real. 'Mrs

Patterson has a baby boy.' I say it again because I still don't believe it.

I wonder: *Where is Mrs Patterson's baby? At nursery school?*

Then I have an idea. Maybe Mrs Patterson's baby stays with a neighbor while she is at work. Maybe Mrs Patterson walked over to the neighbor's house to pick her baby up.

That is it. I know it. Mrs Patterson left the house when I was upstairs or in the basement but she did not drive her car. She went to get her baby from a neighbor's house or maybe from a nursery school down the street. Someplace close. Maybe she picks up her baby and walks home every day because fresh air is good for babies and she can ask him questions about his day even though he can't answer because that is what mothers do.

I am feeling relieved now. I do not know where Max is, but as long as I follow Mrs Patterson, I will find him. As long as I do not lose her, everything will be fine. Maybe Max is in another house with Mrs Patterson's husband. Maybe Mr and Mrs Patterson have a vacation house in Vermont like the one that Sadie McCormick likes to talk about whenever someone will listen, and maybe Max is there right now. Far away from where the police would look.

That would be a smart thing for Mrs Patterson to do.

Take Max so far away that the police would never find him.

Far away from the parents she doesn't trust and the school she thinks he shouldn't go to.

But that is okay. If I stay with Mrs Patterson, she will eventually lead me to Max. Even if he is in Vermont, I will find him.

I check my hand. I hold it in front of my face. I feel bad for doing it, but I remind myself that I am checking for Max's sake even though I know I am checking for my own sake, too. More for my own sake. My hand is still solid. I am okay. I am not disappearing. And Max is okay. Somewhere Max is okay.

I decide to search the house again while I wait for Mrs Patterson to get back. I feel like a police person on television, looking for clues, and that is exactly what I am doing. Looking for clues that will lead me to Max.

I notice a closet in the kitchen that I did not notice before, and I look inside even though I know that Max is not inside. It would be a silly place to hide a boy, and besides, Max would have heard me calling if he was in this closet. It is dark inside but I can see the outline of cans and boxes in the gloom. It is a pantry.

I find more pictures of Mrs Patterson's son, on the mantle over both fireplaces and on the little tables in the living room. I don't find pictures of Mr Patterson, which seems strange at first, but then I realize that Mr Patterson is probably the one who is taking all the pictures. Max's dad does the same thing. He doesn't show up in many of Max's photographs because he is always behind the camera instead of in front of it.

There is not a lot of stuff in Mrs Patterson's house. No piles of magazines. No bowls of fruit. No toys on the floor or baskets of dirty clothes near the washer machine. No dishes in the sink or empty coffee cups on the kitchen table. The house reminds me of our house when Max's parents were trying to sell it. Max was in kindergarten and Max's mom and dad decided that they needed a bigger house in case Max ever got a brother or a sister, so they stuck a big sign in the front lawn, kind of like a price tag without any price, so people would know that the house was for sale. And a lady named Meg would bring strangers into the house when nobody was home so they could look around and decide if they wanted to buy it.

Max hated the thought of moving. He hates change, and switching houses would be a big change. He got stuck a few times when he found out that strangers were coming over, so eventually Max's mom and dad stopped telling him that people were coming over.

I think that is why we never moved. They were worried that Max might get stuck for ever if we moved to a new house.

Every time the strangers came over to look at the house, Max's parents would push all of the papers and magazines into a kitchen drawer and throw all the clothes on the floor into a closet. And they would make their bed, which they never do. They had to make it look like no one in the house ever forgot to put anything away so the strangers would see what the house looked like if perfect people lived inside.

That's what Mrs Patterson's house looks like. It looks ready for strangers to come over. But I don't think that Mrs Patterson is trying to sell her house. I think that this is just how she is.

I check the upstairs and the basement again, looking for closets that I did not see the first time or any clues about where Max might be. I find more pictures of Mrs Patterson's baby and a closet in the upstairs hallway. Max is not inside.

In the basement, I find three cupboards, but they are dark and dusty and too small for Max to be inside. I find boxes of nails and a pile of bricks and plastic containers full of clothes and a lawnmower but no Mrs Patterson and no Max.

It's okay. Mrs Patterson will walk through the front door any minute. Even though I know that Max will not be with her, that will be okay. Just finding Mrs Patterson will be enough. She will lead me to Max.

I am standing in the dining room, looking out the sliding glass doors at the pond, when I hear the door finally open.

The shadows from the trees are dipping into the pond now and the orange sparkles on the ripples of the water are almost gone. The sun is too low to sparkle any more today. I turn and walk into the kitchen, toward the hallway that leads to the front door, when I see that it was not the front door that I heard opening.

It was the basement door.

Mrs Patterson is walking through the basement door. She is coming into the kitchen through the basement door.

I was just in the basement a couple minutes ago, looking at the cupboards and finding boxes of nails. Mrs Patterson was not in the basement two minutes ago and now she is stepping through the doorway to the basement and closing the door behind her.

I am more scared than ever.

CHAPTER 35

My first thought is that Mrs Patterson is an imaginary friend and I did not realize it. Maybe she can pass through doors like me and somehow she came home and went into the basement without me hearing her.

I know right away that this is ridiculous.

But she must be something special, because somehow she was in the basement without me seeing her. Maybe she can make herself invisible or maybe she can shrink herself.

I know that this is ridiculous, too.

I watch as she opens the refrigerator and removes some chicken. She places a pan on the stove and begins cooking the chicken. While it sizzles, she starts making rice.

Chicken and rice. Max's favorite meal. Max does not eat many things, but he always eats chicken and white rice. He likes foods that don't have bright colors.

I want to go into the basement again and find the closet or staircase that I must have missed. Maybe Mrs Patterson has a basement under the basement. Maybe there is a door in the floor that I did not see because I don't usually look for doors in the floor.

But I'm afraid to leave Mrs Patterson again. I will wait. She is making dinner for Max. I know it. I will follow her when she is done.

Mrs Patterson does not make a mess when she cooks. When she is finished with the cutting board, she rinses it and puts it in the dishwasher. When she is done pouring the rice into a glass bowl, she puts the box away in the pantry. Max's mom would like Mrs Patterson if she had not stolen Max. They both like things neat. Max's mom says, 'Clean as you go.' But Max's dad still piles dishes in the sink and leaves them there overnight.

Mrs Patterson slides a red tray on the counter. She wipes it with a paper towel even though it looks clean. She puts two paper plates and two plastic forks and two paper cups on the tray.

Max likes to eat from paper plates and paper cups because he knows that they are clean. Max does not trust people or dishwashers to get his plates and forks and cups clean. Max's mom and dad don't always let Max eat from paper and plastic stuff, but sometimes they do, especially if Max's mom is trying to get Max to try something new.

But how does Mrs Patterson know that Max likes paper plates and plastic forks? She has never come over for dinner. Then I realize that Mrs Patterson has been with Max for three days. She has learned that Max does not trust dishwashers.

Mrs Patterson puts rice and chicken on both plates and then pours apple juice into both cups.

Max's favorite drink is apple juice.

She lifts the tray and heads down the stairs to the basement. I follow.

At the bottom of the stairs, Mrs Patterson turns left into the part of the basement with the carpeting and the green table with the net and the television.

There is a door under the carpet somewhere. I know it. Max is probably right underneath me. In a basement's basement.

Then Mrs Patterson walks across the room, past the green table and to a wall with a painting of flowers hanging from it and a shelf stretching across the top. I wait for her to bend over to pull back the carpet but instead she reaches up and pushes a little piece of the shelf into the wall. It clicks and then a part of the wall moves. Mrs Patterson pushes it until there is space enough for her to enter. She does and then a second later the wall slides back and the shelf clicks again. It has popped back into place. The parts of the wall where the secret door and the wall are are invisible. There is wallpaper on the wall and the place where a tiny space between the wall and the door might be is hidden by the design in the wallpaper. It is camouflaged. Even though I know the door is there, I cannot see the outline of the door anymore. It is a super-secret door.

Max is behind that super-secret door.

I walk across the room. I am finally going to see Max. I step into the door but I do not pass through. I bump into the door and fall backwards onto the floor. The door in the wall is impossible to see so I must have missed it. I move to the left and try again, walking slower this time in case I miss it again. I bump into the wall again. I try this three more times but bump into the wall each time.

There is a door here, but it is like the elevator doors at the hospital. When Max imagined me, he did not imagine super-secret-doors-that-look-like-walls were also doors, so I cannot pass through.

Max is on the other side of this door that is not a door. The only way I can get in is if Mrs Patterson opens the door again.

I must wait.

I sit on the green table and stare at the wall. I cannot step away and cannot daydream. When Mrs Patterson opens that door, there will be just enough space for her to exit, which means I have to squeeze into that space as soon as she is clear of it. If I am too slow, I will not be able to get through.

I wait.

I stare at the painting of the flowers, waiting for it to move. I try to only think about the door that is a wall but I start to wonder what it is like behind the wall. There must be a room behind the wall, and it must be big enough for Mrs Patterson and Max to eat dinner together. But it is underground and has no windows and is probably locked so Max must feel trapped, too. And that means that he might be stuck. Or maybe he was stuck but now he is unstuck.

I want to see Max but I am afraid to see what he looks like after three days behind a wall. Even if he is unstuck, he cannot be good.

I wait.

The wall finally moves. I jump off the edge of the table and step over to it. The wall opens and Mrs Patterson steps through the opening. She looks back after passing through, giving me plenty of time to pass through the opening.

I think she is looking back to make sure that Max is not trying to follow her, but I am wrong. I take one look at the room behind the wall and know that I am wrong.

Max is not trying to escape.

I cannot believe my eyes.

CHAPTER 36

The light is blinding. Maybe it is just because I have been standing in the dimly lit basement for a long time, waiting for the wall to move, but the room is brighter than any underground room I could have ever imagined.

As my eyes adjust to the light, I can see that the room is painted in yellow and green and red and blue. It reminds me of Mr Michaud's kindergarten classroom, with his giant caterpillar crawling over the white board and his students' finger-painting spread all over the walls. It reminds me of a box of crayons. The boxes with just eight or ten different colors inside. The room is an explosion of color.

There is a bed in the shape of a race car. It is painted red and gold. It even has a steering wheel sticking out of the headboard. There is a dresser with every drawer painted a different color. There is a door on the far side of the room with the word *Boys* written on it in red, squiggly letters.

There is a desk with a tall pile of drawing paper and an even taller pile of graph paper, which is Max's favorite kind of paper. Good for drawing maps and planning battles. There are model airplanes hanging from the ceiling on wires. There are toy soldiers and tanks and army trucks and airplanes everywhere. Snipers on a shelf over the bed. A line of tanks on top of a beanbag chair. Columns of soldiers marching across the center of the room. An airfield on the bed with anti-aircraft guns on the pillows surrounding it. A battle has taken place recently. I can tell by the way the soldiers and tanks are spaced out.

Green has defeated gray, I think. It doesn't look like gray stood a chance.

The room is bigger than I thought. Much bigger. There are train tracks running all the way around the room, disappearing under the bed and popping out on the other side. I do not see a train. Probably parked underneath the bed.

There are dozens, maybe hundreds, of *Star Wars* figures standing on the dresser, and *Star Wars* spaceships on one side of the room, organized like Max would like them organized. The X-wing fighters need a runway to take off, so there are no other spaceships parked in front of them. The *Millennium Falcon* can fly straight up, so it is surrounded by TIE fighters and twin-pod cloud cars. There are stormtroopers and Cloud City troopers standing next to each spaceship, waiting for Max's orders to launch.

I've never seen so much *Star Wars* stuff in one place except at the toy store. Neither has Max. He probably has the biggest collection of *Star Wars* stuff of anyone in his class, but this collection makes his collection at home look puny.

There are enough stormtroopers here to make a small army.

There are *six X-wing fighters*. Max has two, and even that is a lot.

There is a television hanging on the wall across from the bed and a pile of DVDs underneath it. A stack almost as tall as Max. It is so tall that it looks like it could fall at any second. There are three green helicopters parked on top of it with snipers guarding the perimeter. The DVD that the snipers are standing on is *Starship Troopers*. Max loves that movie.

There is a carpet on the floor. It is dark blue with stars and planets and moons everywhere. It is new and thick and I wish I could sink my toes into it like Max can. But my feet only touch the idea of the carpet, so they do not sink in. They stay on top.

There is a gumball machine by the bed.

The blue backpack from Mrs Patterson's car is sitting on the bed. It is open. I can see Lego peeking out from underneath the flap.

Lego to keep Max *engaged* while he was in the back seat of the car. To distract him until she got him home.

And in the center of the room, there's more Lego. Thousands of Lego in sizes and shapes that even I have never even seen before. There's large Lego and small Lego and mechanical Lego, the kind that needs batteries and the kind that Max loves the most. There is more here than Max could ever dream of. It has been sorted into piles according to size and shape, and I know right away that Max has made those piles. They look like the kind of piles that Max makes. Lined up like the soldiers on the floor, all the same distance from one another.

And sitting in front of those piles like a Lego general, with his back to me, is Max.

I found him.

CHAPTER 37

I can't believe it. I am standing in the same room as Max. I wait one more second before saying his name, just staring at him like his mom does at night when he is asleep after she has sneaked her kisses. I never understood why she just stares at him like that, but now I do.

I never want to stop staring.

I missed Max but I did not know how much I missed Max until now. Now I know what it feels like to miss someone so much that you can't describe it. I would have to invent new words to describe it.

Finally, I say his name. 'Max,' I say. 'I'm here.'

Max screams louder than I have ever heard him scream before.

His scream doesn't last long. Just a couple seconds. But I am sure that Mrs Patterson will come running in any second to see what is wrong but then I realize that I could not hear Mrs Patterson and Max while I was waiting on the other side of the wall. And Max couldn't hear me when I was screaming his name earlier.

I think this room is soundproof.

There are lots of soundproof rooms on television. Mostly in movies but sometimes in TV shows, too.

Max does not turn around to look at me as he screams, and this is a bad sign. It means he might get stuck. It means that he is getting stuck right now. I walk over to Max but I do not touch him. As his scream starts to fade, I say, 'Max, I'm here.' I say exactly the same thing that I said before he started to scream. I speak softly and quickly. I move as I speak so that I am standing in front of him, with his army of Lego piles between us. I can see that he has been building a submarine, and it looks like the propeller might actually move on its own when it is finished.

'Max,' I say again. 'I'm here.'

Max is no longer screaming. He is breathing hard now. Max's mom calls this hyperventilating. It sounds like he has just finished running a thousand-mile race and now he is trying to catch his breath. Sometimes this will end with Max getting stuck.

I say again, 'Max. I'm here. It's okay. I'm here. It's okay.'

Touching Max would be the worst thing that I could do. Yelling at Max would be bad, too. It would be like pushing him into his inside stuck world. Instead, I speak softly and quickly again and again. I reach for him with my voice. It is like throwing him a rope and begging him to grab on. Sometimes it works and I can pull him out before he ends up stuck, and sometimes it doesn't. But it is the only thing I know that helps.

And it works.

I can tell.

His breathing is slowing down, but his breathing would slow down even if he was getting stuck. I can tell by his eyes that he is not stuck. They see me. His eyes see my eyes. He is not disappearing. He is reappearing. Coming back to the world. His eyes smile at me and I know that he is back.

'Budo,' he says. He sounds happy, and this makes me happy.

'Max,' I say back.

I suddenly feel like Max's mom. I want to leap over the piles of Lego and grab Max by the neck and squeeze him tight. But I cannot. Max is probably happy that the Lego piles are separating us. They let his eyes smile at me without him having to worry that I might touch him.

Max knows that I would normally never touch him, but he might think this is different. We have never been separated for three days.

'Are you okay?' I ask, sitting down on the floor in front of Max, keeping the Lego between us.

'Yes,' Max says. 'You scared me. I didn't think I would see you anymore. I am building a submarine.'

'Yes,' I say. 'I saw.'

I don't know what to say next. I try to think about the best thing to say. The thing that will save Max. I feel like I should be sneaky and try to find out how tricked he is, but then I think that I should just find out what is going on no matter what. This is serious business. Not lies about lost homework or throwing chicken nuggets in the cafeteria.

This is even more serious than Tommy Swinden.

I decide not to be sneaky. I decide not to dance with the devil in the pale moonlight. This is something Mrs Gosk says when she thinks that a student is lying. She says, 'You are dancing with the devil in the pale moonlight, Mr Woods. Watch yourself.'

I am dancing with a real devil in the pale moonlight now and I have no time to waste.

'Max,' I say, trying to sound like a Mrs Gosk. 'Mrs Patterson is bad and we have to get you out of here.'

I don't actually know how to do this, but I know I can't do anything if Max doesn't agree.

'She is not bad,' Max says.

'She stole you,' I say. 'She tricked you and stole you from school.'

'Mrs Patterson says I shouldn't go to school. She says that school is not a safe place for me.'

'That's not true,' I say.

'Yes, it is,' Max says, and it sounds like he is getting upset.

'You know it. Tommy Swinden is going to kill me if I stay in school. Ella and Jennifer are always touching me. Touching my food. Kids make fun of me. Mrs Patterson knows about Tommy Swinden and the other kids and she said that school is not a good place for me.'

'Your mom and dad think school is a safe place for you. And they are your mom and dad.'

'Moms and dads don't always know best. That's what Mrs Patterson says.'

'Max, you are locked up in a basement. That is bad. Only bad people lock kids in basements. We have to get you out.'

Max's voice softens. 'If I tell Mrs Patterson that I am happy, then she will be happy.'

I don't understand what Max means. Before I can ask him, he speaks again.

'If Mrs Patterson is happy, she won't touch me or hurt me.'

'Mrs Patterson told you that?'

'No. But I think it,' Max says. 'I think if I tried to get away she might get real angry.'

'I don't think so, Max. I don't think she wants to hurt you. She just wants to steal you.'

But as I say this, I wonder if Max is right. Max doesn't understand people very well, but there are times when he understands people better than anyone else. He might not see how sucking on his fingers in the middle of class makes

262

him look silly, but he was the only one who knew that Mrs Gosk was sad on the day her mom died. Max knew right away, even though Mrs Gosk did a good job hiding it, and the rest of the kids didn't know until the next day when Mrs Gosk told them. So I wonder if he is right about Mrs Patterson, too. Maybe she is more of a devil than I thought.

'Don't you want to leave?' I ask.

'This is a good place,' Max says. 'It has lots of good stuff. And you are here. You promise that you will never leave?'

'Yes, I promise. But what about your mom and dad?'

I want to say more. I want to list all the things that Max will miss if he stays locked up in this room but I can't. I realize that, in all of Max's life, the only things that he might miss are his mom and dad. He has no friends. His grandma died last year, and his other grandma lives in Florida and never sees him. His aunt and uncles are nervous and quiet around him. His cousins avoid him. All he has is his mom and dad and his things and me. And his things might be just as important to him as his mom and dad. That is a sad thing to say, but it is a true thing to say, too. If Max had to choose between his Lego and his army men or his mom or dad, I don't know what he would choose.

I think Max's mom knows this, too. I think his dad probably knows, too, but he lies to himself and says it isn't true.

'I can see Mom and Dad again,' Max says. 'Mrs Patterson told me. Someday. But not now. She is going to take care of me and keep me safe and keep me away from school. She calls me her little lad.'

'What about her son?' I ask. 'Have you met him?'

'Mrs Patterson doesn't have a son anymore. He died. She told me.'

I do not speak. I wait.

Max looks down at his submarine and tries to fit pieces into the unfinished side. After a minute, he starts speaking again. 'He died because his daddy did not take care of him good enough. So he died.'

I think about asking where Mr Patterson is right now, but I do not. Wherever Mr Patterson is, he is not here. He is not a part of this. I know this now.

'Do you like it here?' I ask.

'It's a good room,' Max says. 'It has a lot of good stuff. It was a mess when I got here but Mrs Patterson let me fix it. All the Lego were mixed up and the *Star Wars* stuff was in the toy box and all the army men were still in their boxes. All wrapped in plastic and stuff. And those DVDs were in a box, too. Now everything is right. She even gave me a piggy bank and a bunch of pennies, and I got to put the pennies inside. There were so many that they almost didn't fit.'

Max points at the desk. There is a small, metallic piggy bank on the corner of the desk. It has tiny metal legs and metal ears and a metal snout. It is tarnished and old.

'It was Mrs Patterson's when she was little,' Max says, seeming to read my mind.

I think that Mrs Patterson was smart to let Max fix the room. I bet that fixing the room helped Max get through the first day. Max can't leave his Lego unless they are sorted into the right piles, and in kindergarten he used to sort the Lego center before he went home or it would bother him all night. I bet that Max stayed busy during his first day here, if he wasn't stuck.

'Max, if you are afraid of Mrs Patterson, then this is not a good place.'

'I am not afraid of her as long as she is happy. And now you are here. I feel a lot better now. As long as you are here, everything will be fine. I know it. I told Mrs Patterson that I needed you, and she said that maybe you would come. And you did. Now we can just be together here.'

That is when I realize it. I will never disappear as long as Max stays in this room.

Max's mom and dad are always pushing Max to grow up, meet new people, try new things. Max's dad wants him to join something called Farm League next year and Max's mom wants to see if he can play the piano. They send him to school every day even though Max told them that Tommy Swinden is going to kill him.

I never thought about it before, but Max's mom and dad are my biggest danger.

265

They want Max to grow up.

Mrs Patterson wants to do the opposite. She wants to keep Max in this room made especially for Max. She wants to keep Max here and keep him safe. She is not going to send a ransom note or chop Max up into tiny pieces. She just wants to keep him here like he belongs to her. All locked up and safe. She is a devil in the pale moonlight, but she is not a movie or television devil. She is a real devil, and maybe I should be dancing with her after all.

If Max stays here, I could live for as long as Max lives. I could live longer than any imaginary friend ever.

Maybe if Max stays here in this room, we could both be happily ever after.

CHAPTER 38

Max and I are playing with army men when the door opens and Mrs Patterson comes in. She is wearing a pink night-gown.

I feel embarrassed. I am looking at a teacher in her paja-mas.

Max does not look at her. His head stays down. He is staring at the pile of army men in front of him. They were just hit by something called a cruise missile. It was actually just a crayon that Max dropped from a plastic airplane, but it blew up all the neat little rows of men by the time Max was done with them.

'You've been playing with your army men?' Mrs Patterson asks. She sounds surprised.

'Yes,' Max says. 'Budo is here.'

'Oh, he is? I'm so happy for you, Max.'

She really does look happy. I think she might be relieved to hear that Max has someone to play with, even if she doesn't think I'm real. She probably thinks that Max is getting adjusted to his new room, and that is why I am back.

She doesn't know how hard it was for me to get here.

'It's time for bed,' Mrs Patterson says. 'Did you brush your teeth yet?'

'No,' Max says, still looking down. There is a gray sniper in his hand. He turns it over and over in his hand as he speaks.

'Will you brush your teeth?' she asks.

'Yes,' Max says.

'Would you like me to tuck you in?'

'No,' Max says. He says this fast. He answers her question fast, and he says the word *No* fast, even though it's just the word *No*.

'Okay but you need to be in bed, lights out, in fifteen minutes.'

'Yes,' Max says.

'Okay, then. Good night, Max.'

Her voice gets higher as she says the last three words, as if she is waiting for him to speak. She is waiting for him to say 'Good night' in return and finish the little good-night song. She stands by the doorway for a minute, waiting for Max to answer.

Max stares at his sniper and says nothing.

When she realizes that Max is not going to answer, her face falls. Her eyes and cheeks and head all drop, and for an instant I feel bad for Mrs Patterson. She may have stolen Max, but she will not hurt Max. In this tiny moment of sadness, I know this for sure.

She loves Max.

I know you can't just steal a little boy from his parents because you lost your own little boy and I know that she is probably still a devil and a monster. But in that split second, she looks more like a sad lady than a monster. I think she thought that Max would make her happy, but so far he has not.

She finally leaves, closing the door behind her without saying another word.

'Will she come back to check on you?' I ask.

'No,' Max says.

'So why not play all night?'

'I don't know,' Max says. 'She won't peek through the door, but I think she would still know somehow.'

Max walks to the door marked *Boys*. He opens it. There is a bathroom on the other side of the door. He takes a toothbrush down off the sink, squeezes some toothpaste onto the brush and begins brushing.

'How did she know to get you Crest Kids gel?' I ask. It is the only toothpaste that Max will use.

'She didn't,' he says between brushings. 'I told her.'

I could ask more about the toothpaste but don't. Either Max got stuck on the first night when she tried to get him to use Colgate or Crest Cool Mint (which happened once when Max's dad tried to change the toothpaste) or she asked him which toothpaste he wanted before he needed to brush.

She probably asked Max. Even though Mrs Patterson changed every single thing in Max's entire life, she also understands that any change is trouble for Max. Max's dad understands this, but he keeps trying to change things anyway, even when he knows that Max will get stuck. His mom understands, too, but she tries to change things slowly, so Max won't notice. Max's dad just changes things, like the toothpaste.

'This room is nice,' I say as Max changes into pajamas. They are camouflage pajamas. They are not the pajamas that he usually wears, but I can tell that he likes them a lot. When he is done putting them on, he walks into the bathroom to look at himself in the mirror.

'This place is pretty nice,' I say again.

Max does not answer.

I keep thinking about the way he turned that army man over and over in his hand when Mrs Patterson was talking to him, and the way he would not look at her. Max said that this was a good room and that we could just stay here together. I believe him, but I think there are words behind those words that Max is not saying.

Max is afraid. Max is sad.

Part of me wants to forget about the way he was staring at that army man. It wants me to wait a few days or a month or even a year because Max will eventually like his new room and maybe even Mrs Patterson. It wants me to believe that Max will be fine like he said he will because that means that I get to exist for ever.

But another part of me wants to save Max right now, before it's too late. Before something happens that I can't see yet. That part of me thinks that I am Max's only chance and I have to do something soon.

Now.

And I am standing in between the two parts of me. Stuck like Max. I want to save both of us but I don't know if I can.

I don't know how much of Max I am allowed to lose to save myself.

CHAPTER 39

Max is finally asleep.

He turned out the lights and climbed into bed after brushing his teeth. I sat in a chair next to his bed and waited for him to arrange the pillows. Just like home.

Except there are nine nightlights in the room, six more than Max has in his bedroom at home, so it isn't very dark.

I waited for Max to say something, but he just lay there, staring at the ceiling. I asked him if he wanted to talk, because we usually talk before he goes to sleep, but he just shook his head. After a little while he whispered, 'Good night, Budo.'

That was it.

After a long time, he fell asleep.

I've been sitting here ever since, wondering what to do. I listen to Max breathing. He tosses and turns a little, but he does not wake up. If I close my eyes and just listen to him, it is almost like we are home again.

If we were home, I would be sitting in the living room by now, watching television with Max's parents.

I already miss them.

I feel trapped inside this room.

I am trapped inside this room. I am a prisoner, just like Max. I stare at the door and wonder how I could ever save Max when I can't even escape myself.

Then I know what to do.

I stand up and walk to the door. I take three steps into and then through the door, and a second later I am standing back in the part of the basement with the little tennis table and the stairs. There are no nightlights in this room, so it is pitch black.

I passed through the door on Max's side of the wall because it looks like a door. Max even called it a door. He had said that Mrs Patterson would not peek through the door, which means that it is a door to Max, and if it is a door, I can pass through it. It is his idea of a door.

But the super-secret door on this side of the wall is not a door in Max's mind, so I cannot pass through it. In Max's mind it is a wall. Just to check, I turn and walk back toward the wall. It is so dark that I bump into it even harder than I had expected.

I was right. It's just a wall on this side.

This might not have been a good idea. If Max wakes up, I cannot get back into the room to let him know I am still here. I won't even know if he is awake. I have left Max alone again, and he will know it. I have made another big mistake.

I turn and walk along the edge of the room, feeling the wall to find my way, until I make it to the staircase. I climb the stairs slowly, holding the railing as I do, and then I pass through the door at the top of the stairs into the hallway between the kitchen and the living room. Mrs Patterson is standing in the kitchen. There are Campbell's soup cans and boxes of Kraft macaroni and cheese on the kitchen table. Mrs Patterson is packing the cans and boxes into a large cardboard box.

Those are two of Max's favorite foods.

Four other cardboard boxes are stacked on the table. The lids are closed so I cannot see what is inside them. For a second I think these boxes are important, but then I know that they are not. I am looking for clues to save Max, except there are no clues. Max is locked in a secret room in the basement and no one knows that he is here. This is not a mystery. It is just bad.

Mrs Patterson finishes packing the rest of the soup and macaroni and cheese into the box and closes the lid. She adds it to the pile of boxes on the other side of the table. She moves to the sink to wash her hands. She hums as she washes.

When she is done, she walks past me and heads upstairs.

I follow. There is nothing else for me to do. I cannot leave the house. Even though the secret room could not hold me, I am trapped inside this house. I do not know where I am or where anything else is. There are no gas stations or police stations or hospitals to visit. Max is here. I cannot leave without Max. I promised him that I would never leave, though I'm starting to think that if I am going to save him, I will have to.

There are cardboard boxes on the floor in Mrs Patterson's bedroom that were not here earlier today. Mrs Patterson opens her dresser and begins moving clothing from the dresser into the cardboard boxes. She is not moving all the clothes. She is picking and choosing. Now I think that the cardboard boxes might be a clue after all. Packing food into a box isn't normal, but it is not as strange as packing clothing into a cardboard box.

After she has filled five boxes with clothing and shoes and a bathrobe, she brings the boxes downstairs and adds them to the pile on the table. Then she goes back upstairs and brushes her teeth. She is getting ready for bed, I think, so I leave. She is the bad guy, but I still don't think it is right to watch her floss between her teeth and wash her face.

I go to the spare room and sit down in a chair to think. I need a plan.

I wish Graham was here.

CHAPTER 40

I hear Max's voice. He is calling my name. I stand up and run into the hallway. I am confused. His voice is not coming from the basement. It is coming from Mrs Patterson's bedroom. I turn and run down the hall. I pass through the bedroom door into her room. The sun is peeking through Mrs Patterson's bedroom window. I look right at it and am blinded for a second. I close my eyes and see orange spots float past my eyes. I can still hear Max calling my name. The sound is coming from this room, but it sounds far away, too, like he is under a blanket or locked in a closet. I open my eyes and see Mrs Patterson. She is sitting up in bed, looking at her telephone. Except it isn't a telephone. It is bigger than a telephone and chunkier. It has a screen that Mrs Patterson is staring at. Max's voice is coming from the not-a-phone.

I walk to the other side of the bed and sit down beside Mrs Patterson. I look over her shoulder to see the not-a-phone. Max is on the screen. It is black and white and gray, but I can still see Max. He is sitting up in his bed, too, and he is screaming my name.

He sounds so afraid.

Mrs Patterson and I stand up at the same time, she on one side of the bed and me on the other. She slides on a pair of slippers and leaves the room.

I follow.

She goes straight to the basement. I am right behind her. I can hear Max screaming on the not-a-phone but I can't hear him screaming through the wall. It's strange. He's right behind that wall but I can't hear a peep, even though I know he is screaming.

Mrs Patterson opens the secret door and steps inside. His screams fill the room.

I stand behind Mrs Patterson. I don't want Max to see me and say my name. He is screaming my name, but that's okay. I don't want Max to see me and say, 'Budo! You're back! Where were you? Why were you with Mrs Patterson?'

If he does, then Mrs Patterson will know that I was outside of the secret room, spying on her.

I know this would not happen, because Mrs Patterson does not believe that I am real, but I forget this in the first few seconds that I am back inside the room. It's easy to forget that people don't believe you exist.

When I first step inside, I am afraid. Afraid of being caught by Mrs Patterson. Mrs Patterson is a bad person and I do not want her to be mad at me, even if she does not believe in me.

'Max, it's all right,' Mrs Patterson says, moving toward his bed but stopping a few steps short of it, which is smart. Getting too close to Max when he is upset is the thing that most people want to do but should never do. Mrs Patterson is one smart cookie.

She really is the devil in the pale moonlight.

'Budo!' Max screams again.

It sounds one hundred times worse in real life. It is the worst thing I have ever heard. I feel like the worst friend in the world. As I step out from behind Mrs Patterson, I wonder how I am ever going to leave Max alone today.

'I'm here, Max,' I say.

'I'm sure he'll be back,' Mrs Patterson says, speaking immediately after me and making me think for a second that she can hear me.

'Budo!' Max screams again, but this time it's a happy scream. He sees me.

'Good morning, Max,' I say. 'I'm sorry. I got stuck outside the room.'

'Stuck?' Max asks.

'What's stuck?' Mrs Patterson asks.

'Budo was stuck,' Max says. 'Right?' He is looking at me when he asks this.

'Yes,' I say. 'I can tell you about it when we are alone.'

One of the things that I have learned is that it is too confusing for Max to talk to me and human persons at the same time, so I try to avoid it whenever I can.

'I'm sure that Budo can get himself unstuck,' Mrs Patterson says. 'Nothing to fear.'

'He's already unstuck,' Max says.

'Oh, good,' Mrs Patterson says. She sounds like she just took a deep breath after being stuck underwater for a long time. 'I'm so glad he's back.'

'Okay,' Max says. It sounds like a strange answer, but Max never knows what to say when people tell him how they feel. Most of the time he doesn't say anything. He just waits for the person to say something different. But *okay* is his safe answer.

'Can you get yourself dressed?' Mrs Patterson asks. 'I haven't even started your breakfast yet.'

'Yes,' Max says.

'Okay,' Mrs Patterson says.

She stands by the door again, waiting. I am not sure if she is waiting for Max to say something or trying to think of something else to say. She looks sad either way. Max does not even notice her. He already has an X-wing fighter in his hands. He is pressing the button that makes the wings spread.

Mrs Patterson sighs and then leaves.

When the door clicks shut, Max looks up from his toy. 'Where were you?' he asks.

I know that he is angry because he is looking at me when he asks this question, even though there is a *Star Wars* toy in his hand.

'I left the room last night but I couldn't get back in.'

'Why not?' Max says. His eyes have returned to the spaceship.

'It's a door on this side but it's a wall on the other side,' I say.

Max says nothing. This means he either understands what I said or stopped caring about my answer. Usually I can tell which, but this time I can't.

He puts the X-wing fighter down on his pillow and steps out of bed. He walks over to the bathroom and opens the door. He turns and looks at me again.

'Promise you'll never leave me alone again,' he says.

I promise even though I know I will be leaving him shortly.

CHAPTER 41

I think about not telling Max that I am leaving. I think that it will be easier for him if I just sneak out. Then I realize that sneaking out would be easier for me. Not Max.

But I'm worried that Max might get so angry at me that he'll start unbelieving in me.

I wish I knew what to do.

I thought that Max would be trapped here for ever, and that I would have time to figure things out. Make a plan. But now I'm worried that Max might not be trapped here for ever, and that I am running out of time to help him before the time has even started.

Secretly I was hoping that Max would fall in love with this place and maybe we could stay here for ever. I know that it would be bad not to help Max, but I know that it would be bad to stop existing, too. Lions eat giraffes so they can survive even though the giraffes didn't do anything to the lions, and nobody thinks that the lions are wrong.

Because existing is so important. It's the most important thing. So I know I should help Max and I want to help Max and I want to make the right decision, but I want to exist, too.

That's a lot of stuff to think about, and now I am worried that I will not have any more time to think.

Max finished breakfast and he is playing with the PlayStation. He is driving a car around a racetrack. I watch him play because Max likes it when I watch him play his video games. He doesn't talk to me or ask me any questions. He just needs me to watch.

The door swings open. Mrs Patterson steps inside the room. She is wearing her school clothes and perfume. I can smell her before I can see her.

Not all imaginary friends can smell, but I can.

She smells like old flowers. She is wearing gray pants and a pink shirt and a jacket. She has a *Transformers* lunchbox in her hand.

'Max,' she says. 'I have to go to work.'

She speaks like she is dipping her voice into water to see how cold it is. She is slow and careful.

Max doesn't answer. It is hard for his mom and dad to get him to answer when he is playing a video game, so I am not sure if he is ignoring Mrs Patterson on purpose.

'I have your lunch packed in your lunchbox,' she says. 'Soup in your thermos and yogurt and an orange. I know it mustn't be fun eating the same thing every day, but I can't give you anything that you might choke on when I'm not here.'

She waits for Max to say something but he just keeps steering his electronic car around the TV track.

'But don't worry,' she says. 'Pretty soon we'll be together all day. Okay?'

Max is still silent. Still staring at the screen.

'I'll miss you today, Max,' Mrs Patterson says, and it sounds like she is reaching to him with her voice now, like I sometimes do. She is throwing him a rope but I already know that he will not reach for it. He is playing video games. Nothing else matters.

'I miss you every day, Max,' she says. 'And I want you to know that everything that I am doing is for you. Pretty soon things will be much better. Okay?'

Now I want Max to answer. I want him to ask Mrs Patterson what she is talking about. How are things going to change? When are they going to change? What is she planning?

Instead he stares at the screen as his car moves around a track.

'Goodbye, Max. I'll see you soon.'

She wants to say I love you. I know it. I can see those three words hanging on her lips. And I believe that she loves Max. Loves him a lot. I feel bad for Mrs Patterson again. She has stolen Max, and even though she says that it is for his own good, I know that she wants to have a little boy again. And the little boy she stole talks only a little bit more than her dead little boy.

Mrs Patterson leaves the room and closes the door behind her. As the door clicks shut, Max looks up. He stares at the door for a moment, and then his eyes return to his game.

I wait by the door, watching Max play his game. I count to one hundred. I open my mouth to speak and then I count to one hundred again.

When I am done counting the second hundred, I finally speak.

'I am leaving, too, Max,' I say.

'What?' Max says. He looks up from his game.

This is not easy because I have to tell Max something important and make him understand, but I also have no time. I was afraid that if I left the room before Mrs Patterson was walking out the door, she might hear Max scream in her not-a-phone and come back to the room. Maybe stay home from work. I need her to be walking into the garage right now but I have no way of knowing if she is. I am just guessing. But I counted to one hundred twice, so she has had plenty of time to get to the car. Probably too much time. I might already be too late.

'I am leaving, Max,' I say. 'But only for the day. I am

going to school with Mrs Patterson so I can check on Mrs Gosk and see if your mom and dad are okay. Then I'll be back with her after school.'

'I want to go, too,' Max says.

I didn't expect this. I don't know what to say. I stand with my mouth open until the words come back to me.

'I know,' I say. 'But I can't get you out of the room. You can't pass through the door like I can.'

'I want to go, too!' Max shouts. 'I want to see Mrs Gosk and Mommy and Daddy! I want to see Mommy and Daddy!'

Max never calls his mom and dad *Mommy* and *Daddy*. When I hear him say these words I think that I will never be able to leave this room. I will never be able to leave Max again because doing so would be too sad and too mean.

'I'll find a way to get you out of this room,' I say to Max.

I say it to make him happy, but as the words come out of my mouth I realize that I did not need any time to decide what to do. I am not a lion and Max is not a giraffe. I am Budo and Max is my friend and there was only one right thing to do all along. It doesn't mean that I have to stop existing, but it means that I have to stop thinking only about me existing.

That means I have to leave now.

'Max, I am going. But I'll be back. And I'll make sure you see your mom and dad soon. I promise.'

This is the second promise I have made to Max this morning. I am about to break the first.

Max screams as I turn toward the door. 'No, no, no, no!' he shouts.

Max will get stuck if I leave.

If I pass through the door, I will not be able to get back into the room until Mrs Patterson opens the door again after school.

I step through the door anyway, knowing that the hard thing and the right thing are usually the same thing.

I ask someone who I know is not listening to forgive me for breaking my promise to Max and leaving my friend behind.

Sound returns as I step into the basement. Max's silent room is behind me and the hum of the furnace and the swish and drip of water in the pipes fills this room. I know that Max is screaming. He is probably pounding on the door right behind me but I cannot hear him. I am glad. Imagining him getting stuck behind the wall fills me with sadness and guilt. Hearing the real thing would be worse.

A door slams upstairs. I suddenly remember what I need to do. I run across the room and up the stairs to the first floor. I turn in the hallway and look into the kitchen. The cardboard boxes that were stacked on the table last night are gone. I do not see Mrs Patterson.

Then I hear the sound of an engine starting, followed a second later by the clankity sound of the garage door opening.

I think about running to the garage but decide that it is too late. I turn right and head to the front door. I pass through it and step outside, falling off the stoop that I did not know existed. I tumble to the ground, bouncing off a stone walkway that wraps around the house and leads to the driveway. I pull myself up, running before I am even standing upright. My knuckles drag on the ground for my first few steps. I run around the bend to the front of the house and see the driveway that stretches down to the road. Mrs Patterson's car is already halfway down the driveway. Her car is facing toward the road so she is not driving slowly like people who are backing up do.

I will not make it to the car in time. It is already too far away. Max never imagined that I could run that fast. He never imagined that I would need to run that fast.

But I run anyway. I cannot imagine spending the day in Mrs Patterson's house knowing that Max is trapped behind a wall and I cannot reach him. I run as fast as I can down the hill, meeting the driveway halfway down. I am running so fast that I am on the edge of falling, half running and half tumbling, and, even so, I will not catch Mrs Patterson.

Then I see it. A car coming down the road. A green car that will pass by Mrs Patterson's driveway. Mrs Patterson will need to slow down and maybe even stop to let the car pass.

I have a chance.

And just as I begin to think that I can make it, I cross over the edge from running into tumbling and I am rolling on the pavement, end over end. I hold my arms against my ears to protect my head, and then somehow I roll over and push up, and a second later I am running again, still out of control but in the right direction, toward the bottom of the driveway and Mrs Patterson's car. My feet are flailing and my arms are outstretched, trying to help me keep my balance, but I am on my feet and moving.

Her car has stopped at the end of the driveway and the green car is passing by. I veer left off the driveway and onto the grass. I will not reach the bottom of the drive-way in time but maybe I can meet the car as it turns onto the street. I point my body at the far corner of the front lawn, where the grass meets a stone wall and a line of trees. I run as fast as I can to that corner as Mrs Patterson's car turns and accelerates. I will not make it unless I jump. As I reach the edge of the lawn, where the grass meets the pavement, I jump and close my eyes, expecting to bounce off the fender or the wheel of Mrs Patterson's car.

Instead, I feel the almost silent *whoosh* that accompanies every passing through a door, and a second later I am lying in the back seat of the car, crumpled on the floor, trying to catch my breath.

I can hear Mrs Patterson. She is singing.

It's a song about hammering in the morning and hammering in the evening.

It sounds like it should be a happy song, but somehow it sounds scary coming from Mrs Patterson.

CHAPTER 42

Mrs Patterson sings the hammer song twice and then turns on the radio. She is listening to the news. I listen to hear if there is news about Max. There is not.

I wonder if she is listening for news about Max, too.

We have been driving on a highway for a long time, which is strange since Mrs Patterson lives so close to the school. Our ride from the school to her house last night took less than fifteen minutes, and I don't remember driving on a highway to get there.

The clock on the dashboard says 7.36. The first bell rings at 8.30 so we still have lots of time to get there, but this highway driving is making me nervous.

Where are we going?

I try not to think about Max. I try to stop imagining Max trapped behind that wall, all alone. I try not to hear his voice crying for me. I tell myself to pay attention to the road and try to read the green signs and watch Mrs Patterson for clues but my imagination keeps imagining Max, screaming and crying and pounding on the walls for help.

'I am helping,' I want to tell Max, but even if I could, I know he wouldn't believe me. It's hard to help when you have to break promises and leave your friend alone behind a wall.

I hear a roar over my head and know that it is an airplane. I have never heard a plane flying so low but I have seen and heard them on television and know that this is a big plane somewhere over our heads. A jumbo jet.

I look out the window. I look up. I want to see the plane but I do not. A green sign above the road reads *Welcome to Bradley International Airport*. There are other words on the sign but I do not read fast enough to read them all. I am happy that I was able to read the word *international*, because that is not an easy word. I look ahead and see low buildings and tall parking garages and buses and cars and lots of signs everywhere. I have never been to the airport before but I expected to see airplanes. I see none. I can hear them but cannot see a single one.

Mrs Patterson turns off the main road and drives down and around to a gate. She stops the car in front of a machine, rolls down her window and reaches out to press a button. There is a sign on the machine that says *Long Term Parking*. I do not know what *Long Term Parking* means, but I am starting to wonder if I have made another mistake. Is Mrs Patterson flying away somewhere? Is she worried that the police are about to find Max?

I have seen people arrested in airports on television before. They are always bad guys trying to leave the country. I don't know why the police don't just leave the country, too, and arrest the bad guys in the new country, but maybe this is what Mrs Patterson is doing. Maybe she knows that Mrs Gosk or the police chief have solved the mystery and know who took Max and now she has to escape or end up in jail.

The machine makes a humming sound and then spits out a ticket. Mrs Patterson drives into a parking lot that is full of cars. There must be hundreds of cars and there is a parking garage right next to the parking lot that is full of cars, too.

We drive up and down the rows. We drive past empty spots but Mrs Patterson does not park in any of them. She is driving like she has a place to go instead of a place to find.

Finally she slows down and parks the car in an empty spot. She gets out. I get out, too. I am too far from home to get lost now. Wherever Mrs Patterson goes, I go.

She opens the trunk. The boxes that were stacked on top of the kitchen table are piled inside. She lifts a box from the trunk, turns, and walks across the aisle to the other side of the parking lot. She walks down the aisle past three cars and then stops at a van. A huge van. A bus, really. It's one of those houses on wheels, I think. A house-van-bus thingy. Mrs Patterson reaches in her pocket and removes a key. She puts the key in a door and opens it. It's like the door on Max's school bus. It's regular sized. Mrs Patterson climbs three steps and turns left into the house-van-bus thingy.

I follow.

There is a living room inside, right behind the driver's seat. There is a couch and a cushy chair and a table that is attached to the floor so it won't move around. There is a television hanging on the wall and a bunk bed over the couch. Mrs Patterson puts the box on the couch and turns around and exits. I follow her back to the car and watch as she removes a second box and brings it back to the bus. She puts the box beside the first and turns to leave again. I do not follow this time. I stay. She has six more boxes to bring over and I want to take a second to look at the rest of the bus.

I walk past the living room into a narrow hallway. There is a closed door to my right and a little kitchen to my left. There is a sink and a stove and a microwave oven and a refrigerator. I pass through the door to the right and am standing in a tiny bathroom with a sink and a toilet.

A bathroom inside the bus.

If Max's school bus had a bathroom, he would never have to worry about bonus poops again.

Actually, I don't think Max could ever poop on a school bus, even if it had a toilet.

I step back through the door and into the narrow hallway. There is another closed door at the end of the hallway. I look behind me and see Mrs Patterson dropping two more boxes onto the couch. Four all together now. Two or three more trips and then she'll be done.

I step through the door at the end of the hallway. As I open my eyes, the first shiver of my life runs down my spine. I have heard this expression before but never understood it until now.

I cannot believe what I am seeing.

I am standing in a bedroom.

It is the same bedroom where Max is trapped right now.

It is smaller, and there are fewer lamps, and there are two oval-shaped windows on either side of the bus that are covered by curtains, but the walls are the same colors as Max's room in Mrs Patterson's basement and the bed is the same race-car bed with the same sheets and the same pillows and the same blankets. The same rug is covering the floor. And the space is filled with Lego and *Star Wars* toys and army men. Just as many as are in Max's room in the basement. Maybe more. There is a television stuck to the wall and another PlayStation and another rack of DVDs just like in the room in Mrs Patterson's basement. Even the DVDs are the same.

This is another room for Max. A room that can move.

I hear Mrs Patterson drop another box onto the couch. I turn to leave. I do not know if she is going to drive this bus or her car or take an airplane, but I need to stay with her no matter what. I would never find my way home from this airport.

As I pass back through the door, I notice the lock on it. A padlock with a latch.

Another shiver runs down my spine. My second ever.

Mrs Patterson moves the last three boxes from her car over to the bus and then she steps off the bus. I follow. She closes the door and locks it. She walks back to her car, climbs in and starts the engine. I take my spot in the back seat. She pulls out, singing the hammer song again as she weaves her way through the parking lot aisles to a set of gates at the other end of the parking lot.

She pulls up to a booth and hands a man inside her ticket.

'Wrong lot?' he asks when he looks down at her ticket.

'No,' Mrs Patterson says. 'My sister asked me to check on her car and leave her a jacket. I think she asked me to leave the jacket just so she didn't feel too silly about having me check on the car. She's a little obsessive compulsive.'

The man in the booth laughs.

Mrs Patterson is a good liar. She is like an actress on a television show. She is playing a character instead of being herself. She is pretending to be a woman with a sister who is obsessive compulsive. She is good at it. Even I would believe her if I didn't know that she is a Max stealer.

Mrs Patterson hands some money to the man in the booth and the gate in front of her car lifts up. She waves to the man as we drive away.

The clock on the dashboard reads 7.55.

I hope we are on our way to school.

CHAPTER 43

Max's desk is still empty. He is the only student absent again today, and it makes his desk seem even emptier. Nothing has changed since I left yesterday, which feels like a million years ago. The police officer is still sitting by the front door. Mrs Gosk is still pretending to be Mrs Gosk. And Max's desk is still empty.

I would sit at Max's desk if I could, but his chair is pushed in, leaving me no room to sit. Instead, I sit in a chair at the back of the room and listen to Mrs Gosk talk about fractions. Even without her spring, she is the best teacher in the world. She can make kids smile and laugh even while learning about something as boring as numerators and denominators.

I wonder if Mrs Patterson would have stolen Max if Mrs Gosk had been her teacher.

I don't think so.

I think Mrs Gosk could even turn Tommy Swinden into a nice boy with enough time.

When Mrs Patterson went to the Learning Center, I came here, to Mrs Gosk's classroom, to listen to her teach for a while. I cannot take my mind off how I left Max, but I was hoping that listening to Mrs Gosk might make me feel better.

It has. A little.

When the kids leave the classroom for recess, I follow Mrs Gosk to the teachers' room. If I want to know what is going on, this is where I will find it. Mrs Gosk has lunch every day with Miss Daggerty and Mrs Sera, and they always talk about good stuff.

There are two kinds of teachers in the world: there are teachers who play school and teachers who teach school, and Miss Daggerty and Mrs Sera and especially Mrs Gosk are the kind of teachers that teach school. They talk to kids in their regular voices and say things that they would say in their own living rooms. Their bulletin boards are always a little raggedy and their desks are always a little messy and their libraries are always a little out of order, but kids love them because they talk about real things with real voices and they always tell the truth. This is why Max loves Mrs Gosk. She never pretends to be a teacher. She is just herself, and it makes Max relax a little. There is nothing to figure out.

Even Max can tell if a teacher is playing school. Teachers who play school are bad at making kids behave. They like the boys and girls who sit in their seats and listen carefully and never shoot elastics across the room. They want all the boys and girls to be just like they were in school, all neat and perfect and sweet. Teachers who play school don't know what to do with kids like Max or Tommy Swinden or Annie Brinker, who once threw up on Mrs Wilson's desk on purpose. They don't understand kids like Max because they would rather be teaching their dolls than real kids. They use stickers and charts and cards to make kids behave, but none of that junk ever really works.

Mrs Gosk and Miss Daggery and Mrs Sera love kids like Max and Annie and even Tommy Swinden. They make kids want to behave, and they are not afraid to tell kids when they stink. And that makes them the best teachers to sit with at lunchtime.

Mrs Gosk is eating something called a sardine sandwich. I don't know what a *sardine* is, but I don't think it is good. Miss Daggerty crinkles her nose when Mrs Gosk tells her what she is eating.

'Have the police talked to you again?' Miss Daggerty asks. She lowers her voice a little when she speaks.

There are six other teachers in the room. A bunch of them are teachers who play school.

'No,' Mrs Gosk says, not lowering her voice. 'But they'd better do their goddam jobs and find Max.'

I have never seen Mrs Gosk cry, and I have seen a lot of

teachers cry. Man teachers, even, but especially the woman teachers. She is not crying now, but when she said those words, she sounded angry enough to cry. Not sad tears but mad tears.

'It has to be one of the parents,' Miss Daggerty says. 'Or one of his relatives. Kids just don't disappear.'

'I just can't believe that it's been … what? Four days?' Mrs Sera says.

'Five,' Mrs Gosk says. 'Five goddam days.'

'I haven't seen Karen all day,' Mrs Sera says.

Karen is Mrs Palmer's first name. Teachers who play school call her Mrs Palmer, but teachers like Mrs Sera just call her Karen.

'She's been locked in her office all morning,' Miss Daggerty says.

'I hope she's doing something to find Max and not just hiding from everyone,' Mrs Sera says.

'She'd better be working to the death and the dirt to find him,' Mrs Gosk says. There are tears in her eyes. Her cheeks are red. She stands up and leaves her sardine sandwich behind. The room gets quiet as she leaves.

I leave, too.

Mrs Patterson has a two o'clock meeting with Mrs Palmer. I know this because she asked to meet with Mrs Palmer when she came into school today but the secretary lady said that Mrs Palmer was busy until two. So Mrs Patterson said, 'Fine,' in that way that means it isn't fine.

I want to be in the room for that meeting.

I still have an hour before the meeting and Mrs Gosk's students are in gym class. Mrs Gosk is sitting at her desk, correcting papers, so I go down to Mrs Kropp's room to see Puppy. I haven't seen him in five days, which is a lot of days in the imaginary friend world.

That's a lifetime for a lot of imaginary friends.

Puppy is curled up into a ball beside Piper. Piper is reading a book. Her mouth moves but she doesn't say the word. First graders read like this a lot. Max used to read like this.

'Puppy,' I say.

I whisper the words at first. It's a habit. Not my habit but everyone else's habit, so I do it, too. Then I realize how silly it is to whisper in a room where only one person can hear me, so I speak in a normal voice.

'Puppy! It's me, Budo.'

Puppy doesn't move.

'Puppy!' I shout, and this time he jumps up and looks around.

'You scared me,' he says, noticing me on the other side of the room.

'You sleep, too?' I ask.

'Of course I do. Why?'

'Graham once told me that she slept, but I never sleep.'

301

'Really?' Puppy says, walking over to me on the other side of the room.

The kids are silently reading and Mrs Kropp is reading with four kids at a side table. These are only first graders but they all read without fooling around or staring out the windows because Mrs Kropp doesn't play school either. She teaches.

'Yeah,' I say. 'I never sleep. I don't even know how.'

'I sleep more than I am awake,' Puppy says.

I wonder if I could go to sleep if I wanted to. I never feel tired, but maybe if I lay down on a pillow and closed my eyes long enough, I would fall asleep. Then I wonder if all that sleeping might make it easier to forget how easy it is for us to stop existing.

For a second, I find myself jealous of Puppy.

'Have you heard anything about Max?' I ask.

'Is he back?' Puppy asks.

'No, he was stolen. Remember?'

'I know,' Puppy says. 'But I thought that maybe he was back.'

'You haven't heard anything about it?'

'No,' Puppy says. 'Did you find him?'

'I have to go,' I say.

It's not true, but I forgot how annoying it is to talk to Puppy. Not only is he dumb, but he thinks that the whole world is like one of those picture books that Mrs Kropp reads to her first graders. The books where everyone learns a lesson and nobody ever dies. Puppy thinks that the world is one big, happy ending. I know it's not his fault, but it still annoys me. I can't help it.

I turn to leave the room.

'Maybe Wooly knows,' Puppy says.

'Wooly?'

'Yeah. Wooly.'

Puppy doesn't have any hands, so instead of pointing he nods his head in the direction of the coatroom. Standing against the far wall is a paper doll. He is about as tall as my waist, and at first I think it is one of those body tracings that Max refused to do in kindergarten when the kids were told to lie down on big sheets of paper and trace one another.

Max's teacher tried to trace him and Max got stuck.

But when I look closer, I see the paper doll's eyes blink. Then he nods his head left and right, like he is trying to say hello without using his hands.

'Wooly?' I ask Puppy again.

'Yes. Wooly.'

'How long has he been here?' I ask.

'I don't know,' Puppy says. 'A little while.'

I walk over to the coatroom to where Wooly still seems to be hanging on the wall.

'Hi,' I say. 'I'm Budo.'

'I'm Wooly,' the paper doll says.

He has two arms and two legs but not much body, and he looks like he was cut out in a hurry. *Imagined in a hurry*, I remind myself. His edges are all jagged and uneven, and he has creases all over his body from where it looks like he was folded up a million times in a million different ways.

'How long have you been here?' I ask.

'In this room?' he asks. 'Or in the whole wide world?'

I smile. He is already smarter than Puppy.

'World,' I say.

'Since last year,' Wooly says. 'At the end of kindergarten. But I don't come to school very much. Kayla used to keep me at home or folded up inside her backpack, but she has been taking me out for a bunch of days now. Maybe a month.'

'Which one is Kayla?' I ask.

Wooly reaches out to point, but as he does so his whole body curls over and slides to the floor, face down, in a rustle of paper.

'Are you okay?' I ask, unsure what to do.

'Yes,' Wooly says, using his arms and legs to flip himself on his back so he is looking up at me. 'This happens a lot.'

He is smiling. He doesn't have a real mouth like me but just a line that opens and closes and changes shape. But the edges are curled up, so I can tell that it's a smile.

I smile back. 'Can you stand up?' I ask.

'Sure,' Wooly says.

I watch as Wooly curls the middle of his body up and then down like an inch worm, pushing himself back against the wall until his head is touching it. Then he curls the middle of his body again, pushing his head against the wall and sliding it up. He does this twice more, reaching out and grabbing the edge of a small bookshelf as he does so and pulling himself up while the middle of his body pushes. When he is finished, he is standing again, but really he is just leaning against the wall.

'That's not easy,' I say.

'No. I can get around okay by scooting on my back or my belly, but climbing up the wall is hard. If there isn't something to grab onto, it's impossible.'

'Sorry,' I say.

'It's all right,' Wooly says. 'Last week I met a little boy in the shape of a popsicle stick with no arms and no legs. Just a stick. Jason brought him to school, but when Mrs Kropp let him try the new computer game first, he threw the popsicle stick boy on his desk and just forgot about him. I stood here against the wall and watched him just fade away and disappear. One minute he was here and the next minute he was gone. Have you ever seen an imaginary friend disappear?'

'Yes,' I say.

'I cried,' Wooly says. 'I didn't even know him but I

cried. So did the popsicle stick boy. He cried until he was gone.'

'I would've cried, too,' I say.

We are both quiet for a moment. I try to imagine what it must have been like to be that popsicle stick boy.

I decide that I like Wooly a lot.

'Why is Kayla bringing you to school now?' I ask.

I know that when a kid starts taking an imaginary friend to new places, it usually means something bad has happened.

'Her dad doesn't live with her anymore. He hit her mom before he left. Right at the dinner table. Right on the face. Then she threw her food in his face and they started yelling at each other. Really loud. Kayla cried and cried, and then she started bringing me to school.'

'Sorry,' I say again.

'No,' Wooly says. 'Be sorry for Kayla. I like coming to school. I think it means that I won't end up like the popsicle stick boy for a while. She is always coming over to the drinking fountain to get a drink, but really she's just checking to make sure I am here. That's why I'm not stuffed in her backpack anymore. I think it would be a lot easier to forget about me if she still had me stuffed inside that backpack. So this is good.'

I smile. Wooly is smart. Very smart.

'I was wondering if you heard anything about a boy named Max,' I say. 'He disappeared last week.'

'He ran away. Right?'

'What did you hear?' I ask.

'Mrs Kropp had lunch in here with two other ladies and they were talking about it. Mrs Kropp said that he ran away.'

'What did the other ladies say?' I ask.

'One of the ladies said he was probably kidnapped by someone who knew him. She said that kidnapped kids are always kidnapped by people they know. She said that Max was too stupid to run away and hide for so long without being found.'

'He's not stupid,' I say. I am surprised by how angry I sound.

'I didn't say it. The lady did.'

'I know. I'm sorry. Anyways, she's right about him being kidnapped. Mrs Patterson stole Max.'

'Who is Mrs Patterson?' Wooly asks.

'She is Max's teacher.'

'A teacher?' Wooly sounds as if he cannot believe it. I feel like I finally have someone on my side. 'Did you tell anyone?' he asks.

'No. Max is the only human person who can hear me.'

'Oh.' Then his eyes, which are just circles inside a circle, widen. 'Oh no. Max is your imaginer friend?'

I have never heard a human person called this before, but I say yes.

'Maybe I should tell Kayla,' Wooly says. 'Then she can tell Mrs Kropp for you.'

I had not thought of this, but Wooly is right. Wooly could be my connection to the world of human persons. He could tell Kayla, and then Kayla could tell Mrs Kropp, and then Mrs Kropp could tell the police chief. I cannot believe I did not think of this before.

'Do you think Mrs Kropp would believe her?' I ask.

'I don't know,' Wooly says. 'Maybe.'

It might work. I used to think that Max was my only connection to his world, but every imaginary friend is a connection to Max's world.

Every imaginary friend can touch the world of human persons. Even Puppy.

Every imaginary friend can touch the world, I think.

Then I have a different idea. A better idea and a worse idea all rolled into one.

'No,' I say. 'Don't tell Kayla.'

I think about Mrs Patterson's bus with the bedroom in the back and the lock on the door and I worry that if she finds out what Kayla said to Mrs Kropp, she might lock Max up in that bedroom and drive away for ever. Mrs Kropp might tell the police, but maybe Mrs Kropp would smile at Kayla and say something like, 'Oh, did Wooly tell you that?' And then she would tell Mrs Patterson about the funny thing that Kayla said in class today, and Mrs

Patterson would panic and run away with Max before I ever found a way to save him.

Wooly's idea might work, but I have a better connection to Max's world.

A much better and a much worse connection.

I feel another shiver run down my spine.

CHAPTER 44

Mrs Palmer looks tired. Her voice is scratchy and her eyes are puffy and they look like they want to close. Even her clothes and hair look tired.

'How are you doing?' Mrs Patterson asks her.

I notice that Mrs Palmer's desk is cluttered with papers and folders and styrofoam coffee cups. There is a pile of newspapers on the floor beside the trash can. I have never before seen anything on her desk except for a computer and a telephone. I can't remember ever seeing a single scrap of paper in this office.

'I'm fine,' Mrs Palmer says, and even those two words sound tired. 'I'll be much better once we find Max, but I know we're doing everything we can.'

'There's not much that we can do. Is there?' Mrs Patterson asks.

'I'm helping the police as much as possible, and I'm handling the media inquiries. And I'm trying to help Mr and

Mrs Delaney any way I can. But you're right. There's not much we can do now but wait and pray.'

'I'm certainly glad that you're in charge and not me,' Mrs Patterson says. 'I give you a lot of credit, Karen. I don't know how you do it.'

But Mrs Palmer is not in charge, and Mrs Patterson knows it. Mrs Palmer answers the phone and makes the announcements over the intercom and reminds Mr Fedyzyn to wear a tie at graduation, but she is supposed to be in charge of making sure that kids are safe. That is her real job. But Max is not safe, and the person who stole him is sitting right here in her office and she doesn't know it.

That is not what I call being in charge.

'This has been the toughest time in my twenty years as an administrator,' Mrs Palmer says. 'But God willing, we'll get through this and Max will come back to us safe and sound. Now what can I do for you?'

'I know this is bad timing, but I'd like to take a leave of absence. My condition isn't improving and I'd like to spend some time with my sister out west. But I have no intention of leaving you in the lurch. I'm in no rush. I'll wait until you find a replacement, and I'll make sure I cooperate with the police in any way needed and stay in Connecticut until they no longer require my assistance. But when it's possible, and as soon as it's possible, I'd like to take the rest of the year off.'

'Of course,' Mrs Palmer says.

She sounds surprised and maybe a little relieved. I think she thought Mrs Patterson was meeting with her about something else.

'I don't know much about lupus, and I feel terrible about it. I would have done more reading about it, had I not been focused solely on Max these past few days. But is there anything we can do?'

'Thank you, but I'm okay. I'm taking several medications that seem to have things under control for the moment, but it's an unpredictable disease. I'd hate to wake up one morning and discover that I don't have the time to see my sister and get to know her kids. Let them get to know their auntie.'

'It must be hard,' Mrs Palmer says.

'I didn't think I'd ever stand up again when I lost my Scotty. But this place has been so good for me. It brought me back from the dead. It reminded me that there is still good in this world, and that there are kids who really need me. There isn't a day that goes by that I don't think about my boy, but I've moved on and done some good, I think.'

'You have,' Mrs Palmer says.

'But Max's disappearance has really got me thinking again about how unpredictable life can be. I pray every night that Max is okay, but there is no telling what has happened. Here today, gone tomorrow. Just like my Scotty.

That could be me someday. I don't want to wait until my life is piled high with regrets before I do something about it.'

'I certainly understand,' Mrs Palmer says. 'I can call Rich tomorrow and have Human Resources start interviewing replacements immediately. I'd do it myself but I just don't think I'll have the time. But there are a lot of teachers on the market without jobs, so hiring a qualified replacement shouldn't be difficult. Do you think you'll want to return next year?'

Mrs Patterson sighs, and it sounds so real even though I know that everything she is saying is a lie. I can't believe how good she is at pretending to be someone else.

'I'd like to think that I'll be back,' she says. 'Would it be all right if I let you know for sure in the spring? It's hard to tell how I will feel in six months. To be honest, it's been hard to come to school each day, knowing Max is not here and knowing that had I been working last Friday, none of this would have happened.'

'Don't be ridiculous, Ruth,' Mrs Palmer says.

'It's not ridiculous,' Mrs Patterson says. 'If I had been—'

'Stop,' Mrs Palmer says, holding her hand out like a crossing guard. 'This is not your fault. Max did not run away. Someone took him, and if they didn't take him on Friday, they would have taken him another day. The police say that random abductions are almost unheard of. Someone planned this. This is not your fault.'

'I know. But it's still hard. If Max comes back to us, I could see myself coming back next year. But if, God forbid, he is still missing next September, I don't know how I could bring myself to walk through those doors ever again.'

Everything Mrs Patterson says makes her seem more innocent to Mrs Palmer and more dangerous to me.

'Just don't blame yourself,' Mrs Palmer says. 'You had nothing to do with this.'

'When I'm lying in my bed at night, thinking about Max and where he might be, it's hard not to think this is all my fault,' Mrs Patterson says.

'Don't. You are too good to be blaming yourself, Ruth.'

Sometimes I ask Max if I exist just to get him to admit that I exist. To remind him that I exist. Now Mrs Patterson is doing the same thing. Mrs Patterson, Max's kidnapper, has walked into Mrs Palmer's office and tricked her into insisting that she did nothing wrong. The bad guy is sitting right in front of Mrs Palmer, and all Mrs Palmer can do is tell her over and over that she is innocent, even when Mrs Patterson admits that she is to blame.

Mrs Palmer is dancing with the devil in the pale moonlight, and she is losing badly.

And now Mrs Palmer has agreed to let Mrs Patterson take the rest of the year off so she can head to a place out west, to visit a sister who probably does not exist. I think Mrs Patterson is planning to leave Connecticut, and she might even be planning to head out west, but it's not to see her sister.

She is going to take Max away, and if she does I don't think that either one of them will ever come back.

I have to hurry.

I have to break another promise to Max.

CHAPTER 45

I ride the school bus home but get off at the Savoys' house again since the bus did not stop for Max. I walk to the house to check on Max's mom and dad, but that is not why I rode the school bus home. I do not know how to get to the hospital from school, so I have to start at the house.

I wish I paid better attention to the streets. Max's dad says that he carries a map inside his head that lets him get anywhere. All of my maps start at Max's house. My map looks like a spider. Max's house is the body and all the places that I go are the legs.

No two legs connect.

I also cannot get to Mrs Patterson's house without driving in her car, which means that if Mrs Patterson decides to never come back to school again, I am in big trouble. I will never find Max again.

If everything goes according to my plan, I will be back in Mrs Patterson's car tomorrow.

Max's parents are home. I saw their cars in the driveway when the bus drove past. Normally Max's dad would be at work and Max's mom would just be getting home in time to see Max off the bus. But today they are both home.

His mom is in the kitchen. She is baking cookies. The house is quiet. No radio or television. The only sound I can hear is Max's dad's voice coming from his office. He is on the telephone.

It is weird. I did not expect cookies and telephone calls.

The house is clean, too. Cleaner than usual. There are no books or mail piled on the dining room table and there are no dishes in the sink. No shoes piled by the front door.

It reminds me a little bit of Mrs Patterson's house.

Max's dad comes out of his office and walks into the kitchen.

'You're baking cookies?' he asks.

I'm glad because I wanted to ask the same thing.

'I'm making them to take to the police station.'

'You think they need cookies?' Max's dad says.

'I don't know what else to do, okay?' Max's mom says.

She pushes the bowl of cookie batter across the counter. It slides over the edge and falls to the floor. The bowl breaks. It makes a cracking sound but most of the bowl stays together. It is held together by the cookie

317

dough. Only a couple pieces of glass separate from the bowl.

Max's mom begins to cry.

'Jesus Christ!' Max's dad shouts.

He stares down at the broken bowl. One of the broken pieces has slid across the linoleum and stopped in front of his shoe. He stares at it and then back up to Max's mom.

'I'm sorry,' Max's mom says. 'I just don't know what to do. There isn't a book that tells you what to do when your little boy disappears. The police tell you to stay home and wait, but what the fuck am I supposed to do? Watch TV? Read a book? You're in there playing amateur detective and I'm stuck in here, staring at the walls and wondering what the hell is happening to Max.'

'The police said that it was probably someone who Max knows,' Max's dad says. 'I'm just trying to figure out who it might be.'

'By calling everyone we know and hoping that they will admit to taking him? Did you hope to hear him playing in the background with the Parker boys or with my sister's kids?'

'I don't know,' Max's dad says. 'I have to do something.'

'You really think my sister could've taken Max? She can't even talk to Max without getting nervous. She can't even look him in the eyes.'

'It's something, goddamit! I can't just sit here and do nothing.'

'And you think baking cookies is nothing?'

'I don't see how it's going to help us find Max.'

'And what happens when you run out of people to call?' Max's mom asks. 'Then what? How long do we put ourselves on hold before we go back to work and resume our lives?'

'You want to go back to work?'

'No, of course not. But I keep wondering what will happen if they don't find Max. How long are we going to sit in this house waiting for news? I know it's awful, but I keep thinking about how we will ever move on after the police tell us to give up hope. Because I'm starting to give up hope. God help me, I am. It's been five days and they have nothing. What's going to happen to us?'

'It's only been five days,' Max's dad says. 'The chief said that people make mistakes. Maybe not in the first week or even the first month, but you can't be careful for ever. Whoever has Max will make a mistake and that's when we'll find him.'

'What if he's already dead?'

'Don't say that!' Max's father says. 'Don't fucking say that!'

'Why not? Don't tell me you haven't thought about it.'

'I'm trying not to think about it,' Max's dad says. 'For Christ's sake, why would you even say that?'

'Because it's all I can think about!' Max's mom says. 'My little boy is gone and he's probably dead and we're never getting him back!'

Now Max's mom is really crying. She throws a wooden spoon covered with cookie batter across the counter and crumples to the floor, her head dipping into her arms. For a moment, she reminds me of Wooly, sliding off his wall and onto the floor. Max's dad steps forward, stops for a moment, and then goes to her. He eases himself down to the floor and puts his arms around her.

'He's not dead,' Max's dad whispers. He is not shouting his words anymore.

'But what if he is?' Max's mom asks. 'What then? I don't know how we'll ever go on.'

'We'll find him,' Max's dad says.

'I can't stop thinking that there was something we did. Or forgot to do. That somehow this is our fault.'

'Stop,' Max's dad says, but he says it gently. Not like a crossing guard. 'That's not how the world works and you know it. Some awful person decided to take Max from us. It doesn't have anything to do with us. It's just an awful thing done by an awful person, and we're going to catch the son-of-a-bitch and bring our son back. He's going to make a mistake. The chief said so. When he does, we'll get Max back. I know it.'

'But what if we don't?'

'We will. I promise.'

Max's dad sounds so sure of himself even though he keeps calling the kidnapper a he.

I suddenly realize that Max isn't the only person who I have to save. I have to save his parents, too.

CHAPTER 46

I start at the Children's Hospital. I have no reason to be here, but I want to see Summer. I'm not sure why, but I do. I feel like I need to see her.

I make my way to the recess room. The elevator drops me off on the fourteenth floor this time. No stairs. I decide that this is a good sign. Things are already working out.

I make my way to the recess room. It is after seven so the kids will probably be in their beds and the imaginary friends who leave the rooms will probably be in the recess room by now.

As I walk in, Klute jumps up out of his chair and shouts my name. His head bobbles uncontrollably as he does so. Three other imaginary friends jump up from their seats in surprise as well. None of them are Spoon or Summer.

'Hello, Klute,' I say.

'You look so real!' says a boy who looks like a robot. Shiny and boxy and stiff. I have seen many robot imaginary friends before.

'He really does,' says a brown teddy bear about half my size.

The third, a girl who looks like a human person except for missing eyebrows and a pair of fairy wings on her back, sits back down and folds her hands in her lap without saying anything.

'Thank you,' I say to the robot and the teddy bear. I turn to Klute. 'Is Summer still here? Or Spoon?'

'Spoon went home two days ago,' Klute says.

'What about Summer?' I ask.

Klute looks at his feet. I turn to the robot and the teddy bear. They both do the same.

'What happened?' I ask.

Klute shakes his head back and forth slowly, but it causes his head to bobble. He will not look at me except when his bobbling head forces his eyes up for a second.

'She died,' the girl with the fairy wings says.

I turn around and face her. 'What do you mean she died?'

'Summer died,' she says. 'And then Grace died.'

'Grace?' I ask. Then I remember.

'Her friend,' the fairy says. 'Her friend who was sick.'

'Summer died *and then* Grace died?' I ask.

'Yes,' the fairy says. 'Summer disappeared. And then a little while later the doctors said that Grace died.'

'It was sad,' Klute says. It sounds like he is going to cry. 'She was sitting in here with us and then she just started to fade away. I could see right through her.'

'Was she scared?' I ask. 'Did it hurt?'

'No,' the fairy says. 'She knew that Grace was going to die so she was happy that she was going to die first.'

'Why?' I ask.

'So she could wait for Grace on the other side,' the fairy says.

'The other side of what?'

'I don't know,' she says.

I look at Klute. '

'I don't know either,' he says. 'She just said that she and Grace would be together on the other side.'

'I wasn't here,' the teddy bear says. 'But it sure sounds sad. I never want to disappear.'

'We all disappear someday,' the robot says. He talks like a robot from the movies. All stiff and choppy.

'We do?' Klute says.

'Did you find your friend?' the fairy asks.

'What?' I ask.

'Did you find your friend?' the fairy asks again. 'Summer told us that you lost your friend and you were trying to find him.'

'I told you, too,' Klute says, bobbling his head up and down. 'I knew Budo before all of you.'

'Yes,' I say. 'I found him, but I haven't saved him yet.'

'Will you?' the fairy asks. She stands up, but the top of her head still doesn't reach my shoulders.

I want to tell the fairy that I'm trying to save Max, but instead I say, 'Yes. I promised Summer I would.'

'Then why are you here?' she asks.

'I need help,' I say. 'I need help to save Max.'

'Our help?' Klute asks expectantly. Excitedly. His head bobbles again.

'No,' I say. 'But thank you. You can't help me. I need someone else.'

CHAPTER 47

Here is what I know about Oswald:

1. He is so tall that his head almost touches the ceiling. He is the tallest imaginary friend I have ever seen.
2. Oswald looks like a human person. He looks as much like a human person as I do, except he is so tall. Ears and eyebrows and all.
3. Oswald is the only imaginary friend I have ever met who has a grown-up for a human friend.
4. Oswald is the only imaginary friend I have ever met who can move things in the real world. This is why I am only pretty sure that he is an imaginary friend.
5. Oswald is mean and scary.
6. Oswald hates me.
7. Oswald is the only person who can help me save Max.

I met Oswald about a month ago, so I am not sure if he is still in the hospital, but I think he probably is. His human person is on a special floor of the hospital for lunatics, which Max told me is another word for crazy people. That's what I heard one of the doctors say. Or maybe it was a nurse. She said she hated working on the floor with all the lunatics.

But another nurse person said that it was the floor for head injuries, which I think are people who break their heads. So I'm not sure. Maybe it's both. Maybe a broken head turns people into lunatics.

Oswald's human person is also in a coma, which Max said means that he is sleeping for ever.

A coma person is like the opposite of me. I never sleep but a coma person only sleeps.

I was in the grown-up hospital when I first saw Oswald. I like to go there sometimes and listen to the doctors talk about the sick people. Every sick person is different, so every story is different. Sometimes the stories are hard to understand, but they are always exciting. Even better than watching Pauley scratch lottery tickets.

Sometimes I just like to walk around the hospital, because it is so big. Every time I go there, I find a new place to explore.

I was exploring the eighth floor that day, and Oswald was walking down the hall toward me. His head was down and he was looking at his feet. He was tall and wide with a flat face and a thick neck. His cheeks were red, like he had just come in from the cold. He was bald. Not a speck of hair on his big head.

But it was the way he walked that I noticed the most. He threw each leg forward like he wanted to kick the air in front of him. Like nothing in the whole wide world could stop him. He reminded me of a snowplow.

When he got close to me, he looked up and shouted, 'Get out of my way!'

I turned around to see who was walking behind me, but the hallway was empty.

I turned back around and Oswald said, 'Get out of my way right now!'

That was when I realized that he was an imaginary friend. He could see me. He was talking to me. So I stepped to the side and he walked right past me. Plowed right past me without even looking up. I turned and followed him. I had never seen an imaginary friend look so real before, and I wanted to talk to him.

'I'm Budo,' I said, trying to catch up.

'Oswald,' he said. He didn't look back at me. He just said the word and kept plowing forward.

'No,' I said. 'I'm Budo.'

He stopped and turned toward me. 'I'm Oswald. Leave me alone.'

He turned and started walking again.

I was a little nervous, because Oswald was so big and so loud and seemed so mean. I had never met an imaginary friend who was mean before. But I had never seen any imaginary friend look so real before, either, so I couldn't help myself. I followed him.

He walked down the hallway, turned, walked down another hallway, turned again, and then he stopped at a door. The door wasn't closed all the way. It was open only a little crack. The doctors keep the doors open a crack a lot so they can sneak into rooms in the middle of the night to check on people without waking them up. The crack in the doorway was too small for Oswald to fit through, so I thought he was going to pass through the door like I would. But instead he reached out and moved the door. He pushed it open with his hand just enough to squeeze through.

When the door moved, I screamed. I couldn't believe it. I had never seen an imaginary friend move anything in the real world before. Oswald must have heard me scream because he turned. He ran toward me. I was frozen. I didn't know what to do. I still couldn't believe what I had seen. As Oswald reached me, he threw his hands out in front of him and he hit me. No one had ever hit me before. I went tumbling to the floor.

It hurt.

I had never really known that I could hurt until then. I had never even known what *hurt* really meant until then.

'I said to leave me alone!' he shouted. Then he turned and went back to the room.

Even though Oswald had yelled at me and pushed me and hurt me, I had to know what was in that room. I couldn't help it. I had just seen an imaginary friend touch a door and move it in the real world. I had to know more.

So I waited. I went to the end of the hallway and stood there, peeking around the corner, never taking my eyes off that door. I waited for ever and finally Oswald came out of the room through the same crack in the doorway that he had made for ever ago. He was walking in my direction, so I went down the hallway a bit and hid inside a closet. I stood in the dark and counted to one hundred and then I came back out.

Oswald was nowhere in sight.

So I went back to the room that Oswald had left and went inside. The lights were off but the light from the hallway gave the room a dull glow. There were two beds in the room. A man was lying in the bed closest to the door. The other bed was empty. No sheets or pillows. I looked around for toys or stuffed animals or little pairs of pants or shoes. Anything that would show me that a little boy or a little girl was staying in this room, too. But I found nothing.

Just this man.

He had a bushy, red beard and bushy eyebrows but his head was completely bald like Oswald's. There were machines next to his bed and wires and tubes connected to his arms and chest. The machines beeped and hissed. Lights blinked and glowed on tiny television screens attached to the machines.

I looked back at the empty bed again, thinking that maybe I missed something. Maybe there were stuffed animals and little pants hanging in the closet and the little boy was in the bathroom. Or maybe the bald man in the bed was a dad, and Oswald was the imaginary friend of his son or daughter (but probably his son). Maybe the bald man's son was sitting in the waiting room right now, waiting for his dad to wake up. Maybe the little boy had sent Oswald to check on his dad to make sure he was okay.

Then I thought that maybe the bald man wasn't anyone's dad. This could be any person. Maybe Oswald was just resting on the extra bed. Or maybe Oswald was looking for a quiet place to sit. Or maybe Oswald was just curious like me.

Then I thought that maybe Oswald was a human person who could see imaginary friends instead of an imaginary friend who could touch the human person world. I was trying to decide which was more likely when three people turned on the lights and came into the room. One was wearing a white coat and the other two were standing behind her, carrying clipboards. They walked over to the man in the bed and the woman in the white coat said, 'This is John Hurly. Age fifty-two. Head trauma caused from a fall. Brought to us on 4 August. Non-responsive to all treatment. He has been in a coma since he arrived.'

'What's the plan for Mr Hurly?' one of the clipboard people asked.

The people kept on talking, asking questions and answering questions, but I stopped listening.

That was when Oswald walked back into the room.

His eyes fell upon the white coat and clipboard people first. He looked annoyed but not angry. He rolled his eyes and snorted a little. I think he had seen them before.

But then he noticed me. I was standing between the two beds, my back against the machines, trying not to move. Hoping that if I didn't move, he might not notice me. His mouth dropped open when he saw me and he froze for a moment. I think he was surprised to see me standing there. As surprised as I had been to see him move that door. He couldn't believe it.

He took a deep breath, pointed his finger at me and said, 'You!'

He didn't run at me, but he was so tall and so quick that he moved from the doorway to the space between the two beds in three or four steps. Before I even had time to think.

I was trapped, and I was scared. I don't think that one imaginary friend can kill another imaginary friend, but I didn't think that imaginary friends could hurt each other either, and Oswald had already proven me wrong about that.

Oswald lunged at me, so I hopped onto and over the empty bed. Oswald followed, rolling over the bed and landing on the other side even before I had a chance to get my balance. He pushed me again. His hands were so big that his push lifted me right off the ground. I fell backwards into a small table in the corner of the room. The table didn't move, of course, but I hit it just the same, and it hurt. The corner of the table dug into my back, and I cried out in pain. The idea of the corner, I mean, but it was just as sharp as the real corner.

I was about to lift myself off the table when Oswald grabbed me by the shoulders and threw me back over the empty bed. I bounced once on the mattress and fell off the edge and onto the floor between the two beds. I hit my head on the way down, on one of the machines, I think, so I was slow getting back up. I just lay there for a second, trying to calm down and think. I looked under the bald man's bed and saw six feet on the other side. The white coat and the two clipboard people. They were still talking about the coma man. Asking questions and looking at something called a chart. They had no idea that a fight was happening

333

right in front of them, except it wasn't a fight, because I was not fighting. I was just getting hurt.

I lifted myself onto my hands and knees and was about to stand back up when Oswald's knee came crashing down on my back. That was the worst pain I have ever felt. It was like something exploded in my back. I cried out and dropped back down to the floor. My face smacked the tile and my nose and forehead blew up in the same kind of pain that was still exploding in my back. I thought I was going to cry, and back then I had never cried before. I didn't even know that I could cry back then, but I thought I might. It hurt so much.

Little kids who get hurt on the playground call for their mommies a lot. I wanted to call for my mommy but I have no mommy, and not having a mommy hurt the most at that moment. Not having anyone who could help me. The three doctor people were still in the room, still talking, still staring at their clipboards, but they had no idea that someone else in the room was hurt.

I wondered if Oswald could kill me or coma me like the bald man.

Oswald kicked me in the legs. He kicked me in the arms.

I wanted to cry out for my mommy again. Instead I thought about Dee. I called out her name instead.

I think I would have started crying then, but there was no time to cry because Oswald was picking me up and throwing me against the wall on the other side of the room. I bounced off the wall and landed on my still-exploding back. Then he lifted me again and threw me in the direction of the doorway. My head hit the wall next to the door and I saw stars. I couldn't tell up from down. Then he lifted me one more time and threw me out of the room and into the hallway. I rolled a couple times and then I started to crawl away as fast as I could. I had no idea which direction I was crawling. All I knew was that I was crawling away and that was good. And the whole time that I crawled I was just waiting for Oswald to pick me up again.

But he didn't.

I crawled for about thirty seconds then I stopped and looked behind me. Oswald was standing in the middle of the hallway, staring at me.

'Never again,' he said.

I waited for him to say something else.

When he didn't, I said, 'Okay.'

'I mean it,' he said. 'Never again.'

CHAPTER 48

'Oswald is my only chance,' I say. 'He is Max's only chance. He has to help.'

'He won't,' Klute says.

The robot shakes his head in agreement.

'He has to,' I say.

I take the elevator to the tenth floor and then I walk down two flights of stairs to the eighth floor.

The lunatic floor.

I walk to the room where I last saw Oswald. The room with Oswald's bald lunatic friend. I walk slowly, keeping my eyes peeled as I turn corners and pass by open doors. I do not want to bump into Oswald by mistake. I still have no idea what I will say to him.

The door to the room is open. I walk toward it. I try not to think about the last time I saw Oswald. The sound of his voice. The way he threw me around the room. The way his eyes doubled in size as he said, 'Never again.'

I agreed with him that day. I promised to stay away for ever. But here I am again.

I step into the doorway, bracing myself for attack.

It comes quickly.

I take in many details before Oswald reaches me.

The curtains are open and the room is bright with sunlight. It surprises me. My memories of this room are dark and scary. In my memory, the room has no corners. Just patches of darkness. The room looks too happy and sunny now for anything bad to ever happen, and yet Oswald is already a few feet away from me and shouting, 'No! No! No!'

The bald man with the red beard is still in his bed, machines still whirring and hissing and flashing. There is a man in the second bed, too. He is young and round and there is something wrong with his face. It looks rubbery and sleepy.

There is a third man in the room. He is sitting in a chair at the end of the sleepy face man's bed. He is holding a magazine in his hands and he is reading it out loud to Sleepy Face. I hear only a tiny bit of it before Oswald is on top of me. It's a story about baseball, I think. Someone threw a low hitter. But before I can hear anymore, Oswald's hands grab me around the neck. He squeezes and turns,

337

throwing me into the room. My body crashes into the bald man's bed. If I was not an imaginary friend, the bed would have slid across the room. That's how hard I hit it.

But I am imaginary so I bounce off the bed and land in a heap at Oswald's feet. My head and chest and neck hurt. I can't breathe for a moment. Oswald bends over, picks me up by the collar of my shirt and the waist of my pants, and flings me over the bald man's bed and onto Sleepy Face's bed. I bounce off him, too, without him ever feeling a thing, and roll off the side of the bed. I land in another heap on the floor against the far wall.

More parts hurt. Lots of them.

This was a bad idea. Oswald is not like a snowplow. He is like one of those giant cranes with the ball hanging from a chain. The kind that knock down old buildings. He just keeps pounding away at me.

I stand up quickly this time. I know that I must or Oswald will pick me up and throw me again or start kicking me again. The man in the chair, a young man with pale skin, keeps reading. He is in the middle of a fight, and he will never know it.

Oswald is moving again, filling the space between Sleepy Face's bed and the wall, blocking my escape. I suddenly wish that I had stayed on the floor and rolled under Sleepy Face's bed and then under Bald Lunatic's bed and then out the door.

Oswald takes two steps forward, closing the distance between us. I still have not said a word to him. I decide that now is a good time to speak.

'Stop,' I say, trying to sound like I am begging. I do a good job because I am begging. 'Please. I need your help.'

'I told you to stay away,' Oswald shouts. He shouts loud enough to drown out the baseball story for a second. Then he steps forward and puts his hands on my neck again.

I try to block him this time but he swats my hands away like they are made of paper. Like Wooly's hands. Oswald starts squeezing. He is choking me. If I breathed air, I might be dying. I breathe the idea of air, but even that is getting squished out of my throat now.

I think I might be dying.

I feel my feet leave the floor when I hear another voice in the room.

'Let go of him, Oswald.'

Oswald lets go, but not because he is obeying the command. He is surprised. No, he is shocked. I can see it on his face.

My feet hit the floor and I stumble for a moment, catch my balance and my breath at the same time, then turn in the direction of the doorway. The fairy from the recess room is standing in the doorway, except she is not standing.

She is flying. She is hovering in place, her tiny wings moving so fast they are a blur.

I have never seen an imaginary friend fly before.

'How did you know my name?' Oswald asks.

I think about taking advantage of the moment and shoving Oswald to the ground and escaping. Hitting him while he is distracted. But I still need his help, even if he wants to kill me, and I think that this might be my one chance to turn things around.

Might be the fairy's one chance to turn things around.

'Budo is my friend,' the fairy says. 'I don't want you to hurt him.'

'How do you know my name?' Oswald asks again. His surprise is quickly turning to anger. His hands ball up into fists. His nostrils flare.

'Budo needs your help, Oswald,' the fairy says.

I don't know how I know, but I am sure that the fairy is avoiding Oswald's question on purpose. I think she might be trying to figure out the best answer.

'How do you know my name?' Oswald shouts the question this time and moves toward the doorway, straight toward the fairy.

I follow.

I will not let him hurt the fairy like he has hurt me. But as I reach out to grab him, to pull him back and give the fairy enough time to escape, the fairy's eyes and my eyes meet, and she shakes her head ever so gently. She is telling me to stop. Or to wait at least.

I obey.

The fairy is right to tell me to stop.

As Oswald approaches the doorway, he stops, too. He does not reach for the fairy with his giant hands. He can throw me around the room and kick me and choke me but he does not touch the fairy.

'How do you know my name?' Oswald shouts again, and this time I hear something in his voice that I missed the first time. Oswald is angry, but I think that he is curious, too. Hopeful, even. Underneath his anger is something else. I think Oswald is hoping that the fairy's answer to his question is a good one. I think he wants help, too.

'I am a fairy,' the fairy says. 'Do you know what a fairy is?'

'How do you know my name!' Oswald roars the question this time. If Oswald was a human person, every window on the eighth floor would have rattled and every single person in the hospital would have heard his voice.

I have never been more afraid.

The fairy turns and points to the bald man in the bed. 'He is your friend. And he's hurt. Right?'

Oswald stares at her and says nothing. I am standing behind him so I cannot see the expression on Oswald's face, but his fists unclench and I can see the muscles in his arms and back relax a little.

'Oswald,' the fairy says again. 'He is your friend. Right?'

Oswald looks to the bald man and then back to the fairy. He shakes his head up and down.

'And he's hurt?' she asks.

Oswald nods slowly.

'I'm so sorry,' the fairy says. 'Do you know how it happened?'

Oswald nods again.

'Can we go into the hallway and talk?' the fairy asks. 'I can't think straight with that man reading that book.'

I have forgotten that Sleepy Face and his pale friend were even in the room. I stopped hearing about the low hitter once the fairy started speaking. It was like watching a lion-tamer calm down a lion with a toothpick instead of a whip and chair.

No, not a toothpick. A Q-tip. But somehow it worked. The fairy has done it.

Oswald agrees to move into the hallway. But as the fairy turns to leave, she notices that Oswald does not move. She turns back.

'What?' she asks.

'He has to leave, too,' Oswald says, turning and pointing at me.

'Of course,' the fairy says. 'Budo is coming with us.'

Oswald turns and follows the fairy into the hallway. I follow behind him. We walk down a little ways to a space with chairs and lamps and short tables piled with magazines. The fairy sits on a chair. Her wings stop moving. When they are still, they look small and weak and flimsy. I can't believe that she can fly.

Oswald sits on a chair opposite the fairy.

I take a seat in a chair next to the fairy.

'Who are you?' Oswald asks.

'I'm Teeny,' the fairy says.

I feel bad. I never asked her name.

'How do you know my name?' Oswald asks again. Anger is now pure curiosity.

Teeny pauses. I wonder if I should say something to give her more time to think. She looks uncertain. But then she speaks before I can think of something to say.

'I was going to tell you that I am a magical fairy who knows everything in the world, and that you need to listen to me. But I don't want to lie. I know your name is Oswald because Budo told me.'

Oswald says nothing.

I open my mouth to talk but it is Teeny who speaks.

'Budo needs your help, and I was afraid that you might be mean to him like the last time you saw him. So I followed him here.'

'I told him to leave,' Oswald says. 'I warned him.'

'I know. But he needs your help. He had to come.'

'Why?' Oswald asks.

'Because Budo said that you can move things in the real world,' Teeny says. 'Is that true?' She asks the question like she can't believe it herself.

Oswald's bushy eyebrows come together like two caterpillars kissing. He has the same eyebrows as the bald man, I suddenly realize. He looks a lot like the bald man. It's easier to see the resemblance now that I'm not being thrown around the room.

'I saw you push the door to that room open,' I say. 'You can move things in the real world. Right? Like this table? Or these magazines?'

'Yes,' Oswald says. 'But it's hard.'

'Hard?' Teeny asks.

'Everything in the real world is heavy. A lot heavier than you,' he says, pointing to me.

'You would know,' I say.

The caterpillars kiss again.

'Never mind,' I say.

'And I could never move a table,' he says. 'Even a little one like this is too heavy.'

'But you can move small things,' I say. 'Right?'

Oswald nods.

'How long have you been alive?' Teeny asks.

'I don't know,' Oswald says. He looks down at his feet.

'What is your friend's name?' Teeny asks.

'Who?'

'The man in the bed.'

'Oh,' Oswald says. 'He is John.'

'Did you know him before he was hurt?' I ask.

I think about the little girl without a name in the Intensive Care Unit. I wonder if Oswald is like her.

'Only for a second,' Oswald says. 'He was on the ground. His head was broken. He looked up at me and smiled and then he closed his eyes.'

'And you followed him here?' I ask.

'Yes.' Oswald pauses, and then he says, 'I wish John would open his eyes and smile again.'

'Can you help Budo?' Teeny asks.

'How?'

'I need you to help my friend,' I say. 'He isn't hurt like John, but he is in big trouble, and I can't save him without you.'

'Will I have to go down the stairs? I don't like the stairs.'

'You will have to go far away,' Teeny says. 'Down the stairs and outside and far away. But it is important and John would want you to do it. And when you're done, Budo will bring you right back here. Okay?'

'No,' Oswald says. 'I can't.'

'Yes you can,' Teeny says. 'You have to. A little boy is in trouble and only you can save him.'

'I don't want to,' Oswald says.

'I know,' Teeny says. 'But you have to do it. A little boy is in trouble. We can't say no to little boys in trouble. Right?'

'Right,' Oswald says.

CHAPTER 49

'How did you do that?' I ask as we walk down the hallway toward the elevators.

I am walking alongside Teeny, who is flying down the hall. Her wings make a humming sound that I did not hear when I was in the bald man's room. Even this close, her wings move so fast that they are nothing but a blur.

Oswald is behind us, head down, looking like a snow-plow again.

'How did I do what?' Teeny asks.

'Everything,' I say, lowering my voice to a whisper. 'How did you know that Oswald wouldn't attack you like he attacked me? How did you convince him to help me? How did you even know where I was?'

'The last question is easy,' Teeny says. 'You told us what floor you found Oswald on the first time. A couple minutes after you left, I decided that you might need some help. So I walked over to the grown-up hospital and flew up the

347

stairs to the eighth floor. By the time I got up here, finding you was easy. The two of you were making such a racket that I knew right where to go.'

'That racket was me getting tossed around the room like a doll.'

'I know,' Teeny says, smiling.

'Okay, how did you know that Oswald wouldn't attack you like he attacked me?' I ask.

'I didn't go into his room,' Teeny says. 'I stayed at the doorway.'

'I don't get it.'

'You told us that Oswald found you sneaking up behind him the first time you met. Right outside his room. And later on he found you in his room. I thought that if I didn't go into the room, he probably wouldn't hurt me. Plus I'm a girl. And a fairy. You'd have to be a real stinker to hit a fairy.'

'You were imagined smart,' I say.

Teeny smiles again.

'How long have you been alive?' I ask.

'Almost three years.'

'That's a long time for someone like us,' I say.

'Not nearly as long as you.'

'No, but it's still a long time. You're lucky.'

We turn a corner and pass a man in a wheelchair talking to himself. I look around for an imaginary friend but see none. I turn to check on Oswald. He is about three steps behind us, plowing away. I turn back to Teeny.

'How did you get Oswald to help me?' I whisper. 'All you did was ask him to help, and he said yes.'

'I did what Mom always does when she wants Aubrey to do something.'

'Aubrey is your human friend?' I ask.

'Yes. She has something wrong in her head that the doctors have to fix. That's why she is in the hospital.'

'What does your mom do when she wants Aubrey to do something?' I ask.

'When Mom wants Aubrey to do her homework or brush her teeth or eat her broccoli, she doesn't tell Aubrey to do it. She makes it sound like it's Aubrey's choice. Like it's Aubrey's only choice. Like not eating the broccoli would be wrong.'

'That was it?' I ask. 'That's all you did?'

I try to remember everything that Teeny said to Oswald but it all happened so fast.

'It was easy with Oswald, because not helping you was a really wrong thing to do. A lot more wrong than not eating broccoli or not brushing his teeth. And I asked him questions, too. I tried to show him I cared, because I thought that he was probably lonely. There aren't too many imaginary friends in a grown-up hospital. Right?'

'You really were imagined smart,' I say.

Teeny smiles again. For the first time since Graham disappeared, I think I may have found an imaginary friend who could be my friend, too.

We reach the elevators and I turn to Oswald. 'Do you want to ride on the elevator or take the stairs?'

'I never rode on the elevator before,' he says.

'Do you want to take the stairs, then?' I ask.

'I don't like the stairs,' he says, looking down at his feet.

'Okay. We'll take the elevator then. It will be fun.'

We stand by the elevators, waiting for someone to come along and press the down button. I think about asking Oswald to press the button, just so I could see him move something in the real world again, but I decide not to. He said that it was hard to move things in the real world, so there is no need to make him work when someone else can do the work for him. He is nervous enough already.

It doesn't take long before a man in a white coat comes along, pushing another man in a wheelchair. The man in the white coat pushes the down arrow and when the door slides open, Oswald, Teeny and I step in behind him.

'I never rode in an elevator before,' Oswald says again.

'It's fun,' I say. 'You'll like it.'

But Oswald looks nervous. So does Teeny.

The man pushing the wheelchair presses the number three and the elevator begins to move. Oswald's eyes widen. His hands bunch into fists.

'The men are getting out on the third floor. We will, too. We can take the stairs from there.'

'Okay,' Oswald says, looking relieved.

I want to tell him that riding from the third to the first floor in an elevator would only take an extra five seconds, but I let him feel relieved instead. He doesn't like the stairs, so he must hate the elevator.

I think Teeny does, too.

The door slides open and we follow the man and the wheelchair into the hallway.

'The stairs are around the corner,' I say.

As I speak, I notice the sign on the wall opposite the elevators. In between the directions for restrooms and a place called *Radiation* is this:

← INTENSIVE CARE UNIT

I stop.

I stare at the sign for a moment.

'What?' Teeny asks when I do not move.

'Can you and Oswald wait here for a minute?' I ask Teeny.

'Why?'

351

'I want to check on somebody. I think she is on this floor.'

'Who?' Teeny asks.

'A friend,' I say. 'Sort of a friend, I mean. I think she is down the hall.'

Teeny stares at me. She narrows her eyes to slits. I feel like she is trying to look straight through me.

'Okay,' she finally says. 'We can wait. Right, Oswald?'

'Okay,' Oswald says.

I turn left. I follow the signs like I did when I found the ICU in the Children's Hospital. After two long hallways and one turn, I find myself standing outside a set of double doors that look a lot like the doors to the children's ICU. The name tag on the doors reads *Intensive Care Unit*.

I pass through them.

I am standing in a large room with curtains along the outside edges of the room. Some of the curtains are closed and some are open. There is a long counter and desks and lots of machines in the center of the room. Doctors are moving around, going in and out of the curtains, typing on computers, talking on the telephones, talking to each other, writing things down on clipboards, and looking worried.

All doctors look worried, but these doctors look extra worried.

I start with the curtain closest to me. It is closed. I crawl under it. An old woman is lying in the bed behind it. She has gray hair and lots of wrinkles around her eyes. She has machines with wires and tubes hooked up to her arms and a thin plastic tube stuck underneath her nose. She is sleeping.

I move to the next curtain and then the next. When the curtain is closed, I crawl underneath. Some of the beds are empty and some have people in them. All grown-ups. Mostly men. Two of the curtains have no beds at all.

I find Dee behind the last curtain. I do not realize that it is Dee at first. Her head is shaved. She is as bald as Oswald's bald friend. She is as bald as Oswald. Her cheeks are swollen and the skin around her eyes is black. She has the most machines attached to her of anyone I've seen so far. Tubes and wires run from bags of water and machines with tiny television screens to her arm and chest. The machines make hissing, beeping, clicking sounds.

There is a woman sitting in a chair next to Dee. She is holding Dee's hand. It is Dee's sister. I know this because she looks just like Dee. A younger version of Dee. Same dark skin. Same sharp chin. Same round eyes. She is whispering words into Dee's ear. She whispers the same words over and over again. Words like *God* and *Jesus* and *Almighty* and *praise*. I can barely hear her.

Dee does not look good. She looks very bad.

Dee's sister does not look good, either. She looks tired and scared.

I sit on the edge of the bed next to Dee's sister. I look down at Dee. I want to cry, except I do not have time to cry. Teeny and Oswald are waiting by the elevators and Mrs Patterson is packing her secret bus with food and clothes. I have to go.

'I'm sorry you are hurt,' I say to Dee. 'I'm so sorry. I wish I could have saved you. I miss you.'

Tears fill my eyes. This is only the second time that my eyes have made tears and they feel strange. Slippery and hot.

'I have to save Max,' I tell Dee. 'I couldn't save you, but I think I can save Max. So I have to go now.'

I stand up to leave. I look back at Dee's pale face and thin wrists. I listen to her raspy, uneven breath and the whispers of her sister and the steady beep of the machine beside her bed. I look and I listen. Then I sit back down.

'I'm afraid,' I say to Dee. 'I couldn't save you, but maybe I can save Max. Except I'm scared. Max is in trouble, but I think his trouble is good for me. If he stays in trouble, I stay alive. So I'm confused.'

I take a deep breath. I think about what I want to say next, but when nothing comes to my mind, I just start talking again.

'It's not like Max is going to be shot by a man in a devil

mask. It's not that kind of trouble at all. Mrs Patterson will take good care of Max. I know it. She is a devil, too, but not the kind that shot you. Max will be fine no matter what I do. But I might not be fine. I don't know what is going to happen to me. And now I have Oswald helping me, so I really might be able to save Max. I never thought that Oswald would agree to help, but he has. Now I can save Max, I think. Except I'm afraid.'

I sit and stare at Dee. I listen to her sister whisper her words over and over again. They sound almost like a song.

'I know saving Max is the right thing to do,' I say to Dee. 'But it won't matter if I do the right thing if I stop existing too. The right thing is good only if you are here to enjoy it.'

I feel more hot, slippery tears in my eyes, but these are not for Dee. They are for me.

'I wish there was a Heaven. If I knew there was a Heaven for me, then I would save Max for sure. I wouldn't be afraid because there would be a place to go after this place. Another place. But I don't think there is a Heaven, and I definitely don't think there is a Heaven for imaginary friends. Heaven is supposed to be only for people who God made, and God didn't make me. Max made me.'

I smile, thinking about Max as a god. A god locked up in

a basement with a bunch of Lego and army men. The god of one. The God of Budo.

'I guess that's why I should save him,' I say. 'Because he made me. I wouldn't be alive without him. But I'm afraid, and I feel bad for being afraid. I feel even worse for thinking about leaving Max with Mrs Patterson. Even though I know I will try to save him, I think about not saving him and that makes me feel bad. Like a real stinker. But it's not wrong to be worried about myself, too. Right?'

'No.'

This is not Dee's sister or a doctor who speaks. It is Dee.

I know she can't hear me because I am an imaginary friend. But the word sounds like an answer to my question. It surprises me. Just Dee speaking surprises me. I gasp.

'Dee?' her sister says. 'What did you say?'

'Don't be afraid,' Dee says.

'Don't be afraid of what?' her sister asks. She is squeezing Dee's hand. Leaning in closer and closer.

'Are you talking to me?' I ask.

Dee's eyes are open now, but they are only teeny, tiny slits. I look to see if she is looking at me, but I can't tell.

'Don't be afraid,' Dee says again. Her voice is thin and whispery but the words are clear.

'Doctor!' Dee's sister shouts, turning her head toward the counter and the desks in the center of the room. 'My sister is awake. She's talking!'

Two doctors stand up and move in our direction.

'Are you talking to me, Dee?' I ask again. I know she is not. She can't be. But it seems like she is.

'Go,' Dee says. 'Go. It's time.'

'Me?' I ask. 'Are you talking to me? Dee?'

The doctors arrive. They pull the curtains all the way open. A doctor asks Dee's sister to step aside. The other doctor walks to the opposite side of the bed as an alarm sound begins ringing. Dee's eyes roll back in her head. The doctors move faster, and I am pushed off the bed and onto the floor by another doctor who has just arrived. He shoved me out of the way without even knowing it.

'She was just talking!' Dee's sister says.

'She's crashing!' one of the doctors shouts.

Another doctor takes Dee's sister by the shoulder and moves her away from the bed. Two more doctors arrive. I move to the end of the bed. I can barely see Dee. The doctors are crowding around her. One of the doctors puts a plastic bag over Dee's mouth and starts squeezing it open and shut. Another doctor sticks a needle into a tube that is connected to Dee's arm. I watch as a yellow liquid moves up the tube and disappears under Dee's nightgown.

Dee is dying.

I can tell by the look on the doctors' faces. They are working hard and fast but they are just doing what they are supposed to do. I see the same look on the faces of some of

357

Max's teachers when Max doesn't understand something and the teacher doesn't think he will ever understand it. The teachers work hard but you can tell that they are just doing the lesson. Not teaching the lesson. That's what the doctors look like now. They are doing the doctoring but they do not believe in the doctoring.

Dee's eyes close.

I hear her words ringing in my head.

Go. It's time. Don't be afraid.

CHAPTER 50

We are standing at the front doors to the hospital. Snow is falling outside. Oswald says that he has never seen snow. I tell him that he will love it.

'Thank you,' I say to Teeny.

She smiles. I know she can't leave Aubrey, but I wish she could come with us.

'Are you ready, Oswald?' I ask.

The lobby is busy. It is full of people coming and going. Oswald looks even bigger now that I can compare him to so many other people. He is a giant.

'No,' Oswald says. 'I want to stay here.'

'But you will go with Budo and help him,' Teeny says. This is not a question. It is a command.

'Yes,' Oswald says.

The word is *yes* but the sound is *no*.

'Good,' Teeny says, and then she flies over to Oswald and hugs his neck, too.

He gasps. His muscles tense. His hands ball into fists again. Teeny keeps squeezing until he finally relaxes. It takes a long time.

'And good luck,' she adds. 'I want to see both of you again. Soon.'

'Okay,' Oswald says.

'You will,' I say.

But I do not believe it. I think this is the last time I will ever see Teeny or this hospital again.

Oswald spends the first five minutes outside trying to avoid the falling snowflakes. He dodges one while ten other flakes pass through him. He doesn't even notice.

Once he realizes that they will not hurt him, he spends the next five minutes trying to catch snowflakes on his tongue. They pass through his tongue, of course, but it takes him a while to realize this, and he bounces off at least three people and a telephone pole while doing so.

'We have to go,' I say to Oswald.

'Where?'

'We have to go home. We have to ride the bus to school tomorrow.'

'I have never been on a bus before,' Oswald says.

I can see that he is nervous. I decide to tell him as little as possible from now on.

'It will be fun,' I say. 'I promise.'

It is a long walk from the hospital to Max's house. I usually enjoy the walk, but Oswald asks questions. Lots and lots of questions.

When do they turn the street lights on?

Does each street light have a separate switch?

Where did all the choo-choo trains go?

Why don't people just draw their own money?

Who decided that red means stop and green means go?

Is there only one moon?

Are all car honks the same?

How do the police stop trees from growing in the middle of the street?

Do people paint their own cars?

What is a fire hydrant?

Why don't people whistle when they walk?

Where do airplanes live when they are not flying?

The questions never stop, and even though I want them to stop, I keep answering. This giant who was throwing me around a hospital room earlier today needs me now, and as long as he needs me, I hope that he will listen to me and help me.

Ever since we left Teeny behind at the hospital, I have been afraid that Oswald would turn into his old, angry self. That Teeny's magic would wear off after we got far enough away. Instead he has become more like a preschooler who wants to know everything.

'This is my house,' I say to Oswald as we finally turn up the driveway.

It is late. I do not know how late, but the lights in the kitchen and the living room are turned off.

'Where are we going?' Oswald asks.

'Inside. Do you sleep?'

'When?' Oswald asks.

'Do you sleep at all?'

'Oh. Yes.'

'This is where we will sleep tonight,' I say, pointing at the house.

'How will I get in?' he asks.

'Through the door,' I say.

'How?'

Then I realize it. Oswald can't pass through doors. In the hospital, when we took the stairs from the third floor to the first floor, we followed two men in blue uniforms through the door to the stairway. When we left the hospital, we followed a man and a woman.

This is why Oswald pushed open the door to the bald man's room. John's room. He had to push it open if he wanted to get in.

'Can you open the door?' I ask.

'I don't know,' Oswald says. But I can see that he is looking at the door like it is a mountain.

'It'll be locked,' I say, which is true. 'Never mind.'

'How would you normally get in?' Oswald asks.

'I can pass through doors.'

'Pass through?'

I climb three steps to the front door of the house and then pass through. I actually pass through two doors. A screen door and a wooden door. Then I turn around and pass back through to the outside.

Oswald's mouth is hanging open when I reappear on the other side. His eyes are gigantic.

'You're magic,' he says.

'No, you're magic,' I say. 'I know lots of imaginary friends who can pass through doors. But I don't know any imaginary friends who can touch the real world.'

'Imaginary friends?'

I realize that I have said too much again.

'Yes,' I say. 'I'm an imaginary friend.' I pause for a moment, thinking about what to say next. Then I add, 'So are you.'

'I'm an imaginary friend?' Oswald asks.

'Yes. What did you think you were?'

'A ghost,' he says. 'I thought you were a ghost, too. I thought you were going to steal John away from me.'

I laugh. 'Nope. No ghosts here. What did you think Teeny was?'

'A fairy,' Oswald says.

I laugh again, but then I realize that this probably helped Teeny convince Oswald to help me.

'I guess you're half right about Teeny,' I say. 'She's a fairy, but she is imaginary, too.'

'Oh.'

'You look upset,' I say.

And he does. He is looking at his feet again and his arms are hanging by his side like wet noodles.

'I don't know which is better,' Oswald says. 'Imaginary or a ghost.'

'What's the difference?' I ask.

'If I am a ghost, that means I was alive once. If I'm imaginary, that means I was never alive.'

There is silence between us as we stare at one another. I don't know what to say. Then I do.

'I have an idea,' I say.

I say this because I really do have an idea, but mostly because I want to change the subject.

'Do you think you could press the doorbell?'

'Where?' Oswald asks, and I can tell by the question that he does not know what a doorbell is.

'This little dot,' I say, pointing at the button. 'If you press it down, a bell will ring inside the house and Max's parents will open the door. When they do, we can slip inside.'

'I thought you could pass through the door?' Oswald says.

'Yes, I can. Sorry. I meant *you* could slip inside.'

'Okay,' Oswald says.

He says *okay* a lot, and I can't help but think of Max every time he does. Max will be alone tonight, locked in Mrs Patterson's basement, and the thought of that makes me feel sad and rotten.

I promised him that I would never leave. Now I am here with Oswald.

But tomorrow night Max will be sleeping in his own bed. I say these words in my head, and they make me feel a little better.

Oswald climbs the three steps to the landing. He reaches out to press the doorbell, but before he does, his entire body stiffens. The muscles in his arms and neck pop out. A vein in his forehead appears and throbs. The caterpillars above his eyes kiss again. He clenches his teeth. His hand shakes as he reaches out with his finger. It touches the button, and for a second, nothing happens. Then his hand shakes even more and I hear Oswald grunt. As he grunts, the button disappears under his finger and the bell rings.

'You did it!' I say, and even though I have seen him touch the real world before, I am still amazed.

Oswald nods. There are tiny beads of sweat on his forehead and he is trying to catch his breath. He looks like he just ran twenty miles.

I hear someone moving inside the house. We stand back so the door doesn't knock Oswald off the stoop. The wooden door opens inward. Max's mom steps into the doorway and peers out through the screen door. She cups her hands over her eyes. She looks back and forth, and now I can see that this was not a good idea.

I can see hope in her face.

She was thinking that this might be good news. She was thinking that it might be Max.

She opens the screen door and steps out onto the stoop beside Oswald. It is cold outside. The snow has stopped but I can see her breath in the freezing air. She wraps her arms around her body to stay warm. I nudge Oswald forward as Max's mom says, 'Hello? Is anyone there?'

'Go inside,' I say. 'Wait for me.'

Oswald does as I say. I watch as Max's mom calls out one more time, and then the hope disappears from her face.

'Who is it?' Max's dad says. He is standing in the kitchen now. Oswald is standing beside him.

'No one,' Max's mom says. Her words sound like boulders. She can barely pick them up to say them.

'Who the fuck rings a person's doorbell at ten at night and then runs away?' Max's dad says.

'Maybe it was a mistake,' Max's mom says. She sounds far away even though she is standing right beside me.

'Fuck that,' Max's dad says. 'No one makes that kind of mistake and then disappears.'

Max's mom starts to cry. She would have cried anyway,

366

I think, but the word *disappears* hits her like one of those boulders. Her tears pour out.

Max's dad knows it. He knows what he has done.

'Honey, I'm sorry.'

He puts his arms around her and pulls her back from the doorway, letting the screen door close behind him. No whack-whack-whack this time. They stand in the kitchen, holding each other, as Max's mom cries and cries and cries. She cries harder than I have ever heard a person cry before.

The door to Max's bedroom is closed, so I tell Oswald to sleep on the couch in the living room. He is so long that his feet hang off the end of the couch. They dangle in the air like two enormous fishing poles.

'Are you comfortable?' I ask.

'When someone is sleeping in the bed next to John, I have to sleep on the floor. This is better than the floor.'

'Good. Sleep tight, then.'

'Wait,' Oswald says. 'Are you going to sleep now?'

I don't want to tell Oswald that I don't sleep. I think it will just make him ask more questions. So I say yes. 'I'll just sleep in this chair. I do it a lot.'

'Before I go to sleep, I always talk to John.'

'You do? What do you tell him?'

'I tell him about my day,' Oswald says. 'What I did. Who

367

I saw. I can't wait to tell him about all the things I saw today.'

'Do you want to tell me about your day?'

'No,' Oswald says. 'You already know about my day. You were with me.'

'Oh,' I say. 'Then do you want to tell me something else?'

'No, I want you to tell me about your friend.'

'Max?' I ask.

'Yes,' Oswald says. 'Tell me about Max. I never had a friend who could walk and talk.'

'Okay,' I say. 'I will tell you about Max.'

I start with the easy stuff. I talk about what Max looks like and what he likes to eat. I tell him about the Lego and the army men and the video games. I explain how Max is different than other kids because he can get stuck and he lives mostly on the inside.

Then I tell the stories. I tell the story about Max's first Halloween party in kindergarten and his bonus poops and his fight with Tommy Swinden in the boys' bathroom and the rock that Tommy Swinden threw through Max's bedroom window last week. I talk about how Max's mom makes Max try new things and how Max's dad likes to use the word *normal* a lot. I tell him about the games of catch in the backyard and the way I help Max choose between a red or green shirt when he can't decide.

And I tell him about Mrs Gosk. I tell him about how she

is almost perfect except when she calls Max *my boy* but that is close enough to perfect to make her perfect.

I do not talk about Mrs Patterson. I'm afraid that if I do, Oswald might be too afraid to help me tomorrow.

Oswald does not ask any questions. Twice I think he has fallen asleep. I stop talking and he lifts his head, looks at me, and says, 'What?'

'Do you know what I like best about Max?' I ask.

'No,' he says. 'I don't know Max.'

'The thing I like best about Max is that he is brave.'

'What did he do that was brave?'

'It's not one thing,' I say. 'It's everything. Max is not like any other person in the whole world. Kids make fun of him because he is different. His mom tries to change him into a different boy and his dad tries to treat him like he is someone else. Even his teachers treat him differently, and not always nicely. Even Mrs Gosk. She is perfect but she still treats Max differently. No one treats him like a regular boy, but everyone wants him to be regular instead of himself. With all that, Max still gets out of bed every morning and goes to school and the park and even the bus stop.'

'That's brave?' Oswald asks.

'That's the bravest,' I say. 'I am the oldest, smartest imaginary friend I have ever met. It is easy for me to go out and meet other imaginary friends because they all look up to me. They ask me questions and want to be like me. When they are not beating me up.'

I smile at Oswald.

He does not smile back.

'But you have to be the bravest person in the world to go out every day being yourself when no one likes who you are. I could never be as brave as Max.'

'I wish I had a Max,' Oswald says. 'I never even heard John talk.'

'Maybe he will someday.'

'Maybe,' Oswald says, but I don't think he believes it.

'Can we go to sleep now?' I ask.

'Yes,' Oswald says, and he does not say another word. He falls asleep almost immediately.

I sit in a chair and watch him sleep. I try to imagine tomorrow. I make a list of all the things I need to do to save Max. I try to predict where my plan might go wrong. I think about what I will say to Max when the time comes.

This will be the most important part. I cannot save Max alone. I will need Oswald's help, but, most of all, I will need Max.

I cannot save Max unless I can convince him to save himself.

CHAPTER 51

Mrs Gosk once read a story to the class about a boy named Pinocchio. The kids laughed when they heard that she was going to read the story to them. They thought it was for babies.

It is never a good idea to laugh at Mrs Gosk.

Once she started reading, the kids realized how wrong they were. They loved the story. They didn't want her to stop reading. They wanted to hear more and more and more. But every day Mrs Gosk would stop at the most suspenseful moment in the book and make the kids wait until the next day to find out what happened next. They begged her to read more and she would say, 'You can take charge of this classroom when pigs fly!' This made them all so mad. Even Max. He loved the story, too. I think Mrs Gosk did this on purpose just to punish her students for laughing at her.

Never mess with Mrs Gosk.

Pinocchio was a puppet who was carved from a magical block of wood by a man named Geppetto. Even though he was supposed to be a puppet, Pinocchio was alive. He could move around on his own and talk and his nose even grew longer when he lied. But Pinocchio spent most of the time wishing that he could become a real boy.

I hated Pinocchio. I think I was the only one in the class who hated him. Pinocchio was alive, but that was not enough for him. He could walk and talk and touch things in the real world, but he spent the whole book wanting more.

Pinocchio didn't know how lucky he was.

I started thinking about Pinocchio tonight because of what Oswald said about ghosts and imaginary friends. I think he was right. Being a ghost would be better. Ghosts were alive once. Imaginary friends are never alive in the real world.

If you are a ghost, you don't stop existing if someone stops believing in you. Or forgets about you. Or finds someone better than you to take your place.

If I was a ghost, I could exist for ever.

I forgot about getting Oswald out of the house this morning. My first mistake of the day. Making a mistake before we even leave the house is not a good sign.

I think we will still be okay. Max's mom goes for a run on

most mornings, and Max's dad usually leaves for work before the bus comes. Plus he sometimes goes outside to pick up the newspaper off the front lawn. Sometimes he just picks it up and brings it to work with him, but sometimes he brings it inside to read while he is eating breakfast. We just need someone to open the door once and Oswald will be able to get outside.

Max's mom walks into the kitchen at 7.30. She is quiet. She is wearing her robe. Even though she just woke up, she still looks tired. She brews a pot of coffee and eats toast with jam. She is not my mother, but she is the closest thing to a mom that I will ever have, and I hate to see her so small and tired and sad. I try to picture her screaming with joy when she sees Max tonight. I try to erase the picture of her from right now, all tired and worn out, and replace it with my picture from the future. I will fix her. I will save Max and that will save her, too.

Max's dad finally opens the door at 7.48 according to the clock on the microwave above the stove. He is still wearing sweat pants. I don't think he is going to work. He looks tired. Even though Max's mom and dad were hugging last night, I can tell that there is something wrong between them. Max's dad does not talk to Max's mom. He says, 'Good morning,' and nothing else. And she does not talk to him. It's like an invisible wall is standing between them.

Max always gave them lots of reasons to fight, but I think that Max also gave them a reason to love each other. But now they are losing hope. They are starting to think that they might never see Max again. And without Max, there is nothing to hold them together. It's almost like Max is still here, except now he is just a reminder of what they have lost.

I have a lot of saving to do today.

The bus stops at Max's house at 7.55, but the bus will not stop at Max's house today. We have to go to the Savoys' house, and that means we will have to run as fast as we can. We cannot miss the bus because I am not sure if I can find the school on my own. I might be able to, but I do not pay enough attention to the streets when we drive. I might not.

Oswald starts to ask questions as soon as we step outside.

'What is that little box at the end of the driveway?' he asks.

'The mailbox,' I say.

'What's a mailbox?' he asks.

I stop and turn. 'If we do not catch that bus, we can't save Max. You can ask me as many questions as you want once we are on that bus, but we have to run as fast as we can right now if we are going to catch it. Okay?'

'Okay,' Oswald says and he starts to run. He is a giant but he can run fast. I can barely keep up with him.

The bus passes us when we are two driveways away from the Savoys' house. I am sure that we will never make it to the bus stop in time. But there are three Savoy boys and a first-grade girl named Patty who all get on the bus at this stop, so they might slow down the bus driver a little while they climb aboard. Probably not enough, but there is a chance.

Then I see our chance. As Jerry Savoy is getting ready to step onto the bus, his big brother, Henry, knocks the books out of Jerry's hands and laughs. The books fall to the ground in front of the steps, and one book tumbles under the bus. Jerry has to bend over to collect them, and he has to get on his hands and knees to reach the book that landed under the bus. Henry Savoy is a big, mean jerk, but today he has done me a favor. Henry doesn't know it, and Jerry doesn't know it, but they may have just saved Max. We reach the Savoys' bus stop just in time to squeeze through the door behind Patty.

Ten seconds later and the bus would have already been moving.

I try to catch my breath as I point Oswald to the seat where Max and I usually sit.

'Why do kids ride buses?' Oswald asks. 'Why don't their moms just drive them to school?'

'I don't know,' I say. 'Maybe some people don't have cars.'

'I've never ridden on a bus before.'

'I know,' I say. 'How do you like it?'

'It's not as exciting as I thought it would be.'

'Thanks for running so fast.'

'I want to save Max,' Oswald says.

'You do?'

'Yeah.'

'Why?' I ask. 'You don't even know him.'

'He is the bravest boy in the world. You said so. He pooped on Tommy Swinden's head and goes to school every day even though no one likes him. We have to save Max.'

Listening to Oswald say these words makes me feel warm inside. This must be how Mrs Gosk feels when she tells a story that becomes a part of her students.

'Except how are we going to save Max?' Oswald asks. 'You didn't tell me that yet.'

I decide it is time. I spend the next ten minutes telling Oswald everything I know about Mrs Patterson.

'You're right,' Oswald says when I am finished. 'She is the devil. She is a little-boy-stealing devil.'

'Yes,' I say. 'But you know what? I don't think Mrs Patterson knows that she is the devil. She thinks that Max's parents are the devils. She thinks that what she is doing is right. I still don't like her, but it makes me hate her a little less.'

'Maybe we are all somebody's devil,' Oswald says. 'Maybe even me and you.'

As he says these last four words, I notice for the first time that I can see the houses and the last few brightly colored leaves flashing by the windows as the bus moves down the street.

I can see the trees flashing by *through him*.

Oswald is fading away.

It makes no sense. What are the chances that Oswald would start to fade away on the very day I need him? On the day that Max needs him?

It doesn't seem fair.

It seems impossible.

It feels like one of those television shows where too many bad things happen at once and the show feels fake.

Then I realize what has happened. It is my fault. Oswald is dying because of me.

Oswald said that before he went to sleep, he would spend every night talking to John. He would tell John what he did and who he saw, and after he was done telling about his day, he would fall asleep.

This must have been what kept John believing in Oswald. John must have been able to hear Oswald tell his stories every night. Either with his ears or maybe just inside his head. Inside his mind. Maybe this is why Oswald existed in the first place. John is trapped in a body that won't wake up, so Oswald is like John's eyes and ears. His window on the outside world.

I thought that Oswald could move things in the real world because John is a grown-up. I never met an imaginary friend whose human person friend was a grown-up, so I thought this was what made Oswald special. This was what gave Oswald his special powers.

But maybe Oswald can move things in the real world because John can't move things anymore. Maybe John is so sad about being stuck in his coma that he imagined Oswald being able to move things because he couldn't. Maybe Oswald is John's window to the world and the way that John can still touch the real world.

Except now I have taken that window away. Oswald was not able to talk to John last night, and now John has stopped believing in his imaginary friend.

Oswald is dying because of me.

Oswald was right. Everyone is somebody's devil, and I am Oswald's devil.

CHAPTER 52

We are sitting in Mrs Gosk's classroom. Mrs Gosk is telling a story about her daughters, Stephanie and Chelsea. She is still not herself. I can see the sadness in her eyes. She does not bounce around the room like the floor is on fire. But the kids are still sitting on the edges of their chairs. Oswald is sitting on the edge of his chair. He cannot take his eyes off Mrs Gosk. I think this is the only reason that he hasn't noticed that he is disappearing. He is disappearing fast. Much faster than Graham. I'm worried that he might be completely gone by the end of the school day.

Oswald turns to me.

I brace myself. He knows that he is fading away. I can feel it.

'I love Mrs Gosk,' he says.

I smile.

Oswald turns his attention back to Mrs Gosk. She has finished telling the story about her daughters. She is talking about something called a predicate now. I do not know what a predicate is. I don't think Oswald knows either, but he seems more interested in predicates than anyone else in the room. His eyes are glued to Mrs Gosk.

I know what I have to do. I don't know how I will do it, but I have to find a way. It is the right thing to do.

It feels impossible to do the wrong thing when Mrs Gosk is in the room.

'Oswald, we have to go,' I say.

'Where?' he asks, still staring at Mrs Gosk.

'The hospital.'

He turns to me. Those caterpillars above his eyes kiss again. 'What about Max? We have to save him.'

'Oswald, you're disappearing.'

'You know?' he asks.

'You know?' I ask.

'Yes. I noticed when I woke up this morning. I could see through my hands. You didn't say anything, so I thought that maybe only I could see it.'

'No, I can see it, and I've seen it happen before. You're going to disappear completely if we don't get you back to John.'

'Maybe,' Oswald says, but he does not believe maybe. He believes definitely, just like me.

'Not maybe,' I say. 'I know it. John believes in you because he hears you talking to him every night. But he didn't hear you last night because you were with me. That is why you're disappearing. We have to get you back to him.'

'But what about Max?' Oswald asks. There is a tiny bit of anger in his voice that surprises me.

'Max is my friend, and I know that he wouldn't want you to die saving him. It's not right.'

'I want to save Max,' Oswald says. 'And I get to choose.'

His fists clench and he glares at me. I can't help but wonder if even Oswald is forced to do the right thing when Mrs Gosk is in the room.

'I know you want to save him,' I say. 'But not today. We have to get you back to John. You can save Max tomorrow.'

'I might not get back to John in time,' Oswald says. 'And even if I did, I can't feel John anymore. I think it's too late.'

I think so, too. I remember what happened when I tried to save Graham. I'm starting to believe that once an imaginary friend begins to disappear, nothing can stop it. But I don't want to be the one to say it aloud.

'You're going to die unless we do something,' I say.

'It's okay. I know.'

'You're not going to become a ghost if that's what you're thinking. You're just going to disappear for ever. It will be like you were never here.'

'Not if I save Max,' Oswald says. 'If I save the bravest boy in the world, it will be like I am here for ever.'

'That's not true,' I say. 'You'll be gone and no one will remember you. Max won't even remember you. It will be like you never even existed.'

'Do you know why I was so angry when you met me?' Oswald asks.

'You thought I was a ghost. And you thought I was going to steal John.'

'Yes, but not really. It was because when I was in that hospital, it was like I didn't exist. I was stuck in that room and in those hallways with no one to talk to and nothing to see or do. Maybe I'm not a ghost, but it was like I was a ghost.'

'This is ridiculous,' I say.

And it is. I feel like Oswald and I have switched places. I am angry and scared and ready to punch someone in the face, and he is so stupidly calm. He is disappearing right in front of his own eyes but he doesn't even care. He doesn't want to fight.

He reminds me of Graham after our plan to save her failed. She quit, too.

Then Oswald does the unbelievable. Oswald reaches out and hugs me. He wraps his giant arms around me and squeezes. He lifts me right out of my seat. It's the first time he has touched me without hurting me, and it makes no sense. Oswald is disappearing but I am the one being hugged.

'I knew I was disappearing this morning when I looked through my hands,' he says, still squeezing. 'I was scared at first, but I was scared the whole time I was in the hospital, too. And now I got to meet you and Teeny. I rode on an elevator and a bus. I got to see Mrs Gosk. And I will save Max. That is more than I have ever done in my whole life.'

'Just think about all you could still do,' I say.

Oswald puts me down. Our eyes meet.

'Not if I have to stay in the hospital every day. I'd rather have one good adventure than stay at the hospital for ever.'

'It's wrong not to try to get you back to the hospital,' I say. 'I feel like we're giving up.'

'It's wrong not to help Max,' Oswald says. 'He's the bravest little boy in the whole world. He needs to be saved.'

'You can save him after you save yourself.'

Oswald suddenly looks angry. It's the kind of anger that I saw on his face just before he started throwing me around the hospital room. His muscles tighten and he seems to grow six more inches.

Then just as quickly I see him change again. His fists unclench. His muscles relax. His face softens. It is not anger anymore. It is disappointment.

Disappointment in me.

'Stop,' he says. 'I want to listen to Mrs Gosk. Okay? I just want to sit here and listen to Mrs Gosk until we have to go.'

'Okay,' I say.

I want to say more but I am afraid. I am not afraid because Oswald is angry or disappointed in me, even though that hurts more than I thought it could. I am afraid because I need Oswald. I cannot save Max without him. I am glad that he wants to save Max instead of himself, but that makes me feel awful inside for wanting it. Like I am the worst imaginary friend who ever lived.

Max is the bravest little boy in the world, but Oswald is the bravest imaginary friend in the world.

CHAPTER 53

Oswald stays with Mrs Gosk all day. He even follows her into the bathroom. I tell him not to, but I don't think he understands about bathroom privacy.

I stay with Mrs Gosk for most of the day, too. I keep an eye on Oswald. I am worried that he will disappear before he can help me save Max. I stare at his transparent body and try to guess how much longer he has. It is impossible to tell. It makes me crazy just thinking about it.

I also check on Mrs Patterson. The first thing I did when we arrived at school was check to be sure that Mrs Patterson is working today. She is. We saw her getting out of her car as the bus pulled into the circle.

Everything is going according to my plan. Except that the most important person for my plan to work is disappearing before my eyes.

Even though the school day ends at 3.20, Oswald and I leave Mrs Gosk's classroom at 3 p.m. Oswald has to climb into Mrs Patterson's car when she opens the door, so I want him to be ready.

He says goodbye to Mrs Gosk before he leaves. He walks up to the front of the room and tells her that she is the greatest teacher in the world. He tells her that sitting in her room was the best day of his life. I am not sure if I will see Mrs Gosk again, but I know that Oswald will not. Watching him wave to her as he steps out of the classroom is almost as sad as watching Graham disappear. Almost the saddest thing ever. I say goodbye, too, but I make my good-bye as quick as possible.

I can't imagine never seeing her again. I love her so much.

Mrs Patterson walks out the side door of the school five minutes after the bell rings. She is carrying a large, cloth bag with both hands. It looks full. Her purse is slung over her shoulder.

'Don't worry about me,' I remind Oswald. 'I can pass through car doors just like the front door of my house. Just get inside. When she opens the door, jump in ahead of her. Don't wait a second. You have to be fast.'

Mrs Patterson stops by her car. She puts the bag down on the pavement and opens the back door. She lifts the bag. It looks heavy. I can see books and picture frames and snow boots inside. Other stuff too underneath all that. She is going to put the bag on the back seat. Oswald is not in position to enter through this door. He is standing in front of the door as Mrs Patterson opens it. But he panics. He tries to run around the door and around Mrs Patterson and sneak in as the door closes but he does not get there in time. He slams into the door and bounces off, landing on the pavement. He grunts, shaking his head.

'Get up!' I yell.

He listens. He pops right back up.

Mrs Patterson steps forward and opens the front door. The one next to the steering wheel. Oswald is still in position to climb in. He is standing a couple steps back from where I told him to wait, but he is close enough to get in, I think.

'Now!' I yell, and Oswald moves, faster than I think he can move, squeezing in and crawling across the driver's seat just ahead of Mrs Patterson's body. I am not sure what would have happened had Mrs Patterson sat on Oswald. Imaginary friends are usually pushed out of the way, like when the elevator gets crowded, but there is always some-place to be pushed into. If Mrs Patterson sat on Oswald, there would be no place for him to go.

I'm glad we'll never find out.

I pass through the back seat door, climb over the cloth

bag and sit behind Oswald, who is now in the passenger seat.

'Are you okay?' I ask.

'Yes,' he says. But his voice sounds far away. After a couple seconds, he adds, 'She doesn't look like a bad person. I thought she would look a lot meaner.'

'That's probably why no one thinks she stole Max,' I say.

'Maybe all the devils look normal,' Oswald says. 'Maybe that's why they can be so bad.'

He sounds so far away now that I am worried he won't survive the car ride.

'Are you sure you're okay?' I ask.

'Yes,' he says.

'Good. We'll be at Mrs Patterson's house real soon.'

Even though we'll be at Mrs Patterson's house soon, we can't save Max until tonight. Oswald has to exist for another few hours, and I am not sure if he will.

I try to put those thoughts out of my mind and pay attention to the streets as we leave the school. I need to draw a map in my head for my plan to work. First we turn left out of the circle. We drive to the end of the road and stop at a stop light. It's a long light. Mrs Patterson starts tapping on her steering wheel while we wait. She thinks it is long, too. Finally the light turns green and Mrs Patterson turns left.

The radio is on. A man is telling us about the news. Nothing about a little boy disappearing from school.

We drive past the park on the left and a church on the right. The front lawn of the church is covered by pumpkins. There is a white tent beside the field of orange. A man is standing underneath the tent. I think he is selling the pumpkins. We pass through two more traffic lights. Then we turn right at another traffic light.

'Left, then left, then three lights and a right,' I say and I repeat it twice more. I try to turn it into a song because songs are easier to remember.

'What are you saying?' Oswald asks.

'Directions. I need to know how to get back to the school.'

'Driving in cars isn't very fun either,' Oswald says. 'But a little better than the bus.'

I wish I could talk to him but I can't. I am trying to memorize directions. But I feel bad. Oswald is fading away fast. The only imaginary friend who I ever met who could touch the outside world will disappear for ever and I do not have time to talk to him.

We drive down a long, dark street. No parks or churches. Just houses and roads on the left and right. We go through two stop lights and then Mrs Patterson turns left and we drive down a small, windy hill. At the bottom of the hill she turns left again. This is Mrs Patterson's street.

I recognize it. The pond is on the right. Mrs Patterson's house is down the street on the right, too.

I try to imagine the drive from the school to Mrs Patterson's street in my mind. Left, left, right, left, left. Traffic lights in between. The park. The pumpkin church. The pond.

I realize that I am not good with directions. I can walk to the hospital and the police station and the gas station because I walk slowly. Cars drive fast. It's hard to notice things when you are driving. And there are more turns to memorize because you go farther.

The car slows down and Mrs Patterson turns right into her driveway.

'We're here,' I say. 'The house is at the top of this hill.'

'Okay,' Oswald says.

We drive up the hill to the house. Mrs Patterson presses the button on the remote control and the garage door opens. She pulls into the garage and presses the button on the remote control again. The garage door closes.

'Is it time to save Max?' Oswald asks.

'Not yet,' I say. 'We have to wait a few hours. Do you think you can wait that long?'

'I don't know time. I don't know how long a few hours is.'

'That's okay,' I say. 'I'm going to check on Max first, because I can pass through the door to his room. But you will see him soon.'

Mrs Patterson slams her car door shut. It's the bang that makes me realize that Oswald is still sitting in the passenger seat with no way of getting out of the car.

I have made another mistake.

After spending six years being able to pass through doors, I have forgotten that Oswald can't.

Again.

CHAPTER 54

'What's the matter?' Oswald asks.

I have not said a word since Mrs Patterson closed the door.

'I messed up,' I say. 'I forgot to tell you to get out of the car.'

'Oh.'

'It's okay,' I say. 'I'll think of something.'

But as I tell Oswald not to worry, I can see a picture of him in my mind. The only imaginary friend who could touch the real world, fading away inside this ordinary car in this ordinary garage, unable to do the last, great thing that he was meant to do.

'I could try to open the door,' Oswald says.

'You can't,' I say. 'I saw how hard it was for you to ring the doorbell at Max's house. You'll never be able to pull the handle and push that door at the same time.'

Oswald looks at the handle and the door. He nods. 'Maybe she will come back,' he says.

It's true. She might. She left the cloth bag on the back seat and she may still need it. But Oswald is fading fast. If she does not come back soon, I am afraid that there will be nothing to come back to.

'Climb back here,' I say. 'If she comes back, she will come back for this bag. This is the door she will open.' I point at the door closest to the bag. 'We have to be ready.'

Oswald climbs into the back seat. I am still amazed at how easily he moves even though he is a giant. He sits between me and the bag. We sit in silence for a while, waiting.

'Maybe you should go inside and check on Max,' Oswald suggests. He sounds a million miles away. His voice is soft and muffled.

I thought about checking on Max but I am afraid to leave the car. I am afraid that Oswald will disappear while I am gone. I look closely at him. I can still see him, but I can also see everything behind him. The bag on the seat. The car door. The rake and shovel hanging on the wall of the garage. When he stops moving, it is easier to see the rake and the shovel than to see him.

'I'll be okay,' he says. It's like he was reading my mind. 'Just go check on Max and come back.'

'You're disappearing,' I say.

'I know.'

'I'm afraid that you will disappear while I am gone.'

'You think that if you leave the car, I will start disappearing faster?' he asks.

'No. I just don't want you to die alone.'

'Oh.'

We sit in silence again. I feel like I have said the wrong thing. I try to think of the right thing to say.

'Are you afraid?' I finally ask.

'No,' he says. 'Not afraid. Sad.'

'Sad about what?'

'I'm sad that we won't be friends anymore. I'm sad that I won't see John or Teeny again. I'm sad that I won't ride in another elevator or another bus. I'm sad that I won't get to be friends with Max.' He sighs and hangs his head. I try to think of the right thing to say again, but he speaks first before I can. 'But when I disappear, I won't be sad anymore. I won't be anything anymore. So I'm just sad now.'

'Why aren't you afraid?'

This is not the right thing to say for Oswald, but it is the right thing to say for me, because I am afraid and I am not even disappearing. I feel bad for not thinking about what is the right thing to say to Oswald, but I can't help it.

'Afraid of what?' he asks.

'Afraid of what happens after you die.'

'What happens?' he asks.

'I don't know what happens.'

'Then why be afraid?' he asks. 'I think probably nothing happens. And if it's better than nothing, that's okay, too.'

'What if it's worse than nothing?'

'There's nothing worse than nothing. But if it's nothing, I won't know it because I will be nothing.'

In that moment, Oswald sounds like a genius to me.

'But what about not existing?' I ask. 'The whole world will go on without you. Like you were never here. And then someday everyone who knows you will be dead, too, and then it will be like you never, ever existed. Doesn't that make you sad?'

'Not if I save Max. If I save Max, I will exist for ever.'

I smile. I don't believe what he has said, but I smile because I like the idea. I wish I could believe it.

'Go check on Max,' he says. 'I promise that I won't disappear.'

'I can't.'

'If I start to disappear, I will honk the horn. Okay? I am sure I can do that.'

'Fine,' I say, and I turn to leave the car. Then I stop. 'You're right. You can honk the horn.'

'So?'

'Climb into the front seat,' I say. 'Honk that horn.'

'Why?'

'I think it might be your way out of here.'

Oswald climbs into the driver's seat. He places both hands on the horn. I can barely see them. I am worried that his power to touch the real world might be disappearing as he disappears.

He presses down, and as he does so, the muscles in his arms tighten. His body shakes. Two veins in his neck grow thick and dark, even as they grow transparent. He groans a faraway groan. A second later the horn honks. It honks for about three seconds before stopping.

The moment it stops, Oswald relaxes. He sighs.

'Get ready now,' I say.

'Okay,' he says between breaths.

We wait for what feels like a long time. Ten minutes. Maybe longer. We stare at the door that connects the garage to the house. It does not open.

'You need to do it again,' I say.

'Okay,' Oswald says, but the look on his face tells me that he is not sure if he can.

'Wait,' I say. 'Mrs Patterson might be in the secret room with Max. Maybe she can't hear the horn from the secret room. Let me go inside and check where she is. I don't want you to honk the horn for nothing.'

'Me either,' Oswald says.

I find Mrs Patterson in the kitchen. She is washing a frying pan with a sponge. She is singing the hammer song again. The dishwasher is open. There are plates and glasses and silverware in the racks. Maybe she just finished eating with Max.

I return to the garage. As I approach the car, I do not see Oswald. He has disappeared. Just as I feared, he stopped existing while I was inside the house.

Then I see him. Almost invisible but still alive. He blinks and I can see his two black eyes and then the outline of his giant body. We can't wait until Mrs Patterson is asleep, I decide. We have to save Max now.

I climb back into the car.

'Okay. She is in the kitchen. Listen. When she comes out, she will open the car door to check on the horn. To see what is making it honk. Get out of the car right away and make sure you get into the house as fast as you can. You can't get stuck in the garage.'

'Okay,' he says. I can barely hear him and I am sitting right next to him.

Oswald returns his hands to the steering wheel. This time when he presses down, he lifts himself up so his bottom is no longer touching the seat. He is using his weight this time to help him. The muscles in his nearly transparent arms pop out again. The veins in his neck return. He groans. It takes at least a minute before the horn finally honks. It honks for only a second this time, but it is enough.

A moment later, the door connecting the garage to the

house opens. Mrs Patterson is standing in the doorway. She stares at the car. Her brow furrows. She leans forward slightly. But she remains in the doorway.

I stare into her eyes. She is not going to check on the car. I know it.

'Do it again!' I shout. 'Honk the horn again. Now!'

Oswald looks at me. I can barely see him but I can still see the exhaustion on his face. He does not believe that he can do it.

'Do it!' I shout again. 'Honk that horn for Max Delaney! You are his only chance. Do it. You will be gone soon and if you don't get out of this car you will have nothing to show for it. Honk it. Honk it now!'

Oswald rises up. He kneels on the driver's seat and leans over, putting all his weight on the horn. And then he pushes, shouting Max's name as he does. Even though every word he says sounds farther and farther away, Max's name fills the car. He doesn't just shout Max's name. He roars it. The muscles in his back rise up with him, joining those in his arms and shoulders. He reminds me of a snowplow again. An unstoppable snowplow.

The horn honks almost immediately.

Mrs Patterson is pulling the door closed when the sound of the horn stops her. She jumps. She releases the door and allows it to swing open again. She stares back at the car. She scratches her head. Then, just as I think she is going to step back into the house and ignore her self-honking car again, she descends the three steps into the garage.

'Here she comes,' I say. 'When she opens that door, get out of the car and get into the house.'

Oswald nods. He cannot speak. He cannot catch his breath.

Mrs Patterson pulls open the driver's door and leans in. She is reaching for the horn with her right arm as Oswald twists his way past her and steps onto the concrete floor of the garage. He pauses, still catching his breath, when I tell him to go.

'Go now,' I say.

He listens. As he passes by Mrs Patterson, she tests the horn, honking it herself. Oswald flinches at the sound but keeps moving. I don't waste a second waiting for her to finish her test. I pass through the door on my side of the car and follow Oswald into the house. As we pass through the washer machine room and into the gloom of the living room, I stop. The sun has set. It is dark outside. We have been sitting in the car longer than I thought. There are no lights on in this room. I have lost sight of Oswald.

'Oswald,' I whisper. 'Where are you?' Mrs Patterson cannot hear me but I whisper anyway.

Television makes you do a lot of dumb things.

'Here,' he says, grabbing my arm.

Oswald is standing beside me but I cannot see him. And

I can barely hear him. Yet his grip is strong. It gives me hope that he can do what must be done.

'Okay. Let's go,' I say.

'I think that's a good idea,' he says. 'I don't think I have much time.'

The door to the basement is open. After all that has happened, we deserve this small piece of luck. I did not know how to get Oswald into the basement if it had been closed. As I lead Oswald through the kitchen and down the stairs, I look at the clock on Mrs Patterson's stove.

6.05.

Later than I thought but still not late enough. Mrs Patterson will not be asleep for hours. But Oswald has no time left. I have to find a way to make it happen now.

The basement lights are on, but it is still almost impossible to see Oswald. As he steps into the room outside of Max's secret room, I can see him only because he is moving. When he stops beside the green table with the tiny tennis court on top, he disappears.

'Max is behind that wall,' I say. 'It's a door, but it's a secret door so I can't pass through it. And Max can't open it.'

'You want me to open it?' Oswald asks from some faraway land.

'Yes,' I say.

'This is where I save Max?' Oswald asks. He sounds

relieved. He has made it. He is going to be able to do the one big thing in his life before he disappears.

'This is it,' I say. 'You are the only one who can open the door. The only one in the whole wide world.'

I show Oswald the spot on the shelf where he must press. He places both hands against the shelf. He leans in and pushes. His whole body presses forward. He becomes the snowplow. The section of the shelf moves in almost immediately and the door slides open.

'That was easy,' I say.

'Yeah,' he says, sounding surprised. 'Maybe I'm getting stronger.'

I can't see Oswald's smile, but I can hear it in his voice.

I step inside Max's room for what I hope is the last time.

CHAPTER 55

The Problems with Getting Max Home

1. Max is afraid of the dark.
2. Max is afraid of strangers.
3. Max will not talk to anyone who he does not know.
4. Max is afraid of Mrs Patterson.
5. Max won't admit that he is afraid of Mrs Patterson.
6. Max does not like change.
7. Max believes in me.

CHAPTER 56

Max is expecting Mrs Patterson to walk through the door. He does not look up when I enter the room. He is building a train with his Lego. The tracks are surrounded by platoons of plastic army men.

'Hi, Max,' I say.

'A choo-choo train!' Oswald shouts.

Max drops the Lego piece in his hand and stands up. 'Budo!'

He sounds happy to see me. His eyes widen as they meet mine. He takes a quick step forward but then stops. His tone quickly changes. His eyes narrow. He frowns. 'You left me.'

'I know.'

'You broke your promise,' he says.

'I know.'

'Tell him you're sorry,' Oswald says.

He has moved across the room and is standing beside

Max. He can't stop staring down at him. It is like the God of One has become the God of Two.

I look at Oswald with wide eyes and shake my head. I hope he understands my meaning. I am not afraid that Max will hear Oswald. I am afraid that Oswald will distract me. I feel like one of those police officers on television who has to talk a crazy person out of jumping off a bridge. I can't have any distractions. It's time for me to do my part. I have only one chance to save Max and I don't have much time.

'Why did you leave?' Max asks.

'I had to leave. If I stayed here, I thought you would stay here.'

'I did stay here,' Max says. His eyes narrow even farther. He sounds confused.

'I know,' I say. 'But I was afraid that if I stayed here, you would stay with Mrs Patterson for ever. You're not supposed to be here, Max.'

'Yes, I am. Stop it, Budo. You're not talking right.'

'Max, you have to leave this place.'

'No. I don't,' Max says.

He is starting to get upset. His cheeks are turning red and he is spitting his words. I have to be careful. I need to get Max just the right amount of upset. If he gets too upset, he could get stuck.

'Yes, you do,' I say. 'You have to leave. You don't belong

here.'

'Mrs Patterson says that I belong here. She said you can stay here, too.'

'Mrs Patterson is bad,' I say.

'No,' Max says. He shouts the word. 'Mrs Patterson takes care of me. She gave me Lego and army men and lets me eat grilled cheese for dinner whenever I want it. She told her mom that I am a good boy. She can't be bad.'

'This is not a good place,' I say.

'Yes, it is. Stop it, Budo. You're not talking right. You're not being a good friend. Why aren't you talking right?'

'You have to leave, Max. If you don't, you will never see your mom or dad or Mrs Gosk or anyone else ever again.'

'I will see you,' Max says. 'And Mrs Patterson said I can see Mommy and Daddy again soon.'

'She is lying about your mom and dad, and you know it.'

Max says nothing. This is a good sign.

'And if you stay here, you will never see me again, either,' I say.

'Stop it. You're not talking right.' Max's hands clench into tiny fists. For a second, he reminds me of Oswald.

'I mean it,' I say. 'You'll never, ever see me again.'

'Why?' Max asks. There is fear in his voice now. This is good.

'I am leaving. And I am not coming back.'

'No,' Max says.

But this is not a command. It is a request. He is asking me to stay. He is almost begging me to stay. Now there is hope.

'Yes,' I say. 'I am leaving. I am never, ever coming back.'

'Please, Budo. Don't leave.'

'I am leaving.'

'No. Please don't leave.'

'I am leaving,' I say, trying to make my voice like cold, hard stone. 'You can leave, too. Or you can stay here for ever.'

'I can't leave,' Max says. I hear panic in his voice now. 'Mrs Patterson won't let me leave.'

'That is why you have to escape, Max.'

'I can't.'

'Yes, you can.'

'I can't,' Max says, and it sounds as if he might cry. 'Mrs Patterson won't let me out.'

'The door is open,' I say. I point to the open door.

'The door is open?' Max says, finally noticing.

'Mrs Patterson left the door open,' I say.

'Liar, liar, pants are on fire!' Oswald says from far away. I smile, wondering where he learned that.

'Listen to me, Max. This is the only time that Mrs Patterson will forget to lock the door. You have to go now.'

'Budo, please stay with me. We can just stay here and play with army men and Lego and video games.'

'No, we can't. I am leaving.'

'Why are you being so mean?' Oswald asks.

His voice is like an old whisper. It is like dust. I want to stop and say goodbye to him. Thank him for what he has done. I feel like he could be gone at any second. But I cannot stop. Max is toppling. I can feel it. I need to finish the job.

I turn and take three steps toward the open door.

'Please, Budo.' Max is pleading now. I can hear the tears in his eyes.

'No. I am leaving and never coming back.'

'Please, Budo,' Max says, and my heart breaks a little to hear him so frightened. This is what I wanted, but I didn't know how hard it would be. The right thing and the easy thing are never the same thing, and this is the truest right now.

'Please don't leave me,' Max begs.

I decide that this is the moment to make my stand. I change my voice from stone to ice. 'Mrs Patterson is bad, Max. You are afraid to say it, but you know it. But she is even worse than you know. She is planning on taking you away from this room. Away from this house. Far, far away. You will never see your mom or dad again. You will never see me again. Everything is going to change for ever and ever unless you go now. You have to go now.'

'Please, Budo.' Max is crying now.

'I promise that if you leave now, you will be safe. You

will get away from Mrs Patterson. You will make it home. You will see your mom and dad tonight. Cross my heart and hope to die. But we have to go now. Will you follow me now?'

Max is weeping. Tears are spilling down his cheeks. He can barely catch his breath. But in between the sobs, Max nods.

He nods.

We have a chance.

CHAPTER 57

Mrs Patterson is in her bedroom. She is packing another box with things from under her bathroom sink. The clock above the stove reads 6.42. It is time to go.

I go back to the basement. Max is standing by the staircase. Right where I left him. He is holding the locomotive from his Lego train in his hands. He is clinging to it like it is a life preserver. His pants pocket is bulging with something, too. I do not ask what.

I wonder if Oswald is still here. I look around but cannot see him.

'I'm here,' he says, waving his hand. The movement catches my eye. He is standing behind Max but it sounds like he is on the other side of the Grand Canyon. 'Did you think you lost me?'

I smile.

'Mrs Patterson is upstairs,' I say. 'In her bedroom. You

are going to walk up the stairs and follow me. We are going to try to get out through the sliding glass door in the dining room. The door should open quietly. I watched her open it once. It didn't squeak. Once we are outside, you are going to turn right and run as fast as you can into the woods.'

'Okay,' Max says. His whole body is shaking. He is terrified.

'You can do this, Max.'

'Okay,' he says. But he does not believe me.

We climb the stairs and enter the hallway. The front door is to the right. I think again about sending Max out this door and decide against it. It is at the foot of the stairs. Mrs Patterson might hear it open.

'This way,' I say, leading Max through the kitchen and into the dining room. 'The handle is on the right-hand side. Just give the door a pull.'

Max shifts the Lego train to his left hand and grabs the handle with his right. He pulls. The door moves a teeny tiny bit and then stops with a thud.

'Oh, no,' I say, feeling the first bits of panic race through me. 'Max, we have to go to—' Before I can finish my sentence, Max has turned a knob on the door. 'It was locked,' he whispers. 'That's all.'

He pulls on the door a second time and the glass slides open with a quiet hiss.

For a moment, I am excited. Not only is the door open but Max opened it. He solved the problem. Max does not solve problems. Max becomes trapped inside problems.

This is a good sign.

But as the door slides open, three beeps ring out throughout the house. The alarm has not gone off, but it is the beeps that tell the person who owns the door that the alarm is working but is turned off. Max's parents' doors make the same sound. I don't even notice the beeps anymore because they beep every time someone opens the door. They beep all the time.

I do not think these three beeps will go unnoticed.

As if to prove the point, I hear something drop to the floor directly above us. A second later footsteps thump quickly across the upstairs floor.

'She's coming!' I shout. 'Run!'

Max does not move. He stands in the open doorway, frozen in place. The sound of Mrs Patterson's charge across the second floor has stopped him in his tracks.

'Max, if you do not run now, you will never escape.'

I realize how true this is as I say the words. I have taken a big chance. If Mrs Patterson catches Max now, she will never give him another chance to escape ever again. This is the one chance I have to get Max home.

And he is still not moving.

I hear Mrs Patterson. She is on the stairs now.

411

'Max. Please run now. I am leaving with or without you. I am not staying here. There is no time. Your mom and dad are waiting. Mrs Gosk is waiting. Run!'

Something I said makes him move. I wish I knew what it was so I could use it again. I think it was maybe the mention of his mom.

Max steps into the night. It is dark and I am worried that this will stop Max again but it does not. Max is afraid of the dark but now he is more afraid of Mrs Patterson. He has admitted that he is afraid of her, and this is good. He crosses Mrs Patterson's deck and walks down the three steps onto the grass. He looks out at the pond. The moon is hanging just above the trees on the opposite side. White light shimmers on the still water.

The pale moonlight, I think. Max is dancing with the devil in the pale moonlight for real now.

'Turn right and run!' I scream as loud as I can. As angry as I can.

Max turns and runs into the trees.

I turn to look back at the door. Mrs Patterson is not there yet. She must have decided to check the front door first.

Oswald is standing in the doorway. He shimmers in the mixing of moonlight and light from inside the house like hot air off a parking lot. He is disappearing. It is happening right now. Right in front of my eyes.

'Run, Budo!' he shouts.

The sound coming from his mouth does not sound like a voice anymore. It sounds more like a distant memory. A memory almost forgotten, except now I know that Oswald was right. He will never be forgotten.

'Save Max,' he says.

He is probably shouting these words. Roaring this all-important final command. The words that have ended his life. But they come to me as a whisper's whisper.

'I have one more thing to do.'

I cannot run. I feel like Max. I am stuck in place. Oswald the Giant, imaginary friend of John the Lunatic, the only imaginary friend to have feet in both worlds, is dying before my eyes.

I am responsible for his death.

Just as I expect him to wink out for ever, he turns and looks back inside the house. He waits a second, drops to one knee and places his hands out in front of him like a boy showing his mother how many fingers make ten. I cannot see the details that once made Oswald real, but I do not need to see them to know that his muscles are popping for the last time. The veins in his neck are pulsing their final pulses. He is Oswald the Giant once again, one more time, preparing for battle.

Then he turns back to me, sees me frozen on the lawn, the pale moon hanging behind me, and says, 'Goodbye, Budo.'

I can no longer hear his words, but they somehow find their way into my mind.

And then, 'Thank you.'

At that moment, Mrs Patterson comes into view. She is running from the kitchen into the dining room and toward the open door. She is running faster than I thought she ever could, and in that moment I realize that Max's escape will not end with his disappearance into the trees.

It has just begun.

Oswald was right. Everyone is somebody's devil, and Mrs Patterson is Max's devil.

And mine.

Then the thought hits me.

Oswald is Mrs Patterson's devil. Oswald the Giant is the devil in the pale moonlight now.

An instant later, Mrs Patterson charges into the open doorway and hits the crouching, shimmering, dying Oswald. Her right knee strikes his right hand and she topples over, head first, flying up and over and down onto the deck with a grunt and a bang and a thump. She slides all the way to the edge of the deck and then rolls down the three stairs to the grass, stopping inches before my feet.

I look up. I look to the doorway, looking for my brave and dying friend, and I already know that he is gone.

'You saved Max,' I say to my friend, but no one is listening anymore.

Then I hear Max shout. 'Budo!'

Mrs Patterson's head rises from the grass. She pulls herself up on one arm. She looks in the direction of Max's voice. A second later, she rises to her feet.

I turn and run.

Max's escape has just begun.

CHAPTER 58

Max is standing behind a tree. He is hugging his Lego train like it is a teddy bear. Some of the pieces have broken off but I do not think Max has noticed. He is shaking all over. It is cold and Max is not wearing a coat, but I do not think this is why he is shaking.

'You can't stay here,' I say. 'You have to run.'

'Make her stop,' Max whispers.

'I can't,' I say. 'You have to run.'

I listen. I expect to hear Mrs Patterson crashing through the trees and bushes, but I do not. She is probably walking slowly. Trying to be quiet. She is probably trying to sneak up on Max so that she can grab him.

'Max, you have to run,' I say again.

'I can't.'

'You have to.'

416

At that moment a beam of light passes through the trees. I look back toward Mrs Patterson's house. There is a dot of bright light near the edge of the trees.

A flashlight.

Mrs Patterson went back inside the house for a flashlight.

'Max, if she finds you, she will take you away for ever and you will be alone for ever.'

'I'll have you,' Max says.

'No, you won't.'

'Yes, I will. You say that you will leave me, but you won't leave me,' he says. 'I know it.'

Max is right. I would never leave him. But this is no time for the truth. I must lie to Max in a way I have never done before. In a way I never thought I would ever, ever do.

'Max,' I say, looking him in the eyes. 'I am not real. I am imaginary.'

'No, you're not,' he says. 'Stop it.'

'It's true. I am imaginary. You are all alone right now, Max. You can see me, but I am not really here. I am imaginary. I can't help you, Max. You have to help yourself.'

The beam of light passes across the trees to the left. In the direction of the pond. Mrs Patterson is moving down the hill, slightly away from Max, but there is not much ground between Max and the pond. Even if she is heading in the wrong direction, she will see him soon. The moon is lighting up the forest and Mrs Patterson has a flashlight.

A second later we hear the first snap of a branch on the ground. She is getting close.

Max startles and almost drops his train. 'Which way?' he asks. 'Which way should I run?'

'I don't know,' I say. 'I'm imaginary. You tell me which way.'

Another branch snaps, this one much closer, and Max turns and runs up and to the right, away from the water and away from Mrs Patterson. But he moves too fast and too loud. The light from the flashlight swerves in his direction and lands on his back.

'Max!' Mrs Patterson yells. 'Wait!'

When Max hears her voice, he runs faster. I run, too.

I lose sight of Max as he runs through a tight bunch of pine trees. But he is headed in the right direction. There are five houses on this side of the road before the end of the street, and he is getting close to Mrs Patterson's closest neighbor. I can see the lights of the neighbor's house through the trees. But somehow I have lost Max. He was twenty or thirty steps in front of me but now he is gone.

I stop running. I walk. I want to listen and look. Mrs Patterson has stopped running, too. She is walking, not too far behind me and off to my left, doing the same thing I am doing.

We are both looking for Max.

'Budo!'

Max calls my name, but this time it is a whisper. The voice comes from my right so I look in that direction. I see trees and rocks and leaves and the glow of street lights at the top of the hill where the forest meets the road, but no Max.

'Budo,' he whispers again and I become afraid. Max is trying to be quiet but Mrs Patterson is too close. He cannot afford to make another sound.

Then I see him.

There is a rock and a tree with leaves piled in between them, probably pushed there by the wind. Max has buried himself in the leaves. I can see his tiny hand waving to me from underneath the pile.

I get down on my hands and knees and crawl to him, leaning against the opposite side of the rock.

'Max, what are you doing?' I whisper as softly as I can so Max will do the same.

'Waiting,' Max says.

'What?'

'This is what a sniper does,' Max whispers. 'He lets the enemy soldiers walk right by them before they attack.'

'You can't attack Mrs Patterson.'

'No. I will wait until— '

Max stops talking as the sound of footsteps rustling in

leaves reaches us. A second later the flashlight passes over the rock where I am sitting and where Max lies buried under leaves.

I look up. I can see Mrs Patterson now. I can see her outline in the moonlight. She is close. Fifty steps away. Then thirty. Then twenty. She is walking quickly as if she knows exactly where Max is hiding. If she does not change direction, she may step right on top of Max.

'Max,' I say. 'Don't move. She's coming.'

As I sit and wait for Max to be caught, I think about Max's decision to hide under the leaves. *This is what a sniper does*, he said.

Max read a book about war. Actually, he has read a million books about war, but now he is using what he read to save himself. In a strange forest. At night. With someone chasing him. And with his best friend insisting that he is not real.

He is not stuck.

It is almost unbelievable.

Mrs Patterson is now ten steps from Max. Five steps. Her flashlight shoots ahead. Not at the ground but straight ahead. Two steps before she would have stepped on Max, she turns left and heads up the hill toward the road. It makes sense that she turns. Otherwise she would have had to climb over the rock or squeeze between the rock and the tree, but it was still close. If she had shined her flashlight on the pile of leaves, I am sure that she would have seen Max's shape under those leaves.

'How long are you going to wait?' I ask, once Mrs Patterson is far enough away that I cannot hear her footsteps in the leaves.

'Snipers wait for days,' he whispers.

'Days?'

'Not me. But snipers do. I don't know. In a little while.'

'Okay,' I say.

I don't know if this is a good idea or a bad idea, but Max has made a decision. He is solving the problem. He is escaping on his own.

'Budo,' he whispers. 'Are you real? Tell me the truth.'

I pause before answering. I want to say yes, because yes is the truth, and yes will keep me safe. Yes will keep me existing. But Max is not safe, and he cannot afford to believe in me now because I cannot save him. He needs to believe in himself. He has depended on me for too long. He needs to depend on himself now. I can't get him home.

This is not choosing between chicken noodle or vegetable beef. Blue or green. This is not the Learning Center or the playground or the school bus or even Tommy Swinden. This is the actual devil in actual pale moonlight.

Max has to get himself home.

'No,' I say. 'Cross my heart and hope to die. I'm imaginary.

You imagine me to make things easier for you. So you'll have a friend.'

'Really?' he asks.

'Really.'

'You're a good friend, Budo,' Max says.

Max has never said this to me before. I want to exist for ever, but if I had stopped existing at this very moment, I would have at least been happy. The happiest ever.

'Thanks,' I say. 'But I'm only what you imagine. I'm a good friend because you made me a good friend.'

'Time to go,' Max says. He says it so fast that I am not sure if he was listening to me.

He stands up but stays bent over in a crouch. He starts moving up the hill but to the left of where Mrs Patterson went.

I follow.

As I step past the leaf pile where Max was buried seconds ago, I see the Lego train sitting by the rock. Max has left it behind.

In a minute we are on the edge of the neighbor's lawn. The long, stretch of grass is split in two by a gravel drive-way. On the other side of the lawn is another patch of forest. Smaller, I think. The lights of the next house look close. They shine through the tree line.

'You should go to that house and knock on the door. The people will help.'

Max says nothing.

'They won't hurt you, Max,' I say.

He does not answer.

I did not expect Max to get help from Mrs Patterson's neighbors or anyone else. I think Max would rather melt every Lego piece and army man and video game in the world into a pile of gooey plastic before he ever talked to a stranger. Knocking on a stranger's door would be like knocking on the door to an alien spaceship.

Max looks left and right across the lawn. He looks like he is getting ready to cross the street, even though he has never crossed a street alone in his entire life. Then he bursts out of the trees and runs across the lawn. He is visible in the moonlight, but unless Mrs Patterson is watching, he is going to make it across the lawn to the other side without being noticed.

As he reaches the driveway, spotlights on the house switch on. They light up the front yard like the sun. They are the lights that switch on and off when people move. Max's parents have them in the backyard, and they turn on sometimes when a stray cat or a deer passes by.

Max freezes when the lights come on. He looks behind him. I am standing on the edge of the trees. I have been watching Max but not following. I have been standing and staring in amazement at this boy who once needed help deciding on which pair of socks to wear.

Max turns toward the trees on the other side of the lawn and starts running again, and that is when Mrs Patterson bursts from the trees to my right and runs like lightning across the lawn. Max does not see her at first, so I shout.

'Max! Look out! She's behind you!'

Max turns to look but does not stop running.

I start running. I shake off my amazement. I am suddenly filled with fear. I follow behind Mrs Patterson, who is now closing in on Max. She is faster than Max. She is faster than she should be.

She really is the devil.

Max reaches the trees on the other side of the lawn. He takes two steps into the trees and then jumps over an old stone wall. His foot catches a rock and he tumbles to the ground behind the wall, out of sight. A second later he pops up and begins running again.

Mrs Patterson reaches the trees about ten seconds later. She jumps over the wall, too, but she clears it, landing and running again in one smooth motion. She pumps her arms, the flashlight turned on but not pointed at Max any longer. She can see him now. She is getting closer and closer. The beam of the flashlight flies wildly through the trees.

'Run, Max!' I scream as I jump the wall.

I am seconds behind Mrs Patterson but I can do no good. I am helpless. Useless.

I scream again. 'Run!'

Max reaches the front lawn of the next house. It is not as wide as the first, and the driveway is made of street stuff instead of gravel, but otherwise it is the same. He sprints across the grass, no spotlights turning on this time, and he disappears into the gloom of the trees on the other side.

Max is running out of houses and trees and pond. Two more houses and he will reach a street that he must cross. A street that he has never been able to cross alone before. Then he will be in a neighborhood with houses and sidewalks and street lights and stop signs. No more leaf piles and stone walls and tall trees. No more gloom. No more hiding places. He will have to find help or be caught.

But none of that will matter if Mrs Patterson catches him first, and it looks like she will.

Mrs Patterson reaches the tree line just seconds after Max. I am about twenty steps behind her when I see a thick, bare branch swing out wildly from the gloom and smash Mrs Patterson in the face. She cries out and drops to the ground like a rock. A second later I see Max. He has changed direction. He has turned right. He is running through the trees toward the road instead of into the forest toward the next house.

I come to a stop where Mrs Patterson is lying on the ground. Her nose is bloody. Her hands are pressing down hard on her left eye. She is moaning.

Max has danced with the devil in the pale moonlight, and he has won.

I turn and run in the same direction as Max, not bothering to enter the trees. I can run faster if I stay on the lawn. When I reach the street, I stop and look left and right.

No Max.

I turn left, toward the main road, and run, hoping Max has kept moving in the same direction. A few seconds later I hear him call my name.

'Over here!' he shouts in a whisper. He is on the other side of the street, in a small patch of trees, crouched behind another stone wall.

It takes me a moment to realize that he has crossed a street on his own.

'What did you do?' I ask, climbing behind the wall with him. 'Mrs Patterson is hurt.'

'I set a trap,' he says, panting and shaking and sweating but grinning, too. Not smiling, but so close to smiling.

'What?' I ask.

'I pulled a branch way back and let it go when she got close,' he says.

I stare in disbelief.

'I learned it from Rambo,' he says. '*First Blood*. Remember?'

I do remember. Max watched the movie with his dad, and then his dad made Max promise not to tell his mom.

Max told his mom when she got home because Max is a terrible liar. Max's dad slept in the guest room that night.

'She's really hurt,' I say. 'Bleeding.'

'It wasn't really a Rambo trap. His trap had spikes that stuck in the police's legs. I didn't have any rope or a knife, and I didn't have time even if I had that stuff. But it's where I got the idea.'

'Okay,' I say. I don't know what else to say.

'Okay,' Max says. He stands up and moves along the stone wall, staying low, in the direction of the main road.

He does not wait for me to lead or even ask me for a direction. Max is moving on his own.

He is saving himself.

CHAPTER 59

Max reaches the end of Mrs Patterson's street and stops. He has stayed in the woods on the opposite side of the street, walking slowly and quietly between the trees, but when he turns off this street, he will no longer have patches of forest where he can hide. The houses with the long driveways and enormous plots of land along the pond will be gone. He will be on a street with short driveways, bunched-up houses, street lights and sidewalks.

If Mrs Patterson is still chasing Max, he will be easy to see.

'Go right,' I tell Max.

He is standing on the corner. His body is pressed against a tree. He looks unsure about which way to go.

'The school is to the right,' I say.

'Okay,' Max says, but instead of stepping out from behind the tree where he is hiding, he turns into the back-yard of the first house on the street.

'Where are you going?' I ask.

'I can't walk on the sidewalks,' he says. 'She might see me.'

'So where are you going?' I ask.

'I'll stay behind the houses.'

This is what Max does. We walk for almost thirty minutes this way, crossing from one backyard to another. When the space between the houses is not guarded by fences or trees or garages or cars, Max runs. He stays low to the ground and moves fast. When a backyard is fenced, he walks around the outside edge, pushing his way through bushes and weeds. He scrapes his hands and face on shrubs and soaks his feet in puddles and mud but he keeps moving. He sets off six more spotlights along the way but no one inside any of the houses sees him.

Max is not like the Rambo guy in that movie. He can't swim through abandoned mines or break into police stations or climb mountains, but that is because there are no mines or police stations or mountains here. Max has houses and backyards and fences and trees and rose bushes, but he uses them just like Rambo would.

When we reach the next intersection, Max recognizes where he is.

'The park is across the street,' he says. 'Over there.'

He points left in the direction of the park. The school is behind the park. But instead of turning left, he turns right.

'Where are you going?' I ask. He is already moving along a fence, making his way behind another house.

'We can't cross the street there,' he whispers. 'That's where Mrs Patterson would expect me to cross.'

Max crosses the street two blocks down, and he does not cross at an intersection. Instead he waits behind a parked car until no cars are coming and then he runs across the street without the help of a crosswalk.

Max just broke his first law, I think.

Unless there is a law against pooping on someone's head.

Once he is on the other side of the street, Max keeps running. He is using the sidewalk this time instead of sneaking behind houses, and he is running as fast as he can. He wants to get to the park as quickly as possible, I think. The park feels safe to me, too. The park is a place for kids, even in the middle of the night.

Max crosses one more side street and then he turns right into the park, running off the footpaths and toward a soccer field between two steep hills. Max's dad once tried to take him sledding on these hills. The hills are made for people to sit on while watching the soccer games, but they are great for sledding, too. There are tons of kids on the hills after every snowstorm. But Max refused to get on the sled and complained the whole time that his mittens were wet. His dad finally drove him home without saying a word.

Max flies down the hill today, faster than a sled, it seems, and runs straight across the soccer field. Near the goalpost he turns right toward the baseball field, but he stays off the footpaths, running on the grass and through the trees on the edges of the trails instead. After he is past the baseball field, Max turns right past the playground toward the trees.

There is a small patch of forest that stands between the school and the park. There are trails covered by woodchips, and the teachers sometimes take the students on these trails in the fall and spring. Mrs Gosk took her class for a walk a few weeks ago so her students could write some poetry about nature. Max sat on a stump and made a list of all the words that rhymed with *tree*.

There were 102 words on his list. It wasn't a poem, but Mrs Gosk was still impressed.

Max heads in the direction of the forest. He runs along the edge of a small pond on the edge of the trees, daring to step on the path for a moment before he reaches the entrance of the forest and disappears into the gloom.

Fifteen minutes later, after getting lost on the trails twice, we stand on the other side of the forest. A field stands between us and the school. It is the same field where Max has refused to run and jump and throw softballs on field day. The moon has risen higher in the sky since we left Mrs Patterson's house. It hangs over the school like a giant, blind eye.

I want to tell Max that he has made it. I want to tell him to crawl into the bushes along the edge of the forest and wait until the morning comes. I want to tell him that once the buses start pulling into the circle at the front of the school, all he has to do is run across this field to the school and go through the front doors like it was a regular school day. He could even walk down to Mrs Gosk's classroom if he wanted. Once he is inside the school, he will be safe.

Instead I ask, 'What's next?'

I ask because I am not in charge anymore. I don't think I could be in charge even if I wanted to be.

'I want to go home,' he says. 'I want to see Mom and Dad.'

'Do you know the way home from here?' I ask.

'Yes,' he says.

'You do?'

'Yes,' he says again. 'Of course.'

'Oh.'

'When should we go?' I ask, hoping he says that we will wait for morning. That we will let Mrs Gosk or Mrs Palmer or the police bring him home.

'Now,' he says, turning and starting to walk along the edge of the field. 'I want to go home.'

CHAPTER 60

I do not know how long we have been walking when we pass the Savoys' house. The moon has moved across the sky but it is still hanging over our heads. Max has not said much. But this is Max. He may have turned into Rambo overnight, but he is still Max, too.

We have been walking for a long time, staying behind houses and bushes and trees whenever possible. I have followed Max the whole way, and he has not complained once.

I can't believe that Max will be home in a few minutes. I have stopped imagining the look on Max's parents' faces when they see him standing on the stoop. It is about to happen for real. I did not think it would ever happen.

I stop just before our driveway and stare at my friend. For the first time in my life, I understand what it feels like to be proud of someone. I am not Max's mom or dad, but I am his friend, and I am bursting with pride.

And then I see it.

Mrs Patterson's bus. The bus with the room in the back just for Max.

Max is about to turn up his driveway and take the final steps to his house, but he doesn't know that Mrs Patterson is waiting for him. He doesn't know that parked down the street, a little bit past the house, in the dark space between two street lights, is Mrs Patterson and her bus.

He doesn't even know that Mrs Patterson has a bus.

I open my mouth to shout a warning but it is too late. Max is four or five paces up the driveway when Mrs Patterson steps out from behind the giant oak tree where Max and I have waited for the bus every day since kindergarten. The tree that Max touches until the bus comes.

Max hears the footsteps before he hears my voice, but both sounds are too late. He sees Mrs Patterson closing in on him and he runs. He is more than halfway up the drive-way when Mrs Patterson's arm comes down on Max's shoulder and grabs hold. The force of her arm causes Max to trip and stumble to the ground, and for a second Max is free. He crawls toward the house on his hands and knees, but Mrs Patterson is on him in seconds, reaching down and grabbing him by the arm. She lifts him up like he is a doll.

Max screams. 'Mom! Dad! Help!'

Mrs Patterson presses her free hand over Max's mouth to silence him. I do not think that Max's parents would hear him anyway. Their bedroom is upstairs and in the back of the house, and it is late. They are sleeping, I think. But she does not know this. She wants him to be quiet so she can get away with him for ever.

Finally I move, running up the driveway, stopping in front of Max. He is wriggling, trying to break free. His eyes are wide. I can see the terror in his face. He tries to scream through Mrs Patterson's hand but all that comes out is a low hum. He kicks at Mrs Patterson's shins. Some of his kicks connect, but Mrs Patterson does not even flinch.

I stand there like a helpless fool. I am inches from my friend, watching him fight for his life, and I can do nothing. Max stares into my eyes. He is pleading for help but there is nothing I can do. I can only watch my friend be dragged away for ever.

'Fight!' I yell at Max. 'Bite her hand!'

He does. I watch his jaw drop open and then shut. Mrs Patterson winces but does not let go.

Max's arms flail. His feet continue to kick. He grabs onto the hand that is pressed over his mouth and tries to pull it free. He strains, eyes bulging even more, but he cannot. He pounds his fist on her hand. Then I see something in his eyes change. The panic is replaced by something else for just a second. Max reaches into his pocket and removes the object that has caused his pocket to bulge all night. It is the piggy bank that was sitting on his desk in his room. The tarnished pig filled to the brim with pennies.

I was wrong. When Max crossed the street without the crosswalk, it was the second time he had broken the law.

He was a thief first.

Max holds the piggy bank in his right hand and brings it down on Mrs Patterson's arm. The pig's tiny, metallic feet bite into her skin. She flinches and cries out this time, but her grip remains in place.

She is not going to let go. I realize this now. Bitten and beaten and stabbed by pig's feet, she knows that she needs only to drag Max back to her bus and then she will be safe again. And that is what she begins to do. With Max hammering on her arm with his piggy bank, she backs up, dragging Max back down the driveway toward the oak tree and her bus.

I want to scream and yell for help. Wake up Max's parents. Let the world know that my friend has made it all the way back to his driveway and just needs a final bit of help to finish his escape. He has made this trip on his own and he just needs someone to step in and save him now.

Then the idea strikes me.

'Tommy Swinden!' I yell at Max.

And even as he continues to batter Mrs Patterson's arm with the piggy bank and try to wriggle free, he furrows his eyes and stares at me.

'No, I don't want you to poop on her head,' I say. 'Tommy Swinden. He broke your window on Halloween. Break a window, Max!'

Max cocks his arm, ready to smash Mrs Patterson's arm again with the piggy bank, when he stops. Understanding fills Max's eyes. He has only one shot, but he understands.

He looks up at the house. He is halfway down the driveway now and still being dragged on the back of his heels. He will have to throw it now or he will be too far. There is a picture window in the living room. It is big. It is smack in the center of the house. But it will be a difficult throw. It is far away and his feet are barely touching the ground.

And Max can't throw.

'Bite her first,' I say. 'Bite her *hard*. As hard as you can.'

Max nods. While being grabbed and dragged, with his chances of ever seeing his mom and dad again disappearing, he nods.

And then he bites.

He must bite harder than before, because as he does, Mrs Patterson yells this time and pulls her hand away from his mouth, shaking it like it is on fire. More importantly, she stops dragging Max down the driveway. She is still holding

Max by one arm, but Max's feet are now on the ground. He has a chance.

'Step into it,' I say. 'Throw with your body. Give it your all.'

'Okay,' Max says between breaths. He reaches back with the piggy bank and throws it into the night.

Mrs Patterson sees the piggy bank leave Max's hand and her eyes widen as the pig soars snout up and then down toward the picture window.

When pigs fly, I think.

For a moment, it seems as if the entire world stops. Even the moon's blind eye turns to watch that tiny metallic pig fly through the air.

The piggy bank hits the window in its center. It is a throw that would make Max's dad forever proud. It is a throw that will make me forever proud. A throw better than Tommy Swinden could have ever hoped for. The glass explodes and, seconds later, the alarm screams into the night.

Mrs Patterson reaches out with her free hand. It is bleeding where Max has bitten her. She wrenches it around Max and grabs him by the neck. Then she lifts him off the ground and runs as fast as she can with a wriggling, screaming boy in her arms. She is now running across the front lawn toward her bus.

Max has made the throw of his life. The picture window

is broken. The alarm is screaming. The police are on the way. And still Mrs Patterson is getting away with Max. She is seconds from escaping for ever.

All I see is a blur as Max's dad flies past me and slams his body into Mrs Patterson's back like a runaway train. She cries out as he drives her body toward the ground. Mrs Patterson releases Max before she strikes the ground, trying to brace her fall. Max falls forward and rolls to the side, panting, heaving, clutching at his throat, trying to catch his breath.

Mrs Patterson was choking him to death.

Mrs Patterson crashes into the ground with Max's dad still on top of her, his arms wrapped around her body like steel cables. He is wearing boxer shorts and a T-shirt, and his arms are torn and bleeding. Long gashes stretch up his arms and across his shoulders. His T-shirt is torn in the back and already covered in blood. I am confused, but then I look back at the house. The door to the house is still shut. Max's dad jumped through the broken picture window. The broken glass cut him on the way through.

'Max! My God! Are you okay?' Max's dad asks, still not letting go of Mrs Patterson. He has her pinned to the ground but still he presses all his weight into her back. 'My God, Max. Are you okay?'

'I'm okay,' Max says. His voice is hoarse and scratchy and weak but he is telling the truth.

Max is okay.

'Max!'

It is Max's mom. She is standing in the picture window, looking out at the scene on her front lawn. Her bloody husband. Max's kidnapper. And Max, sitting beside his father, rubbing his neck.

'Max! Oh my God! Max!'

She disappears from the picture window. A few seconds later, the lights come on, brightening the front lawn. The front door flies open and Max's mom runs out of the house, down the stoop and across the lawn. She is wearing a white nightgown and it looks like she is glowing in the moonlight. She drops to her knees and slides the last few feet over to Max, wrapping him in her arms and kissing his forehead one million times. I can tell by the look on Max's face that he does not like this many kisses, but for once he does not complain. His mom is crying and kissing all at once, and Max does not even wince.

I look to Max's dad, who is still holding Mrs Patterson to the ground. She is not moving, but Max's dad has watched too many detective shows to let her go now. He knows that just when you think the bad guy is gone or dead, she can pop out from behind an oak tree and grab you.

Still, he is smiling.

I hear sirens in the distance. The policemen are coming. Max's mom, still holding Max in her arms, scoots over to

Max's dad and hugs him even as he holds Mrs Patterson down. Max's mom is crying rivers.

Max looks up at me from his mother's arms. He is smiling. Max is not grinning. He is smiling.

Max Delaney is smiling.

I am smiling, too. I am crying, too. These are my first happy tears ever. I give Max a thumbs up.

Through my fading thumb, I watch Max kiss his mom on her teary cheek.

CHAPTER 61

'Do you know that you are—'

'I know,' I say. 'I've been disappearing for two days.'

Teeny sighs. She does not say anything for a moment. She just stares at me. We are alone in the recess room. There were other imaginary friends in here when I arrived, but Teeny took one look at me and sent them away.

I guess everyone really does listen to a fairy.

'Does it feel …?' she asks.

'It doesn't feel like anything,' I say. 'If I was blind, I would have no idea that I was fading away.'

Actually, this is not true. Max has stopped talking to me. It's not that he is angry with me. He just doesn't know that I am around anymore. If I stand right in front of him and speak to him, he will notice me and talk back. But if I do not speak to him, he does not speak to me.

It has been sad.

'Where's Oswald?' Teeny asks. But I can tell by the way she looks down at her feet that she already knows.

'He's gone,' I say.

'Where?'

'Good question,' I say. 'I don't know. Wherever I'm going, which probably isn't anywhere.'

I tell Teeny the story of Max's escape and how Oswald the Giant broke open Max's basement prison and touched the real world one final time to slow down Mrs Patterson and knock her off her feet, giving Max time to run. I tell her about the chase through the forest and Max's trap at the tree line and the final battle on the front lawn of Max's house. I tell her how Max's dad held Mrs Patterson down until the police arrived, and how his father was bragging to the police officers about how his son had 'matched wits with that crazy bitch and won'.

Then I tell her how Oswald knew that he was dying, and how I tried to bring him back to the hospital to save him.

'But he wouldn't come back,' I say. 'He sacrificed himself to save Max. He is a hero.'

'So are you,' Teeny says, smiling through her tears.

'Not like Oswald,' I say. 'I stood around and told Max to run and to hide. I can't touch the real world like Oswald could.'

'You told Max to throw that pig through that window.

And you told Max that you were imaginary so he could save himself. You sacrificed yourself, too.'

'Yes,' I say, feeling anger boil up in me. 'And now I won't exist anymore because of it. Max is free and safe but I am dying. And when I'm gone, he won't even remember me. I'll just be a story that his mom tells him someday. How he once had an imaginary friend named Budo.'

'I think he'll always remember you,' Teeny says. 'He just won't believe that you were ever real. But I will.'

But Teeny is going to die someday, too. Probably soon. Her human friend is four years old. Teeny will probably be gone in a year or less. Kindergarten will kill her like it kills so many imaginary friends. And when she dies, that will be it. No memory of Budo ever existing. Everything I ever said or did will be gone for ever.

Teeny's wings flutter. She lifts off the couch and hovers in the center of the room.

'And I will tell others,' she says, seeming to read my mind. 'I will tell every imaginary friend I meet, and I will tell them to tell all the imaginary friends they meet. I will tell them to keep the story going from one imaginary friend to the next, so that the world will never forget what Oswald the Giant and Budo the Great did for Max Delaney, the bravest little boy in the world.'

'That's nice,' I say. 'Thank you, Teeny.'

I don't have the heart to tell her that it doesn't make

dying any easier. Or that I don't trust the imaginary friends of the world to carry our story. There are too many imaginary friends out there like Puppy or Chomp or Spoon.

Not enough Teenys or Oswalds or Summers or Grahams.

Not nearly enough.

'How is Max doing?' Teeny asks, landing back on the couch beside me. She wants to change the subject and I am glad that she is.

'He is good,' I say. 'I thought that after everything that happened, he would be different. But he's not. Maybe a little different, but not much.'

'What do you mean?'

'Max was great in the forest and even in his front yard because that was what he is good at. He has spent his life reading books about war and weapons and snipers. He has planned a thousand battles with his army men. There were no people in the woods to bother him. No one to talk to or make eye contact with. No one trying to shake his hand or punch him in the nose or zip up his coat. He was running away from a person, and that is what Max always wants to do. Run away from people. He was great out there, but it was almost like that is where he belonged.'

'And now?' Teeny asks.

'When he went back to school yesterday, it was really hard for him. Everyone wanted to talk to him. It was too many people, too fast. He almost got stuck. But Mrs Gosk saw what was happening and told all the other teachers and older kids and even the school psychologist to "Scram!" Max is still Max. Maybe a little braver now. A little better at taking care of himself. But still Max. Still worried about bonus poops and Tommy Swinden.'

Teeny furrows the spot on her face where her eyebrows would be if she had any.

'Never mind,' I say. 'Long story.'

'How long before—'

'I don't know,' I say. 'Maybe tomorrow, I think.'

Teeny smiles, but it is a sad smile. 'I'll miss you, Budo.'

'I'll miss you,' I say. 'I'll miss everything.'

CHAPTER 62

I was right. It is happening today. When Max turned on the light this morning, I could barely see myself. I said hello to Max and he did not answer. He did not even look in my direction.

And then I started having this feeling a little while ago. I am sitting in Mrs Gosk's class. Max is sitting on the rug with the rest of the kids. Mrs Gosk is reading a book called *The Tale of Despereaux*. It is a book about a mouse. I thought it was going to be stupid because it is about a mouse, but it is not stupid at all. It is great. It is the best book. It is about a mouse who loves the light and can read and must save the Princess Pea.

Mrs Gosk is only halfway through the book. I will never hear the end of the story. I will never know what happens to Despereaux.

Despereaux is a little like me in that way. I will never know Despereaux's fate and no one will ever know mine.

I will stop existing, stop persisting, today, but only I will know it. I will die a silent, unknown death in the back of this classroom, listening to a story about a mouse whose fate I will never know.

Max and Mrs Gosk and everyone else will go on like nothing has happened. They will follow Despereaux on the rest of his adventure.

I cannot.

I feel like there is a soft, gooey balloon in my belly. One of the balloons that float all by themselves. It doesn't hurt. I just feel like I am being pulled up, even though I am still sitting in this chair. I look at my hands and can see them only if I wave them in front of my eyes.

I am glad to be in Mrs Gosk's classroom when I die. Max and Mrs Gosk are my two favorite people in the whole wide world. It is nice to think that they will be my last memory.

Except I will have no memory. It is nice to die with Max and Mrs Gosk only until the moment that I die. At that moment, nothing will matter anymore. Everything from that second on will never mean anything to me ever again. But not just everything after I die, but everything before I die, too. When I die, everything dies.

It all feels like such a waste.

I look at Max, sitting at Mrs Gosk's feet. He loves this story as much as I do. He is smiling. He smiles now. That is the one big difference between the Max who believed in Budo and the Max that doesn't. He smiles. Not much, but sometimes.

Mrs Gosk is smiling, too. She is smiling because Max is back, but she is also smiling because she loves this story as much as anyone else in the room. Despereaux has been thrown into the dungeon with the rats for being different than the rest of the mice, and in a way Max is like Despereaux, too. He is different than everyone, and he was trapped in a basement, too. And, just like Max, I think Despereaux will escape the dark and save the day.

The balloon in my belly is getting bigger now. It feels warm and good.

I move over and sit at Mrs Gosk's feet. I sit right beside Max.

I think about all the people I have lost over the last two weeks. Graham and Summer and Oswald and Dee. I imagine each one standing before me. I try to imagine each one of them when they were at their best.

Graham sitting beside Grace as she faded away.

Summer making me promise to save Max.

Oswald dropping down on one knee in that doorway, hands outstretched, toppling Mrs Patterson.

Dee shouting at Sally because she loved him like a brother.

I loved them all.

I miss them all.

I look up at Mrs Gosk. When I am gone, she will have to protect Max. She will have to help him with the bonus poops and Tommy Swinden and all the other little things that Max cannot do because he lives so much of his life on the inside. That big, beautiful inside that once made me.

And she will. Oswald the Giant was a hero, and maybe even I was a little bit of a hero, too. But Mrs Gosk is an everyday, all-the-time hero, even though it's only kids like Max who know that she is a hero. She will be a hero long after I am gone because she has always been a hero.

I turn to Max. My friend. The boy who made me. I want to be angry at him for forgetting about me, but I am not. I cannot be angry at Max. I love Max. Nothing will matter when I stop existing, but somehow I think I will still love Max.

Death is not scary for me anymore. It is just sad. I will never see Max again. I will miss all the thousands of days in his future, when he will grow up and become a man and have a little Max of his own. I think if I could just sit somewhere, quiet and still, and watch the little boy who I love so much grow up and live his life, I would be happy.

I do not need to exist for me anymore. I just want to exist for Max. I want to know Max's story.

My tears are warm. My body is warm. I cannot see myself, but I can see Max. His beautiful face stares up at the teacher he loves, the only teacher he has ever loved, and I know that he will be happy. He will be safe. He will be good.

I will not see the rest of Max's life, but I know it will be long and happy and good.

I close my eyes. Tears stream down my cheeks and then they are gone. The warm, wet streaks are no more. The gooey balloon in my belly grows to fill every nook and cranny of my insides, and then I feel myself start to rise.

I am no longer whole. I am no longer me.

I soar.

I hold the image of Max's face in my mind for as long as I can. Until I am no more.

'I love you, Max,' I whisper as his face and everything else in the world fades to white.

EPILOGUE

I open my eyes. I am staring at eyes. I have seen these eyes before. They are dark and warm. They know me.

I cannot place them. And then I can.

I do not understand.

I say her name.

'Dee?'

And then I know.

ACKNOWLEDGEMENTS

Stephen King suggests writing the first draft of your novel with the door closed.

I suspect that Mr King, who I respect a great deal, did not spend his youth toiling away in the dim confines of an arcade or sitting in front of a television with an Atari 5200 controller in hand. Videogame junkies become hooked on immediate feedback and require it constantly. Though I have overcome my addiction and play sparingly nowadays, the need for immediate feedback has not left me.

As a result, I write every sentence with the door open. In the process of completing this novel, I invited about a dozen friends and family members to read along as I wrote. While their helpful suggestions, generous praise and private counsel were critical to my success, the most important thing for me was the knowledge that someone was reading and anxiously waiting for the next chapter.

For that, I am forever grateful.

Most important of all those early readers is and always has been my wife, Elysha Dicks, the person for whom I write every word. Writing for me is little more than a continual, unending effort to impress the pretty girl who I love. I am fortunate in that Elysha likes more of what I write than she doesn't and offers me the time and support to accomplish my goals. She is both the reason I want to write well and the reason I am able to write well enough.

A special thanks to Lindsay Heyer for suggesting that my childhood imaginary friend might serve as inspiration for a novel. I have been fortunate enough to spend a great deal of time with Lindsay over the past four years, and this book would have never happened had she not been such a good listener, confidant, and friend.

Thanks to my in-laws, Barbara and Gerry Green, for their constant support and love. They can be overwhelming at times, and their dogs can drive my wife and me batty most of the time, but their presence has been a blessing in my life. Never before have I understood or experienced the sense of pride that parents can feel for a son. I am fortunate to have found this gift so late in life.

Thanks to the real life Mrs Gosk, who differs only slightly from her fictional counterpart. I was lucky enough to be mentored by Donna when I entered the teaching profession fourteen years ago, and since the first day, we have been close friends and kindred spirits.

Donna is one of the finest teachers I have ever known and I have watched her change the lives of countless children over the years. My desire was to give Max and Budo the best possible teacher, and I quickly realized that reality had provided me with a character much greater than any I could have ever imagined.

Great appreciation goes to Celia Levett, the copyeditor for this book. I believe that editors' names should appear on the cover of every book, in recognition for all the work that they do in bringing a story to the finish line. Her expertise has spared me countless moments of grammatical embarrassment. Her invisible but vital imprint is hiding, much like an imaginary friend, on every page of this book.

Undying gratitude to Daniel Mallory, who I have yet to meet in person yet feel a deep affinity for despite a relationship that consists of a few phone calls and a plethora of emails. I suspect that if Daniel was living nearby, we would be fast friends, but with an ocean between us, I must settle for his sage wisdom and cherished counsel. I am fortunate to have someone as skilled as he helping to bring Budo to life.

Lastly, everlasting appreciation to Taryn Fagerness, my agent and friend who believed that I could write this story when I did not. Without her urging, Budo and his friends would remain on the heap of untested ideas that litter my hard drive. Taryn has been the invisible friend of my writing career for a long time. She is the person who makes every bump a little less jarring, every success a little more joyful and every sentence that I place on the page a little less unfortunate. She is the Teeny of my life. My guardian angel.